STORM OF MIST AND MONSTERS

A FAE FANTASY SERIES

STORM OF CHAOS AND SHADOWS
BOOK FOUR

C.L. BRIAR

Copyright © 2023 by C.L. Briar

All rights reserved.

No part of this book may be reproduced in any form or by any electronic or mechanical means, including information storage and retrieval systems, without written permission from the author, except for the use of brief quotations in a book review.

Map Design © 2023 by C.L. Briar

Cover Design © 2023 by Artscandare Book Cover Design

Identifiers:

ISBN: 978-1-956829-14-3 (Ebook)

ISBN: 978-1-956829-13-6 (Paperback)

ISBN: 978-1-956829-15-0 (Hardback)

*To the reader who uses books to escape:
Here's to making the darkness a little less lonely.*

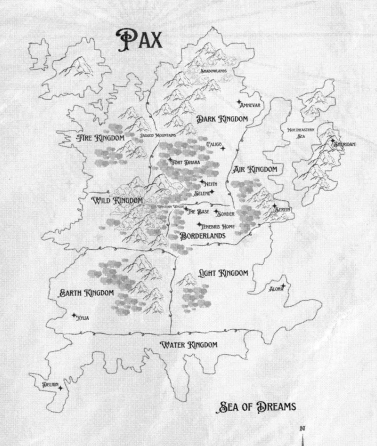

AUTHOR NOTE
CONTENT WARNING

This book is intended for readers 18 years and older. It contains graphic language, violence, gore, death, homophobia, vague reference to sexual assault, and depressive throughs, sexual situations, graphic sexual encounters, blood play, and shifters.

1

ELARA

Our brother's salvation resides in Neith.

Words swirled through my mind, close and distant all at once. My body knelt along the mossy banks of The Seven Sacred Pools, my fingers drifting down of their own volition to graze the surface of the cool waters. Ripples rocked outward, disrupting the malicious smile staring back any me. My reflection's grin stretched, the tips of my fangs peeking out beneath blood-red lips.

"Come now, Elara," Levana said, holding my gaze through the tranquil pool. The balmy air was heavy with the scent of night-blooming jasmine, the nap of my neck slick with humidity despite winter being only weeks away. Zaeth had thought to save me by bringing me here—to her. He hadn't had much of a choice, what with Draven's blade hilt-deep in my stomach, but I wondered if he would've made the same choice had he known the true cost.

Levana, the enchantress of these waters, *had* healed my wounds, but she'd also taken possession of my body and trapped my consciousness.

It was my body—my voice—but Levana controlled everything.

"Stop fighting me," she snapped. "Erebus's shadows may have shrouded you in a thin layer of protection, but you will not reclaim this body, Elara. You will never be free of me."

I'll find a way to defeat you.

I screamed the words inside my head, but the deafening silence remained unblemished in the darkness surrounding me. Gentle tendrils swirled along my legs, my chest, beckoning me to rest. Urging me to leave the horrors of my present and succumb to the peace the shadows offered.

My body stood, batting away playful fairies, their luminescent wings shimmering in the soft light of the crescent moon. Clouds rolled across the sky, remnants from the storm two days prior—the one that had cracked the barrier between realms. Silver-blue lightening had fissured along the rift, drawing the massive ice wyvern through. It had been the first of many beasts to breach Pax's wards.

"Don't you worry about that, Elara." Levana cooed, her silver-blue mist rising to brush along the cocoon of shadows in my mind. The darkness intensified, bracing against her onslaught, and bringing with it a slow urging to heed their command and sleep. "My monsters are awaiting orders. Ice wyverns, bats, dark birds of prey—these are nothing compared to my children still contained in the otherworld. My beautiful creations deemed too cruel for the light of Pax."

Images flashed, dozens of them clashing: Dark fae, pale and confined to the night, slaves to their bloodlust, earth fae staring at the full moon, bodies bending and cracking until great, howling beasts stood in their place, a beautiful water fae luring a human into the vast expanse of the sea with only the sound of her voice. Other visions showed creatures beyond recognition, too horrid to place.

"Yes," Levana said, our boots crushing jasmine blossoms as

we stalked away from the pools, toward the quiet surrounding forest of the Earth Kingdom. "Eunoia couldn't see their beauty, either. No matter. You won't be here long enough to see them returned to their rightful place among their cousins."

You won't get away with this. I meant to shout the words, but my mind was already drifting, sinking deeper into the darkness.

I felt my lips tug into a wicked grin, felt the vibrations of my voice ring through me. "Oh, but I already have. In fact, I believe our mate is eager for our return.

Zaeth.

Surely, he would know something was off. He realized it when I first woke up—hadn't he? It was growing harder and harder to remember... to remain present.

"I'll be sure to give our king a kiss for you," Levana cooed, flitting into the forest.

Her wild laughter haunted me as my vision blackened, my consciousness blending into the shadows cradling me, until I could no longer tell where I ended and where the darkness began.

2

GREER

"I can still smell it," I whispered across the sitting room of Queen Halcyon's countryside cottage.

Zaeth met my concerned look from his position on the cushioned seat with a quirked brow, swirling a glass of amber liquid. He lifted the glass to his lips, draining half its contents before shrugging a single shoulder in dismissal.

"Don't act so nonchalant. I know you smell it too. Like night-blooming jasmine."

Ryuu's wings bristled behind me near the door, and I could practically hear his jaw tick. "It's the lingering effects of the pools. Whatever Levana did, it has affected Elara. She's even removed her necklace."

Zaeth's gaze lifted, pain lashing through them as he studied the grey crystal encasing Will's ashes abandoned on her nightside table. His brown eyes flicked to Ryuu's as my winged fae prince came to my side. The soft undercoat of Ryuu's feathers grazed my shoulder, but this time the small touch did nothing to calm my frantic mind.

"What deal did you make?" Ryuu asked, his voice low as if he, too, were worried about being over heard. My hand automatically sought the long chain around my neck with two sapphire dragons twisted together. It'd become a comfort, something I could focus on when it felt like things were spiraling out of control.

I knew El was still in the same kingdom as us, but miles away, probably near The Seven Sacred Pools, just as I knew Lannie was still safe in Caligo, the capitol of the Dark Kingdom. Ever since we'd aligned the three pieces of the Spear of Empyrean, I'd been able to sense them. Not that it had done us any good. It was true El had managed to kill Alderidge and stab Draven, but with each passing day it seemed more and more likely the red-eyed commander had survived.

It had been three days since we fought the brothers. Ryuu had taken possession of the spear as he was the only one unaffected by its ability to siphon power. We all wanted revenge but had no immediate plans to launch a counterstrike.

Things had been off, to say the least. El had insisted on traveling to The Seven Sacred Pools. Again. While her motivations behind going worried me, it offered a chance to speak freely. She was miles away, the distance too great for any fae to hear.

No, my elder sister wouldn't be aware of what we were discussing. So, why was I so on edge?

"Look, I don't care what you had to do to save my sister." Ryuu stiffened, but I continued before he could interject. "She's alive because of you. I would have done the same thing, whatever it took, but I think she may still be in danger."

Zaeth sighed, finishing the rest of his glass before setting it down on the low wooden table with a *thunk*. Searing brown eyes met mine as he spoke, his voice barely more than a whisper. "She's still gone?"

Closing my eyes, I concentrated on the faint pull that linked me to my sisters. Lannie's strong connection was thrumming, where El's was muted, but both confirmed they'd yet to move locations. Blinking, I met Zaeth's waiting gaze. "She's near the pools."

"I offered Levana my life for El's. She accepted."

"You asked for her life, but what of her soul?" Ryuu breathed, the sorrow in his tone worse than anger.

The rings around Zaeth's eyes blazed as his anger spiked. "If Elara's soul was forfeited, I'd know."

"Would you?" Ryuu pressed, meeting Zaeth's glare.

"Yes," he gritted between clenched teeth. The tension broke as he leaned forward with his elbow braced on the arm of the chair, his fingers massaging his temple.

"Did Levana say anything else before El was healed?" I asked.

"'When I have need, the Dark Phoenix will be sacrificed.' I expected her to claim my life right away, but..." Zaeth shook his head. "Levana plunged beneath the water with El clasped in her arms. When El resurfaced, she was healed—unconscious—but the wound had mended, and Levana had vanished. You know the rest."

The feel of El's presence flickered, the string connecting us flaring with life. I reached for her, following that tug of familiarity, only for the line to cool before I reached the end. Turning to the window, I pressed a hand to my chest, attempting to ease the cold ache where El's burning presence had been only moments prior.

"What is it?" Ryuu asked.

"It's El. I felt her, almost as strongly as I felt Lannie... It was only a flicker before it ebbed back into a weird, numbed feeling." I swallowed, eyes searching the horizon. "She's there, I know she is, but it's like something is shrouding her presence from me. Like something—"

"Is keeping her consciousness caged," Zaeth finished.

I nodded. "You feel it too?"

"Yes and no. I can sense spikes of fear or anger and then... nothing. Even in sleep, she was still *present*, but this last sleep felt like a forced slumber. Almost as if the darkness itself was hiding her from me." After a long moment, Zaeth's eyes found Ryuu. "What do you know about Levana?"

Ryuu's spine stiffened. "I know little more than you do. She is the enchantress of The Seven Sacred Pools. Has been for millennia. She makes bargains with desperate fae or mortals, but all end up paying a far greater price than intended."

Zaeth huffed a harsh laugh. "So it would seem."

"So, what does that mean for my sister?" I asked, cutting in before Ryuu could start on another lecture. "El's body was healed, but her soul was imprisoned. How is that even possible?"

"I'm less concerned about the how and more concerned about the why," Zaeth said, pushing from the cushioned chair, glass in hand. He flitted the few steps to the decanter filled with amber liquid, took the stopper off the crystal top, and poured. Only once he had drained another glass did he turn. "Why control El? What purpose does it serve?"

"Unless she isn't controlling Elara," Ryuu said, voice far too gentle. "Levana may have healed her body but allowed El to pass from this world."

Zaeth's eyes narrowed.

"You mean El—the real El—could be dead?" I asked, my voice pitching.

Ryuu flinched from the pang of panic lashing through me but nodded.

"No," I breathed, already shaking my head. "I know my sister. She's there, just trapped."

"Greer—"

"No," I said again, this time more firmly. "I know you think it's a possibility, but Zaeth and I both know she's here, or at least a part of her. We need Lannie. She'll be able to sense Elara, too, and maybe, together, we can figure this out."

Forest-green flecks blazed in Ryuu's dark gaze, the bond

between us allowing him to sense the storm of emotions tumbling through me.

"Okay," he answered. "When Jarek returns, we'll ask him to lux to Caligo and bring Lannie here. We all agree it's best to keep Elara away from others until we know what's going on?"

"Agreed," Zaeth muttered around another swig. "Whether Elara has been stripped of her soul or if another is in control of her actions, we can't trust her knowledge will remain her own."

"El is on her way back," I breathed, feeling her presence grow closer. The churning pool of unease twisted in my stomach as a wash of malicious mirth flared down her line. I met Ryuu's piercing gaze. "She's happy about something."

"Veles?" Zaeth asked. "Could Levana be working for the brothers?"

"I don't know," answered Ryuu, his frown deepening. "But if Veles and Draven have been meeting at the pools, perhaps it wasn't their brother, Olysseus, they were speaking with."

El's presence flitted through the wild jungle of the Earth Kingdom, growing nearer every second. "If there's a way to bring her back, we'll find it."

"And if there's not?" Ryuu asked, breathing life into words I was much too afraid to speak. "If Elara is lost to the darkness beyond this life?"

Zaeth threw back his drink, the empty glass clattering loudly on the tablet before he padded across the cottage toward the window beside me. The scent of whisky clung to him as the ring of light around his irises blazed.

"If she is beyond this world, I will go into the next and find her, obliterating any god who tries to stop me."

3

LANNIE

My stomach clenched as I felt my body piece itself back together. Jarek had warned me luxing wasn't agreeable with everyone, but I hadn't anticipated feeling like every cell in my body had exploded.

"Not a fan?" Jarek asked as I bowed forward, bracing my hands on my knees. "The nausea should pass in another moment."

Working on taking deep breaths, I focused on the site before me. The jungle of tortuous vines and thick, waxy leaves opened to allow for a large but cozy cottage. A field of ferns stretched around it, the front portion currently serving as a sparring arena for Queen Freya, Zaeth, and El. Jarek filled me in on their theories about my eldest sister, including the concern her soul was in jeopardy. As if another, more powerful being could suppress it.

Though my initial reaction was skepticism, it *had* felt like she was off. Discovering logical reasons for unexplainable situations was what I did best. Being fae was new to me, being linked with my sisters even more so, but as I watched El deliver a particularly ruthless punch to Queen Freya's gut, that sense of worry grew.

"Has she been like this the whole time?" I asked, my voice low enough to not be overheard.

Jarek nodded, matching my tone as Zaeth intercepted a round kick aimed at the Wild Queen's head. "She asked to burn off some extra energy."

Zaeth grunted with the force of the deflection, narrowly avoiding an elbow to the nose. The Dark King matched her, spinning and avoiding whenever possible, but never attacking.

"Stop running from me," Elara spat, her chest heaving as she turned her full attention on Zaeth. They moved in a slow circle, two predators sizing each other up. "Afraid of what would happen in a real fight, King?"

Elara launch forward, battering Zaeth's body with punch after punch. His arms stayed locked against his sides, offering what protection they could until El's attack eased, ever so slightly. That was all the opening Zaeth needed. He spun, twisting El's arm until there was a sickening *pop*.

My sister gasped as he stumbled away, the sound turning into unhinged laughter as she noted the deformity of her shoulder and the odd angle of her arm.

"Perhaps there's a king in you, after all," El said with a crazed grin. With a quick jerk, she popped the joint into place, and then raised her fists to go again.

"That's enough," Jarek called as we approached through the tangle of vines. "We have matters to discuss."

A dramatic pout tilted Elara's lips, so at odds with the stoic sister I knew. Her eyes met mine, the hazel-blue flashing black as she grinned. I blinked, but the color of her irises had returned to normal. *Odd.*

"Sister." Elara relaxed her fighting stance and pushed past Zaeth to greet us. "It's been too long."

I kept my expression blank as she came to a stop before me,

assessing her with a cool detachment. If this had been any other person—any other patient—I'd look at the situation from all angles. Even the impossible ones.

"I suppose a lot has changed in the space of a few days." I glanced to the cottage. It was a collage of wooden beams and river stones, vines and moss growing along the base and working their way up, perfect for the Earth Queen. "Should we wait to discuss our next steps until Greer and Ryuu return with Queen Halcyon? Greer will either be able to undo the wards around the underground passage or she won't. They should be along quickly."

A twisted giggle rang through Elara's chest as she looped her arm through mine. I fought the urge to recoil from her, but it was like my body intrinsically sensed a threat.

"Don't be silly," she said as she guided us through the cottage door and onto the plush couch of the sitting room. "There's more than enough of us to have a discussion without them."

Zaeth stayed close, taking a seat opposite my sister, while Jarek and Queen Freya leaned against the table on the far side of the room—keeping their distance, I noticed. The queen's nose had a trickle of blood running down, but I could sense most of the internal damage was repairing itself.

Since Mother's binding spell had failed and my fae affinities had surfaced, I could sometimes catch glimpses of injuries... could somehow *feel* the extent of the damage done by a blade or a disease. The lotus flower brand seared into the skin along my right shoulder was a constant reminder of her betrayal... and of my identity. My power.

Being that everyone within the Dark Castle had been healed once I'd shifted, I'd ventured into the heart of Caligo these last few days, doing what I could to help. Keeping my mind busy was the only way to keep grief at bay.

Losing loved ones wasn't a foreign concept to me. At a young age, I had to watch my elder brothers die. My parents soon after. I'd seen countless families fall prey to illness, famine, and war—all of it a never-ending struggle to survive in a world intent on delivering death.

But then Will died, my little brother not yet having completed his first decade of life, and the world had ceased to make sense.

A part of me wondered if that was why this world had taken *her* from me. Had Ser's death been a punishment for finding a glimpse of happiness after Will? Maybe I wasn't meant to laugh. To hope. Maybe my ongoing battle with sustaining life in this harsh, cruel reality... was doomed.

"Yes," I said, focusing on the task at hand. I couldn't let my mind wander. The places my thoughts traveled were too unpredictable. Too unforgiving. "I wanted to see you after hearing what Draven did, but Naz thought it best I wait."

I'd understood my sisters' concerns about me not jointing them in battle. I'd even agreed at first, but then we joined the Spear of Empyrean, and I was suddenly aware of their presence like I'd never been before. Bits of their emotions bled through, all mixed together with the added burden of feeling all the emotions of my fated mate—Queen Halcyon.

Each spike of fear and pain and loneliness... It had been nearly unbearable. At least if I had gone with them into battle, I would've known what was happening. I could've helped.

"Nazneen," Elara cooed, her gaze flitting to Zaeth. "Princess of the Dark Kingdom. She seems to be making all the decisions these days. Tell me, sister, did you feel the blade pierce my flesh? Did my pain reach you despite our distance?"

I hadn't felt her physical pain, but I had been aware of El's fear. Her heartbeat pitched as shock took hold, and then everything had started to spiraling descent. Until everything was whisked away and replaced by a resounding numbness.

"I was told of your injuries," I said carefully, having the nagging urge to keep the extent of our connection a secret. I wanted to believe this was El, my sister, but everything about her seemed wrong. "Just as I was informed you'd been healed."

Her lips twitched, as if knowing I was avoiding her question. She held my gaze a moment longer before reclining, the posture not at all relaxed. "Yes, my mate was smart enough to deliver me to the goddess Levana. It was with her blessing that I was spared."

"Enchantress," Zaeth corrected, his searing gaze watching Elara's every movement. "Not goddess."

Elara's spine stiffened before she forced a shrug. "Either way, I am recovered."

"Are you?" I asked, tone a polite inquiry. I could feel my sister still lingering beneath the numbness, but I didn't want to think about why she felt so far away when she was here before me.

"Such brilliance in that mind of yours." Her smile stretched, amused at my candor. "If you doubt my recovery, sister, perhaps you should ask Queen Freya how she is feeling. My sparring skills alone should prove my strength has returned."

The Wild Queen shifted, her arms crossing over her chest, but she offered no rebuttal. She didn't need to. It wasn't my sister's physical recovery I was worried about.

"We need to be discussing our next steps for eradicating the brothers." Elara pushed to a stand, making her way to the table. She laughed as Queen Freya stiffened with her approach. "Relax. If I wished for another match, I'd have taken you in the clearing. No point in damaging this quaint residence, now is there?"

Elara reached across the table and dragged the map of Pax toward her. Zaeth and I peered over her shoulder as Jarek and Queen Freya lean forward to see what she was pointing at.

"You stabbed Draven with the spear," I said, watching as she brushed aside markers, unbothered as they pinged across the floor. "I thought that was enough to kill him."

"Tsk. I thought you were the smart one. The spear did not pierce his heart. As such, Draven lives... For now." Elara pressed the map flat, the surface now bare except for one red marker she positioned near the Dark Kingdom's southern border. "We need to focus our attention on Neith."

"Neith fell." Zaeth spoke from beside her, his face a careful mask of control. "The streets were bathed in blood, and its people slaughtered."

"It's true," Jarek added with a shake of his head. "Evulka's blessing failed."

Elara's lips quirked as if Jarek had said something amusing. "The beings once occupying Neith are gone, but the power of the site remains. The brothers are positioning themselves there, intent on taking it. We need to stop them before they become even stronger."

"How do you know this?" Queen Freya asked, arms crossed.

Elara lifted an expectant brow. "Can you not feel the concentration of Pax's energy, Wild Queen?"

"I can," Queen Freya confirmed. "But how would the brothers? Furthermore, how is it you claim to know where they will be?"

It was clear by her clipped tone Queen Freya wasn't bothering to hide her skepticism. There was something off with my sister, but I didn't think it wise to make an enemy of her—not until we knew what we were dealing with. Maybe this was a side effect of The Seven Sacred Pools' healing powers.

"Did you overhear them during battle, or..." I asked. El's eyes snapped to mine, no evidence of the flash of black that I'd seen previously.

"I overheard the brothers talking while I was at the pools," she said offhandedly.

"You didn't think to tell us?" Zaeth gritted out.

El shrugged. A soft smile graced her lips as her gaze fixated on the round, red marker placed atop the ancient city. "I'm telling you now. We need to move quickly, Dark King. If the brothers harness the primal forces residing within the city, the boundaries between this world and the next will continue to deteriorate."

"What does that mean?" I asked, the words little more than a whisper.

Her grin widened as her eyes gleamed with a hidden challenge. "Pax will fall."

4

GREER

"She said what?" I shrieked, barely able to dampen the shrill note to my voice.

"Shh," Lannie hissed, glancing around the plant-covered cottage as if we'd be overheard, but our sister was miles away. Queen Freya insisted they return to the Seven Scared Pools to confirm Elara's lead on the brothers. Unsurprisingly, Zaeth accompanied them. He'd yet to allow Elara out of his sight after she's given him the slip and returned to the pools on her own. I wasn't sure if his intent was to keep her safe or to keep everyone else safe *from* her.

"Focus on the pull within, Lannie. They're still at the pools."

She shot me an annoyed look.

"What?" I asked, sending my own narrowed-eyed glare back at her. Elara hadn't wanted to waste time returning there, and she definitely hadn't seemed happy about being asked to show us where she overheard the brothers, but Queen Freya insisted we attempt to validate her story. "We have another hour, tops, before they return. No time to waste."

Lannie sighed but conceded. "I agree Elara is different."

I suppressed the urge to roll my eyes. Lannie was nothing if not methodical. She'd look at this from a hundred different angles before coming to the most logical conclusion. It was a process that yielded results, but one that took time.

"We're all agreed on that," Ryuu said as he passed Queen Halcyon's position at the head of the table and took a seat beside me. The wooden chair creaked under his weight, but his wings fit nicely around the short back. "The question is, *how* is she different?"

Lannie tilted her head to the side, her gaze growing distant as her mind whirled. I felt Lannie tap into our bound, my own essence responding to hers. Our two strings linked, searching for El, following the thread, only to come to the edge of it shroud in frosted darkness.

"I don't think she's gone," Lannie panted, catching her breath as we returned to ourselves. Ryuu's pulse quickened, our mating bond affecting him just as Queen Halcyon was affected by Lannie. My little sister swallowed, carefully avoiding the Earth Queen's glance. "We're still tethered to her but blocked."

Nodding, I replayed all that had happened in the last few days. "Something happened at the pools. Is the enchantress, Levana, able to craft binding spells? It feels like El's essence has been locked away."

Queen Halcyon's brows furrowed. "Why would the enchantress do such a thing?"

I shrugged. "Maybe she wanted El weakened."

"No," Lannie said. "If anything, Elara is stronger. Her speed has increased, her healing even more so. Zaeth dislocated her shoulder, and it took only moments for her to fully recover. Even a normal fae would have had pain for a few minutes."

"Zaeth attacked her?"

"They were sparring," Lannie answered. "If anything, he was protecting Queen Freya from Elara's ruthlessness. She's always been a little battle hungry, but not like this."

"True," I agreed. "Killing off monsters gets her going, but she's never relished pain."

Lannie met my gaze. "That is a key shift in who she is. Not an absence of her fae affinities, but a glorification of them. Like her humanity has been stripped."

"Sort of like a reverse binding?" I asked, trying to follow along.

"It's one theory," Lannie said, shaking her head. She looked as if she might elaborate, but then stopped herself. "Either way, she can't be trusted."

"Agreed," Ryuu rumbled, the soft under feathers of his wings grazing my shoulder. "Trustworthy or not, do we heed her advice and travel to Neith?"

"It sounds like a trap," Queen Halcyon said, glancing up from the map. The battle leathers I'd come to expect her in had been exchanged for a long shirt-and-shorts combination. Her light violet hair was tugged into a high, manicured bun just behind her dark ram horns with a few free pieces framing her face. Queen Halcyon was brave and brilliant, having done much for the people of the Earth Kingdom, but when she was like this, in lounge wear sitting at a dining table, it was a glaring reminder she was only barely older than Lannie.

"Neith has been destroyed," I said. "What could be the harm in checking it out?"

"It would be nearly impossible to fit a sizable army within the city limits," Ryuu added. "Now that Alderidge is dead."

"Perhaps," Queen Halcyon said, eyes drifting back to the map. "She claimed to have overheard the brothers speaking at the pools?"

"Yes," Lannie said. "As if the waters had the ability to link to the brothers' consciousness."

"If that were the case, how could she have 'overheard'?" I asked, meeting Lannie's troubled gaze.

She shook her head. "She wouldn't have, unless—"

"Unless her mind was linked with theirs," Ryuu finished.

All eyes turned to him as the tension in the air thickened.

"I know you want to believe your sister is well," he said, "But we have to consider the possibility that what resurfaced may not be her."

"Not entirely her," Lannie correctly. Her head cocked to the side, a gesture she did when she was working through a particularly difficult problem.

"If her humanity was repressed…" I started, only to fall silent when Lannie's dark gaze focused on mine.

"That wouldn't explain how she heard the brothers, or the extent of her personality changing. She isn't bound."

"Veles has possessed others," Queen Halcyon warned. "What's to stop him from controlling your sister?"

"He's only ever controlled another when he's resided in their body," I said, looking to Ryuu.

"Veles was very much alive and fully formed." He shook his head. "He was busy flitting Draven to safety."

"Why would that not have been to the pools?" Queen Halcyon asked. "If they frequented them as often as the mortal traitor suggested, why not seek the enchantress's help as Zaeth did?"

"Cadoc never said anything about Levana," Lannie mussed. "Only that the brothers used it to speak with each other."

"Suggesting Olysseus, the third brother isn't with them," I nodded, seeing where Lannie's mind had gone. "At least not yet. Maybe they didn't know about Levana."

"Unlikely," Ryuu disagreed. "The pools have been around for eons."

After a quiet moment, Queen Halcyon spoke. "They could have believed the myths of the enchantress to be just that: a story."

"And Levana just, what? Left them alone and let them talk to their brother in another realm?"

I meant it as a joke, an outlandish accusation, but Lannie tilted her head to the side, studying me. "Maybe. The barrier between realms *has been* cracked, as confirmed by that giant fissure in the sky. Either way, Levana would have had access to the brothers' conversations."

The storm that raged only a few nights ago *had* looked as if the lightening were born from the realm beyond ours. It had felt like something had intrinsically shifted as the sky cracked, and though Queen Freya agreed the *feel* of Pax had changed—growing colder, wilder—neither of us were sure how to stop it.

"You think more of those armless dragon monsters are going to come through the rift?"

Lannie lifted a brow. "Wyverns, Greer. And yes. If the wards surrounding Pax are compromised, we'll be fighting a war on two fronts."

"Whatever Levana did, El's alive because of it." The chair scraped across the wooden floors as I pushed to stand, rounding the table toward the Earth Queen and the map of Pax set before her. "Elara's not herself, but she's still trying to warn us. Maybe she had access to Levana's memories when she was healed, or—or absorbed some of her powers. I don't know, but I believe our sister is still on our side."

"You believe that because you want to," Queen Halcyon said, voice soft but cutting all the same. She leaned back, allowing me to turn the map toward myself as I glared at her.

"Yes," I snapped as Lannie and Ryuu gathered behind. "But we're also bound, now. You forget I can sense her, just as Lannie can."

The Earth Queen's gaze shifted to my little sister. It was calculating and curious, an expression I'd seen hundreds of times on Lannie's face. After a long moment, Queen Halcyon nodded.

With a long exhale, I pointed to the small dot, now crossed through with a harsh slash, demarcating it as another location yielded to Veles's wrath. "Neith is along the southern border of the Dark Kingdom. It wouldn't be too far out of the way to validate Elara's claims."

"Claims of what, exactly?" Ryuu rumbled. "She's shared the brothers have fled to the fallen city, but what of their army? What of the Fractured?"

"We have to expect the worst," Queen Halcyon said. "If Veles felt comfortable enough to retreat to Neith, we must assume it is his acting base. We'd need armies—as many warriors as possible. A battle like that takes time. Strategy."

"Time we don't have," breathed Lannie.

Frustration flared as I scoured the map. The Air and Dark Kingdoms were closer together, but Neith was a long way from the Earth Kingdom. Even if armies were ready to deploy at a moment's notice, we'd have to unite our forces before approaching the town. El had made it sound like the brothers were on their way to Neith now. If that was the case, we'd be too late.

"Then what are our options?" I gritted through clenched teeth.

The three of them shared a look, and though Lannie was the practical sister, the logical one, it still stung to see her so emotionally removed from the situation. Her brown eyes met mine, unbothered by my narrowed brows and the slight frown of my lips.

"We need El to give us more information," Lannie said. "If we can intercept Veles and Draven before they're able to reunite with Olysseus, we should take the risk. The three of us are a lot stronger together, especially after the spear. We've been linked only a few days and I can already sense your and El's affinities. There's no telling how the brothers will be affected when they're rejoined—especially if they're able to tap into whatever power is in Neith."

"And if we can't?" I asked. "If El doesn't have any further information to give, what then?"

Queen Halcyon stood, lifting her chin as she met each of our gazes. "Then we prepare for war."

5

ELARA

Something was wrong.

It was harder and harder to surface, to remain present in what Levana was doing with my body. Harder to remember the lives she planned to destroy.

"The pools are dying." A feminine voice reached me through the darkness.

"A shame," I heard myself say with mock concern. "With the essence of the pools waning, I doubt there is enough energy for the brothers to use them. Though, as I said, Veles is already on his way to Neith."

"You overheard them while Levana submerged you?" Zaeth's rich voice pierced through the fog of my mind.

I blinked, forcing myself to pay attention. Slowly, the bright rays of the sun cut through the haze. Sounds became sharper. My vision clearer. Zaeth was here, surrounded by the same mossy banks and bubbling pools he'd brought me to when Draven's blade had been lodged in my stomach, but rather than the lush greens and shimmering lights of darting fairies, the ground had turned yellow, the muddy banks soggy with dead leaves. Even the pools looked dimmer. Darker.

"That's right, Dark King." My lips pulled back in a too-wide grin as my gaze fixed on Zaeth. His beard had grown in thick, framing his strong jaw, but there was a tightness to the set of his lips. His eyes were bloodshot, the cinnamon depths swirling with worry, and the bright rings that I'd come to expect framing his irises were absent. My boot squished through the soft earth as I stepped toward him, turning my back on the waters. "Are you thinking about the last time we were here? About how you cradled me in your arms, begging for my body to be healed."

Zaeth tensed, his shoulders drawing back, but he made no move to pull away. Jealousy and panic roared within me as I watched Levana trace my hand across Zaeth's chest, her touch drifting up to clasp his jaw between my fingers.

Queen Freya made a disgusted sound in the back of her throat. "I'm going to inspect the surrounding area. So far, there's nothing here to prove your story."

My gaze shifted for a moment, flashing with darkness as I caught sight of the Wild Queen flitting through the trees, before fixing my sights on Zaeth.

"Lucky for you the goddess spared my life." Levana leaned in, her fingers drawing his mouth toward mine.

No.

I thrashed, hatred and a mounting wave of fury crashing through me. My grip eased, allowing Zaeth to jerk free. My chest heaved as I opened my mouth to speak. A moment, that was all it took. I had a moment where I could see him, scent him. Where my body was my own again.

Zaeth's eyes flashed, the flicker of rings igniting. I thought he might reach for me, that he might have seen... But my heart beat, and Levana had forced me into submission once again.

"Naughty," she said. I knew she was speaking to both of us, but I felt the rise of malicious joy as she closed the distance to Zaeth. "Do you not care for me, mate?"

Get away from him! I screamed in my mind, raking my nails

through the silver-blue mist restraining me, but the awful grin etched across my face only grew.

Zaeth's cinnamon gaze bored into me, searching. "I would follow you anywhere, love. In this world and the next."

His lips crashed into mine, harsh and demanding. I felt him reaching for me as Levana was distracted by her own arrogance. Zaeth had called me 'love'. I had to believe he'd felt me. Seen me.

He jerked my head to the side, the bite of his fangs sharp as they sank into the soft curve of my neck and drank. My body hummed as he sucked, each pull drawing more of myself into him.

Levana snarled, my palms slamming into Zaeth's chest, and thrusting him back. The flesh at my neck tore, warm blood gushing from the wound. "You dare to bite me?"

The rings around Zaeth's wide eyes were bright and his mouth was coated in a wash of scarlet with fat streams dripping down his chin. He swallowed, settling a cocky smirk in place. "My apologies, Elara. You enjoyed it last time. Was I too rough?"

"Not at all," she said, indignation flaring at the thought of being weak. "As I said, the brothers are converging. We have no time to waste."

Zaeth nodded, his face a mask of control. "As you said, we need to return to Neith."

She lifted my chin, the bleeding along the wound slowing to a trickle and then stopping as our fae healing took over. "Yes."

"We need to go to Neith because you overheard a conversation while the enchantress healed you?" Zaeth pressed.

Levana scowled. "The goddess Levana restored my body, granting me life when death was moments away. I am your mate and I've explained to you my reasoning, yet my words are met with skepticism."

"Enchantress," Zaeth corrected, his head cocking to the side as he studied each shift in expression. "Not goddess."

"No," my voice thundered as Levana's temper flared. "I said

'goddess' and I meant it. Do you know how long these pools have been present, or how vast their powers are?"

Zaeth only stared, watching, Waiting.

"Eons," I felt myself say as Levana stalked among the withering foliage.

Anger spurred on by an unrelenting wave of injustice ripped through me as I met my reflection in the too-still waters. It was me, but my hazel-blue eyes were entirely black, a vicious glower twisting my lips. Levana spoke to the pools, to Pax itself.

"Who determines what beings are gods and which are monsters? The two are just as easily interchanged, depending on beliefs. This world worships Eunoia, the great light goddess who created Pax."

My reflection blinked, the darks of my eyes receding as Levana stifled her rage a moment before turning to meet Zaeth. "Tell me, Dark King, how is it a goddess of light, one born only of the sun and earth was able to create beings from darkness?"

"Erebus joined with the goddess," Queen Freya interjected, the large waxy leaves of the trees behind her still swinging from her return into the clearing. "He coupled with Eunoia to form Pax."

A harsh laugh ripped through me, the stark sound jading. "Yes, I suppose that is a nice way to wrap up loose endings. And the other gods and goddesses of Pax? What about Thetis of the oceans, Iris of the skies? What about the great forges of north with the ever-burning ember, or the immortal responsible for blessing humans with forethought and cunning? Where have they been?"

Queen Freya shot an unsettling glance toward Zaeth, but his gaze stayed fixed on me with cool detachment.

"The minor gods are known—"

"*Minor*," I felt myself sneer. "All other powerful beings fail in comparison to the great Eunoia. Strange to think how an entire realm of semi-intelligent creatures could believe such a ridiculous lie.

"I ask again, Dark King, who determines which beings are pure and which are cursed? Any tale repeated for centuries would seem like the truth to those who weren't there at the beginning. A myth, given life by repetition would cease to be a story, would it not? Gathering strength through mortals' believes, until it became a part of history. And, as such, beyond contestation."

My lungs were heaving, Levana's grip on my consciousness easing as her own resentment seared through my body. I blinked, reaching for Zaeth, but my hand only twitched, before clenching into a fist.

His sharp gaze tracked the small movement, and I could've sworn the rings of light that had yet to fade flashed a shade brighter, but Zaeth looked away before I could be sure.

"I suppose liberties could've been taken," Queen Freya hedged, uncertainty clear in her voice, "with regards to gods—"

"Oh, stop your blabbering," I cut in, Levana fully in control. "I don't have time for useless conversations. It's beneath me."

Queen Freya's lips pressed thin, but she didn't move to speak as Levana carried my body past Zaeth and into the trees, flitting away before I had a chance to scream.

6

LANNIE

Elara returned moments before Zaeth and Queen Freya, her face a fury of emotion as she crashed through the door. Greer and I had felt her coming, had been able to shift the conversation around the table to talk of Neith and what we might find there. Anything else would have been too obvious a slight.

"I'm glad you've seen reason. We must leave at once," Elara said, closing the door to the cottage behind her just as Zaeth arrived. He shot El a glare, holding it open for Queen Freya, before the three of them joined us around the table.

Greer lifted a brow toward our older sister. "Leave for Neith, now?"

Elara shot her a look suggesting Greer had all the intelligence of an earth worm. "Waiting only increases Veles's chance at power."

"Jarek and Evander are due back at mid-day," Ryuu interjected. "They're updating Naz and Soter about the situation. Even so, it will take time to amass an army."

"An army," Elara huffed, a harsh smile tilting her lips. "The brothers may very well already be at the ancient city, and you think to what? Spend weeks coordinating a strike?"

"Yes," Queen Halcyon answered. "If what you say is true and Veles intends to become even more powerful. We can't hope to defeat him with half-a-dozen warriors."

"No," Elara agreed, cocking her head to the side as she slowly circled the wooden table. "Not if he is successful. Do you know what resides beneath the city? What the stones were truly guarding?"

Zaeth matched her steps, his voice carefully neutral. "Something lies beneath?"

She dipped her head once. "A grand temple, one slashed from history."

"What does a temple have to do with power?" I asked, searching for the missing.

"Temples are more than points of worship," Ryuu said as Elara's grin stretched. "Most sit atop collections of energy. Some believe them to be resting places of minor gods, others think they're sites where the goddess Eunoia is closest to the surface."

"Lore aside," I said, contemplating all I'd learned of Pax's history and my new understanding of the way energy shifts in the earth. "You're saying a temple beneath the city of Neith holds power strong enough to unraveling the world?"

Elara met my gaze with an offhanded shrug. "Or reforging it. The brothers have already managed a crack large enough for ice wyverns."

"Yes," I said, glancing toward Greer and then Queen Halcyon. The three of us had discussed the monsters and concluded that the crack wasn't so much a rupture of Pax's wards, but a bridge to the otherworld, one known for unforgiving cold and endless shadows. "Are you suggesting the pool of power beneath this temple is capable of sealing the rift?"

"Impossible," Queen Halcyon breathed. "We'd need a god to rebuild the realms."

"It wouldn't be rebuilding," I countered, my gaze returning to Greer. Her silver curls were piled atop her head in a messy bun, and I was surprised to see she'd donned thin, practical pants beneath her dark red dress, hiding the dragon brand on her left thigh. "Only repairing. Like stitching a tear."

"Oh no." Greer shook her head, seeing where I was going with. "I can't fix the world, Lannie. I'm a cursebreaker, not a goddess."

"Actually," Queen Freya said, disbelief coating her words. "That's not a bad idea."

"You can't be serious," Greer retorted.

"It's better than any of our other ideas," Queen Freya shrugged.

My sister's crystal-blue gaze swung to her mate as Ryuu's wings closed protectively around her. "Is that even possible?"

"In theory," he finally answered, jaw ticking as he pulled her close. "It would take more than a warding spell. You'd need it to last, which requires anchoring it to the foundations of Pax."

"More similar to a binding spell than wards," Zaeth supplied.

"Something of that magnitude would take great strength." Queen Freya met my gaze. "Perhaps the spear could help amplify Greer's affinities, but we'd need all three of you to ground the power, returning it to the earth."

"I thought only Ryuu could wield the spear," I countered.

A frown cut through Greer's blossoming hope as she turned toward Elara. "You used the spear to stab Draven. It's possible for others to wield it."

"I did," Elara smirked. "And how did that go?"

Greer flinched, but my eyes narrowed, focusing on my eldest sister. "Not well. You don't seem like yourself, Elara."

"Is that so?" She asked, her grin shifting to one of amusement. "I suppose you need to decide if you trust me enough to heed my warning, or if you'd rather let Pax fall further under the control of the brothers."

Ryuu bristled as if he sensed a threat, but before he could answer Jarek luxed into the room. His normally pristine appearance was rumpled, the typical light shading around his eyes and pop of color staining his lips absent. His light blond hair was loose, a few of the longer pieces tumbling forward.

"No Evander?" I asked before I could contain the question.

The tension around Jarek's eyes tightened. It seemed I wasn't the only one worrying about him these days. "He hasn't been sleeping well and wished to remain in Caligo."

My stomach lurched as I read beneath the lie. Evander had been avoiding me since I'd healed him—since I'd stollen him from death's claws and returned him to the living. He hadn't mentioned my eldest brother, hadn't dared to whisper Jem's name, but I saw the anguish in his eyes churn each time he looked at me.

I hadn't thought much as to what lay beyond this world, beyond this reality of skin and bones. My intent had always been to save lives, to prevent death through every means possible. I never thought prolonging someone's life could be seen as a slight, but Evander had seen something in the beyond. It was probably nothing more than a vision concocted by his dying brain tissue, some trace of electrical activity conjuring his most cherished desires perhaps, but Evander believed Jem was waiting for him—and that my meddling had ripped them apart.

Ignoring the weight that had settled in my stomach, I swallowed and gave a small nod.

Jarek turned, finding Zaeth. "Naz and Soter have managed to round up the rest of Silas's men. All confirm Silas has proclaimed his right to the Dark Kingdom. He has crafted a new throne, one born of shadow crystal as he intends to rule from the Shadowlands."

Zaeth's jaw ticked, but I caught the slight twitch of Elara's lips. How could she view this as a good thing?

Greer wanted to believe our sister was still with us—I did too—but *this* wasn't Elara. I risked a glance toward Greer, keeping my voice low so that the two of us weren't overheard. "Anything?"

She shook her head. "No binding. Nothing but the thick fog blocking my advancements."

We'd hoped this was simply a matter of Levana trapping El's humanity, something easily reversible now that we'd had practice breaking binding spells—now that we had a true cursebreaker.

No binding, meaning Elara was free to be herself. I cocked my head to the side, cautiously reaching for our bond, easing through the heaviness that pushed against it the closer I got to her.

Elara's eyes snapped to me, the pupils expanding to cover the entirety of her gaze. She blinked and when she opened them, all was normal.

"Just making sure you're well," I breathed, my heartbeat hammering with having been caught prodding.

Her face twisted into a warped smile, the illusion of kindness seeming to mock me before she focused back on the conversation.

"Naz has sent scouts to gauge his army, but they haven't return yet. She offered to go herself, but with shadow crystal being in abundance, I didn't think it wise."

Zaeth shook his head. "I'm glad she heeded your warning."

"Shadow crystal?" I asked, needing the distraction from the growing worry about my sister.

"She can't shadowwalk through it," Zaeth explained. "Just as Jarek can't lux through fire opal."

"Something about the density of the stones and the specific wavelength we tap into when traveling," Jarek added, some of his normal cadence returning. "All very boring… you'd love it."

I flushed.

"Shadowwalking and luxing are exceedingly rare and the stones costly," Ryuu added. "Millennia ago, the Merged took precautions against such affinities, but being that Naz and Jarek are the only two in existence today, no fae bothers fortifying their kingdoms with the material."

"Unless they are attempting to overthrow the ruling Dark King and his shadowwalking sister," Greer supplied, her voice growing more strained by the second. "Just to clarify, we have a war brewing in the north with Silas's presence forcing The Dark Army to respond, meaning even our immediate source of soldiers will be split. Is that correct?"

"That's correct," Jarek sighed. "And let me guess: The murdering brothers are moving quickly?"

"Too quickly," Queen Freya supplied.

"According to Elara," Greer said. "We have today to decide on a course of action or they'll reach Neith, tap into an ancient power beneath its soil and become invincible."

Jarek's brows shot up. "I knew there was something off about that place."

"What do you mean?" I asked as the rest of the room quieted for his response.

He glanced around, sharing a long look with Zaeth, before he answered. "When we first encountered the humans from the base, Naz informed us Alarik and his Select Guard were defending Neith from Draven and a swarm of Fractured. They were protecting the city, but still the barrier held.

"Wards are not a strong affinity for me, but I'm able to sense them, and the ones surrounding Neith were unlike any I'd felt before. They're colder… harsher somehow."

"But wards are normally warm," Greer interjected. "Like particles of light."

Jarek nodded before his stormy blue eyes met mine. "Whatever lies beneath Neith is not only powerful, but dark. It's not of Pax's making."

"Not the Pax you're familiar with," Elara interjected, her voice low.

The others proceeded to talk over the risks associated with going immediately and delaying our trip to Neith, but my gaze narrowed on Elara. She was barely pretending to conceal her emotions, all her eagerness, her mounting excitement clear for any to see.

Logical explanations for what happened to her warred with the evidence before me. There were no binding wards, or other influences we could see, but her scent had changed, her thoughts and actions, her personality—as if she were someone else entirely.

My gaze bounced to Zaeth, the only other fae with a connection to her beside Greer. I blinked, startled to realize he'd been watching me, waiting for me to glance his way. There was caution in his eyes as he darted a quick look to Elara.

A warning.

Zaeth felt it, too—knew the truth, despite the absurdity of it: Elara was being controlled by another.

"It seems we have no other choice," Queen Halcyon spoke, her voice resigned. I meet her silver gaze, knowing she felt my mounting disquiet, just as I was privy to her growing angst. "We leave for Neith in the morning."

GREER

"Would anyone like a drink?" I asked, pouring a small measure of the amber liquid into a glass for myself. I wasn't a huge fan of spirits, but I was going to need something for this conversation. Lannie and Ryuu declined right away. "Zaeth?"

"Thank you, but not tonight," he said, taking a seat with the others.

"Suit yourself." I placed the decanter down and retreated toward Ryuu, choosing to climb into his lap rather than sit beside him. "She didn't even try to act normal."

Queen Freya, Queen Halcyon, Jarek, and Elara had gone to bed hours earlier, but there was still much to discuss before we left in the morning. I'd crept down the cottage hallways, gathering Lannie and Zaeth under a sound-proof ward before returning to Ryuu waiting for us in our room. The domed ward stretched above us, ensuring our conversation remained between the four of us.

"That's not Elara," Zaeth said.

The cushioned seat shifted as I pushed off Ryuu's warm chest, gaze zeroing in on Zaeth. He reclined in the wooden chair at the small table across from Lannie, the wall behind them a collage of vines and hanging plants, but his eyes we sharp.

"Despite it being farfetched, I agree." Lannie sat forward, her spine straight.

I lifted a brow in her direction. "You do? I had a hard time convincing you Veles possessed the Light King, but you're willing to believe our sister is under someone else's control after one day?"

She shot me a glare. "That was different. It was far more likely that the Light King was carrying out Veles's orders rather than a partially formed, ancient fae king taking control of his body."

"And now?" I asked, not sure how I felt about El being another victim of the brothers. "Veles is fully corporal. How could he be controlling her?"

Lannie frowned, but Zaeth answered without hesitation. "It's not Veles or his brothers. It's something else. Something ancient and angry."

"How do you know this?" Ryuu rumbled.

Zaeth's hand twitched, looking as if he was rethinking declining the drink I'd offered earlier. "I drank from her."

"*Drank* from her?" I asked, my voice squeaky.

"Yes," he continued brushing aside my startled response. "But the connection this time was different—"

"*This time?*"

Zaeth shot me an exacerbating glare, causing me to hold up my palms in surrender.

"No judgment on the types of kinks you two are into—"

"Greer," Lannie quipped.

"*But,*" I continued, shooting her a look back before meeting Zaeth's glower. "El is not herself. You can't just go biting her—"

"I wasn't taking advantage of her, if that's what you're suggesting," huffed Zaeth, looking entirely offended.

I lifted my chin, response poised, but Ryuu cut me off.

"Dark fae can derive pleasure from drinking, but sometimes, more powerful dark fae can gain access to a person's essence," Ryuu explained. "Especially if the partner or partners in question have already connected in a similar manner."

"Oh." I blinked, shrugging apologetically toward Zaeth as Lannie massaged her temples and muttered something about knowing too much about her sisters. "You bit her for research purposes?"

"Yes," growled Zaeth. "When we were at the pools, there was a moment where I felt her—the real El. It was fleeting, but I took a chance and what I found was disjointed and disturbing. There were flashes of a dark temple, the pillars marbled with shadow crystal. Silver-blue mist hung heavy in the air. There were also glimpses of a place consumed by frosted darkness, home to creatures who'd never felt the warmth of the sun. Even the air was painful to breathe."

Silence stretched around us. It was Lannie who broke it, her voice laced with uncertainty. "I've seen her eyes flash a few times. I thought it was a trick of the light at first, but it happened again when I was following the tether between us."

"What did they look like?" Zaeth asked.

"Black. Entirely black."

"What does all of this mean?" I asked, looking between them. "If this isn't Veles, then who?"

Zaeth's face fell, torment raging in his eyes as he looked to Ryuu. "I had to risk it. She would have died if I hadn't."

Ryuu shook his head, his shoulders tensing. "Then she would have gone with the goddess—"

"Don't," Zaeth snapped, the cushioned chair crashing to the floor behind him as he stood. "I'll never regret saving her life, whatever the cost."

Ryuu's jaw ticked, looking as if it took all his self-control to not retort.

Lannie's eyes narrowed a moment before widening with

understanding. "You think the enchantress did this, the one from The Seven Sacred Pools."

Zaeth's gaze cut to her. "I think Levana may have invaded her body. The pools were dying when we returned."

Lannie nodded slowly as my mind whirled.

"The enchantress mustn't be allowed to leave the pools," Ryuu's voice was low but humming with warning.

"Don't you think I know that?" Zaeth growled, running a hand through his hair. "The deal I made with her was for my life. I said nothing of Elara's."

"That's not exactly true," Lannie said, and I could practically see the wheels in her head turning.

"You offered the Dark Phoenix's aid," I said, realizing what my youngest sister was getting at. "You never specified who that was, meaning El..." The words lodged themselves in my throat as my breathing quickened.

"Elara is the Dark Phoenix." Lannie spoke the words and I felt the truth of them ring through me. It had always been her—been us.

"The prophecy," I breathed, meeting Lannie's dark eyes swimming with concern. Her new brand of the lotus flower along her shoulder had unnerved me, but I couldn't figure out why. And with everything going on, that concern fell to the wayside. But now...

"It's us, Lannie. If El is the Dark Phoenix and Will was the raven protecting Pax, we must be the others."

Ryuu's arms tightened around me, reflexively trying to keep me safe from what my next words would bring. I met his concern with a sad, resigned smile and continued.

"*Driven by pride, brothers wandered deep,*
Through splintered realms to the shadowed keep.
Severing bonds, they ventured too far,

Enduring pain and harrowing scars."

"THE BROTHERS," ZAETH SUPPLIED. "THEY MUST HAVE GONE TO the otherworld, the one of ice and darkness. Levana's world."

"A RAVEN'S WINGS PROTECT THE REALM,
   The final shield of the human's helm.
   But creatures' crushing blows shall reign,
   Shattering shelter, unleashing pain."

"WILL," BREATHED RYUU, HIS VOICE CRACKING AS I CONTINUED.

"FIERCE DRAGON'S TEARS, RELEASING, FREEING,
   Breaking constraints, finally seeing."

"I WAS THE FIRST TO BREAK THE BINDING ON OUR FAE AFFINITIES. Seeing you injured—" Swallowing the wave of tears, I stared into Ryuu's dark eyes, the green flecks smoldering around vertical slits. "The pain of that moment was enough to undo Mother's spell."

"SILENT LOTUS, SPROUTING REDEMPTION,
   Flourishing without compensation.
   A flicker of light preserving hope,
   Gripping fiercely to the savior's rope."

. . .

My gaze turned to Lannie. "That must be you. You're the anchor, the tether to Pax." Lannie opened her mouth to speak, but then closed it again, and I took it as a sign to continue.

"Dark Phoenix vengeance, harsh, unbending.
　Torment abounds, unchecked, unending.
　Immense powers merge, blending pooling.
　Great storms of chaos twisting, spooling."

"The 'powers merge' must be the three of us uniting the pieces of The Spear of Empyrean," Lannie said, disbelief coating her voice. "And El…"

"Finish it," Zaeth said, his voice hollow.

I opened my mouth to speak but couldn't force the last stanza of the prophecy out. Despite the truth staring me in the face, I didn't want it to be true. Ryuu cleared his throat, tugging me into his arms. I buried my face in his chest, the hard planes rumbling as he finished the prophecy that has haunted us, the lullaby Mother had sung every night until she stripped the memory from our minds.

"When wrongs are righted and wounds mend,
　When fear is conquered at battle's end,
　Darkness will spring, devouring all,
　With malicious tendrils none can stall.

When wicked forces of old arrive,
　Death will reign among the ancient hive."

. . .

"I guess Levana, the enchantress of The Seven Sacred Pools, *would* fill the requirement of 'wicked forces of old,'" I said, realizing what it meant. Realizing just who my sister was being controlled by.

"Yes," Zaeth said grimly. "Meaning the war we've been spending the last few years trying to avoid is finally upon us."

Lannie looked at me, her face crumpling as fear broke through her controlled countenance. In little more than a whisper, she repeated the last of the prophecy, the one line that stirred fear in my heart more than any of the others. "'Death will reign.'"

8

GREER

I didn't trust Elara—Levana—any farther than I could throw her, and let's be honest, my upper body strength was terrible. But it made no difference. The risk of her telling the truth and us not stopping Veles and his brothers from acquiring more power was too great. We were stuck.

Jarek luxed to just outside the city limits, before returning to the Earth Kingdom minutes later to confirm the well of power kept beneath Neith was still there. There was further debate as to if we should wait, but with the source of power confirmed, we couldn't risk it.

"Neith awaits," Jarek said, hands outstretched for Zaeth and Elara—Levana.

She flashed us a triumphant grin as they disappeared.

"There are things you need to be updated on," I breathed, turning toward the queens before we joined Zaeth and Elara at Neith's gates. Lannie, Ryuu, and I used the spare moments to fill them in on all that we'd discovered last night, including our theories about Levana.

Queen Freya scoffed. "Wouldn't it make more sense if the enchantress's healing saved your sister's body but not her essence? I know you want there to be a way to save her, but there's nothing *left* to save."

"There is," I insisted, glancing toward a frowning Lannie. "We can feel her—"

"You feel what you want to feel," Queen Freya said, waving off my protests as Jarek returned. "It's fine, Cursebreaker. We'll do things your way, but if it comes down to my life or hers, I won't hesitate to kill her."

With that, she reached for Jarek, the light fae lifting a blond brow in our direction before luxing with the Wild Queen.

"She's right, you know." Queen Halcyon's face was twisted into a frown, mirroring Lannie's expression. "We see what we want to see. I know you feel her, but you can't deny that tug toward Elara has changed from the connection it originally was."

"A difference is expected if Levana is suppressing El," Lannie said defensively.

Queen Halcyon only shook her head, luxing immediately when Jarek returned.

"There's truth to the queens' words," Ryuu rumbled.

"Not you too," I said with a groan. "We decided last night not to give up on her."

Jarek returned in a flash, looking slightly out of breath. Ryuu seized upon the opportunity to explain about the Elara situation, thereby avoiding further discussion with me.

I lifted a brow at my dragon but couldn't find it in myself to be upset. We had disagreements all the time over small things with most of the conversations turning into mental sparring matches, but this was different. This was my sister. I would fight for her until there was no strength left in my body.

"That sounds terrifying," Jarek said as he looked between Lannie and me. "The enchantress is ancient, her powers untested and unknown."

"That could be a good thing," I said, voice clipped. "She's old and out of practice."

Jarek huffed a laugh. "Or restless and eager to play. If what you say is true, she can't be fully formed, or Elara's body wouldn't be able to contain her. She must have a plan in place to be reborn, like how Veles was."

"What do you men, 'reborn,'" Lannie asked, brows furrowed. "You think Elara could be a stepping stone of sorts?"

"A being as powerful as Levana can't be contained by a normal fae. I'm surprised El's body hasn't already collapsed from the strain." Worry churned in Jarek's gaze as he dragged a hand across his face. "Gods, Evander can't handle anything else. He's already sleeping through most of the day and barely eating. If I had to tell him Elara was dead, that any of you were—"

"It won't come to that," I soothed.

"You can't promise that." Ryuu's voice was gentle, pacifying almost, but he couldn't feel what I did.

"I can, and I will," I said, lifting my chin in challenge. "Let's go, Lannie. We have a sister to save, a temple to find, and a band of brothers to murder."

Naz met us in the field across from the arching stone bridge. She had shadowwalked two dozen guards, the entirety of what the Dark Kingdom could spare. It wasn't much, but it was something.

"Has anyone gone in yet?" I asked as Naz brushed the sheen of sweat from her brow.

"Not yet," she answered. "The last time I was here, the wards kept us out until daybreak."

I glanced up, the bite of fall dulling the rays of warmth from the rising sun. "We're good on that front."

"Exactly," she said, shooting me an exacerbated look. "Why

would the wards keep us out but allow shadow wraiths in? The people of this peaceful town were slaughtered. Most had never seen a weapon in their lives, as they believed Evulka's sacrifice would be enough to keep them safe."

Elara told me the story when she'd first return from Neith. Evulka had fallen in love with a mortal, Khrysaor, and upon his death siphoned her life force into the surrounding lands rather than live without him. Elara had thought it ridiculous. I'd found it romantic.

"They were wrong," Zaeth finished.

He followed El's line of sight to the village set before us. The winding cobblestone streets and vacant shops were no longer a thriving home to fae and humans... but a tomb frozen in time.

My gaze dipped to the silver stones on this side of the river, the rounded, blue-tinged edges linking together into an arching bridge and a ring surrounding the village. The walls loomed ahead, still giving off the appearance of being strong and imposing, but the large door set at the mouth of the bridge was slightly ajar.

"Enough with the preamble." Elara said, an unusual giddiness to her voice as she started toward the bridge.

Zaeth was there in a flash, flitting in front of her. Elara's lip curled back, looking as if she might snarl, might launch herself at Zaeth, but he remained cool in the face of her fury. Detached even.

"Shadow wraiths sacked this city. Veles and his brothers have had days to regroup. It would help if the men were briefed on what to look for."

Elara studied him a long moment before nodding, the tension in her shoulders easing just a little.

Naz exhaled, the small sound drawing my attention to the way the grip on the hilt of her blade lightened. I lifted a brow in her direction, anger clear in my expression.

"He's my brother," she said, meeting my gaze without trepidation.

"Yes, and *she's* my sister."

She only shrugged before answering in a voice nearly too soft to hear. "Is she?"

"There will be a clearing of wildflowers with stone columns," Elara said, her voice carrying across the tense silence as she spoke to the warrior of The Dark Army. "Neith was founded because fae and humans felt the power of such a place, despite its meager appearance. It has been seen as a site of refuge, a temple of its own sort. If any make it to the stones, they are to set up a perimeter, but not get too close."

Zaeth nodded once, turning away from Elara only long enough to address his men. "I trust that Naz has filled each of you in on what we face today. The goal is to be quick in discovering the stone columns and guard it while we work to destroy the brothers. You all know what Veles and his brothers have done to our world."

There was a murmuring of agreement, the warriors growing restless as Zaeth held them, poised on the tip of a blade.

"We will not let him gain this power."

Nods and growls of agreement filled the air. Ryuu and Jarek shifted, humming with their own pent up energy. Lannie glanced to Queen Halcyon and Queen Freya, noting much of the same. Everyone had had enough of loss and mourning. Enough of defeat.

"Today, on this soil slick with fae and human blood, we will make a stand and turn the tides of war." Zaeth pointed to the silent city, meeting Elara's gaze as he turned.

She grinned, like a cat having been given the finest cream.

"After you," Zaeth said, arm sweeping out before him.

She leaned forward, tracing a sharpened nail down his cheek with a feline grin, before flitting toward the bridge. The men rushed forward, swords at the ready.

We had no choice but to follow. No choice but to listen to her tales about an ancient temple with the power to destroy Pax, but as the others surged forward, as I started after Levana controlling my sister's body, I couldn't help the cold shudder of fear that gripped me.

9

LEVANA

FOOLS, ALL OF THEM.

I didn't bother to hide the sinister smile curving my lips or the excited gleam in my eyes. I was so close. After everything—thousands of years of plotting and biding my time—I was mere minutes away from achieving all that I'd planned.

The silver stones pulsed a faint blue as I stepped across the bridge toward the towering walls of Neith. It felt that same as it had when my temple was first constructed, but everything else had changed. Pushing through the wooden gates left ajar from the last attack, I followed the familiar path, the once dirt road now lined with vacant homes and corpses. Flies and blood sprites swarmed the bodies, the air heavy with the scent of rotting, spoiled meat.

That's all fae and humans were—flesh and decay. Weak. An endless plague on this world. They thought my creatures were monsters, but the Fractured were merely a means to an end. A learning experience on the way to correcting the course of Pax's future. I'd tried to revert the fae into what they were meant to be, but the transition was too much. Stripping a fae of their humanity left them twisted and damaged—left them *fractured*—though, still better than Eunoia's creatures.

My boot slid on the entrails of an opened abdomen, the goo pressing between the cobblestones of the street. Disgustingly frail things.

They thought they were clever, assuming their whispered words and side glances had gone unnoticed. Had they truly believed they could misdirect *me*, the ultimate deceiver? The Goddess of Chaos?

The arrogance. The naivety. It would be their downfall—I'd make sure of it.

Even the sisters. Elara would be discarded as soon as I was reborn, despite Erebus's shadows, but the others would need to be dealt with.

Eunoia had blessed the two of them, despite their half-human lineage. They were following now, aware that I wasn't their sister but helpless to do anything about it. They were but budding blossoms in a freshly planted field, while I was the endless forest stretching toward the horizon. Really, it was amusing they thought they stood a chance.

I hadn't pretended to be more like their sister because I hadn't needed to. All that had been required was to get the sisters here, to this ancient site surrounded by the power of my stones. I'd allowed Neith to prosper because it had served my purpose, keeping Eunoia's attentions elsewhere.

When that ridiculous fae, Evulka, had given up her essence to be with her human lover, Khrysaor, it hadn't been the land she'd been feeding. It was me. I'd used her sacrifice as an excuse to stretch my power, letting whispers of it surface as a test.

Eunoia was none the wiser.

My sister never did understand this world, at least not the world Erebus and I had intended. In time, he would've come to embrace the fierceness of my children.

Erebus, that lying, cheating disgrace of a god. His betrayal had hurt, but Evulka had been the one to shatter my heart.

The Merged, fae, *humans*—each of them had grown weaker under my sister's influence. *Pax* had grown weaker, governed my morality rather than strength.

No matter.

They never understood the vastness of my power, the lengths I would go for my freedom.

Glancing behind me, I checked to make sure the sisters had followed. They were toward the back, flanked by the Air Prince, Wild Queen, and Earth Queen, but they were here—trapped—just as their sister was inside the shadows of her own mind.

I let my power flare, casting a ward around the city, stretching up from the stones surrounding it. My sister's prophecy had warned them, had nearly stopped my return. And that meddling seducing mother of theirs placing the binding spell...

All would have been lost.

Elara had grown strong enough to house me with their affinities awakened, but it had also created a vulnerability. I was not immortal in this form. Outside of this village, my vessel could have been killed, returning my essence to the void in the process. It would have taken thousands of years for my body to rise again, but here, on this patch of land that would be my rebirth, I was nearly invincible.

The barrier between realms was splintered, some of my children already finding the rift. The wards would continue to crack, and then the rest of my darlings would join me. Together, we would take this world back, just as soon as I shed this form.

Excitement hummed within me at the thought of finally being free. Elara was more determined than I'd intended and blessed by Erebus himself. No doubt the God of Night meant only to hinder me by keeping her consciousness intact. I hadn't intended to have the strain of my returning power put to the test so thoroughly, but it would be no matter soon enough.

The figures shifted in the shadows a few paces further along the narrowed street as I followed the decaying bodies into the heart of the city. Swaying grasses of the field marking the start of the temple were visible just beyond.

Perfect.

"This way," I called loudly, altering my creatures to our presence. I'd kept them here, my children of shadows. My wraiths. Kept them waiting until I returned.

The Dark King stiffened as the rest of the fae followed, like a flock of sheep delivered to a pack of hungry wolves. With one last, delighted glance behind my shoulder, I slipped passed my concealed creatures with their bony hands clasped around scythes poised to strike.

"Shadow wraiths!" The Dark King screamed, intercepting a swiping blade aimed at another's neck.

Chaos ensued as metal clashed. My children blocked the fae from following, flooding the street behind me in waves. I inhaled deeply, the scent of fresh blood misting the air, mingling with the rancid decay of bodies long since dead. *Delicious.*

"Naz," the Dark King shouted. "Don't let her out of your sight."

The princess's attention snapped to mine, her body wavering before solidifying in place. Confusion marred her pretty face for a moment, her eyes searching for shadow crystal to explain why she couldn't travel. But my stones—my power—was beyond shadow crystal.

"I can't shadowwalk," she breathed, meeting Zaeth's worried eyes.

He cursed. "Jarek, to Elara. Now!"

The light fae's skin shimmered, a pulse of power rising, only to be snatched away, bleeding into the earth. I grinned There would be no shadowwalking or luxing here. Not on my land, on the first site of worship where I'd once received sacrifices of the tallest order... on the hallowed ground of my imprisonment.

I paused long enough to find the Dark King, waiting for him to realize. Fury twisted his features, the bright rings around his irises proof of Eunoia's favor. I wondered if he knew my sister was the reason the brands of the Dark Throne hadn't appeared. Eunoia's power was greater than his fae father's—far greater than any force in this world.

That fact needed to change.

Lifting my hand in a mocking wave, I turned from the battle behind me, flitting toward the field and the cluster of silver-blue stones at their center.

Toward my release.

10

LANNIE

Howls sounded in the distance as the clash of steel rang. Shadow wraiths attacked from every corner of the narrowed, cobblestoned street, their scythes swiping across bodies in great arcs. Greer's wards of protection wrapped around us like a bubble, impenetrable unless she purposely pulled back the light-woven net as she was doing right now.

"Do you have him?" Greer asked, palms raised as she maintained the barrier.

"Yes," I said, peeling off the split edges of the fae's sleeve. A shadow wraith had slashed at his arm, the scythe sinking through muscle until it hit bone. Some of his fae healing had started, but flushing the wound with a tonic and applying a quick salve would have him feeling better in minutes. My fingers worked nimbly until a fresh dressing was in place. The fae pressed up with a 'thank you' and returned to the fray. "On to the next."

We worked in tandem, Greer navigating through swinging blades as I healed those in need. Naz and Jarek guided the dark fae warriors among the swarm of wraiths, but Ryuu remained by our side, never straying far. My stomach clenched as I watched the shadow wraiths part for Elara, Zaeth slicing through them moments later as he flitted after her.

Elara had planned this—no, not El. Levana. She'd set us up, dragged us to this city for what? Why not kill us on the way when we had been less prepared?

My mind raced as I bent to heal another. Tucking bands of intestines back inside his abdominal cavity, I poured the clear tonic into the open wound, before stitching him up. Though fae could ward off most diseases, the tonic would prevent infection and seal any major bleeding. He'd been lucky. Another minute, another inch deeper, and he would have bled out... just like Ahmya.

The image of her split in two by a scythe was something I'd never forget. I hadn't been able to save her then... probably couldn't now, but I was determined to unlock the key to my healing affinities and become just as useful as Jarek was.

Ryuu returned to our sides, his tunic stained with sweat and blood. Shadow wraiths didn't bleed, their gaunt figures crafted from bone, shadows, and sickly grey skin. The gore marring Ryuu's tunic, the pools of blood littering the streets—they were from fae.

"Zaeth has gone after Elara," Ryuu called, decapitating a wraith with a swipe of his sword. A cacophony of howls erupted in the distance, snapping our attention to the north. Dozens of cú sídhe crested the hill set before us, blocking our direct path to chase after El. Their numbers fanned out, howls sounding from the west, east, behind—we were surrounded.

"We thought this was a trap," Greer acknowledged, sending a sheet of light barreling into a wraith. The creature stumbled back with the blow, allowing a dark-haired fae to finish it off. "But why is Levana running away? Her monsters are here, why flee?"

The largest of the malicious wolves stepped forward, throwing its head back in an ear-splitting howl, before launching forward. The rest of the pack followed, the cú sídhe joining the shadow wraiths. Jaws bit into flesh, bones snapping from the impact as blood sprayed.

"Stay within your shield," Ryuu called with a curse, flitting into the mayhem.

We heeded his command, aiding those we could as we navigated the street, slowly working our way toward El. I focused on the tether, sensing Greer doing the same. As long we could feel her, we would fight. As long as she remained trapped, a voyeur in her own body, we'd find a way to bring her back.

Her essence seemed to flicker, the connection growing stronger for a fleeting moment.

Hold on just a little longer, El.

I gasped as pain tore through my chest, my knees buckling under the pain. It was like every nerve ending in my body had been ignited, like a million cuts had sliced through each layer of my skin only for alcohol to be poured over the open wounds. My stomach turned, chest heaving as my meager breakfast joined the spoiled pools of rot on Neith's streets.

Greer's body writhed beside mine, the cover of the shield forgotten.

"It's El," she panted, arms wrapped around herself. Her silver-blond curls were matted to her forehead, her crystal-blue eyes closed tight in a grimace. "Something's wrong."

I opened my mouth to respond, but a deep growl from behind cut me off. My head snapped up, spotting the large wolf responsible meters away. Its haunches were raised, sharp, blackened fangs bared and snarling.

"Greer..." I started, but before I could utter more, the beast pounced.

11

ELARA

My consciousness fluttered as a pulse of power rocked through me. I blinked, focusing on the cluster of silver stones vibrating with a light blue energy, the sight made all the more menacing by the body of corpses surrounding it.

"How nice of you to join me, Elara." Levana spoke with my voice. My mouth. "Just in time to watch my rebirth."

The largest slab dropped, the weight buckling under the pressure of the other stones. Rocks tumbled into the darkness as the scent of stale air and damp earth rose, mingling with the distant sounds of howls and clashing metal.

I looked up, Levana seeming to allow me to view the field of wildflowers littered with bodies surrounding us and the quaint city beyond: Neith.

The glow of a shield flashed amid the homes of the city. I could feel the tether of my sisters' connection thrumming as Greer's wards deflected the blow of an arching scythe. They were here, caught in the fray of battle, darting among the injured. It looked like Lannie was healing our fallen warriors, ensuring that despite our fewer numbers, we had a chance at victory.

Seeing the mayhem around my sisters sent a spike of worry through me, but my attention was redirected toward the deep tugging that sent my heart fluttering. It was warmth and love. Darkness and unchecked fury.

Zaeth.

I focused on the shadow wraiths and wolves just beyond the field, and the blur of darkness cutting through them.

He was a coming for me.

Another howl pierced the morning sky, the sound drawing my lips into an unbidden grin as Levana wrenched away what little control she'd allowed me to hold.

"Make your peace, Elara. That was the last time you'll look upon this world, though I have little doubt that your sisters will soon join you in the after."

Levana forced my body through the stone opening and into the earth. Sounds fell away as my feet followed the cold stairs, each step taking me further from my sisters... further from Zaeth.

I could feel his rage, his longing. His fear. Somehow, he must have realized what had happened. The connection between us flared brighter, banishing more of the haze around my mind. I hadn't even realized the shadows had started to gather again.

I only needed to remain present long enough to see him, and hope he knew a way to save me... Or, at the very least, kill Levana along with me.

"Tsk," Levana reprimanded with my voice. "The Dark King may have figured out you're not yourself, but make no mistake, Elara, nobody can help you now."

I wasn't sure how long my feet continued finding step after step in the infinite darkness, moving past fallen boulders as the earth rose, but eventually my strides slowed. I blinked, attempting to shake off the rising darkness that had started lulling be back to sleep and focused on the large door crafted from shadow crystal set before me. The forgotten passage

Levana led me down was still cold, but the oppressive weight of the narrowed tunnel had eased as it opened into an antechamber of sorts.

Levana held my hand out, my fingers brushing along groves of the door before us. Words in a language long since forgotten spilled from my lips, the purple stone flaring with a silver-blue light. There was a build in energy, electricity humming around us as scripture of the ancient language illuminated carved groves along the door's surface.

Line after line came to life, the text traveling from the thick slab of shadow crystal to the looming, rounded pillars on either side. The primal language stretched further into the chamber, igniting each pillar with a silver-blue glow, until a grand temple came into view.

The light pierced through the last of the fog hovering around my mind, allowing me to be fully present in this moment.

"It seems even Erebus's shadows tire of our game, Elara."

Erebus? Yes... I remember Levana mentioning his name when I'd first been possessed. The shadows had protected me then, cocooned me in a shroud separate from Levana's influence, but they'd shifted after a while. Rather than protect, it had felt like the shadows were dragging me under, urging me to fade into the darkness and never remerge.

"You thought the shadows lulling you into the darkness were of my making?" A harsh laugh bubbled in my throat as the shadow crystal door trembled and then split. Swirling silver mist rose from the jarring crack down the middle, the scent of stale air and damp earth suffocating. "Your blessed father may have saved you, but there's a reason behind his actions—one that always benefits him.

"I knew what my sister was planning, but she never would have had the power to imprison me without him—without

Erebus. So, I tied his fate to mine. An insurance policy of sorts. If I was to be bound, then so would he."

My pulse raced as my mind spun, recalling a time not too long ago when I'd tracked and destroyed a group of goblins with Zaeth. Ryuu and Jarek had all but confirmed I was fae even before Mother's curse had been broken, but it had been Zaeth who'd known I was dark fae. Zaeth who had always been quick to point out how powerful my dark affinities were, how I was able to sense the essence of Pax in the north, and how I was one of the few dark fae in all of existence gifted with bloodlust.

Panic seized me, its talons sinking into to my consciousness as realization dawned. *I* was the Daughter of Darkness, born from the God of Death and Torment. If that were true, if I was blessed by the God of Night, then did that mean…

My fingers gripped the split edges of the glowing shadow crystal door, thrusting them away from each other. Silver blue mist swirling toward us in great clouds, pricking with energy as I stepped forward under Levana's will.

"Yes, Elara. You've almost unraveled the truth of things."

Levana guided us through the silver mist, the walls of the temple coated in scripture still glowing a faint blue and casting the space in a soft light. Thick columns were spaced along the periphery, the mosaic floors shimmering with cut gems— diamonds, I realized, hundreds of diamonds set within obsidian fragments. The two of them looped together in large swirls, until they joined in an infinite circle surrounding a great black alter in the center of the room.

Levana halted, palms hovering over the surface of the large obsidian slab. My gut twisted as electricity pricked along my spine.

Feeling my mounting panic, Levana smirked, lowering my hand another inch. The black stone surface flared a bright silver as my fingers neared, the pulse of energy dimming again when Levana pulled away.

There was something dangerous about that alter. Something that held the power to destroy everything I knew. Everything I was. It felt like my worst nightmares had been complied, like the essences of fear itself had been lumped together and then pressed into the obsidian stone set before me.

I wasn't sure what this place was, but I knew one thing for certain: I didn't want to go anywhere near that alter.

Pebbles tumbled down the stairs behind me, pinging off their smooth edges. Levana heard them too, my head cocking to the side as she focused on the sound.

My heart stuttered as the heavy footsteps drew nearer. It was Zaeth. It had to be.

"You're right," Levana answered my thoughts. "The Dark King comes for you, drawn to the darkness of your soul. The two of you have always been joined, if not by your shared shadows than by my sister's blessing. His light to your dark. Two halves of a whole."

His light? Zaeth was a dark fae—the Dark King.

"Yes," Levana said. "I am proud how the darkness blossomed in him, but it's tempered by my sister's light. Haven't you seen the rings around his eyes? All my best creatures... ruined."

Your creatures? Zaeth has nothing to do with you. I shouted in my mind, suddenly feeling like rather than coming to save me, Zaeth was walking toward his own demise.

His footsteps grew louder, their pounding racing in time with my frantic heartbeat.

"El!" Zaeth shouted from the antechamber, the tether between us strengthening. Gods, he was so close.

I thrashed against Levana's will, bucking and fighting the silver mist caging my consciousness, but it was no use. There was nothing to fight against. She was more mist than monster, an immortal jailer who had crafted the perfect cage.

"There's no use in fighting," she said, loud enough for Zaeth to hear.

He stepped through the cracked pieces of shadow crystal, the silver-blue mist parting for him... ushering him forward as if by Levana's command.

No. Run! Zaeth, you have to leave.

But my lips only tilted at the edges. I could feel the prick of my fangs extend as Levana called on my fae affinities. She allowed me one moment to meet Zaeth's gaze, one pump of my heart to stare into his blazing cinnamon eyes and impart all the love and regret churning inside of me, before her grin stretched in a grotesque mockery of a smile.

"You're too late, Dark King. Nothing can save her now."

With one last, taunting grin, Levana turned away, pressing the flat of my palms through the swirling silver-blue mist and against the great obsidian alter.

12

ELARA

For a moment, I felt only the pulse of electricity stinging the tips of my fingers and the silver-blue mist caressing my skin before it erupted into a wash of purple flames. My body remained fixed to the alter, immovable as the unnatural fire grew. Violet flames coated my hands, my arms, my chest, until all that remained was the feeling of my skin melting away under the scorching heat of the fire.

Zaeth's frantic shouts were muted, the intensity of his screams silenced by a silver sphere surrounding me—wards. They'd ignited when my hands connected with the alter, like a trap sprung. The purple flames reflected in the glow of the silver wards encased me, playing back my own torment as I trashed against Levana's control.

The wards flared with each beat of Zaeth's fists, his ebony wings exploding out from his shoulders as he tried again and again to reach me.

Agonized screams tore through my chest, the flames growing hotter, burning deeper. Skin bubbled along my fingers, my forearms, the top layers giving way to juicy bands of tissue beneath—until the fire split.

Purple flames danced across the surface of the alter, linking and thickening into a distorted mirrored image of hands. The fire climbed in the air before me, dragging pieces from my body with it. As the tissue along my arms charred, the pair of limbs across me solidified, as if partaking in some macabre exchange of life.

Each part of my body burned, until the traitorous flames crafted a figure with pale skin, a head with long, ebony hair. Plump red lips appeared next as mine withered away, the monster finishing as cold, black eyes came into focus.

Levana grinned as the wards flared under Zaeth's incessant battering, his anguished cries growing more frantic with each passing second. I caught flashes of the scene through his eyes: my hair consumed, my body charred and smoldering, covered in cursed violet flames as he slammed into the barrier over and over again.

His knuckles were bleeding, the bones of his hands crushed as if more than one had broken. But he delivered another blow, the brands along his arms and chest pulsing with power, his wings thrown wide.

This time, the wards cracked.

I felt Zaeth redouble his efforts as a wave of warm, foul air blasted out, ruffling the disheveled strands of his matted hair—the smell of me burning alive.

He was coming, but I was already lost. The flames surrounding me had started to shrink, unable to continue to burn with the same vigor now that most of my body was covered in a thick layer of blacken flesh.

Another pull of my essence drained away. There was only a flicker of life remaining... trapped in my burnt shell of a body. The images in my mind grew dim, some from my perspective while others were witnessed through Zaeth's eyes.

Levana consumed more, her skin flushing as my body

bowed over the alter, held standing only by the force of the spell she was casting.

She inhaled deeply, pulling the last of the purple fire into her lungs. Her skin was glowing with power, the blackness of her eyes absolute as she leaned forward and held my faltering gaze.

"Even now, he thinks he can save you." Her scarlet grin stretched. "You are little more than ash. Your essence remains grounded in this world by my will alone, and *still* the Dark King thinks he can undo your fate."

"Get away from her!" Zaeth snarled, his voice more beast than fae. Another crack sounded, the wards flickering under his raging assault as a piece of the barrier crumbled. He was so close to breaking through... I could see the wards splintering. But I could feel that small kernel of hope Zaeth clung to start to waver as he looked upon what was left of me.

I'd never heard Zaeth afraid before. Even when Draven had stabbed me, when I was slumped in his arms bleeding out, his endless resilience had never lessened. He refused to believe I could be taken from him, had vowed to destroy this world and all others if the gods even attempted. Zaeth was unbreakable. Fearless... but *here*, in this moment, the unhinged pitch of his voice dripped with terror.

"Do you think this will break him?" Levana cocked her head to the side, her cold eyes fixing on Zaeth behind me. "He bargained with me for your life, not understanding the phoenix I required was you. I had planned on killing him, but I think forcing him to live will be more entertaining."

I focused on the tether connecting me to Zaeth, not allowing myself to dwell on how quiet my body had gone or the absence of the steady rise and fall of my chest. I ignored the detachment I felt toward my mangled limbs, the growing coolness surrounding my charred torso despite the embers still searing my skin, and pushed all my energy—all my love—into Zaeth.

He gasped, the pounding on my cage faltering a moment

before starting anew. Zaeth grunted and he shoved through the widening crack. "Hold on, love. I'm coming."

With one last glace toward Zaeth, Levana withdrew her hands from the obsidian alter, releasing my body from its forced position and allowing the last of the wards to collapse.

She looked down on me, the cruelty of her smile chilling. "Only the strong survive."

13

GREER

I MANAGED TO RAISE MY HANDS IN TIME TO STOP THE BEAST FROM sinking its fangs into my little sister. Doing my best to concentrate through the invisible pain lashing through me, I sent a pulse of light woven into a point at the creature's chest. It pierced fur and flesh, blasting out the other end as the rabid wolf collapsed at Lannie's knees.

"Are you okay?" I asked, reconstructing our shield as I pulled away from my tether to El. Her pain faded into the background. It was still there but tolerable. Ryuu caught my gaze, his wings protecting him from a cú sídhe's attack while he engaged a wraith. I gave him a nod, letting him know the pain he felt was not my own.

When I turned back to Lannie, it seemed she'd pulled back from El as well. Her skin had taken on a sickly hue as she used the back of her sleeve to wipe away bile from her lips. Worried brown eyes, the same shade as our father's, met mine, swirling with fear and something dangerously close to resignation. "I think she's dying, Greer."

Her words sent a pang of grief through me. We'd lost too many family members to this storm. To Levana and Veles, to the horrors of a war not of our making. Unable to stand the terror staring back at me, I turned to the chaos surrounding us. We were nearly at the end of the street, the field of wildflowers and swaying grasses surrounding silver-blue stones visible just beyond.

"She went this way," I called, unwilling to believe the three of us wouldn't make it out of this.

Ryuu fell in beside us as we cut through the sea of wraiths and wolves. His wings flexed and whirled as his sword spun, the golden barbs glinting beneath his soft, white-speckled feathers.

Ryuu hacked through the onslaught of Levana's creatures as I maintained the shield, adjusting it as we went, until we reached the edge of the clearing and left the raging battle behind.

Corpses were clustered around the stones, the faint trace of night-blooming jasmine and cedar indicating this was where Zaeth and Levana had vanished. Levana, the mysterious enchantress possessing my sister. The one who insisted we go to Neith to stop the brothers only to be attacked not by them, but by a team of monsters who seemed to sense Levana beneath the skin of my sister. Monsters who appeared to be in allegiance with her.

"There must be a temple beneath," Lannie said, joining my side to stare at the descending stairs.

I followed her as she took the first step, feeling Ryuu close behind us. His wings obstructed the little bit of light reaching the first few steps, even though they were tucked in tight, plunging us into darkness as we descended.

"Something primal and powerful is down here," Lannie whispered. "I can feel it humming in the walls, feel is vibrating beneath my feet. I don't think Veles and his brothers are going to show. Levana wanted the power for herself."

I couldn't sense the ground the way Lannie could, aware only of the charge thickening in the air. "But why have us come along? Levana controls El. She could have flitted away at any time."

Lannie was silent for a moment, as we continued in the darkness. "She must have needed us here—the three of us. This city... Ryuu, you said it was warded the first time you battled Draven?"

"Yes," Ryuu said, his voice seeming loud in the surrounding quiet. "We couldn't enter until daybreak."

"Daybreak or until the battle was over?"

I considered my sister, trying to puzzle out what she was considering. "You think the wards aren't from Evulka?"

"No. I think Levana has been controlling the wards around Neith all along. The stones surrounding this place are nearly identical to the ones at The Seven Sacred Pools and the ruined temple by our childhood home."

Ryuu inhaled sharply. "Only an extremely powerful being would be capable of spanning multiple areas of Pax at once. Only a..."

"A goddess?" I finished. "I know Levana has been insisting she's more than an enchantress, but is it possible our sister is possessed by an actual goddess?"

When Lannie answered, her voice was eerily calm. "Yes. It's the only logical explanation. When El first came to Neith, she was still bound by Mother's curse. Levana admitted she needed a strong enough vessel to house her, but El's human form wouldn't have been able to sustain a being of such power."

"Possession is not something that can be forced," Ryuu added. "Like the Fractured, the being housing another's consciousness must grant access to themselves. That's why I was worried when Zaeth made a bargain with Levana. He agreed to be her tool, exposing his body and soul to her bidding."

"He offered the Dark Phoenix," Lannie said, reminding me of the prophecy and our roles in it. "On his mate's behalf."

Zaeth, who had done everything he could to protect my sister, offered his life, his very soul for hers... and still it wasn't enough. We'd ended up here, despite everything it had cost him.

We neared a landing of packed earth bathed in a silver-blue glow coming from a space just out of view. The light was beautiful, but my gut twisted at the scent of burned hair and skin that came from it. "Ryuu, how *was* Veles reborn?"

A part of me already knew the answer. I'd been trying to deny it, to look away from what was awaiting my big sister, but as I felt Ryuu tense, felt the pulse of fear-tinged alarm ring down our tether, I knew my worst fears were correct.

"I killed the Light King he was possessing, freeing his soul."

"There's power in death," Lannie breathed.

My stomach clenched as I joined Lannie at the foot of the stairs. Thick columns glowed with a pulsing, silver-blue script, illuminating the antechamber set before us. A temple was visible beyond, a large shadow crystal door split in two. Mist swirled from the crack, flickering with a faint purple light from whatever lay inside.

Dread spiked as Ryuu adjusted the grip on his sword, poised and ready for what awaited us beyond this point.

I turned inward, searching for my eldest sister. Lannie's tether was buzzing, too, both of us needing to reach Elara, despite the pain we'd last felt. Needing to know she was still here, waiting on the other side of the foreboding mist gathering around our ankles.

But as I reached for my sister, for her soul... I found only emptiness.

14

ELARA

Levana grinned as Zaeth flitted forward, her eyes blazing with malicious delight, before she turned and flitted through the darkness. I watched from above as my burnt, charred body fell, as pieces of skin and muscle flaked off. Zaeth's arms came around me, but I was already fading into an endless darkness.

It felt like I was floating, suspended between this world and the next before my soul was pulled into the beyond.

The shadows that had been shielding me through Levana's control fell away, exposing a vast expense of darkness.

"My brave, beautiful daughter, please forgive me."

My heart lurched as I turned to face the familiar, forgotten voice of my childhood. "Mother?"

She was there, her hair the same silver blond of Greer's, and her frame petite and willowy just like Lannie's. Crystal-blue eyes beamed at me, causing the edges to crease with laugh lines as her pale-pink lips split into a smile.

"You can't stay long, but I begged the Goddess of the After to grant me time to explain."

A cry shook my chest as I raced toward her, but my body

didn't move. I looked down, only to find that I was more smoke than form.

Her smile grew sad. "As I said, we don't have long."

"What does that mean?" I implored, glancing around but seeing nothing but an impenetrable blackness. "Am I dead?"

"All will be revealed soon, but you must listen," she insisted.

The ghost of my mother started forward, her hand grasping mine in a cold, but firm clasp. It was like holding on to a whisper of a memory, one buzzing with a foreign type of power.

Then the darkness shifted. Mother remained the only consistent presence, her grip in mine tight, as the world changed around us.

We were drawn back to the night of the storm. Jem and Torin were crouched over Greer and Lannie, their bodies trembling with pain. Father used his own body to shield me from the worst of it, while Mother held a baby with the beginnings of silver-blond curls: Will.

"This was the day I realized your fate was sealed."

I met Mother's sad gaze with a question. "The storm?"

"The curse," she nodded. "The storm was, indeed, a magical attack, one meant to weaken the barriers around Pax. The brothers were searching for a way to return. Too long had they been trapped in the otherworld, their desire for power too costly, even for them.

"The Dark King told you of my involvement in the Warriors of Vita?"

My brows furrowed as I searched through memories of a conversation with Zaeth many weeks ago. All the while I stared at the scene before me, watching the nightmare of a day replay. Lannie, Greer, and I had crawled out, now staring helplessly as our brothers and father were plagued by the invisible effects of the twisted storm.

"Zaeth said the Warriors of Vita believed the prophecies

weren't warnings, but requests from the goddess. That you and a group of others sought to fulfill them."

Mother flinched. "We were wrong, but by the time I realized what I'd done, it was too late."

The memory of our cottage faded away, replaced by crisp, open skies. The scent of moss and fresh water clung to the air as warm swirls of wind whirled toward us. A young woman, no older than I was now, clung tight to the dark traveling cloak wrapped around her, the ends of her sleek blond hair spilling from beneath the drawn hood. A large mare stomped a hoof on the packed earth, its tail swishing as she secured the last of her possessions to his back. She shot a worried glance behind her, scouring the winding road that led to a large city rising from the jungle in the distance: Xyla.

My eyes widened as I took in the contour of the young woman's face, the set of her eyes.

"You've been to the Earth Kingdom?" I asked, my gaze bouncing between the ghost of my mother to the memory playing out before my eyes.

"Quite often in my younger years," she nodded.

I gaped at her, waiting for the explanation that was sure to come. Young Mother swung her leg over the saddle, the movement causing the wind to catch the edges of her cloak, tugging them back to expose her rounded belly.

"Don't worry, my daughter," Young Mother cooed, her hand rubbing gentle circles across her swollen stomach. "I'm taking us far away from here. We'll carve out a life for ourselves away from all of this. It may not be glamorous, but you will be safe."

With a deep breath, she secured the cloak around herself, and spurred the horse into the waiting jungle, not bothering to look back.

"Were you—"

"Pregnant?" Mother answered, an amused lift to her voice.

"Yes. With you. Everything I had done up until this point was for the betterment of Pax."

"Why did you run?"

Mother's face grew somber as the shadows swirled once more, depositing us in a vast cavern composed fully of a dark stone with bright red inflections: bloodstone.

It stretched high, hollowing out into an open space. A narrowed stream cut through black sand, looking as if it were made from ground obsidian. Set a few paces from the edge of the gentle waters was a dark temple, the columns made of the same bloodstone as the cavern—except for the pulsing silver script covering them. It was the same script that had appeared in Levana's temple. The same intensity of flaring brilliance.

I opened my mouth to ask Mother what they meant, but her eyes were fixed on something over my shoulder, wide with fear and regret, and something that looked dangerously close to shameful longing.

Following her line of sight, my gaze snapped back to the temple, watching as the image of my mother, nearly the same age as the last vision, entered from the far side of the cavern. She carried a golden lantern, the burning flame within reflecting off the shards of bloodstone surrounding us.

As if expecting her, the shadows on the steps of the temple condensed, shaping into a tall, solid form. The hard planes of his chest were imposing, chestnut curls cropped short to reveal ears tipped into the slanted points of a fae. Shadows swirled around him, but they were denser than normal shadows. It looked like he'd harnessed the perfect absence of light—the darkest moment of a night without a moon, one devoid even of stars. The hint of fangs could be seen, but it was his hazel-blue eyes that I couldn't look away from—the same shade as *my* eyes.

"Is that—"

"Yes," Mother interrupted, finding her voice at last. We

watched as he extended a hand, his fingers tipped into claws before the scene dissolved. "Erebus, God of Night, King of Shadows, Eunoia's chosen partner... and the being who gifted you your affinities."

My mouth opened but my mind was racing with too many questions.

"I don't understand. I thought Eunoia and Erebus were separated by a great darkness," I breathed. Flashes of beautiful mosaics from the underground hot springs of the Dark Kingdom rose to the surface. "There are historical accounts, tales, even artwork."

Mother dipped her head in grim acknowledgment as the scene around us changed once more. "The myths speak of a powerful being who broke Erebus and Eunoia's love, but it wasn't until it was too late did I understand. This world *was* born from light and darkness, but it was not Erebus's darkness."

I sucked in a sharp breath, the pieces falling into place. "Levana. She was the dark power to Eunoia's light. The balance."

"Her sister in everything," Mother added, her eyes focusing on the shifting flashes around us. "You must understand, when we speak of children of the gods, it's always in reference to their creations, extension of their power shaped into autonomous forms. I won't call him your father, because he's not in the way that matters. You and I were only ever stepping stones for him. Tools to be used to end his imprisonment, but—"

A scream pierced the darkness as the shadows once again cleared. Mother was panting, her riding cloak stained and frayed at the edges as she stalked though the late autumn forest. A groan tore from her chest as she braced herself against the thick trunk of a nearby tree. She didn't appear to feel the bite of the rough bark grating against her back, nor the sharp lash of the cold, twilight breeze across her cheeks. All her attention was focused on her contracting belly and the blood and clear fluid leaking between her thighs.

"Who's there?" a deep, familiar voice called. My head snapped to the left, focusing on a tall man with a thin frame and dark curls dashing through the trees. There was a dagger poised in his hand, and the blurry outline of a modest home just beyond the tree line: Papa.

My heart squeezed as Mother stilled. Her brow was damp with pain and the effort it took to remain upright, but when the next contraction rolled through her, she cried out.

"Gods," he breathed, his eyes going wide as they landed on Mother's trembling form. His gaze darted to the darkening forest and then back, noting Mother's lack of possessions. "Where's your partner? Your family?"

"Gone," she gritted through clenched teeth as another wave overwhelmed her, her belly lifting with the strength of it.

"Oh gods," Papa said, his voice taking on a frantic edge. "Jem, Torin! Help me get her inside before the baby comes."

"Baby?" Torin said, the two of them popping their dark curly heads out from the doorframe.

"What are *we* going to do with a *baby*?" Jem added, eyes going wide as Papa looped an arm around Mother's waist. "You say all the time the two of us drive you mad. Just imagine what a baby must be like."

"Not now, Jem. Go put a kettle of water on if you can't be bothered to help. Torin, set out fresh linens and as many clean rags you can find." Papa's attention bounced from the young boys heeding his command to Mother, his dark brown eyes swirling with kindness. "You're safe, miss. Everything is going to be okay."

"I thought you were already married when I was born," I breathed as he helped her inside.

"We changed the date on the license so there wouldn't be any question as to who your father was. Living in the woods had its advantages." Mother's voice was mournful and happy all at once and I wondered if she saw Papa often in the after.

This time when the images changed, they came in a rush, each one more alarming than the next. Terrifying ice wyverns flew through the sky, breathing frost and ice into a forest of thick pines. Veles and Draven stood before Levana, a contemptuous smile twisting her scarlet lips as silver-blue mist curled around them. A cold, marshy kingdom filled with Fractured, shadow wraiths, goblins, and more—bowing before their queen seated on a throne of purple shards. And then an army of Levana's dark creatures stretched far into the horizon, all making their way south.

The scene blurred, returning Mother and me to the endless darkness and swirling shadows. "There are so many things left unsaid between us. A lifetime worth of words I wish to give you." Mother gave me a proud, sad smile, lifting her hand to cup my cheek. "I'm sorry I couldn't save you from this fate. I bound your powers to keep you safe. If your affinities were suppressed, your fae abilities wouldn't have fully manifested."

My heart raced, the ringing in my ears drowning out everything else Mother said. *I* was the reason we were bound. The cause for Will not being able to stand the power of prophecy. I flinched away from her touch, from the love underlying her confession.

"You forced us to live without our fae halves, knowing who we were. If you had your way, we would've grown up thinking we were human. We would've been bound to a mortal life, weak and fragile, ghosts of what we were meant to be."

Mother only stared; her expression of sad understanding unwavering as I fought to catch my breath. "Yes."

Anger rose within me. "How could you? That wasn't your choice to make. And Will—he might've lived if you hadn't forced him to heed the goddess's prophecies as a human."

"Will's fate was sealed before he was born." Her loving countenance cooled, the soft edges of her lips pressing into a thin line as fire blazed through her eyes. "I did everything in my power to change it. *Everything*. I even offered up my eternal soul when I'd first understood his role in the prophecy, but Eunoia refused. Once a soul has passed into the world beyond, there is no going back."

My throat bobbed as I tried to ignore the twisting of my stomach. "I'm stuck here, in the after?"

Mother shook her head. "This is a sitting room of sorts. You're able to communicate with specific spirits for a limited time but are only permitted to pass through the gates once."

"Levana killed me."

"Yes, but phoenixes rise from the ashes, my daughter, as long as their mate is able to guide them back to the living."

My stomach flipped. "Zaeth and I could continue to save each other?"

"Though the tether between you two is unbreakable, no one knows if there's a limit to rebirths. I would advise against testing it." Her eyes searched mine, her somber tone growing. "The last of the prophecy is upon us."

"We realized," I said, fighting back a flinch as the foreboding stanzas came flooding back. "The three of us are a part of it."

"Yes," Mother confirmed. "And Levana is the 'forces of old', the great evil foretold. Now, I know the prophecies are, indeed, warnings from the goddess, but not in the way I thought."

I stilled, the shadows surrounding me seeming to do the same. "What do you mean?"

"The prophecies cannot be undone, Elara." My mouth dried as I stared at the image of my mother, her features starting to blur around the edges. "Levana is strong. Even now her children of chaos bleed into this world, but she is not invincible. Stay grounded to your sisters. Trust in the strength of the mating bonds. Power must be anchored. It must be shared. Together, the three of you might make it out of this alive."

Mother's form shifted and then slipped away, like smoke on the wind, her voice echoing in the darkening shadows. "Prepare for war but make no mistake: Pax as we know it will fall, and nothing you do will stop it."

15

LANNIE

I FOLLOWED THE SCENT OF SCORCHED FLESH AND BURNT REMAINS through the split shadow crystal door. The silver-blue script that had been pulsing along it had dimmed, giving way to the natural purple color. Something so beautiful shouldn't be here —in this place of death. Because I knew based on the vile scent clinging to the air, death was ahead of us.

Ignoring my growing trepidation, I forced myself into the swirling mist, growing closer to where I knew El must be. Greer and Ryuu followed as the massive columns of silver-blue stones pulsed with lingering power, casting a soft glow around the bowed figure crumpled at the base of an obsidian alter. Zaeth's ebony wings stretched from his shoulders, feathers bent and creased as he knelt on the floor, cradling a blacken husk of a body to his chest.

Greer stilled behind me, and I could practically see her alarm mimicked in Ryuu moments later. Bile singed the back of my throat, but I needed to see.

The tether connecting me to my eldest sister had changed, the threads disappearing into a vague emptiness, but it didn't feel as if it had been cut. Approaching slowly, I stepped around Zaeth's hunched form and compelled myself not to look away.

I should have expected it. I knew it had to be El in his arms, and yet the shock of seeing my sister's face coated in charred swaths of skin clinging to singed muscle beneath... it was my undoing.

My stomach lurched, emptying a pool of bile, as I stared at what remained of my sister.

"Levana used her to recreate her own body," Zaeth spoke, his voice eerily calm. The ring around his eyes was the brightest I'd ever seen, nearly eclipsing the browns of his irises. He cradled El in his arms, silent tears coating his cheeks, but a cold detachment had descended on me.

It was El's body, her frame, but I couldn't quite believe this was how it ended.

"Levana created a ward, one of pure power," Zaeth continued. "I couldn't get in."

"Where is she?" Greer asked, her hands glowing with the shimmering light of a ward not yet cast as.

"The scent of jasmine trails off this way," Ryuu said, raising his blade.

I tore my attention away from Zaeth and the body he clung to, scouring the darkness at the far end of the temple. Ryuu stalked forward, past the obsidian alter and flitted through the dimming columns stretching far into the back of the cave.

"That's not El," Greer whispered. My heart clenched as I saw she had yet to move from the threshold of the temple. Her crystal-blue eyes were ringed with red, but whatever tears had fallen had been wiped away. She looked up from El's burnt remains and met my eyes with fierce determination. "Search for her, Lannie. Follow the tether. It's there, only distant."

"I watched her die," Zaeth said, his voice taking on a crazed undercurrent as he reflexively pulled El's body closer. Flakes of ash fell away, joining the large pile at the base of the alter.

"I don't know what you saw," Greer countered, taking a step toward him. Zaeth's fangs elongated, his shoulders shifting as his dark wings flexed. "It must have been horrific, but the connection between us isn't cut. Search for yours."

He shot Greer a glare, still desperately holding on to El. It wasn't possible. El's body was clearly before us, her chest unmoving... and yet I closed my eyes and reached for her.

That same vagueness greeted me, like trying to see through muddy water.

"See?" Greer asked, hope dripping from the word. "She's still here, right? Somewhere."

I blinked, zeroing in on the rings of light flaring around Zaeth's irises, to the cracks in the ash coating El's skin. There was no blood, no oozing fluid from beneath the top layers of tissue as I'd expect there to be with a burn injury. But that was most likely due to Levana taking everything she needed from my sister before she let her die.

"Levana is gone," Ryuu said, returning from his search. His eyes fixed on Greer as he spoke. "The tunnel at the back of the temple splits into dozens. I followed the first with the strongest scent, but it was a dead end. I promise to avenge—"

"El's not dead," Greer cut in, her voice strong. I wish I had the same blind hope that she did. But the proof was too great.

Ryuu lifted a dark brow, the green specks in his eyes questioning as he glanced from Greer to El's still form as if to say, *'Are you seeing what I'm seeing?'*

Greer looked on the verge of protesting further, but a rush of energy stilled her tongue. The fine hairs on the back of my neck pricked as I felt the pulse of electricity in the air, like a great wave swelling on the horizon.

Zaeth must have felt it, too, because his spine straightened, the small movement shifting some of the ash covering El's body.

Her blackened skin splint—and the tissue beneath it expanded. Layers of debris slouched off as muscle grew beneath, covering exposed bones and thickening into strong limbs. All the mangled remains fell away… leaving areas of pristine skin. Hair sprouted from her skull, her eyebrows, the blank spaces filling in with the same chestnut hue El's hair had been.

I inhaled sharply as my body stilled, barely daring to hope. To breath. The others mirrored my apprehension, all of us stunned into fascinated silence.

Slowly, Zaeth shifted El's regrown form to rest in the crook of his arm, using his other hand to brush away the remaining ash.

"It can't be," I breathed, watching as Zaeth raised a hand to brush away a streak of ash along her cheek. It crumbled under his touch.

"Come back to me, love," Zaeth breathed, pressing a kiss to her brow.

El's body jerked, her chest expanding in a vicious gasp as her hazel-blue eyes ringed in black snapped open.

16

ELARA

SHADOWS RUSHED FORWARD, SLAMMING INTO MY CHEST AND hurtling me through the darkness. I was lost, the endless void of nothing pressing in all around me, until I felt the brush of something. It was a searing warmth against the frigid cold, a glimpse of life and love.

I clung to that feeling, dragging myself up through eons of blackness until the weight of the universe lessened.

A gasp torn from my lips as I was thrust into my body, my eyes flying wide as I fought to control the wave of nausea rocking through me. It felt like I was buried beneath sand, like my skin had suddenly grown too tight.

Arms held me, voices called to me, but everything was at a distance. The scent of burnt flesh mixed with traces of night blooming jasmine lingered in the air, confirming I was back in the world of the living. But there were still swaths of charred flesh lingering atop my new skin.

It all came rushing back: the feeling of the flames licking my arms, their blistering heat searing down my throat as I screamed...

I don't remember standing, but I blinked and found myself

poised above the alter. The obsidian stone was cool to the touch, Levana's violet flames absent. I stared through blurry eyes at my hands, at the layers of ash and blacken skin splitting and flacking off as my fingers flexed.

With renewed frenzy, I tore at the outer layers of my burnt skin, desperate to remove every bit that had been scorched by Levana's fire. Great ribbons fell away, until I was left panting and naked.

I rolled my shoulders, trying to dissipate the heavy weight that had gathered along my spine. There was a prickling sensation along my phoenix brand, expanding into a buzzing of power along my shoulder blades—And then a glorious release. My body shuddered as a set of feathered wings shimmered into place.

Instinctually, I curved them around myself, allowing the soft, violet feathers to sooth the torment of emotions whipping through me.

I'd died.

Levana had killed me, and in the darkness my mother had been waiting.

"El?" The low murmurings behind me stilled. "It's us. You're safe."

Inhaling a deep breath, I turned toward the sound of Greer's voice, not surprised to find my sisters waiting for me.

And Zaeth.

My mate. He had a haunted look in his eyes, the rings of light blazing. His ebony wings were tucked in close, his chest heaving as shock and disbelief seared through our bond.

Something like triumphant was shimmering in Greer's crystal-blue gaze as my sisters stepped forward, but Lannie remained composed, detached even—the same look she got when she was presented with a gruesome patient that had a fifty-fifty chance of survival.

"I'm not sure what happened," Greer said as if she were

talking to a child teetering on the edge of a cliff. "But I can guess it was terrible."

"How is it that you're here?" Lannie asked. Greer nudged her with an elbow, but Lannie shook her off. "Your body was burnt, all the superficial layers of tissue turned to ash. Nobody could survive that—not even a very powerful fae."

Disbelief rocked through me. Dropping my gaze from hers, I focused on the soft feathered wings covering my body. A variety of dark violet hues glimmered in the subtle light, the silver barbs beneath gleaming as they twitched.

Wings. I had wings. They were smaller than Zaeth's and Ryuu's, but they fit my frame perfectly.

"I'm a phoenix.," I breathed, my raw voice cracking. Clearing my throat, I glanced up, finding Zaeth's eyes fixated on me. He hadn't moved, but the incredulity of the situation racing down our bond was starting to wane. "The Dark Phoenix, at least one half of it."

"Three pairs of fated mates," Ryuu said, his gaze flashing between me and Zaeth. "As in, the rest of us are each half of the prophecy?"

With grim understanding, I nodded.

No one spoke for a long moment.

"Mother told me." My stomach clenched. "She showed me things. Things that were, things that will be—all of it was horrible."

"She shared prophecies with you?" Greer asked, eyes bouncing to Ryuu. "The goddess must be warning us, right?"

Ryuu's lips pressed thin, his gaze never leaving mine.

"No," I breathed, focusing on Greer's crystal-blue eyes, the same shade as Mother's. "She said the downfall of Pax is unpreventable."

Greer flinched as if I'd struck her. "That can't be right. You must've heard her wrong—"

"I didn't," I insisted, my tone harsher than I'd intended. "She said nothing we do will stop Pax from changing forever."

"Then why tell us?" Greer pressed, brushing away Ryuu's wing that had come around her shoulder. "Why warn you at all?"

"What *did* she show you?" Lannie asked, sparing me from Greer's onslaught. "If this truly was Mother and she told you we are part of some goddess's prophecy, what did she think was important enough to show you in the after?"

"I learned that Erebus blessed me with his darkness." My sisters' eyes went wide but it was Ryuu who balked as if I'd slapped him.

"Erebus blessed you?" Ryuu asked.

"Blessed?" Greer repeated. "You mean, he's your father?"

But Ryuu shook his head before I could answer. "Gods and goddesses create, but don't reproduce. Erebus granting Elara a sliver of his powers explains her dark affinities. She's blessed by the God of Night, himself.

"What else did you see," Lannie asked, cutting to the core of the conversation.

Swallowing, I lifted my chin, meeting my youngest sister's intelligent gaze. "War. Draven and Veles are working with Levana somehow. All three of them were surrounded by her silver-blue mist near a marsh."

"Where?" Ryuu pressed, his expression tense with worry as he noted Zaeth's silence.

"I'm not sure. Somewhere dark and cold."

I stared at my mate, my heart twisting at the shocked look in his eyes. Disbelief had given way to anguish and denial. He was reliving the fire. I knew he was—I could feel it.

I took a step toward him, meaning to show him that I was alive. I'd come back to him, just as I always would. But I felt a spike of panic shoot down our bond as I took a second step— panic and *anger*. Stilling, I desperately tried to give him time to process everything while also knowing we'd handle this better together. In each other's arms.

"She sat on a throne of shadow crystal shards, one that resembled Zaeth's throne."

"The shadowlands," Ryuu bit out. "What of an army? Did you see how many she has on her side?"

"No. It was only flashes, but there were ice wyverns and other monsters. Creatures I've never seen before. She was leading them—the Fractured, shadow wraiths, goblins, and others—all of them south."

"Toward Caligo?"

"I'm not sure."

"When? Which route?" Ryuu pressed.

"*I don't know.* There were pine trees."

"And you couldn't see how many were with her or how they might attack?" Ryuu asked, eyes narrowed, his blade still clutched firmly in hand.

I blinked, surprised by the hostility in his words. Cocking my head to the side, I took in the scene before me, realizing how it must appear. "I'm not under Levana's control."

Zaeth sucked in a loud breath but Ryuu's grip on the hilt of his sword only tightened.

"I'm not," I insisted, anger rising. "I was, but then…"

"You died." Zaeth's broken voice rang throughout the temple, twisting something in my chest. I allowed myself to look at him—to really look—and I felt the weight of his anguish lash through me. His cheeks were still damp from previously shed tears, his knuckles stained with dried blood, and there was an unhinged, haunted look to his blazing cinnamon eyes that I knew would never fade entirely.

Zaeth had fought for me, that much was clear. Even as he watched my body go up in flames, smelt my flesh melt away, heard each and every scream rip through my chest, he'd never given up.

Ryuu tensed, seeming to feel the shift in the room, but Greer's hand on his shoulder stilled him.

"She's herself," Greer breathed, more to Ryuu than anyone else. "I can feel her. Lannie and Zaeth can, as well, if they allowed themselves to believe it."

From the corner of my eye, I saw Lannie nod. "I don't understand how, but El is alive."

My wings bristled at the accusation glaring back at me in Ryuu's eyes.

"And she requires clothes," Greer added, her attention snagging on my exposed collarbones peeking out from the top of my wings. "Zaeth? Now would be a great time to do the gentlemanly thing and offer her your shirt."

He blinked, looking puzzled before letting his gaze sweep down my violet feathers. Zaeth's wings vanished a moment later as he slowly neared.

Ryuu was led quite firmly by Greer as the three of them turned around. They made their way to the stairs as Zaeth started unbuttoned his battle leathers.

Glancing to make sure the others were out of the chamber, I allowed my wings to pull back, exposing my naked body.

The rings around Zaeth's eyes flared a bright white, his fangs glinting beneath his top lip. My stomach fluttered as I felt his emotions change. He was still in shock, but he desperately wanted to believe this was the truth. That I was here. His mate returned to him.

His dark fae affinities were raging, the furious desire for revenge against Levana spurring on his growing hunger to feel me in his arms. To taste me and know that I was his completely.

"I don't know how to get my wings to go away," I breathed, feeling my nipples pebble against the cold. My own body responded to his, both of us pushed to the extreme in what we'd been through in the last hour.

A vulnerability has opened between us, a wound only just

created. I wanted to feel him, to inhale his scent and imprint my soul with the filigree of his, showing without a doubt that I'd returned to him—had followed the pull of him back to the realm of the living.

"If she's an air fae, they won't," Ryuu called from the stairs, reminding me that fae hearing would detect all that was said between us. Zaeth's lips twitched as I glanced behind him, my wings bristling with the lack of privacy.

"That's not possible. She's the other half to my phoenix." Zaeth answered Ryuu, looking like it took every ounce of willpower to maintain eye contact with me as he stepped near. Zaeth's fingers trailed down the exposed part of my spine, along the phoenix brand nestled between my great wings. "Concentrate on the weight of the wings between your shoulder blades, love. Can you feel where the darkness pools?"

Feeling the stretch of muscles across my spine, I focused on the caress of shadows mingling with Zaeth's touch. It felt like part of my essence was expanding outward, expanding into my dark, violet-hued feathers and the silver barbs beneath.

"I can feel it."

"Good. Now, draw it into yourself."

Closing my eyes, I beckoned the darkness to return, spooling thin tendrils of power back one at a time. The weight lessened, the strain along my spine easing, until only a prickling, tingling sensation remained.

"Close it off, like the last breath before diving under water."

Heeding Zaeth's advice, I urged the rest of the dark energy to retreat, the force of it settling just beneath the surface.

"Perfect," Zaeth rumbled as I blinked my eyes open.

The brush of his thumb across my cheek sent my pulse hammering. I leaned into his touch, a moan escaping me as I relished the warmth of his palm.

"Don't get any ideas," Greer called, a playful note in her voice. "We can hear everything."

I exhaled a frustrated huff as Zaeth's lips quirked, his fingers dropping away from my cheek to finishing unbuttoning his battle leathers. My fangs throbbed with the need to taste him, my hunger only growing as the hard planes of his chest coated in brands came into view as he slipped the tunic beneath off in one fluid motion.

"Soon, love," he rumbled, the bemused half-grin fading as he handed me the black fabric. "But first we need to leave this place."

Nodding solemnly, I slipped into his top before taking Zaeth's outstretched hand and turned toward where my sisters and Ryuu were waiting. There'd be time to bask in our bond—our joined affinities—but it wasn't now.

"We need to make our way to Caligo as soon as possible to prepare for an attack," Ryuu said as we started our assent. "It's the most likely place for Levana to strike."

I felt more than saw Zaeth agree in the darkness as we started up the stairs. "Just as soon as we make it out of Neith alive."

17

GREER

"It's over?" I asked, meeting Jarek's exhausted, but relieved grin as I stepped onto the field of wildflowers surrounding the pile of stones. His crystal blue eyes were bright, despite the splatter of blood matted in his hair.

Ryuu and I emerged first from Levana's underground temple, worried the battle would still be raging, but as we grew nearer to the surface, no sounds of war reached us. The lack of snarls from the cú sídhe let us know our side had won, even before we were above land.

Now, the only sounds were of felled bodies being dragged and piled for burning. Queen Halcyon and Queen Freya were making their way in between clumps of wolves and wraiths, putting flame to each as they passed. Decaying bodies of humans and fae from the original slaughter of Neith were mixed with Levana's monsters, but at least all were being put to rest.

Naz stood before the fae battalion at her back, blades still unsheathed. She was poised, eyes fixed on the opening in the earth Ryuu and I had just emerged from. The bodies that had been surrounding it had been cleared, the smoldering embers a few paces away being all that remained.

Lannie surfaced next under Naz's watchful gaze, glancing around until she spotted Queen Halcyon. I wondered if she even realized she'd gravitated toward her fated mate. I wondered if the two of them would ever grow to be friends.

"It seems like we missed everything," I said, giving her a nod toward Queen Halcyon. "Everyone is either healed by Jarek or already beyond your help, but feel free to ask if they need your help."

A faint blush rose to her cheeks at having the bond between her mate acknowledged and I made a promise to myself to not to bring it up again. I didn't want to make Lannie uncomfortable, especially so soon after Ser, but I did hope her heart would open to the possibility of finding happiness again. If not now, then in the future.

"All over," Jarek confirmed, forcing a smile for Lannie as she dipped her head and headed off toward Queen Halcyon's direction. His smile faltered as his gaze met mine, as if the small gesture was too much of a façade to keep up. "You missed the finality, though. The wards surrounding Neith surged, trapping us in like flies in a web. There was such power coursing through them—I'm not sure even you would've been able to break them."

I glanced around, reaching out for the familiar particles of light. They hummed beneath my touch, free and unencumbered. "Everything feels normal."

"That's because a few minutes ago, all that power was whisked away. I can't be sure, but it felt like it was siphoned beneath the earth. The wards weakened until the stones surrounding Neith, the one pulsing with a silver-blue glow, dimmed."

"The power transferred a few minutes ago?"

My stomach twisted as Jarek nodded, his expression growing wary at my question. He glanced toward Naz, drawing my line of sight to how her jaw ticked while her eyes remained fixed to the now powerless stones surrounding the stairs.

Two synchronized heartbeats were growing as the sounds of El and Zaeth's soft footsteps reached the last of the buried steps.

"I didn't say anything about 'transferring' power," Jarek said, his voice carefully controlled. "Only a draining. I thought Pax was reclaiming it."

"Maybe," I said, my attention fixed on the way Naz's grip flexed around her blade as Zaeth and my sister surfaced.

El was clad only in Zaeth's dark tunic, the course fabric coming to her mid-thigh. The dark rings around her irises were still blazing and I could see a pair of small, sharp fangs beneath her upper lip as she offered Naz a tentative smile. At least both of their wings were hidden.

El had been through a lot—to death and back if she was correct in all that had happened. She'd also confirmed that we were, all six of us, involved in the great prophecy. And that, despite being warned, Pax was destined to fall to the prophecy's fate.

It was a lot to take in. Too much after the day we'd had.

I wasn't sure about the rest of them, but I didn't have the energy to get into all of it right now, and definitely not here surrounded by rotting bodies.

My eldest sister stiffened as she met Naz's intense-boarding-on-hostile stare. Maybe it was because of how close we were, but I felt El's dark fae essence swell. Fury stirred within her, rising to the surface with such force, that I could feel it through our bond. A small gasp across the field confirmed Lannie felt the same thing.

The air pricked with electricity, drawing the attention of the fae warriors at Naz's back. All stilled, sensing a threat but uncertain where to look.

Zaeth stepped forward, El's hand firmly clasped in his. He met Naz's stare with a leveled look before lifting his chin and speaking to the men at her back. "The being who led us into this trap was the enchantress, Levana. She was controlling Elara's mind and movements, but she has been cast out. I witnessed it myself."

Naz's dark gaze darted from Zaeth toward my sister, boring into El's hazel-blue eyes. "You're changed."

El's spine stiffened and I caught the twitch of her hand as if seeking a phantom blade. "Yes."

Another long moment passed before Naz nodded, finally looking away from El toward Zaeth. "Levana?"

"Reborn," he answered loud enough for the others to hear.

"She will be a problem," Naz said.

"She's stationed somewhere in the north and intends to attack," El said, drawing everyone's attention back to her. "We think her target will be Caligo. Evacuations must start immediately."

"Where would you have them go?" Naz asked, her voice hollow as she sheathed her sword. The tension throughout the dark fae warriors behind her eased, but it was replaced with a desolate hopelessness. "All of Pax has been ravaged, and now you offer warning of another threat we're to face."

"All those from the base can be offered sanctuary in the Wild Kingdom."

Queen Freya's voice carried across the field. Her proclamation was met with stunned silence. To my knowledge, none had been welcomed into the Wild Kingdom in all the time I'd been alive. Ryuu said they were notoriously secretive, with Queen Freya one of the only wild fae seen in other kingdoms. We didn't know even basic information like where their cities were, where the palace was—if they had a palace. Everything was warded by either the mist or vast stretches of undisturbed forest. And here she was offering a huge number of *humans* safety in a world growing more dangerous by the day.

"Humans can pass through the mist?" I asked, daring to

break the silence. "Or do you mean to keep them just outside its reach?"

I hadn't meant it as a slight. There were vast portions of the Wild Kingdom not touched by the mist or sacred forests, though most of that was said to be harsh deserts along the western coast.

"Any can pass, when portaled through the worst of the Western Woods." Queen Freya drawled, her honey-gold eyes flashing. The wind caught a few strands of her long blond hair, most of it contained in an array of small braids and ties decorated with various pieces of jewelry. The wind shifted again, clinking a few of the beads together, and I wondered if any of the items woven into her hair were made of bone.

"And you'd be willing to do that?" I asked, not bothering to hide the skepticism from my voice. She was the Queen of the Wild Kingdom, the most mysterious and guarded of all the seven kingdoms and now she'd welcome refugees in with open arms?

The Wild Queen lifted a blond brow. "Yes."

"Why now?" I pressed. "Why not before when the world was falling apart?"

"We don't have time for this," Ryuu rumbled, his wings bristling. "If what Elara has seen is correct, we need every viable army. We must return to the Air Kingdom as soon as possible and speak with my father."

"We?" asked, my gaze swinging toward him.

Green embers flared around vertical slits. "You're my mate. I'd prefer to face the future together, but it's your choice."

I looked at Ryuu, at the intensity of his beseeching gaze, and realized that if I wanted any possibility of being a future ruler to the Air Kingdom, I'd need to go with him.

There were so many unanswered questions between us. His father had yet to see us post-bond, and our claim to the throne had still not been addressed. But Cress knew of our bonding, and she didn't strike me as the quiet type. The entire city probably knew Ryuu and I were bound, at this point. If I had any hope of them accepting me, I needed to be present. I needed to *show* them I would put the good of the Air Kingdom before my own comforts. Which meant I'd have to leave my sisters. Again.

"I must return to the Earth Kingdom, as well," Queen Halcyon said, her eyes flicking to Lannie with hopeful expectance. The Earth Queen had yet to demand Lannie fulfill her deal to help find a cure for the mysterious illness plaguing her court. I had no doubt she would play that card if she needed to, but I could tell by the way she looked at my younger sister that she was hoping Lannie would choose to join her of her own accord.

The wind shifted, sending a cloud of ash-tinged wind in our direction. A heartbeat later, Lannie sighed as her eyes met mine and then El's. "There are plenty of healers in the Dark Kingdom, and with Queen Freya's offer, it seems all those who fled from the base will be well tended to."

"I, too, must first ensure my court is safe," Queen Halcyon added. "But my warriors are fierce and unencumbered thus far. I should be able to offer a sizable force."

"Understood," Zaeth answered and El and I nodded with grim smiles. He turned his attention to Queen Freya. "I appreciate your offer to help our refugees. As you can gather, I must see to preparation for a possible strike against Caligo. We'll see to specifics once I run the offer through General Alarik."

Zaeth waited for Queen Freya to nod before looking toward Ryuu. The two of them exchanged a loaded look, conveying more than words could offer in the space of a few seconds. "Brother, speak to King Dragcor. Send word to Naz as soon as you have an answer."

"I guess this is good-bye, then?" I asked, the tether between my sisters betraying the worry that shot through me.

"Seems like it," Lannie answered. "With any luck, I'll have the illness controlled and mending in no time."

"I'll stay with Zaeth in the Dark Kingdom," El said. "It sounds like Queen Freya will keep us updated on all that transpires in the Wild and Earth Kingdoms."

"If anything happens, use the tether," I said, feeling my own trepidation mirrored through my sister's bonds.

El gave a small shake of her head, her jaw clenched. "That won't happen."

"But just in case," I insisted. "We know how to find each other."

The connection between us wasn't as transparent as the fated bond I had with Ryuu. I could sense him all the time, where I had to seek my sisters out. Still, I took comfort knowing I'd be able to sense if they were in trouble.

"I'll stop by in a fortnight for an update," Naz said, looking between Queen Halcyon and Queen Freya. "It should give us and the Wild Kingdom enough time to structure evacuations before I return for news from the Earth Kingdom. Would that due?"

The Earth Queen nodded.

"Perfect. We'll see you then." Naz looked El over one last time, something shifting in her gaze as she did so before meeting Zaeth's narrowed-eyed stare. "I'll see you at home, brother."

With her palms outstretched, the fae warriors behind her clasped hands, all of them folding into darkness.

18

ELARA

JAREK LUXED ZAETH AND I TO THE DARK KINGDOM AFTER I'D said goodbye to my sisters. Fear coiled low in my stomach at the thought of being separated from them, especially when I knew what Levana was planning, but there was no way around it. We needed the whole of Pax if we were to defeat the enchantress, not to mention the brothers.

The humming vibration of luxing faded as a wide, dark chamber came into view. Sharp-angled windows stretched to the ceiling, the glass framed by polished onyx and dark, spiked vines that grew from a large potted plant at the base of the room. Books were stacked haphazardly along the bordering shelves, the colored spines and thick volumes worn and read through. A grand, roaring fireplace sat on the opposite side, the rough edges looking as if it was carved from the mountain the Dark Palace was built upon.

And there, in the center of the room was the largest bed I'd ever seen. Black silk sheets reflected the light from the fire, making the fluffed pillows all the more alluring.

My stomach flipped. This must be Zaeth's room.

"I thought you two could use a moment alone," Jarek grinned "I'll leave you to it."

Silence stretched between us, making me keenly aware of the fact that I wore nothing but Zaeth's tunic. Though I'd been to death and back, my body was clean, reborn from the fires. Daring a glance up, I found Zaeth's cinnamon gaze fixed on me.

"I followed you back," I breathed, taking a few hesitant steps forward. He'd kept his distance in front of the others, but I wanted him to show me that nothing had changed between us. That him and I—we—were eternal.

Zaeth's gaze darted between my eyes, as if marveling that I was really here as the heat of his body warmed the small distance between us. I wanted nothing more than to close the gap, to press my body against his and let our affinities communicate everything I couldn't put into words… but the worried look in his eyes gave me pause.

"I can feel you," he said, his voice little more than a whisper. It felt like a confession, one uttered into the night like the most desperate of wishes. "I *felt* you—your blood thrumming in your veins as if it were my own. Our hearts beating with the same rhythm. The same warmth."

He swallowed, cinnamon eyes shining.

"But then your heart stopped. And mine shattered."

A silent tear tracked down his cheek as a pang of grief shot through my chest. I reached a tentative hand up, brushing it away.

"You were screaming—burning—and I couldn't reach you."

The vastness of his anguish blasted through our mating bond as he pulled me close. The contact only heightened the emotions swirling between us, sending my dark affinities into overdrive. The darkness along my spine gathered through my phoenix brand, and then expanded in a wash of shadows as my wings sought release.

His essence flared with mine, the light around his eyes

igniting as his own wings shimmered into being. His hands slid up my back, holding me close as he pressed soft kisses along the curve of my neck.

"You're the only reason I'm here, Zaeth," I breathed. "Our bond... our love... it led me back to you."

He drew in a sharp breath as the meaning of my words rocked through him. Great ebony wings, so much larger than my own, expanded to wrap around us in a blanket of protection. Zaeth's eyes searched mine as his hand cupped my cheek. Heart fluttering, I leaned into his touch.

I knew what I felt for Zaeth. I wasn't sure when I'd come to accept it, but I loved him.

Zaeth, my beautiful Dark King, every bit of the mess that I was and then some, but we fit. His shards matched my splinters, the two of them fitting together into a patchwork of shadows built on grief and anguish and... hope. Whatever our essences were crafted from, his and mine were kindred. Our souls recognized each other—*would* recognize each other in every life. In every existence.

Zaeth's gaze seared into mine, his fangs peeking out beneath a tilted smile. "Our love or our bond?"

My heart thundered, but I'd come far too close to being taken from him. We'd wasted so much time already... Zaeth hadn't wanted the bond. Just days ago, he was raging against it, convinced he was going to be my ruin, while all this time, *I'd* been the weight dragging us beneath the waves... and Zaeth had been the rays of sun guiding me back toward air.

Meeting his gaze with unflinching clarity, I let my fingers trace the edge of his strong jaw, savoring the scrape of his beard, before linking my hands behind his neck. "Both."

The playful tilt to his lips evened out. "Loving me isn't an easy thing—"

"But it is," I interrupted, my voice soft and sure. "Loving you has been the easiest thing, so easy it wasn't even a choice."

Zaeth swallowed, his eyes closing briefly as my words washed over him. He leaned in resting his forehead against mine. We stood like that, breathing in each other's scents, basking in the sound of our hearts beating as one.

"I didn't think it was possible," he said so softly I almost missed it. "I didn't think I'd ever be granted a partner, let alone a mate. But you—" His breathing hitched. "Gods, Elara, you are more than I deserve."

I pulled back just far enough to look into his eyes. We'd slept together before, but sex and love didn't always go together. Though a piece of me knew the answer, I still needed to hear him say it.

"Does that mean you love me, too?"

His lips quirked, but the passion in his eyes blazed stronger. "I love you, Elara. More than that, I need you, like the trees need the sun. Before you, I was nothing. I was a withered, gnarled root surviving in the cold darkness, always one step away from death. You brought me back to life."

His lips pressed to mine, desperate in their intensity. Our bodies ignited, the connection between us linking. Every kiss—every touch—was shared. I could feel his love humming in each nip of his fangs, feel the way his body responded as I arch into him. Our pleasures were linked, our sensations feeding one another as we fought for more of each other.

Zaeth's hands fisted in my hair, tugging hard. I gasped, the sound turning into a moan as his tongue swept through me. My fangs throbbed, eager to feed spurred on by Zaeth's own hunger.

"Bite me," I breathed, voice dripping with need. "Feed from me."

A wicked smirk stretched across Zaeth's lips as he pressed a chaste kiss to my forehead. "I will, but first..."

He flitted away, the warmth of his body barely dissipating before his was back. Water sounded from a room in the back.

"A shower?"

His smile grew. "Care to join me?"

I placed my hand in his, an excited laugh bubbling in my throat as Zaeth flitted us to the already steaming water. My eyes widened as I took in the picturesque space.

A small cove was crafted from ebony stone, the surfaces smoothed into a large, open area. Two overhead facets were thundering, the pressure of the water adjusting as Zaeth fiddled with an inconspicuous knob on the wall. A large obsidian bench sat in the center of the overhead streams, the water gently pattering down on either side of it. The scent of cedar hung heavy in the air, and I could now see half-a-dozen small alcoves where various jars held soaps and oils.

Set in the back corner was a wide bath carved into the dark-stoned floor. The golden facets along the edge and the large collection of bathing supplies were the only indication it wasn't a natural hot spring.

"Shower first," Zaeth said, undoing his ties and stepping out of his pants. My pulse raced as my gaze snagged on the proof of his intentions. His lips twitched. "Then we can enjoy the bath."

Licking my lips, I dragged my gaze up and nodded.

"Good," Zaeth grinned. His essence reached for me, the dark caress sending a shiver of pleasure through my body. "Now, take off your clothes, love."

My nipples tightened as I did what he instructed, letting his tunic tumbled to the ground. The light around his eyes flared, mirroring my own dark rings. With a mischievous smirk, I flitted to the shower, letting the hot waters spill over my skin. I raised my hands, smoothing back the hair from my face as I tilted my chin up, knowing Zaeth was tracking my every movement.

A low growl escaped him as my hands trailed down, cupping my breasts before drifting further.

"Join me," I said, the words breathy and filled with longing.

Zaeth smirked before flitting to the shower across from me, the wide, low set bench the only thing between us. His hands lathered soap across his body, through his hair, and washed away all the horrors of the day.

My hands stilled as I opened stared at him, at the network of tattooed ruins across his body tapering into an alluring 'vee', and the impressive length just below.

"I didn't tell you to stop, love."

A blush stained my cheeks as my fangs throbbed with the urge to drink. But two could play this game. With deliberate slowness, I allowed my fingers to wander down my body. Cinnamon eyes tracked my ministrations, a frustrated groan scraping his throat as I brushed the inside of my thighs. It was thrilling to tease him. Freeing knowing that he loved me just as much as I did him.

"I might need some help," I teased, taking deliberate slowness as I neared my heat.

Zaeth flitted around the low set bench, abandoning his own shower to join mine now that he was clean. The warmth of his chest heated my back, his thick length pressing against my ass. Scented oil gleamed across his palms, before Zaeth's strong hands rubbing it up my arms, across my back, working my body with gentle pressure. Tension I hadn't been aware of eased, my body lulled into relaxation.

A moan escaped me as I leaned further back against him, his skilled hands trailing down my thighs to caress my center. Steam rose around us, the soothing water plastering my hair against my slick body. I arched my back, grinding against him, begging him to take more.

His lips were at my neck, the scrape of his fangs sending my pulse racing as he smirked against me.

I whimpered, bucking against his hand that offered only the lightest of touches, needing friction.

"So needy," he purred, but then his fingers dipped lower.

They parted me, pressing in with a tantalizing thrust. A deep moan rumbled through him as he explored the slickness between my thighs, my body revealing just how badly I wanted him.

"Like this, love," Zaeth commanded as he guided my hand toward my center.

My breathing hitched as he pressed our fingers in. This was a new level of control, one that had me feeling exposed and vulnerable, and alive all at once.

His other hand was flat against my stomach, holding me up as our pace increased, our fingers pumping in and out. My thighs clenched as that coil of pleasure tightened. My head dropped back as I gave myself over to him, too lost to heed his instructions.

Zaeth didn't seem to mind as he added another finger, stretching me as his dark fae affinities rushed through to spur my pleasure on, winding my body tighter.

The heel of Zaeth's palm pressed against the sensitive bundle as his fingers curled, causing my knees to buckle.

Delectable fire raced through my veins, heightening every sensation. The heat of his body against mine, the scrape of his fangs, the teasing, prodding length of him pressed against my ass.

"Ride my fingers, love. Take what you want."

I glanced down, realizing at some point I'd begun holding on to his hand, urging him deeper, begging for more. I did as commanded, letting my body take over. The sight of his fingers splitting me, my hips undulating against him, pulled a wanton whimper from my lips. Another pulse of his dark affinities had it shifting into a gasp, my body tightening against him as his fangs scraped along my neck.

"Good girl, love. Now, come for me," he whispered as the sharp prick of his fangs pierced my skin.

My body detonated, waves of ecstasy rocking through me as

I shuttered around him. He drank, the draw of blood causing another explosion of pleasure to crash over me. Zaeth's fingers kept working as he consumed me, wrenching every last drop of ecstasy from my body. Only once the waves of bliss had slowed did his fangs withdrawal.

Slowly, his tongue licked away the beads of blood along my healed flesh as he muttered sweet words against the shell of my ear.

I was floating, nothing but particles of pleasure soaring high. I vaguely recalled him wrapping me in a plash towel and carrying me from the shower, and the feel of silk sheets beneath me as he laid me down on his bed.

The scent of cedar mixed with fresh eucalyptus swirled in the air. Candles were now lit, casting subtle shadows around Zaeth as he stood before me at the edge of the bed.

Pressing my palms down, I sat up, my knees curving over the side as I blinked up at him. Water glistened along Zaeth's chest, the runes pulsing with a faint glow as droplets linked together, dripping down his naked body to the hard length between his thighs.

Savoring the sight before me, I took in the way his muscles shifted as he stepped forward, committing every tantalizing dip and cut of his thighs, his chest, his arms to memory, until I met his eyes.

They were hooded, the rings of light shining as he drank in the sight of me just as I was doing him. A gentle caress of Zaeth's shadows licked up my spine, pulling a gasp from my lips as his dark affinities allowed me to feel just how desperately he wanted me. Heat shot through me, my breasts growing heavy as my back arched.

Zaeth stepped between my open thighs, pressing them further apart, exposing all of me to him. I made to lean forward, needing to taste him, but he knelt before I could.

His palm traced the edge of my arm with reverent tenderness, continuing along the dip in my collarbone, the slope of my neck, before cupping my cheek. I leaned into his touch, staring deeply into his cinnamon eyes, feeling every wave of adoration and love he felt down the bond.

"I watched you die," he whispered.

I felt the pang of his loss beginning to take hold. I knew this would be something that took time, a scar we'd be left with when this was all over, but we'd figure that out later.

Pressing up, I captured his lips with mine, wrapping my arms around his neck and imparting all the love I could. All the desperate longing I felt for him, needing him to know this was real. We were real.

"I'm here, Zaeth. We're both here."

An agonized sound scraped against his throat as his hand fisted in my hair, holding me against him. Before had been gentle, delicate even compared to the pent up storm of emotions I could sense swirling within Zaeth. But I didn't need him to be gentle.

"Take me," I breathed against his lips, knowing this was what he needed—what I needed. "Prove to me we're alive. Show me they can never separate us."

Zaeth wrenched his lips from mine, his hand tugging firmly on my hair. I gasped as my neck arched. But his fangs were at my throat before I had time to think.

The sharp sting sent a wash of electricity crashing through me, the force of his dark affinities touching every inch of my body.

I moaned as he drank, his other hand teasing my nipple, twisting and pinching the peaked tip until it was sore and throbbing, until the pressure along my neck eased. His mouth replacing his hand at my breast, soothing the ache as his tongue swirled.

"Zaeth," I panted, arching into his touch, wanting more even with the remnants of pleasure still humming through my body.

Zaeth obliged.

His hands came to the inside of my thighs, thrusting them open. I braced myself on my elbows as he gazed down at the slickness of my core, his pupils dilating as he bent.

With reckless abandon, he tasted me. Zaeth licked up my center, his hands gripping my ass, holding me to him as he feasted. My head fell back, my back bowing as moan after moan escaped me.

That delicious tightening started again, spurred on by his dark fae affinities, mounting until I couldn't stand it. Until his fangs grazed that sensitive bundle poised at the apex of my thighs. Another blast of dark ecstasy cascaded through me as I shattered.

Before the waves of pleasure ended, Zaeth was there, his cock poised at my entrance.

"You're mine."

Not waiting for a reply, Zaeth buried himself within me, the painful stretch tempered by my arousal.

"Never again will I be parted from you," he growled, his words accentuated by deep thrusts as he held my legs open, watching as he took me.

I couldn't find the words to answer him, my thoughts a tangled array of blissful post-climax haze and a deep tightening starting again. Instead, I sent my own pulse of darkness through him, allowing him to feel just what he did to me. A wicked grin tilted my lips as he threw his head back with a groan.

Zaeth pulled out, flipping me onto my stomach and wrenching my hips up. He spread me, licking up my center with a primal growl before burring himself once more. The silk sheets were fisted in my hands, the fabric smooth against my cheek as his fingers dung into my ass. He set a punishing pace, each pump of his hips splitting me further. Gods, did I want it. I wanted to feel him tomorrow, to know the soreness between my thighs was from our bodies worshiping each other —from him.

Zaeth's hand circled my throat, pulling me up as he continued. With firm but gentle pressure, he tilted my neck to the side, his fangs sinking deep into the flesh along my collarbone, claiming me completely.

My body clenched around him as release called to me once more. Just as I teetered along the edge, Zaeth's wrist was before me, his veins already nicked and bleeding as his lips moving against my ear.

"Drink."

Without any hesitation, my throbbing fangs sank into his flesh. The flood of rich metallic warmth coated my tongue and my body shuddered. Ecstasy found me once more, my climax spurring on Zaeth's. I felt his cock swelled as I sucked, a guttural groan vibrating through him as he pumped, emptying himself inside me as my body clenched greedily around his.

I was vaguely aware of the warm slickness between my thighs as he withdrew. The taste of Zaeth's blood still hot on my lips. The euphoric buzzing of our combined release had me floating, my body and mind transfixed in an elated daze.

Strong arms linked around waist, drawing my close as black wings came into being. They settled around us, creating a comforting blanket of protection as Zaeth pressed a kiss to the top of my head. He draped a necklace around me, the hollowed crystal settling between my breasts.

"I kept this safe for you," Zaeth said as I reached up, feeling the ash-filled neckless with my fingers. Zaeth had given this to me after Will's funeral. It was a traditional token among dark fae to fill with a loved one's ashes, keeping a piece of their essence with you forever.

"I thought I'd lost it," I whispered, relief flooding through me. "Thank you."

Zaeth simply pressed a kiss to me head and held me as our bodies calmed.

A small smile tilted my lips as I listened to our heartbeats, the gentle thrumming in sync with one another. The pads of my fingers traced the soft underside of his feathers, an array of deep cobalt among the midnight hues. They were so beautiful, despite the lethal barbs hidden beneath. "Next time, I want these to stay out."

His chest shook with a sultry laugh, his arms tightening to draw me closer. "I'll show you mine if you show me yours."

My lips quirked as I thought about all the way we could take each other once I mastered my wings. "Deal."

19

LANNIE

The particles of my body zapped themselves back together as I stepped through Queen Freya's portal. My stomach flipped, but it was nothing compared to the terrible nausea that rocked through me with luxing. Despite the number of times I'd traveled through a portal, I still managed to trip upon arrival.

Queen Halcyon was waiting on the other side, hand outstretched and catching me as I stumbled forward.

"It's the moss," she said with a sheepish smile, eyes glancing down. "It's wonderful throughout the day but it can give a little too much when portaling."

"Thank you, Queen Halcyon," I mumbled, releasing her hand with a little too much eagerness. I didn't like the way electricity seem to linger in the places her skin touched mine. It felt too intimate. Too exposing.

Her full lips dipped into a frown as an ember of her embarrassment flickered through our bond. I gritted my teeth against the incessant reminder that *this* was my fated mate.

Tears pricked at the edge of my eyes as images of Ser flashed through my mind: Her gentle nature. Her vibrant red hair and freckled cheeks. The way her whole body seemed to flush whenever she caught me staring. We were going to have a life together... but that future was cut short, replaced by the wash of crimson against her alabaster skin and the arrow protruding from her neck.

Queen Halcyon flinched as I swallowed against the raw misery of Ser's memory. When she spoke, it was with forced lightness.

"Please, call me Halcyon. We're fated to be in each other's lives, at least in some regard. No need to waste time on formalities."

I gave a tight nod.

"I'm sorry about your lover," she said softly, the kindness in her voice soothing despite my illogical urge to scream. "Serephina sounded like a wonderful person—"

"Don't," I snapped, barely managing to control the onslaught of tears threatening to break free. Blinking them back, I forced a calm control to my voice. "She wasn't my lover."

"I thought—"

"No," I said, focusing on facts. They were so much easier to process than emotions. "We were together but hadn't reached that point, yet. Thank you for caring. I can feel that your concern is authentic, but there's no point in talking about it. She wasn't the first to be taken by this war and she won't be the last."

Halcyon's brows furrowed, her mouth parting as if she were contemplating saying something further.

"This is your room?" I supplied, eager for a change in topic. There was nothing to be done. Ser had died and I'd lived. Nothing anyone could say would change that, and as terrible as it sounded, I didn't want to be comforted by the woman who thought to one day replace her.

"This is a sitting room," Halcyon answered, allowing the shift in conversation. "I wasn't sure you'd feel comfortable in my chambers."

Giving a tight nod, I glanced up from the moss-covered

floors. The spacious room was cast in natural light shining from the large, diamond-shaped windows set throughout. A spiraling staircase opened to the second floor, obscured from view by lush, green vines wound among the banisters. Books were set into built-in shelves along the walls, the edges of which came precariously close to the fireplace—or what looked like a fireplace.

Curious, I took a step forward, marveling as a draft of chilled air swirled out.

"It's a cooling system," Halcyon explained. "Summers are sweltering in the Earth Kingdom, the humidity making it unbearable at times. Even though we are well on our way to winter, we still don't have need for heat."

I lifted a quizzical brow, studying the structure. "Does this extend underground?"

Halcyon laughed. "Of course. Most of the Earth Kingdom resides beneath."

"And you never have need of heat?" I asked, thinking about how converting this into a fireplace would cut off air supply to those below.

"Thermal pools heated by deep rivers of magma keep us warm."

I blinked. "Being close to forces that could kill you with a slight shift in pressure doesn't concern the earth fae?"

Her smile softened. "No. Fae from each kingdom have distinct affinities. One of the common affinities among earth fae is a connection to the ground around us. We can sense shifts in moisture, temperature, density, and depth. A select few can even feel lines of power emanating from Pax itself."

"Yourself included?"

She nodded. "It's why I've been so concerned about the illness sweeping through my court. There's a very powerful line linking each of the affected fae that has recently changed."

"Weakening?"

"No, but it's grown dimmer," she mussed, tilting her head to the side as she thought. "Like the power contained within it retreats and then lashes out in bursts. I believe these great pulses of power may be what's causing members of my court to fall ill."

"It sounds reasonable that blasts of primal power could cause a number of things," I nodded, grateful that I had something clinical to focus on. "What are the symptoms of those affected?"

"They've all fallen into a deep sleep. I'd hoped to show you but thought bringing you here would be an easier transition. Most who live above land don't take kindly to being thrown into the heart of the earth without proper warning."

My lips twitched. "I don't mind being enclosed in small places."

"Enclosed it is, but small it is not."

Halcyon swept past me, guiding us through a door and followed a large staircase down. The rails were crafted from jade, the rich green of the stone mimicking the vines in the previous room. We descended, the air growing cooler as the stairs opened onto a large balcony framed by twin stair cases set on opposite sides, arching further down to the world beneath. Our steps slowed as we neared the edge of the railing, gazing out at the cityscape before us.

Great buildings stretched high, their craved pillars and pointed tops set among streets adored with various precious stones. Bio-luminescent stalks and clusters of berries grew from numerous vines their glow glinting along rubies, diamonds, emeralds, sapphires, and more. Dark roots stretched from the ceiling, winding down from what must have been massive trees overhead. They were integrated in the expanding city, built into the sides of homes and structures, the entirety of its citizens living in harmony with their surroundings.

Rolling chatter of the boisterous beings below reached us,

and everywhere I looked, I could see pairs of ram horns designating their earth fae status.

"Are those crops?" I asked, stunned that plants of any sort could thrive under the earth, let alone produce fruit.

Halcyon's full lips lifted into a proud smile, her silver eyes sparkling. And a part of me hated that the sight was not unpleasant.

"They are. We have farms above land too, but we are careful to grow enough food below in order to sustain us should anything happen. It's a necessary precaution under my rule. Those who wish to return to the old ways have been quiet recently, but I'm glad I've invested in safety measures with the enchantress Levana now at large."

"Do you know much about her? Most of what has been relayed to me is built on myth," I said, studying her features for any tells. She remained opened as she answered.

"That's because she *is* a myth. Or, at least, she was until now." Halcyon turned her gaze back to the thriving city below. "Each kingdom has slightly different accounts of history. Ours hedges Levana wasn't always bad. Dark, yes, but there are shadows within all of us. She was once thought to be a great creator, possibly even a sister to Eunoia, the one most believe to be the main goddess of Pax."

"History or myth?" I asked.

"The two are often one and the same. It's simply a matter of perspective. Which brings me back to those taken by the sleeping curse. Can I show you?"

Her silver gaze blazed with challenge, as if a group of fae mysteriously thrust into a cursed sleep would scare me, but it was nothing compared to the horrors I'd seen at the base. At least there wouldn't be any arrows.

"I'm not sure how they're being affected," Halcyon continued, mis-interrupting my silence for hesitation. "And I can't know you'll be safe, but I promise to join you, every step of the way."

Her heart gave a small flutter, the vibrations of anticipation and something else humming down the cord between us. The feeling was a ripple of *her* emotions—not mine—but it was hard to differentiate between the two of us.

"Lead the way," I said.

AFTER WHAT FELT LIKE HOURS OF DESCENDING STAIRCASES AND navigating great stretches of caverns with glinting gems, Halcyon and I arrived at a locked door. She pressed her palm to the center, her touch sending the black crystals spanning the sealed wall glowing with a faint light, before an oval edge appeared and swung inward.

"Have you seen a crystal door before?" Halcyon asked.

I shook my head.

"They are linked with one's essence. Only myself, General Xavier, and you have been granted access," Halcyon said as we stepped forward. "I trust General Xavier with my life. He's been a constant support in my rule, which as you know, has been lonely."

I *did* know, not only had Soter explained Halcyon's revolution of the Earth Kingdom in favor of equality for women—humans and fae alike—but there were also the flickers of longing for companionship that came through our bond at time. Halcyon was strong, powerful, and capable, but she was still flesh and bone. She still desired to find someone in this terrible world who would see her and choose to stand beside her.

"You'll meet General Xavier eventually," Halcyon continued. "But he's my eyes and ears above. I'm telling you this to assure you, you can trust those under the sleeping curse have not been moved since being placed inside."

"Gods," I breathed as the chilled air rose to greet us. It was musty and slightly tinged with a hint of amber despite how deep in the earth we were. I'd expected a small room, like the infirmary at the base, but this was a vast cavern. The faint light cast from glowing stones set throughout the space reflected off sharp, dark planes streaked with scarlet, the entire room carved from bloodstone—and filled wall-to-wall with slumbering bodies. The gentle rise and fall from each chest were the only indication that all the fae here weren't dead.

"It's quite the sight," Halcyon said.

"There are dozens of them—hundreds."

"Yes."

My gaze snapped to hers. "The way you spoke, it sounded as if there were only a few cases, the beginning of a new affliction, but this…"

"This has been going on for years," she whispered. "Even before I became queen."

"May I?" I asked, gesturing toward the bodies.

"Please," Halcyon said. "That's why you're here."

Stepping among the rows of stagnant life, I studied each of the fae who had descended into an unwaking slumber. Only thin, black sheets separated them from the ground, giving the appearance of warped burial shrouds half completed.

"Why are they on the ground?" I asked, dropping to a knee by one who appeared to be among the newest to join. Arching ram horns were set amid tangles of her dark hair, and her skin had a slight sheen of sweat, as if a fever still clung to her, but when I pressed the back of my hand to her brow, it was cool.

"They do better when connected to the earth." Halcyon answered, coming to my side. "When I was first told of the sleeping sickness, those afflicted were laying in the hospital wing above, but I noticed newly afflicted fae declined quickly. The life remaining in them waned, their skin growing pale and their flesh gaunt. When we allowed them to remain in the earth, they stabilized, as if drawing strength from the earth itself—which is common among earth fae."

"And the gem?" I asked, my gaze flicked up to the cavern of dark blacks, greens, and reds. "Why Bloodstone?"

"*That* is something I'd hoped you could uncover. We know they do better when surrounded by it, and each fae preyed upon was found alongside a vein of it."

"A vein?"

"Yes, meaning a sheet or a small sliver of bloodstone that is found within other parts of the earth, sometimes within other stones."

My brows furrowed as I pressed my palm to the chest of the nearest earth fae. As faint as it was, I could hear the steady beating of her heart, could see the sunken hollows of her eyes and the paleness to her complexion... but I couldn't detect a cause for such findings. All her other organs appeared to be working fine.

"I could try a few teas, maybe some gentle stimulants to see if they would wake."

"Most have already been tried. Nothing dangerous, of course, but the families of those first affected are growing desperate." Halcyon's eyes glanced toward the back of the expansive hall.

Following her gaze, I stood. "You said this has been happening for years?"

"Yes," she sighed, and I could feel the weight of that answer as if the burden were my own. "And every year there are more. Just recently ten succumbed at once—the most we've had at a single time."

Striding toward the back, I studied each body, each trapped mind. "Do they ever respond to stimuli?"

"No," Halcyon answered, her voice close behind me as we reached the back wall. The bodies were thinner here, little more than atrophied muscle and skin draped over bones. As if hearing my thoughts, Halcyon spoke. "They deteriorate to a point and then enter a sort of arrest."

My mind whirled, searching for the source of their suspended animation. "The bloodstone must be maintaining them somehow, connecting them to Pax and, therefore, their fae essence. Their innate fae healing and each body's low energy output has allowed them to survive, but we have no way of knowing what their mental status is."

Halcyon nodded, silently urging me to follow my spiraling thoughts.

"When was the first? You said it was years ago, but when exactly?"

Her silver eyes found mine. "Summer, a little over eight years ago."

"When the storm hit," I breathed, my own wide-eyed gaze reflected in Queen Halcyon's worried expression. "And the last surge, the one that claimed the largest number of fae. It matches up with—"

"Levana's rebirth."

20

GREER

I twisted and turned, studying every inch of my reflection in the mirror. The shimmering fabric looked like molten gold and clung to every inch of my body before flowing into a long skirt. My silver curls were left down, the tips covering the beaded straps crisscrossing along my back. The deep slit exposed the dragon brand climbing my thigh, and my legs were made to look longer with the five inch heels Cress had tied me into.

One good thing about others being able to scent our mating bond was that she'd dropped any preamble of seducing Ryuu. She'd also taken nearly an hour to perfect my make-up, complete with the matching modest stud earrings and quaint golden crown set atop my head—a symbol announcing my acceptance as future Queen of the Air Kingdom.

"You look stunning," Ryuu purred, his voice low.

A smile quirked my lips as I turned to face him, finding vertical pupils peering out beneath smoldering green eyes. He was dressed to match, his own golden tunic hanging loose to expose the top of his bronzed chest.

"You're looking particularly delicious, as well, husband."

His hands came around my waist as his lips met mine before drawing back. I shifted self-consciously, as Ryuu's eyes snagged on my crown, adjusting the golden points as I turned back toward the mirror.

"Do you think it's over the top?"

The warmth of his chest heated my back as he leaned down, speaking against my cheek. "Gold represents the rising dawn, the birth of a new day. It's tradition to wear the color when new unions are established between lovers at their joining."

"Are we getting married today?" I snarked, lifting a brow.

"We are already mated," Ryuu chuckled, the deep rumblings in his chest shuddering against my back. "And I would never deprive you of the wedding planning."

"Good," I said, lifting my hand to loop around his neck. The position forced me to arch my back, my ass pressing against his hips. My lip quirked, feeling his fingers dig into my waist as I stretched. "Maybe we can be a little late?"

"Greer," he warned, his growing length betraying his desires despite the reprimand.

"What?" I asked, mock innocence dripping from the word. "You haven't renewed your vows today, husband."

He groaned as I wiggled, his wings bristling as he fought to maintain control. "I know you're nervous, but I'd never trap you here. The crown is a symbol of your status. You are my mate, my soul-bound partner. That's what it represents. If you chose to leave this place tomorrow and never come back, I'd follow you."

"You know I'd never ask that of you, right?" I said, all pretense of flirting forgotten. I turned in his arms when he didn't answer. "This kingdom is a part of you, Ryuu. You are its rightful heir. You've needed space, but I don't think you have ever forgotten that *this* is your kingdom. Now that you know you *are* worthy of your title, I assumed we'd stay, Levana or otherwise."

"You'd stay?" he asked, and I didn't miss the hint of hesitant hope drifting beneath the question. "You would leave your sisters and join me in ruling a foreign kingdom?"

"I wouldn't have to leave them, not really."

My fingers traced the filigree along the hem of his gilded tunic. I'd been thinking about what becoming queen of the Air Kingdom would mean, the good and the bad, ever since Ryuu's dragon had flown me to that ancient island off the coast and made me his. The idea of being responsible for an entire nation was terrifying. There were so many things I had to learn... but I realized I *wanted* to learn them. Being queen would allow me the opportunity to help thousands, to make this world a better— kinder—place, especially for any child left without parents.

"Naz will be El's sister-in-law at some point," I said, tracing the edge of his sleeves. "And she can shadowwalk. I'm not sure where Lannie will end up, but if it is in the Earth Kingdom, Queen Freya seems pretty close to Queen Halcyon, and I'm sure Jarek wouldn't mind luxing us a few times."

He lifted a skeptical brow. "Veles and his brothers are still at large, Silas has announced his play for king in the north, and Levana has been reborn. There won't be much time for casual drop-ins."

"True," I sighed. "I wouldn't want to be queen for some time, though."

"Agreed," Ryuu rumbled. "Father is strong still. He could easily live for another few centuries before he tired of the throne."

"Wonderful," I grinned. "Because I can't see myself being anywhere but at your side as we face the end of the world."

Ryuu's chest heaved at my words, his lips capturing mine in a fierce kiss. "Together."

"Together," I echoed.

"Announcing the Tamer of Winds, General of the Sky Warriors, son of King Dragcor, and sole heir to the Air Kingdom, Price Ryuu Virtus. And his fated mate, Greer Tenebris."

My hand was draped over the crook of Ryuu's elbow as we started forward. I did my best to lift my chin and compose my expression as dozens of eyes fixed on us.

And his fated mate.

I was seriously going to need to add a few taglines to my name. I'd start with, 'Pax's one and only cursebreaker', or 'Sister to the Dark Phoenix', or something of the sort. Ignoring the blow to my pride, I stared ahead and forced my breathing to remain even as we continued toward King Dragcor.

He was as intimidating as I'd remembered. His wings were spread wide, the soft browns and midnight blacks on full display as he stood to welcome us. Sleek, dark locks were unbound, the thin golden crown sitting atop his brow similar to the ones Ryuu and I wore. The blazing orange specks in his eyes complimented the burnt sienna of his tunic, the vertical slits zeroing in on Ryuu's and my matching gold outfits.

"My son," King Dragcor beamed, his authentic smile stretching as he lowered his chin in a nod of respect. "You're looking well. Lady Greer, it is an honor to see you, again. Am I correct in noting you two are fully bound, dragon and all?"

A blush heated my cheeks as Ryuu answered. "Yes. The goddess has blessed us with a mating bond. My dragon has accepted."

"I can see that," King Dragcor said, his gaze finding the brand along my thigh. "It would seem you have a dragon of your own, Lady Greer, one strong enough to withstand the beast within my son."

"He's not a beast," I said, the words spilling from my lips before I could think better of it.

King Dragcor lifted a brow in challenge, as if daring me to explain.

"He's not," I continued, taking the bait, despite Ryuu's flicker of caution down our bond. "The dragon is a little intense but he's really sweet, underneath it all."

"Greer," Ryuu muttered at the same time his father smirked.

"I can see the two of you are well paired," King Dragcor said, turning toward the waiting fae with a tray of drinks. Rising a glass filled with clear, bubbly liquid, he addressed the crowded court room. "To my son and his striking mate. The goddess has seen fit to bless our kingdom with strong leaders in our time of need."

Accepting an offered drink, I took a sip as glasses clanked, welcoming us with cheer. The crisp flora notes of the alcohol were refreshing and helped to steel my nerves in a room where I was the only one without wings.

"That's actually what we came to talk to you about," Ryuu said, focusing his gaze on King Dragcor. "We have need of the Sky Warriors."

The orange embers in the Air King's reptilian eyes seemed to glow brighter as he swallowed his drink. It was unnerving how I could almost see King Dragcor hatching a plan as he stared between the two of us. Ryuu stiffened beside me, no doubt sensing much of the same.

"Lords and ladies of the court, enjoy the feast I've prepared for you tonight," King Dragcor called, ignoring Ryuu. "Tomorrow, we shall welcome your new king and queen."

21

ELARA

"Are you sure this is the best option?" I asked as another wave of refugees from the base stepped through the portal Queen Freya had opened. There were only a few dozen left, the remaining sectioned into groups to allow Queen Freya time to recover between portals as she'd been at it all day.

"This is our *only* option," Zaeth replied, his own gaze filtering through the masses and snagging on Alarik.

I hadn't spoken to the general, despite the close confines we'd shared these last few weeks. There seemed to be too much and nothing to say all at once. There wasn't tension between us. It was more a mutual apathy that we'd both embraced.

With planning for relocating to the Wild Kingdom, Alarik had been working closely with Queen Freya over the last few weeks. He'd insisted on inspecting where they'd be taken to before any of the humans had been portaled, something that was unheard of given how secretive the wild fae were of their territory.

Somehow, after countless meetings and a few long nights, Queen Freya agreed to give him a tour. A few days later, here we were, transferring the last of the refugees.

"I can hold the portal for two more groups," Queen Freya panted, her brow damp with concentration.

Alarik nodded, ushering the next two waiting clusters of fae and humans through as quick as possible.

"Thank you, Queen Freya," Zaeth said. He'd shaved since returning to the Dark Kingdom, but the stubble along his jaw was already growing in. He looked in his element here, among the dark obsidian stone and harsh towers, freely giving commands and knowing they would be followed. "If Levana does come for Caligo, at least the causalities will be far fewer."

The last of the second group disappeared into the shimmering silver light, the portal vanishing seconds later. Queen Freya doubled over with her hands braced on her knees as she fought to catch her breath.

"I'm not used to this," she panted as Zaeth and I flitted toward her, but Alarik was there, helping her into a chair before we were needed.

"Thank you," he said, those emerald eyes fixed on the Wild Queen. "For everything. The humans of Pax have little left to believe in, but you've given them hope they might survive this."

"Careful, General." Queen Freya's lips twitched. "You keep talking to me like that, I might make you thank me properly."

Alarik grinned, the unguarded expression catching me by surprise. "If we survive this, Queen Freya, it would be my pleasure."

Queen Freya glanced over Alarik's shoulder toward us, a small smile playing on her lips as her honey-gold eyes meeting mine. Slowly, the ruins pulsing across her forehead and stretching down her cheeks faded.

Zaeth and I closed the distance toward them. "How are you feeling?"

"Tired, but I should be able to get the rest of them through by night fall. General Alarik has been a huge help in getting everyone settled in the Wild Kingdom."

Alarik's green eyes turned to me for the first time, filled with nothing but a friendly peace. "It's good to see you again, Elara."

"You as well," I said, and meant it. His hair was longer, the scruff along his jaw thickening into a full beard, and his chest and shoulders had filled out. If the expression on Queen Freya's face meant anything, she'd noticed the changes as well.

"I'm glad those from the base are being welcomed," Zaeth said, before turning toward Alarik. "How have you been, General? How are your men doing?"

"As good as they can be, under the circumstances."

My stomach twisted as I searched behind Alarik for the member of the Select Guard who'd first welcomed me to the base all those months ago. "Is Vidarr doing any better?"

Alarik's face fell. "Ahmya's death has been hard on him. Focusing on training helps for a time, but he's not ready for anything further."

I nodded, wishing there was anything I could do to help but knowing grief wasn't something that could be wished away.

"He's looking forward to confronting Veles and his brothers," Alarik continued.

"As are we," Zaeth said.

"Most of the men wish to stay to aid you against them," Alarik added, focusing on Zaeth. "But there are a lot of unanswered questions with Levana introduced to the playing field. What's her role in all of this?"

"We're not sure," I answered honestly.

"We think it reasonable that she's been orchestrating the brothers' attacks," Zaeth said.

"Levana controls the brothers?" Queen Freya asked. "You don't think it's the other way around?"

"No," I answered, my voice steady. "She's far too powerful."

"Our spies confirm an upwelling of dark creatures in the north around the Shadowlands," Zaeth continued. "Suggesting she may be league with Silas, as well."

Queen Freya stood, looking much recovered. "As I've mentioned to General Alarik, the mists around the Wild Kingdom haven't been breached for centuries. Any who seek refuge inside will be safe. I only wish we could extend it."

"The Wild Kingdom's resources will be stained with the added refugees," Alarik added with a glance toward Queen Freya. Her eyes narrowed, but she didn't contradict him. "Living supplies would be helpful, but food is a must."

"We've done fine on our own for centuries," Queen Freya countered, but Zaeth shook his head.

"You shall have all that you need. I'll have Naz prepare supplies as soon as our business here is concluded."

"You and your people have no problem welcoming humans into your realm?" I asked, and not for the first time. Queen Freya usually found a way of evading the question but asking in front of Zaeth and Alarik put her in a unique situation. "The people of the base have been through a lot. They deserve a place of complete safety—"

"They're safe with the wild fae, Elara." The offended rebuke from Alarik drew me up short. "You really think I'd trust my people to be portaled by a ruler I've only just met into an unknown situation?"

Queen Freya lifted a brow. "I don't know about that, general. I think we've gotten to know each other fairly well."

Zaeth's lips twitched at seeing the blush creep up Alarik's face.

"Really not the time, Freya," Alarik muttered.

"On the contrary," she grinned at him before turning to me. "I think now is the perfect time. The humans are safe because we've been saving humans for centuries. Our entire kingdom was closed off millennia ago when fae thought humans little more than slaves."

"I thought most humans were swallowed up by the sea," Zaeth asked, his voice low.

"Some were," Queen Freya conceded, "but the majority of them have been kept safe, integrating into the Wild Kingdom. Most of our humans have some level of fae abilities, but we insisted on keeping them concealed. With the way the brothers targeted humans on the outside, we're one of the only reason Pax hasn't completely lost its tether to humanity."

"I've seen it," Alarik confirmed, tilting his chip up just a hair.

"Why keep it a secret?" I asked. I knew I should trust her, or at the very least, trust Alarik. But trust wasn't something that came easy to me. I would rest easier if I knew this wasn't some sort of trick.

Queen Freya's face grew serious. "By your own account, you've already been possessed by Levana once. We have no idea how much information she's gleamed from you. Maybe she only peered out of your eyes while she controlled you, but she might've had access to your memories, your visions. Even now, there could be some connection."

"She's gone," I said, my jaw clenching at her implications.

"The connection between Elara and Levana is severed," Zaeth added, a bite to his words. "She is herself, fully."

Queen Freya's shrewd, honey-gold gaze cut to him. "While I trust your mating bond is truthful, we still don't know if the enchantress is able to take possession of Elara again. I can't risk my kingdom. I've already said more than I wish."

Zaeth looked like he meant to argue, but I shook my head. "No, she's right. I'm not sure how much Levana had access to while she was inside my head. The less I know the better, just in case."

Zaeth's hand came to the small of my back, pressing soothing circles through the fabric of my tunic. He knew what it was like to worry over a nation, and though I wasn't a queen, I was the Dark Phoenix—at least half of it. I had a responsibility toward protecting the innocents of Pax to the best of my ability.

"They're safe," Alarik repeated, his voice gentle. "And happy.

It's beautiful there. The land, the trees, even the skies seem more welcoming. Animals I've only ever seen in books, ones long since killed off in other kingdoms, they live there, in harmony with fae and humans."

I nodded, hearing the sincerity of his words. "Thank you."

"Yes," Queen Freya huffed. "Now that we've established I'm not carting off humans for slaughter, can we get back to our plans for dealing with Levana? When will she attack?"

"I'm not sure," I said, replaying images of the vision through my mind. "But no leaves were on the trees. With Yule only two weeks away, it could be any day, now."

Queen Freya nodded grimly. "I trust extra wards have been placed around Caligo?"

"Yes," confirmed Zaeth. "As much as possible, according to Jarek."

"Where is he?" Queen Freya asked, looking over our shoulders. "I could use the help transporting."

"He's gone with Evander to the Earth Kingdom touching base with Elara's sister. As you know, Lannie has been working with Queen Halcyon to try to cure the sleeping sickness."

"Any progress?" Alarik asked.

"We'll know as soon as he returns," Zaeth answered. "But for all our sakes, let's hope so. Queen Halcyon won't leave her people until the sickness is righted and Caligo would fare much better if we had her warriors at our side."

"Even if the seven kingdoms were united," Queen Freya mussed. "We're facing the enchantress, a goddess in her own right. What chance do we have of surviving this?"

"A slim one," Zaeth answered honestly, his candor turning my stomach.

Queen Freya let out a harsh, humorless laugh. "We need gods to fight gods, or at least monsters like the Merged—anything and everything this world has to offer—if we're to stand a chance against her."

"Even then, it *still* might not be enough," Zaeth breathed.

Queen Freya shook her head. "Makes you wish the legends about Eunoia and Erebus were true. That we could somehow wake them, and the world would be saved."

"If only," Zaeth sighed. "As it were, we'll coordinate the army we have, relying on strategy rather than strength. Together, we might get through this."

Together.

That word held a lot of possibilities. We needed all of Pax, and while we had the Wild Kingdom's support and what remained of Alarik's men, their numbers were small compared to what we'd seen of the Fractured. Greer had yet to send word from the Air Kingdom and Lannie had been so consumed by the sleeping sickness that her letters were one or two lines just to tell me she was alive and working. We were still significantly outmatched.

With one last nod, Zaeth and I turned from Alarik and Queen Freya to start our journey back to the city center. New perimeters had been established with various alarms and wards set, but I couldn't help feeling like this was all playing right into Levana's hand.

"Something feels off about this," I whispered, careful to not let anyone else overhear. "Why didn't Levana attack right away?"

"I'm not sure," Zaeth said, his hand finding mine. "Maybe she needed to regain her strength. Maybe she's busy amassing her armies. Either way, I'm glad for the time."

I let him draw me in for a kiss, allowing his lips and hands to whisk away some of my worries for a few moments.

"No matter the outcome," I said, peering into his cinnamon eyes.

Zaeth's palm caressed my cheek, tilting my lips up for him to taste once more. "We'll find our way back to each other, love. No matter what comes."

22

LANNIE

Every tonic, salve, infusion, and repositioning proved futile against the sleeping sickness. Halcyon and I had been at it for weeks and nothing had changed—at least nothing for the better.

We confirmed that when fae were taken away from the cavern crafted from bloodstone, they significantly dropped in function. Their breathing slowed, the slight flush of color still clinging to the recent victims faded, even their muscle tone appeared to degenerate. For fear of losing one of them, we hurriedly returned all to the cavern, watching amazed as they stabilized within minutes.

"We know being near bloodstone maintains them," I said pacing the length of the underground garden.

I'd thought the herbs and foliage beneath the earth would have been sparse, to say the least, but there were entire groves of flourishing fruit trees, thronged berry bushes, and fields of flowers.

Halcyon had taken me through the heart of the Earth Kingdom, showing me everything with General Xavier in tow. I'd protested at first, thinking it a waste of time when there were fae suffering, but Halcyon had pointed out that we knew very little about the illness. Any bit of information could be vital, including the medical properties of what thrived below the surface.

The city was divided into provinces, each section dedicated to a different gem: diamond to the north, ruby to the east, sapphire to the west, emerald to the south, and amethyst for the palace at the heart of them all. There were other streaks of gemstones, such as citrine and lapis lazuli, along with various metals including silver, gold, and copper, all of them woven together into the glimmering city.

Today, we were in the Diamond Province. Its garden contained plants thought to be more dangerous and enduring than the others. It was home to various thorny bushes and deadly flowers, some so potent that one prick could kill a human.

Halcyon, General Xavier, and I had explored the other gardens as well. The soothing presence of the Emerald garden, the thriving foliage of the ruby, and the symbiotic plant life in the sapphire garden were all marvelous, but if we were to find any aid from the earth, it thought it would've come from the diamond garden where every plant was a little bit vicious. Though at this point, I was starting to wonder if there was a cure at all.

"And with more falling ill at Levana's rebirth, we know the sleeping sickness is connected to her," General Xavier added, his dark braids swinging in front of his eyes as his umber colored ram horns dipped forward to avoid a low handing vine.

"But how?" I pressed, coming up against the same question for what felt like the hundredth time. I passed beneath the dark vines, too short to bother with ducking, as we came to a round sitting area in the center of a crossroads, complete with diamond-encrusted benches. "What is Levana getting out of this, and why only a few at a time?"

General Xavier's lips pressed thin as Halcyon shook her head. Her light purple hair shimmered around the dark ram horns sweeping back over her head, as her silver eyes stared back at me, glinting like the diamonds around us. Gods, was she beautiful—heartbreakingly so.

The thought sent a ripple of guilt shooting through me.

Not yet three months ago, Ser had been killed. While I wasn't the type of person who believed the living should punish themselves for surviving, I still couldn't shake the feeling that I was betraying Ser each time I allowed myself to appreciate anything that drew me to Halcyon.

It would have been easier if the attraction was based solely on her appearance, but these last few weeks had shown me how strong she was. Halcyon was fierce and protective when it came to her people without striping her ability for kindness. And her mind—gods, the level of cunning intelligence it took to wield words like sharpened blades, to coax your enemies into understanding your view and prevent civil war every other day—she was extraordinary.

Her breathing hitched, only slightly, but I knew she'd gotten a read on my emotions. It sent another burst of guilt through me.

"With Levana reborn," she continued, allowing us to pretend she hadn't been aware of my attraction. "I don't understand why she would keep drawing from them."

Not wanting her to see the blush staining my cheeks, I turned away, slipping around General Xavier, to stroll along the pristine diamond path ahead of us. The precious gem had been crafted into trestles, allowing for dark vines and silver flowers to climb up their intricate lattice. My fingers trailed along a cluster of tall black flowers sprouting along the garden's edge, their petals soft and shimmering in the bio-luminescent glow from afar.

I was careful not to touch the thrones along the stems, but

I'd come to appreciate the feel of the earth. It had a soothing effect on me, one I was indulging in more and more as I spent time below.

"Drawing but not using," I said when Halcyon and General Xavier didn't answer. I turned, fixing my gaze on Halcyon. "You can feel the bloodstone drawing the fae's essence into it, but the power hasn't gone anywhere, right?"

She tilted her head, her graceful hands picking at the cuticles along her polished nails—something she did when she was unnerved.

"I can't read stones often," she said after a time. "And when I can it's only a glimpse, but it feels like all the power is there."

"We're missing something," General Xavier said with a shake of his head. "The power should have waned when Levana was reborn, but it didn't."

I stilled.

"You think she's storing it for something?"

"For what?" he said. "She's already regained her corporal form."

"Maybe for exactly what you described—a power source. If there was enough power held in the bloodstone and if Levana could tap into that power, maybe it would give her abilities a boost."

"Like a type of explosive burst?" Halcyon asked, the slight tilt of her head showing her skepticism.

I shrugged. "What other reason is there?"

"I don't know," she answered, her gaze turning toward the approaching footsteps to the south as General Xavier stepped in front of us. "And that's what worries me."

A pair of guards turned down our path with three others behind them. I blinked, my eyes widening as I recognized the flash of auburn hair and pointed ears.

"Evander," I breathed, flitting toward them. The guards

stepped aside as I approached, exposing the rest of the group: Jarek and Soter.

"My queen," Soter said, his molten gold eyes darting over my shoulder to Halcyon as he bowed. "And General Xavier, it's good to see you."

Halcyon and General Xavier responded with courtly pleasantries, the three of them striking up a conversation, but my gaze was fixed on Evander.

He'd changed.

His hair was longer, well past his shoulders, and looking as if it hadn't been brushed recently. A beard had grown, a few shades darker than his auburn hair, but the most troubling thing was the hollowness in his eyes. It was a look I'd seen far too often as a healer: grief.

My stomach twisted as realization dawned on me. This was from seeing Jem in the after, from me pulling Evander back from the brink of death.

"We came to see how progress has been with the sleeping sickness," Jarek offered, his dazzling smile lacking its normal luster. From the darkness under his eyes, it looked as if Evander wasn't the only one suffering.

"And to transport any available troops to Caligo," Soter added.

Halcyon stiffened. "I can send another hundred, but without a cure for the sleeping sickness or a way to prevent new fae succumbing, I must retain the majority of my warriors here."

Why?

I could sense Halcyon's worry radiating through our bond, but I didn't understand the reason for it. The only threat was the bloodstone, but it had been removed from every piece of jewelry, mosaic, or decoration crafted throughout the kingdom and added to the cavern of the sleeping years ago. So, why prepare for an attack here?

"King Zaethrian also wished to know your thoughts on seeking aid from the Water Kingdom." Jarek's words hung in the air as General Xavier and Halcyon shared a look. The Earth Queen's face was a mask of control, but I felt flashes of emotion beneath the surface, coming and going too fast for me to discern.

"Why don't we continue this conversation in my sitting rooms?" Halcyon said, turning to head up the path before anyone could respond. Left with no other option, we followed.

Halcyon flitted along the diamond mosaic streets toward the great tree palace at the center of Xyla. The world seemed to sparkle as we flitted after her, dashing across the precious jewels as we neared the palace and the amethyst stones surrounding it.

"How has the Earth Kingdom avoided war with such riches?" I asked, catching up to Halcyon as we flitted. I could tell she was still feeling shaken, and I had an irresistible urge to lessen some of her worry. "One glance at the jewels surrounding you, and I would've thought every kingdom would be here demanding a share."

She was quiet a heartbeat longer as the diamonds shifted to amethyst beneath our feet, but then she spoke.

"There was a curse placed on all the stones of the Earth Kingdom. Any not freely given would spell misfortune for the thief and ultimately lead to their death. There are tales long ago of the Ice Kingdom stealing a specific type of diamond."

"Ice Kingdom?" I asked. "I've never heard of it."

Halcyon grinned. "Exactly."

We flitted up the winding steps, the diamonds beneath my feet seeming more precarious than before, until great ebony roots wound through the ground.

Each time I looked upon the Earth Palace, I was awed. It was, in fact, a living tree, the interior hollowed out long ago. We stood at the base of the trunk, my eyes flicking up to note thick branches stretching into the earth overhead. Sprawling roots carved paths into the gemstone-studded streets, the tree's onyx bark lightened by glowing silver veins. Leaves stretched high above, their silver sheen causing it to look like the night sky up above.

"This way," Halcyon beckoned, guiding us through the open double doors and into the open foyer. We continued up the spiral staircases and into the canopy, until we reached her rooms. "Please prepare the troops to lux to Caligo, General Xavier."

"Yes, my queen," he said with a slight bow before he was gone.

With only Jarek, Evander, Soter, and myself remaining, Halcyon pushed open a set of carved black doors crafted from the tree's exterior bark and beckoned us into the well-lit sitting room.

Cozy, silver couches were positioned along the sides, centered around a low-set wooden table. Bookshelves were all around us with various vines draped from the ceiling. Ferns were clustered in corners, the soft moss at their feet stretching to line the main floor way.

The earth was everywhere, thriving in this space. I could sense the way Halcyon connected to it, could practically feel her body humming with energy.

"Please," Halcyon said, sitting in the chair at the far end of the room. "Take a seat."

Soter and I claimed chairs on one side of the table, leaving Evander and Jarek to the other. There was a moment of tense silence before Jarek spoke.

"Levana must be mobilizing troops. It's the only explanation for why she hasn't attacked yet."

"*One* of the possible reasons," I countered.

"Either troops or she's gathering her strength," Soter added.

Halcyon and I shared a look, both of us thinking about the bloodstone.

"Regardless," Jarek continued. "We need to prepare, and we'd stand a much better chance with fae from multiple kingdoms."

"More affinities do allow for better versatility," I said with a reluctant glance toward Halcyon. "Is aid from the Water Kingdom so farfetched?"

"You know my kingdom's history of oppression?" She asked, her silver eyes hard.

I shook my head. "Only small bits of information I've heard the last few weeks and some from Soter."

"It's a long and bloody tale, one that would take years to learn. While the Earth Kingdom is only now coming out of that darkness, a large portion of the Water Kingdom remains trapped in the past. Their queen, Isla, was forced into an arranged marriage, essentially transferring all her ruling power to her husband, King Kai."

"I can see why they wouldn't take kindly to a meeting you," I said. "Strong, independent women don't sound like they would be welcomed."

Queen Halcyon's chin lifted, just a hair, some of the tension seeming to ease from her shoulders.

"I see your point," Jarek said. "And agree wholeheartedly they're seriously behind the times, but Queen Isla might be just as ready for change, and you were. You might be able help her navigate her kingdom's policies in a more suitable fashion, while also establishing a strong ally against Levana and the brother. And Silas," he added after a moment. "We have plenty of enemies. We need to start making a few friends."

"I doubt the Water Kingdom and I could ever be friends. Women's rights are only a sliver of the problem." Halcyon pressed the pads of her fingers to her forehead, massaging her temples. "But with what we're up against, I guess it's worth a try."

"Wonderful," Jarek said, nudging Evander who had been staring absentmindedly at the edge of the wooded table. He blinked, glancing toward Jarek. "Did you hear that? Queen Halcyon has agreed to go to the Water Kingdom and ask for help."

"That's great," Evander said with forced effort.

"Who will join you?" Soter asked. "I must return to Caligo to aid Naz in tracking the whereabouts of the brothers. Jarek and Evander are traveling to the Air Kingdom next with hopes of luxing portions of King Dragcor's army."

"I'll ask Queen Freya," Halcyon said. "She has just as much invested in this war as we do, and she'll be able to portal us."

"Us?" Jarek prompted.

The Earth Queen's silver eyes found mine. I knew what she was going to ask, knew that I'd accept even though every ounce of my being wanted to stay… but for what? To sit in my grief over Ser or spend another hundred hours staring at the barely breathing bodies who had yet to show any signs of higher brain function?

There was nothing more I could do here. I gave Halcyon the smallest of nods.

She grinned. "Lannie will join us in the Water Kingdom."

23

GREER

"He didn't know we decided on ruling the kingdom," I seethed, my breath puffing out in front of me as I paced the length of the plateau. The wind was cold, whipping and tugging at my braided silver curls, but it was the only place Ryuu and I could go. My rooms were full of gowns for me to choose from for our upcoming wedding, and Ryuu's rooms were stacked with various blades for his selection. Apparently, brides were gifted gowns while husbands were offered weapons, as if marriage were a battle they needed to be armed against.

Ryuu stood close by while I fumed with his hand patiently folded over his tanned tunic embossed with red filigree. There were small flutters of snow in the air, and the entire canyon was cast in darkening clouds, but still he waited for me.

"And to just proclaim it like that," I huffed. "Your father hasn't listened to a word we've said. His sole focus is getting you on that throne. I know we agreed to rule, but I thought we would have centuries before we *actually* had to do anything."

Ryuu's lips twitched. "You see now why I've been so hesitant to return home."

"Yep," I said with extra emphasis on the 'p' as I kicked a few pebbles off the cliff. They tumbled down, reminding me just how high up I was and how far I had to fall. "At least he sent a battalion to the Dark Kingdom."

"True," Ryuu agreed, coming to my side to gaze into the valley surrounding us. His arms wrapped around my waist, the dragon within heating his palms just enough to keep the cool from sinking into my bones. His wings wrapped around us, the soft inside feathers caressing me as the wind picked up and keeping the rest of the chill away.

I wanted to stay here in his arms and bask in the silence. So much had changed in such a short period of time.

Before returning, I'd found myself open to ruling, excited even, but that was when it was a far-off distant future. Not right now. Not in the middle of a war.

With a sigh, I turned in Ryuu's arms to rest my head on his chest. "It's not that I don't want to be queen, I just..."

"Want to feel like it's your decision." Ryuu's chest rumbled as he spoke, and I nodded against him.

"You would be a wonderful king."

He leaned back, tilting my chin up to look at him. "And you an unrivaled queen."

A soft smile tilted my lips. "We *would* look phenomenal with crowns."

Ryuu's lips quirked before he pressed a kiss to my brow. When he met my gaze again, the vertical slits of his dragon were staring back at me. "King Dragcor cannot force us, darling. He is strong, but unmated."

"Being mated gives you strength?"

"Mated dragons can draw on each other's essence. We can heal each other and bolster each other's powers when they wane." The green flecks in Ryuu's eyes smoldered as a little more of his dragon crept to the surface. He dragged a thumb down the center of my bottom lip, his nail shifting into a tipped talon that almost pierced my flesh. "We have something worth fighting for."

My pulse quickened, but I'd long since stopped being afraid of Ryuu's inner beast. No, my blood was heating for an entirely different reason.

"A kingdom isn't enough cause to fight for?"

I'd meant it as a light joke, something to distract us from the growing desire between us, but it hit too close to the truth. Both of us were aware that the entire court was waiting for our decision.

"A kingdom is nothing compared to what I feel for you, darling," Ryuu's dragon rumbled. The intensity with which he looked at me was breathtaking. "You are light. Life itself. I'd gladly sacrifice a thousand kingdoms to keep you."

His lips met mine in a biting kiss, his desire showcased in every lash of his tongue, every searing pulse of need shooting down our bond. I clenched my thighs together as another blast of yearning rocked through me.

With a deep groan, Ryuu pulled back. "Gods above, will my need for you never be satiated?"

"Let's hope not," I grinned, nipping at his lower lip. "I could cast a shield…"

I let my lips graze his neck, sucking lightly. His fingers clenched, gripping my ass and pressing me against his growing desire. "Nobody would see or hear us." Another kiss along his collarbone. "And you could keep us warm."

A predatory growl rumbled through him.

"They're waiting for us," he protested, but he didn't pull away. If anything, he leaned in closer, gripping me tighter.

I leaned back, tugging the silk string along my bodice until the bow loosened to expose the tops of my breasts. The green embers of his eyes flashed, his nostrils flaring as I knit together a ward. It was second nature now, something I could maintain in my sleep… or while otherwise occupied.

I pulled the strings, further freeing myself, until my dress slipped down to my waist, my skin pebbling against the air.

"Then be quick."

~

"Where have you been?" King Dragcor snapped as we returned to Ryuu's rooms. His eyes narrowed, taking in the state of Ryuu's hair and the rosy flush to my cheeks. Before either of us could answer, King Dragcor held up a hand, shaking his head in exacerbation. "Don't answer that."

Snickers sounded from the few servants polishing the various weapons, their fae affinities no doubt scenting *exactly* what we'd been up to.

"Leave us," King Dragcor said, more annoyed than angry. Only once the last of them had left, the door clicking closed behind them did he speak. "I understand ruling has never been particularly important to you, but I expected at least the facade of caring."

Ryuu stiffened. "Sorry to disappoint you, father."

"Then don't," King Dragcor gritted through clenched teeth. "Choose your weapon of blessing. And you, Greer, your gown of fortune. If not for yourselves than for the people of the Air Kingdom."

"I love the dresses," I offered, wanting to break the growing tension. "They're a bit more conservative than I'd pictured for my wedding, but any will do."

In truth, when I'd thought of my wedding day, I'd pictured designing my own gown with Ahmya being the one to make it. We would've gone through fabrics and cuts, discussing complimentary gowns for my sisters… it would have taken months. Nothing rushed, no expectations attached to it, just me, Ryuu, and our love.

"Alter them." King Dragcor's dark eyes fixed on me. "We

have access to the finest seamstresses in the seven kingdoms, but I need you to select one."

Feeling like a child being scolded, I nodded.

"Greer doesn't need to do anything she doesn't want to," Ryuu interjected, but I shook my head. I knew he felt the flicker of grief for Ahmya, knew he understood the swell of emotions tied to this one decision.

"It's okay. Ahmya isn't here." King Dragcor's eyes flashed with something akin to sympathy. "I'll choose tonight."

"The kingdom thanks you."

Ryuu huffed a laugh devoid of humor. "*The kingdom* needs us discussing war tactics, not wedding preparations. After all that has transpired, Veles and his brothers, Silas in the north, and Levana's rising, you've hardly said a dozen words regarding the impending war."

The king's wings bristled. The mannerism was so like Ryuu when he was flustered that it almost made me laugh. But when King Dragcor spoke, it was with cold control.

"Which weapon do you choose, my son?"

"None," snapped Ryuu.

I could practically see the king's fury ignite. "Your mate may not understand the implications of this ceremony, but you do—"

"If we lose this war, there won't be a kingdom to rule." Ryuu's jaw clenched. "This, all of this, doesn't matter—"

"It does," King Dragcor thundered, the bite of his words hanging heavy in the growing silence. "I will give you the entire army, all of the weapons and supplies of the Air Kingdom, if you accept your throne."

Ryuu's chest heaved, and I felt his anger shift into alarmed caution as he eyes narrowed. "A dragon bargain?"

King Dragcor nodded, the two of them not breaking eye contact.

"What does that mean, a dragon bargain?"

"It's unbreakable," Ryuu answered, still studying his father. "Why is this so important? You've never been one to underestimate an opponent before. Why start now?"

King Dragcor's spine stiffened, almost bringing him to Ryuu's height.

"Unless," Ryuu breathed, his eyes watching King Dragcor for the smallest tell. "Unless you aren't."

"Proceed with the wedding. Accept your rightful place on the throne." King Dragcor held Ryuu's unflinching gaze, but the fire of his words had cooled. "And you will have all that you need."

Ryuu took a step back, his eyes widening. "You're... afraid."

"If this world is to end, I will see my only son crowned and married."

I blinked, my own anxiety spiking as Ryuu continued to stare at his father, unspeaking. After another drawn out moment, I spoke. "You... think we we're going to lose?"

King Dragcor's reptilian eyes found mine. For once, they were open, his trepidation alarmingly clear.

"Levana is a creature more powerful than you understand. The last time she walked this earth I still in my first century of life, but I knew the darkness she created. It took both her sister and her former lover to trick her into submission. Even then, they were only able to imprison her. Tell me, Cursebreaker, Fated Mate of the Dragon. If two gods with power unrivaled couldn't stop Levana, what chance do we have?"

24
ELARA

Steel clashed. The strength of Zaeth's blow reverberated up the hilt of my blade, stinging my arm. I kicked off him, my boot finding purchase in his chest as I used my wings to propel me backwards, affording me a moment to regroup.

"Good," he called. "But use your wings to shield. The barbs will absorb the brunt of the blow, allowing you to angle your blade up through your opponent's chest."

Panting, I adjusted my grip and nodded. Sparring with Zaeth was helpful, but our bond allowed impressions of our decisions to pass through moments before we made them. Naz was typically the one to meet with me but she was following a lead on Veles this morning before the sun rose and had yet to return.

"Again," Zaeth called as he flitted toward me.

His ebony wings expanded, pulling him to the side, just as his blade descended. A flicker of intention shot through me, letting me know he was aiming for my left thigh.

I flitted right, my wrist twisting to position my blade at the tip of his throat.

"Saw my moves?" he asked, the bright rings around his irises glowing.

"How did you guess?" My lips tugged into a grin, revealing the tips of my fangs as I sheathed the sword. "Let's switch to flying lessons."

Zaeth laughed. "I'm glad to hear heights no longer frighten you, love, but flying takes months to learn and years to master. We should be focusing on utilizing your wings during battle."

My violet wings flexed, eager for movement. The weather had turned for the year, the vibrant colors of fall long since gone, and I was still adjusting to the feel of the cool breeze rustling the downy underside. Tucking them in against me, I realized Yule was next week, the longest night of the year.

Still, Levana had not attacked. Perhaps what I'd seen in the after had only been a dream. I wanted to believe it hadn't been real—that I hadn't actually died and Levana, a primal goddess, hadn't used me to be reborn. But I'd never been one to believe in fantasies.

"Please?" I asked, letting my wings expand, marveling at the ebony undertones.

We'd only spent a few hours on flying, focusing mostly on wing control for short bursts like in battle. I'd heard his rationale before about not flying. I understood it, but there was no point in sparring when I could predict his moves. As if reading my thoughts Zaeth sighed.

"Okay," he said, sheathing his sword. My pulse jumped as a smile spread across my face. The black leather of his battle gear matched my own, the durable material shifting across his sculpted torso as he neared. It was practical and necessary, and gods did he look good in it. "We can practice flying only until—"

The shadows of the bare trees around Zaeth expanded, depositing a strong, feminine figure with dark eyes and tight curls: Naz.

"It's Vesna," she breathed, her eyes wide. "The cousin to the late Light Prince—she's left the Light Kingdom and is flitting north. We think she could lead us to Veles."

There was no time to call for others. Even now, Vesna was getting further away from the point Naz shadowwalked from. If we had any chance of following, we needed to go. Now.

Naz held her hands out. Zaeth and I spared only a moment's look for each other before we stepped toward her and folded into the darkness.

~

SNOW CRUNCHED BENEATH OUR BOOTS AS WE APPEARED. The scent of pine and ice lashed through the air, the forest stretching up the side of the vast mountain range to the west. Inhaling deeply, I caught the faint hint of embers and brimstone—the Fire Kingdom. We were at the base of the Jagged Mountains, just inside the border of the Dark Kingdom.

"She went this way," Naz called.

Without a word, the three of us flitted through the trees, following the subtle scent of roses. Small clumps of snow clung to spots of shadows, the sun melting away all that it touched. The soil was soft, easily capturing footprints a fae had been too foolish or too arrogant to avoid leaving—sounding exactly like the light fae Greer had described.

We caught up to Vesna quickly, flashes of her blond hair and pale blue cloak all too easy to spot among the trees. She slowed as we headed north, the three of us careful to keep our distance.

My fae affinities were on full alert, my ears picking up two heartbeats closing in before Vesna even realized she'd found who she was after. There were hundreds of sluggish heartbeats further off, but we'd have time to flee before any had the chance to attack.

Zaeth gave a quick jerk of his chin. He'd heard them, too. Forging a path through the trees so as not to be detected, he led us closer to the meeting.

"There you are," she breathed, her voice more whine than

relief. "I was so worried when you didn't come back, but a few from The Legion said they saw evidence of the Fractured and I knew if there was a chance, I had to find you."

The Fractured. That must be the distant lethargic pulses we'd picked up on.

We crept closer, still several yards away, but able to peer through the thinning trees. A cloaked figure stepped forward, his towering form and sleek, silver hair giving away his identity even before he pushed back his hood: Veles.

"Vesna," Veles said. "You're here. How... surprising."

"I'm sorry it took so long, Your Greatness. The prince proved more formidable than anticipated, but I have everything sorted."

"The prince was of no consequence," another spoke from behind. My spine stiffened as the sound of that voice lashed through me. I'd heard it in my nightmares, watching as his black tipped claws pierced Zelos's neck, unable to forget the way his red eyes gleamed when he plunged the blade through my stomach. He was the red-eyed commander, the reason Will was gone: Draven. "Has any progress been made on locating our brother, Olysseus?"

Vesna's breaths quicken, her fear casting a heavy sourness in the air. "No, commander. I thought Olysseus asked you to meet him after you spoke at the pools."

"He did," Veles confirmed. "But when we arrived at Neith, he was nowhere to be found. Instead, we discovered fae and shadow wraiths locked in battle."

"As well as the enchantress," Draven added, his red eyes flashing. "Levana was fleeing for the north."

"The cú sídhe followed after her," Veles said, his voice low. "Being that we'd left the Fractured at our base in the Shadowlands, and with Alderidge gone, we were left without protection."

"You should have returned to the Light Kingdom," Vesna

said, her light green eyes wide. "I would have protected you. The Legion of the Light is yours to command."

Naz flashed us looks to say that the Legion had, indeed, been monitored and had yet to pose a threat. She held both hands up, drawing them toward one another before pointing to Vesna—letting us know the Light Kingdom's army had remained within their borders. All but Vesna.

Veles's lips twitched as if he found the idea of her defending him amusing, but the flash of rage in his pale eyes hadn't dimmed. "We were following our brother's instructions, as we have for nearly eight years. He was unable to cross when we'd first arrived, but cracking the realm was supposed to allow him to return home."

"Following his orders would've gotten us killed had the battle started minutes earlier." Draven shook his head. "Levana must have taken him. He hasn't reached out since."

"Perhaps," Veles admitted with reluctance. "But we saw her flit north without him."

"Then she had him taken before we got there," Draven snapped, his fist colliding with the nearest tree. Bark flew as the trunk fissured but remained upright. The commander doubled over, his hand coming to his stomach.

"Control your temper, brother," Veles said coolly, as he knelt next to Draven. "You are weak enough as it is."

Draven spat, the hint of blood stark against his pale lips. "I'm still here, aren't I?"

Veles drew back, poorly concealed disgust on his face. "Barely. A few inches above and The Spear of Empyrean would have claimed your life."

My eyes flashed to Zaeth, my surprise clear. Draven was still injured from the blow I'd dealt him. Zaeth nodded as his fingers flexed. We were treading on delicate ground listening in. Veles had lost the allegiance of the cú sídhe to Levana and without

Alderidge to portal him, had been separated from his army, until just recently.

"Is this why you didn't return?" Vesna asked, the whine creeping back in. Draven flash her an irritated scowl. "I've been waiting on word of your victory at Caligo, but nothing came."

"I can't very well attack when my commander can barely stand," Veles snarled, gesturing toward Draven. "Not to mention it took us weeks to locate the army without Alderidge."

Draven stood, his pulse a little elevated, his breaths slightly shallow. "The bitch and her sisters can wait. We first must ensure Olysseus is found. We've summoned the Fractured to us, leaving Levana weakened. Now is our time to strike."

"You mean to attack the enchantress?" Vesna asked, her voice pitching.

I glanced at Zaeth, watching as his eyes narrowed in speculation. Veles and Draven were our enemies. They were responsible for the death of Will, for the desolation across all of Pax... but if we could use them to split Levana's focus, we might stand a better chance against her.

Ignoring Vesna, Veles faced his brother. "She doesn't have the allegiance of the Fractured, but she is not weak. The cú sídhe remain at her side, along with the shadow wraiths and several other dark creatures."

"And Silas," Vesna added, clearly not liking being left out. They turned to her, waiting for her to continue. "Silas, the Dark King of the North. He's challenged King Zaethrian and hasn't been opposed."

Zaeth's jaw ticked but he otherwise remained in control. We'd had bigger concerns than Silas, but if he had, in fact, joined Levana, he needed to be dealt with. Soon.

"Another self-righteous fae of little concern." Draven waved Vesna away. "We must push our advantage before she discovers our location and launches her own counterstrike—"

"I think it's a little late for that, boys."

Draven spun, unsheathing his blade as the feminine voice cut through the trees. Her midnight hair had been tied in a single tie stretching down her spine. A dagger was strapped to her thigh, her top a lattice of linked metals hugging her bust, but it was the same cold, black eyes, the same scarlet lips tilted into a wicked grin showing pointed teeth that I remembered.

"Levana," Veles breathed as Vesna trembled beside him.

Chilled air shifted on the breeze coming down from the mountains, carrying with it a hint of night-blooming jasmine. My wings pricked, eager for release, but Zaeth's hand found mine before they could burst free and give away our position. A wash of calm flooded through our bond, easing my spiraling need for vengeance.

Patience, Zaeth pleaded.

"Thank you, Silas." Levana turned toward the trees where a collection of shadows waited, just beyond my sight. "Your tracking skills are much appreciated. I can't believe they were foolish enough to remain with our army."

"Where's Olysseus?" Draven demanded, his body coiled and ready for battle.

Levana's musical laugh was echoed by a group of men at her back. I felt Naz and Zaeth stiffen beside me. All our enemies were here, and we had no way of stopping them.

"Poor, sweet child," she cooed stepping toward Draven with mock concern. "Your brother isn't here."

"Liar," Draven called.

"Hold, brother," Veles warned.

Levana's smile only widened. "We *have* had fun together, haven't we?"

Veles and Draven shared a look, neither of them responding.

"We've spent centuries together, just the four of us." She tilted her head to the side as if recalling fond memories. "You three were so pathetic when you first sought my aid."

"We've never asked you for help," countered Veles, but there was an apprehension lining his words now, worry flashing in his eyes. "We've never met."

Levana's white, sharpened teeth glimmered as she grinned. "Who did you think aided you all those years ago? Did you really think you were powerful enough to cross realms? That you had simply stumbled upon the otherworld—my world—by chance?"

Veles's breathing quickened but he stood, unmoving as Levana paced leisurely in front of them.

"I offered you a reprieve from this world, granted you a piece of my darkness, my power, so that you were able to become all that you desired. And when it was time to return, who do you think crafted the storm? Who weakened the borders between our worlds?" She turned to face them, lifting her chin high. "Me."

"No. *We* did that." Draven shook his head, looking to his elder brother, but Veles remained silent, his gaze lock on the enchantress.

"Where is Olysseus?"

"He was the anchor to the otherworld." Levana shrugged. "Power always finds a balance: One returned, one forced to remain, and one divided. Draven was gifted a body yielded from the storm's power—the one returned. You, Veles, were meant to exist as a shadow of a king, one able to jump into various hosts, but unable to sustain your own form—one divided. I admit, I was surprised you gathered the power to reform completely. Another unforeseen side effect of what was done."

"Our brother, enchantress." Draven demanded.

Unfazed, Levana continued as if having a pleasant conversation among old friends. "Olysseus was to remain with my children of darkness, his soul given over to their world in exchange for Draven's here. Balance must be upheld, you know."

"And when the wards separating our two realms cracked?" Veles promoted. "Was Olysseus released then?"

"Yes." Levana's sharp teeth gleamed. "Death is a release for us all."

25

ELARA

DRAVEN LAUNCHED TOWARD LEVANA WITH A GUT WRENCHING cry. Had he been anyone else, I might have felt bad for him, but this was the fae who'd led the Fractured on a killing spree, ravaging The Seven Kingdoms. He and his terrible brothers were responsible for countless families ripped apart. For thousands of innocents slaughtered.

I hoped he suffered. As hollow and lost as I felt when Will had been stabbed before my eyes, as grief-stricken as I'd been when I dragged my father into the grave I'd been forced to dig with my own two hands—and then my mother's soon after—I wanted Draven and Veles to feel every barb of loss *tenfold*. And I prayed the wounds festered.

"Not like this," Veles pleaded, grabbing his brother's arm, yanking Draven back. The two grappling with one another, the red-eyed commander eager for his vengeance while Veles fought to keep him alive.

"Not like *anything*," Levana sneered. "When I heard your pleas centuries ago, begging for the strength to liberate yourselves from the harsh realities of this world, I thought we could help each other. It was a longshot, but if you three survived and returned to Pax after years spent with my banished children, perhaps you would be strong enough to weaken my bonds.

"I hadn't realized that by blessing each of you with a piece of my darkness I would be weakening myself. Not until our storm rolled through Pax, returning two of you and essentially ending the need for Olysseus."

"The storm?" Veles questioned as Draven stilled, brows furrowing. "You killed Olysseus over eight years ago?"

"Yes," Levana answered. "It was upon his death that a sliver of my darkness retuned to me. You see, I'd been weakened for so long… thousands of years spent trapped beneath Pax, my essence bleeding into the earth. I hadn't realized what I was missing.

"Though I was first imprisoned in Neith, The Seven Sacred Pools were where my bindings were weakest. It wasn't much, but over the centuries I gained the ability to float throughout Pax, more ghost than anything. When I killed Olysseus in the otherworld, a current of power stretched across the realms and returned. I was able to visit ancient temples, previous places where I'd been worshipped, and project into the minds of others for brief periods of time—the smallest taste of what I used to be."

"That can't be true," Draven whispered, shaking his head with obvious disbelief. "We've spoken to him. Just a few weeks ago he told us—"

"To go to Neith?" Levana interrupted, her eyes tracking the length of Draven's body, snagging on the fresh stain of red along his abdomen. "Yes, I thought it was worth a try to see if the two of you were stupid enough to get yourselves killed. Afterall, you've been teetering on the verge of death for a while now, Draven."

Zaeth drew in a sharp breath as hundreds of feet shifted in

our direction. Gentle vibrations tracked through the earth, and if I concentrated hard enough I could hear their synchronized, sluggish pulses... the Fractured were on the move, led by some unforeseen command.

Naz jerked her head toward Veles, the light of his eyes now fully black.

"It's a shame really," Levana sighed, retrieving the dagger from the hilt along her thigh. "Then again, I've always enjoyed getting my hands dirty."

Her head snapped to the forest behind her just as the cries from Silas's men echoed through the trees.

"They're attacking," Naz breathed, her words nearly drowned out by the chaos unfolding before us. "The Fractured are following Veles's command *against* Levana. That's the darkness she's talking about reclaiming. Veles and Draven must have pieces of her power. She can't lead the army without reclaiming them."

"She can't lead the Fractured," Zaeth corrected. "There are plenty of monsters already at her disposal."

The Fractured swarmed, a sea of black-eyed fae with grey skin moving as one as they followed Veles's unspoken command. Levana's dagger sliced through decaying flesh, severing limbs and heads with ease as she spun.

"Should I call the cú sídhe, goddess?" Silas called, cutting his way through the masses.

"No." Levana's dagger carved through the belly of the nearest Fractured, its entrails spilling out in thick ropes. "Return to the Shadowlands and gather the goblins. The cú sídhe are needed to guard those who have recently crossed."

"As you wish, goddess." Silas retreated toward his men, the group slowly working their way north as corpses littered the forest floor at Levana's feet.

Another slice of her dagger. Another spray of blackened

blood misting the air. She was dazzling to watch—the skill with which she wielded her blade, the way she anticipated their moves, always one step ahead.

I'd once described battle as a dance between myself and my enemy, but Levana was a soloist. War was her stage, the cries of the dying and the swipe of steal through flesh her music.

"Enough, Veles." Levana swept her hands out before her, a burst of shadows blasting out in a circle. The tendrils of darkness slashed through the nearest Fractured, rendering them little more than flayed skin and strips of bloody meat.

My mouth ran dry. She could wield shadows. I knew of only one other fae who could do that. Not daring to look away, I reached for Zaeth's hand, feeling his disquiet ripple through our bond.

Draven wrenching his arm away from his brother at the edge of the forest where Veles had been dragging him toward the Jagged Mountains.

"She killed him," Draven seethed, turning to face Levana. "We can't run."

Levana opened her arms, palms up. "I'm waiting."

"*Drepa*," Draven's red eyes flashed, his pale lips curling back as he thundered a command.

The Fractured rose, surging toward Levana in a torrent of blades. She deflected every blow, the black sludge of their blood painting her body in wide spurts.

Draven flitted forward, leaping into the air with his sword drawn, the tip angled for her head.

She spun before his blade made contact, lashing out with a hand to grip his neck. Black nails dug into alabaster flesh, the trickle of scarlet the same color as his eyes.

"Do not fear, Draven." Levana's dagger jerked forward, cutting through skin and slicing between ribs to pierce his heart. "Soon, Veles will join you and Olysseus, and the three of you will be united once more."

Scarlet bubbled from his mouth, his body giving one last thrash as Levana yanked her blade back and let him fall. She threw her head back, inhaling deeply as she consumed the sliver of shadow that rose from Draven's bloodied chest.

Veles's body was shaking, his black eyes wide as he stared at the growing scarlet stain across Draven's white tunic. He took a step back, as the Fractured paused, waiting for a command.

"It's time to unite the brothers of legend." Levana exhaled, her black eyes fluttering open. Her ruby lips stretched into a malicious grin as she met Veles's gaze from across the heads of the Fractured. "Your sacrifice is appreciated."

Veles bellowed a command at the same time Levana threw her dagger, the blade and hilt turning end-over-end. The blade sailed through the air, passing through the slow-moving Fractured attempting to throw themselves in front of him.

But Levana had been too quick. There was no out running the blade whirling through the air.

"No!"

A flash of light blond hair flitted forward, her shoulders rounding as her chest absorbed the full impact of the blade. Vesna's brows furrowed over her green eyes, her thin hand shaking as it reached for the hilt, seemingly confused at what it was doing lodged between her ribs.

Without a word, Veles turned his back on her and flitted toward the Jagged Mountains.

A clump of Fractured broke from their mission of destroying Levana to follow him as the enchantress let loose a furious shriek.

My heart was pounding, my eyes wide as Levana let loose another deadly blast of shadows, one explosive enough to rock the trees near our hiding place.

"Amazing," I breathed, both horrified and awed by her power. But I could see darkness collecting around her once more, poised for an even larger attack as the Fractured regrouped.

"We need to go," Naz muttered, her hand finding mine just as Levana's shadows unleashed.

Darkness folded in on itself and we were gone.

26

LANNIE

Emeralds glimmered along every surface. The precious stone was embedded in the ebony bark of underground trees and had also been smoothed into wide sheets to construct cobblestoned walk ways. Where the Diamond Province was flashy, showing off the wealth and strength of the stone at every opportunity, the Emerald Provence utilized the gem innocuously. Its presence was not to stimulate, but to sooth. Their gardens were the same, complete with gentle trickling streams supplied from the underground freshwater springs.

Jarek and Evander were set to leave today, arriving at the Air Kingdom on the eve of Yule. It was an honored holiday among the Earth Kingdom, one in which the Provinces of Xyla had been preparing for. Fae had risen early to start cooking various meats and stewing pots of vegetables. Decorations clung to nearly every surface, their finery adding to the already spectacular surroundings, and everywhere I turned I found friends chatting happily and families holding each other tight. This was a time for celebration, an evening to rejoice with loved ones... but I found the pit in my stomach twisting as I neared Evander.

He was poised on a small, wooden bench set before a

narrowed stream; the black surface was studded with splashes of water lilies, bordered by growing moss along the banks. Evander's auburn hair was at least brushed, the long strands now reaching his mid back. The tips of his slightly pointed ears peaked out as his eyes fixed on the gently rolling waters before him.

"Did you hear Greer is getting married?" I said, taking a seat beside him. "It's kind of ridiculous since her and Ryuu are already mated, but her letter said King Dragcor was insisting. She thinks the ceremony will be in the spring and was asking if I wouldn't mind sharing my birthday month with her special day."

Evander didn't move. He hardly blinked. Okay, time for a different approach.

"Jarek said you're leaving soon,"

He nodded but his eyes remained fixed on the fern-covered banks.

Fidgeting with my nails, I took a deep breath and forced the questions I had to the surface. "He also says you've stopped training, that you hardly eat, and that you haven't been to the stables in months. Ember and Colt are doing fine, by the way."

Most of the horses who had been kept at the base had escaped the worst of Veles's attack. Some had acclimated to life with herds of wild horses, but the majority had been given new homes throughout the Earth Kingdom. I'd thought the humidity and lush jungle of this kingdom would've been a deterrent, but the horses seemed more relaxed. Halcyon said it was something to do with the Earth Kingdom's relationship with Pax that allowed animals of all sorts to feel at ease.

"Jarek's been talking a lot," Evander said, his face remaining impassive despite the bite to his words.

"He's worried about you. We all are."

"What's there to worry about? I'm here." Bitterness dripped

from his voice, the strength of it twisting my stomach. "I'm breathing."

"It sounds like you're grieving," I said, taking a steadying breath. "It's perfectly normal—"

"*Nothing* about this is normal," Evander snapped, his raging copper eyes finding mine. "I lost Jem. I already mourned once when half my soul was ripped away. I'd learned to live without him because you four were young and Jem would've kicked my ass in the after if I'd left you. But Will is gone from this world and you're all grown, now." Evander took a few steadying breaths, his gaze fixed on the stream before us. "He was there... waiting for me."

My breathing hitched.

"He reached for me..." Evander lifted a trembling palm as if waiting for someone to take it, staring at it like another might appear, before his fingers turned inward, forming a fist. "But then you pulled me back."

Swallowing the burn of bile at the back of my throat, I focused on finding a way to speak through the tears threatening to overwhelm me. "I couldn't lose you. I'm—I'm so sorry."

"I don't want your apologies," Evander cut in, jerking to a stand. He ran a hand through his auburn hair, uncaring how pieces of it bunching along the edges. "Gods, Lannie, I know you meant well. I'm not mad at you. I'm just... trying to make sense of a life without *him.*"

Evander's voice broke on the last word, his control shattering along with it. Tears tumbled down his cheeks, the misery in his eyes forever damaging a piece of my heart.

"You loved Ser, did you not?"

I nodded, unable to speak.

"Imagine years with her, planning a wedding, a life together. And then she's gone." Evander started pacing, shaking his head as his eyes took on a manic gleam. Then finally—finally—it's over. You can be together—*are* together for a split second.

Before you're thrust back into a life of emptiness. And then Jarek is here and he's perfect and—and it's just all too much."

He came to a halt, the wild spark in his eyes flashing with gut-wrenching hopelessness. "How can I find a reason to live when I know my love is waiting for me, just out of reach?"

My stomach churned, threatening to upend the meager breakfast I'd had. I opened my mouth to speak. I'd seen patients like this, despair taking hold after a harsh loss… but no words of comfort came. Everything felt hollow. Each turn of phrase a sentiment without enough meaning.

"I couldn't lose you." It wasn't quite right, but at least it was honest.

Evander flinched, another pair of tears escaping as he dipped his head and flitted away, leaving me staring at the vacancy he'd left behind.

I sat on the bark bench, letting the subtle scent of damp earth and fresh water sooth me. Emeralds shimmered beneath the surface of the stream, their presence seeming to ease portions of my guilt.

Time passed. Fae came and went along the garden path, but I sat there until the rawness of the moment stung a little less. Despite how I felt, I knew my entire world wasn't falling apart —only most of it.

It must have been growing close to dusk, because small faeries with glimmering skin winked into to life, their glowing bodies buzzing with the excitement of Yule eve. Sweets and trinkets would be placed under the trees tonight in offering to the faeries to bring good fortune and I could practically feel the swell of anticipation.

It wasn't until the scent of muted wine and roasting meats hung heavy in the air that a familiar set of footprints neared. I didn't bother turning around, the pulse of empathy through our mating bond already confirming who it was.

Halcyon took a seat next to me, the slit up her silky black

dress revealing the toned muscles of her thigh. Her scent of vanilla swirled in the air, soothing and enticing all at once.

Stop it, I chided myself, knowing I didn't need anything else to feel guilty about.

"Queen Freya has agreed to travel with us to the Water Kingdom. She's skeptical but will do her best to see things through. There are rumors the Queen Isla, unlike her husband, sympathizes with humans. Queen Freya thought it best if the human general, Alarik Holt travel with us."

I nodded, letting the words wash over me. The sleeping sickness had yet to dissipate, and the power reserves stored in the bloodstone veins had grown, according to Halcyon's last read. I wasn't giving up, but I'd gone through every resource available here. Maybe the Water Kingdom would offer something new.

"Jarek and Evander left."

My spine stiffened. I knew it had been hours, but I couldn't hide the flash of pain at hearing Evander had chosen to leave when things were left so wrong between us. But I'd brought him back, stolen away his salvation, his earned respite. I guess there wasn't much else to discuss.

"I never thought saving a life was a selfish act," I whispered. Halcyon stilled beside me, giving me the silent support I hadn't realized I needed. "People are injured, and I heal them. Vessels torn, bones broken—it's like a puzzle made of flesh and tissue. I figure out ways to put everything back together... but the mind. The heart. They stay injured far longer than the body."

"I didn't want to lose him," I breathed as a sob escaped, the intensity of it startling even me.

"You did what any healer would do," Halcyon said, her arms wrapping around my shoulders and tugging me close.

I didn't bother resisting her touch, allowing myself this one moment to push aside any thoughts of Ser and be comforted by the one being who could possibility understand how I felt.

"You gave him a second chance at life. Evander will see its benefits in time."

"And if he doesn't?"

She was quiet for a long time, the Yule eve celebrations growing louder in the distance. By the sound of it, the Earth Kingdom was already well underway with celebrations for the evening.

"If he doesn't, you'll know you did everything in your power to save him."

My cheeks were damp, my body sore from sitting for so long. I righted myself, wiping away the tears along my cheeks. "We should be returning to the palace. Aren't you expected to lead the city in the Yule eve celebrations?"

"Yes," Halcyon answered.

Then she slipped her hand into mine and we sat, watching the gentle waters of the stream tumble on.

27

GREER

We were fucked. If King Dragcor thought we were outmatched when it came to Levana, I had no idea how we were going to survive this. I'm all for teaming up to defeat the bad guy, but I didn't want my life to end in some grand, self-sacrificing move.

I realized with alarming clarity that I may not get a choice in the matter, seeing as how the all-powerful enchantress was already freed.

"She really killed Draven?" I glanced away from the balcony overlooking the valley of Serein, the burnt sienna cliffs dusted in white as Yule flurries fluttered through the early-morning air. Ryuu's warm embrace was there, keeping me steady as I turned to face the room.

El, Zaeth, and Naz had shadowwalked just minutes ago, interrupting a perfectly good plate of pastries.

Luckily, Jarek and Evander had arrived late last night from the Earth Kingdom, the four of us having agreed to an early morning Yule breakfast. Most mornings Ryuu and I were otherwise engaged, and *that* would've been awkward for everyone.

My gaze swept through the room, noting how the golden

wedding items draped across every surface were so at odds with the subdued mood. Evander reclined on the sofa, wedged between yards of gaudy tulle and satin while Jarek sat opposite him with a worried crease between his blond brows.

Naz was pacing the floor, her dark eyes glancing up to meet my waiting gaze.

"She did," she confirmed. "Levana snatched Draven right out of the air and plunged a dagger through his chest."

"Draven *was* wounded," El added, her attention focused on the lavish fabric and puffy dresses. Zaeth was leaning against the rounded armrest of El's chair, his lips twitching as she brushed a particularly itchy dress away.

"Maybe Levana took advantage of the situation," I offered. "Maybe she's not as powerful as we fear."

El's hazel-blue snapped to mine, full of skepticism, but tempered with a yearning to accept the lie.

"I'd love to believe that," Zaeth said, his arm coming around my sister. El leaned into him, resting her head against his torso in an uncharacteristic display of trust. Her latest letter mentioned things between them were good. I just hadn't realized *how* good. "But the way Levana wielded shadows, her reflexes and skills with a blade…"

"It wasn't luck that ended Draven's life," Naz finished, her pacing coming to an end as she looked between us. Her gaze shifted behind me, settling on Ryuu. "Do we have the Air Kingdom?"

Ryuu tensed, a ripple of frustration resonating down our bond. "We will after Greer and I are wed."

Naz blinked. "Aren't you mated?"

My cheeks pinked as I realized I'd updated Lannie in my last letter but not El. "King Dragcor wants a marriage ceremony. Something about the air fae accepting me as their queen."

"Queen?" El said, her ability to cut to the heart of the situation uncanny.

I fixed my smile, loosing up the edges that had tightened. "Cursebreaker, Fated Mate of the Dragon, Queen of the Air Kingdom, I'm gathering many titles."

El raised a brow at my forced nonchalance.

Leaning further into Ryuu, I let out a long breath. "Both of us had just come around to the idea of us ruling in the distant future, but…"

"My father promised us the backing of the Air Kingdom in full if we wed," Ryuu said, his grip tightening slightly on my hip, the small gesture calming my rising nerves.

"And as long as we accept the throne following our wedding," I added, glancing over my shoulder at him.

"Those were his initial stipulations, but if what they witnessed about Levana is true, we must move quickly. There won't be time for a joining ceremony and a coronation, not like how he imagines."

Turning to face him, I stared into his dark eyes, the green embers and vertical slits never letting me forget the beast within. "You're thinking we should move up the wedding?"

He dipped his head, half of his sleek ebony locks tied back. "If you're okay with it. We could have the ceremony within the fortnight, then insist on mobilizing troops to Caligo. The coronation would be postponed, not canceled, but it would buy us some time."

I looked at him then, realizing how far he would go to ensure I not be forced into something I wasn't ready for. A quick look around showed me that the others were waiting, ready to back my decision, regardless of the cost. It seemed decisions like these weren't uncommon. Kingdom before self and all that. I wondered if El would willingly join Zaeth at the head of a nation, one day. I wondered if Naz would be happy to yield the responsibilities.

"It's settled then," I said, turning back to my mate. "Let's get married tonight."

The room erupted in a cacophony of protests.

"We need to secure Caligo against attack," Zaeth muttered, looking to El for understanding.

"We shouldn't even be here, now," confirmed Naz. "Veles fled with the Fractured near the Jagged Mountains. It's on the opposite side of the Dark Kingdom, but he could be plotting something."

"And Levana is in the Shadowlands with Silas," El added, before looking toward me. "Besides, don't you want Lannie here?"

"I assumed Jarek could pop over there and get her."

"I could," Jarek said, sitting up straighter as all eyes turned toward him. "But really, none of these dresses are ready to be worn. The whole point is to make an impact on your future court. You can't just toss something together the same day."

My eyes dropped to Evander who seemed to be only half listening.

"Veles is still alive," Ryuu observed. "While I don't like the idea of another enemy on the run, he is severing to distract Levana. As long as he's alive, she remains weakened and the Fractured won't follow her."

"Which buys us at least a sliver of time to prepare." Zaeth finished. "Elara and I can travel to the edge of the Shadowlands and gauge Levana's army. Other creatures have joined her side. We need to know what we're up against and how long we have till she attacks."

"I'll take us," Naz said, weariness creeping into her voice. "It'll be safer if we shadowwalked. There's less chance of being detected and it's easier to escape, if needed."

Zaeth gave a small nod of thanks in her direction.

"The new year then," I said. "That gives you all a week to prepare."

"A week," Ryuu agreed, the faint hint of a smile showing.

I reached up, pressing a quick kiss to his lips. "Then we'll have our honeymoon in the Fire Kingdom convincing the creatures born of lava and brimstone to join us against Levana."

Ryuu's lips twitched, the dragon within seeming to ignite with the prospect.

A knock sounded on the door, the room stilling. We weren't ready to share this information with the Air Kingdom, not until we had their loyalty guaranteed.

"Is your little secret war meeting wrapping up?" Cress's voice sounded from the hall, more annoyed than suspicious. "Greer needs her monthly tea since she is refusing to produce an heir, which, by the way, the kitchen staff has gossiped to the entire court about. And she has yet to pick a dress, further provoking the ire of the royals."

My cheeks flared as everyone in the room turned to me. Ryuu's grip on my waist tightened, his anger flaring as our personal business was broadcast so easily by Cress, but it was El who staked over to the door and flung it open.

"You are never to speak about my sister without her express permission or you'll find yourself relocated to the Dark Kingdom for the foreseeable future under my watch. Are we clear?"

Cress's wings bristled as my sister's whole body hummed with pent up power. Gods, she was strong. She always had been, but her little bout in the after had made an impact. The outer lays of civility that she'd worn her whole life had been burned away—literally, I reminded myself. She was every bit the Dark Queen Zaeth needed. And all her fury was currently directed toward Cress.

Seeming to sense the deadly promise underlying her words, Cress held out a mug for El to take. To her credit, her voice barely wavered when she spoke. "If she is to hold the kingdom's loyalty, we need the royals support."

El's fingers flexed along the handle of the mug, her affinities showing as the dark rings around her eyes flared. "Are you saying there's a threat to my sister's life?"

"Not yet," Cress said, holding her gaze.

"Not *ever*," Ryuu snapped.

"Then at least *pretend* to respect our customs." Cress's bright eyes found his, her long legs locking as she glared. "You've been gone for years, openly shunning your throne only to return mated with a wingless half-mortal who is insisting we join a war against a goddess to support her sister—A sister who is suspected of being the Dark Phoenix of prophecy."

"Levana is a threat to all of us," Ryuu growled. "She's been the force guiding the brothers through their reign of terror these last eight years."

"She splintered the barrier between realms," I added. I hadn't figured out how to repair the damaged yet, but when Ryuu was sleeping and I was alone with my thoughts in the early hours of the morning, it called to me... It felt similar to how light particles buzzed beneath my touch when I constructed wards but the vastness of it remained just out of reach.

Undeterred, Cress looked over El's shoulder to find me. "You may not know this, but we are an isolated people. Our cities are built on mountain tops. Sure, our outlying villages have been decimated like any other kingdom, but the royals haven't been affected like other nations. Some will come to understand the threat of the enchantress, but others worry we're going against the goddess's prophecy by supporting the Dark Phoenix."

El tensed, the shadow of violet wings flashing before she rolled out her shoulders and forced the ghost of them away.

Cress's eyes narrowed. "If I didn't know the gravity of the devastation throughout Pax, I might be inclined to believe the whispers."

"Is that so?" El snapped, the challenge clear in her tone.

Ignoring her, Cress fixed her gaze on Ryuu. Though she was

a royal pain in my ass, I was impressed by the backbone she displayed while coming face-to-face with my sister.

"I've traveled with you for years. I've returned to you through countless situations, dozens of battles, so *I* understand." Jealousy reared her ugly head as images of Cress and Ryuu flitting about Pax flashed through my mind. Cress continued, though I was sure she knew she was getting a rise out of me. "*They*, however, do not. It's your job as their future ruler to help them see. Both of you."

Ryuu's jaw ticked, but he felt the truth of her words as much as I did.

"You can start by joining your people during the traditional Yule service," she said, turning toward the hall and striding down it. Her voice reached us a few paces away. "It starts in ten minutes."

"Services?" I asked as El slammed the door shut.

Ryuu nodded. "Just a lot of listening to thanks given to the goddess. Our people believe Yule is a time for self-reflection. The longest night of the year is meant to allow our minds and souls to weather the darkness and return to the goddess's light."

Our people. The idea of ruling this kingdom just got a lot more real.

"Is what Cress said true? Can the royals turn against us?"

Ryuu's jaw ticked, the only answer I needed.

My stomach clenched as I accepted the tea from El. Without the royals' backing, it sounded like we would forfeit the army. And without the army, not only would we lose any chance at ruling this kingdom, but we'd lose all of Pax along with it.

28

ELARA

"I don't like this," Soter objected for the third time. "We know an attack is coming. We should strengthen our defenses as best as we can and prepare."

"We can better prepare if we know what we're up against," Naz countered.

"She killed Draven, Naz." Soter shook his head. "One of the brothers. Even the Spear of Empyrean didn't kill him."

"Technically, Elara missed his heart," Zaeth added.

"Hey!" I grumbled, shooting him a look that conveyed how helpful I thought his comment was.

Zaeth shrugged, flashing me an unapologetic grin.

"I had a lot going on at the time. Mainly, his sword in my stomach."

Zaeth's smile vanished, instantly cooling my heated temper.

"My point is," Soter said through gritted teeth, "is that we already know Levana is strong. Confirming she has an army at her back won't change that."

"No, but it could help us prepare," I countered. A smug smile crossed Naz's face as she gestured toward me. Soter glared at both of us, but I pushed on. "Hear me out. We know the Fractured fight as a swarm. They are slow and clumsy, only posing a threat by sheer numbers. We also know that the goblins and shadow wraiths think independently."

"But we've faced them before—" Soter started.

"Exactly," Naz cut in. "We know how to handle those creatures, but what about all the others? An ice wyvern crossed through the crack in the realms, one that was nearly three times larger than any dragon found in the Air Kingdom. There were other monsters, too, most of them unheard of. We need more information."

Soter looked like he wanted to protest but couldn't find a convincing enough argument. The two of them shared a long look, one in which I couldn't quite pinpoint the meaning of, but after another tense moment, Soter sighed. "Please, be careful."

Naz's shoulders relaxed, her stoic gaze softening. "We'll be back before you know it."

Zaeth and I gripped her hands and then we were gone.

The throne room of Caligo fell away, replaced by silver blue mist hovering over boggy wetlands. The scent of sulfur was thick in the air, nearly causing me to gag.

I wasn't sure when my anger had changed. It might have been when the tip of Levana's blade pierced Draven's heart, or it might have been when Levana's searing flames had consumed me, burning away skin and muscle until my body was nothing but charred remains, but somewhere along the way my thirst for vengeance had evolved into a resigned knowledge that Levana couldn't be allowed to live.

After what we'd seen two days ago on the eve of Yule, I wasn't sure we were strong enough to kill her. As much as the thought disgusted me, Veles needed to stay alive until Levana was dealt with.

We skirted through black ash and white oak trees. Winter had stolen the leaves from their branches, offering little coverage. A thin sheet of snow clung to the sticks and long grasses of the swampy banks, forcing us to proceed at a human pace in order to avoid detection. It was slow, but the trees thinned after a while. The cool winter sun was nearly midday when we discovered a large patch of dry land stretching into the distance —every bit of it filled with troops.

Goblins along the edges stoked massive fires with the remains of splintered trees that once must have filled the open wetlands. Shadow wraiths and packs of cú sídhe moved behind them, along with groups of light fae, each proving to be problematic, but my gaze was drawn to the massive ice wyvern nestled in the center. Its hide was a pale blue, shards of crystals jutting from every surface. Its wings were tucked under for now, its talon-tipped knuckles folded, but the power contained within such a creature couldn't be hidden.

"By the goddess," Naz breathed. "How are we going to defeat that? Especially if it can freeze the air around it?"

"I'm hoping Ryuu will have an answer," Zaeth said, his face grim. "That's not our biggest problem, though."

"It seems pretty big to me," I muttered.

Zaeth's jaw clenched, his eyes fixed on the horizon. "Look."

I followed his line of sight, not understanding why the flock of black birds in the distance was concerning, but the tremor of dread flashing down the mating bond had me studying them closer.

"They're flying against the wind."

Zaeth nodded, his eyes not leaving them.

Naz sucked in a sharp breath. "They aren't birds."

My brows furrowed, her allegation snapping my attention back to the sky. They were moving fast, their forms now in focus. Thin frames were held aloft by large, bat-like wings, the pale creatures laughing and darting through the cloud-covered sky.

"Are those... fae?"

"Yes," Zaeth answered.

"Almost fire fae with the leathery wings, but it looks like a few of them have fangs." Naz's gaze narrowed as the group reached the edge of Levana's base. "They *do* have fangs."

My stomach flipped as a dozen of them dove, snatching up a few light fae and tearing into the soft flesh along their necks. Scarlet sprayed the air in a cloud of red mist, the metallic scent swirling toward us as it was caught on a breeze moments later.

"Gods," Zaeth said, the bright rings around his eyes flaring. "They love drinking blood, just as we do."

"No," Naz said, shaking her head. "They're all blooddrunk."

The winged creatures gorged themselves. Once every drop had been consumed, they tossed the drained bodies to the ground without a care. Some chose to share, yanking limbs from sockets and lapping up all the blood that spilled. With their faces flushed and irises stained red, they took to the skies once more, their speed somehow increased.

"It makes them stronger," Zaeth said, a note of awe in his voice. I felt the same, a horrified amazement at what these creatures were.

"We need to leave," I breathed, taking a few steps back and stumbling along the water's edge. "We don't know what their limitations are. They might be able to hear us."

"Agreed." Naz turned with her hand outstretched.

My boot squelched in the mud, the wet ground giving way quicker than it should. I tried to pull free again, but the waters churned around me, somehow rising along the bank and dragging me toward the deeper part of the bog.

Zaeth lunged for me, eyes wide in alarm, only to be thrown back by a strong current—And a dagger sinking into the front of his tunic.

29

ELARA

My pulse thundered, adrenaline spiking as my violet wings burst free. They pumped, great torrents of wind fighting the unnatural pull of the water. All so I could get to him. To my mate.

Naz flitted into the trees where the dagger had come from, shadowwalking around branches and pools of water. Cries of the dying were left in her wake, sounding all around us. We were surrounded.

Zaeth held my gaze a moment longer, shock and disbelief dissolving into rage as he jerked the dagger free. Pure, unfiltered fury blazed to the surface, his ebony wings snapping free as mine fought to keep me above water. He was by my side in the blink of an eye, the red stain across his chest slowing as he flew over the water.

I felt a slimy tentacle grip my ankle just as Zaeth's hands came around my waist, the force of his hold tugging me free.

Pulse racing, I glanced down, trying to peer through the bog below. It was quick, but I could have sworn I saw a large pale eye in the darkness. It winked out of view as the surface of the water calmed.

Another time, Zaeth seemed to promise the monster as we circled back toward where Naz should be.

"Are you hurt, love?"

"No," I breathed, unsheathing the sword along my back as we landed. My fear mounted as I saw a few of the winged fae slow their play, heads cocking in our direction. "We need to get to Naz and leave."

"Agreed," Zaeth said, his blade already in hand. "It's time to put our training to the test."

We flitted toward the trees, careful to avoid pools of water as we searched for the vanishing shadows and splayed bodies that signified Naz's presence. The scent of sulfur grew thicker, nearly suffocating as we closed in on dark fae loyal to Silas.

My vision sharpened, fangs elongating as the familiar black clouds hovered over my enemies, evidence of their corruption... their dark blessing from Levana. Zaeth mirrored my movements, the two of us working in tandem as we cut through our traitorous citizens.

Despite these being fae from his own kingdom, Zaeth didn't slow. Never flinched. He embraced the bloodshed, like The Dark King he was purging his kingdom of the rot festering within.

"Show yourself, Silas!" he thundered, ripping through the neck of another with his bare hands before retrieving his sword in the belly of corpse. Spurts of blood covered him, the fat droplets linking together to drip down his neck. "You claim to be a king and yet hide behind your men like a coward."

"Zaeth," I warned, glancing toward the group of winged fae. Most were hovering over the ice wyvern now, but a few curious ones were headed in our direction. They had no doubt scented the blood, meaning the rest of the swarm would be here soon enough. "We don't have time for this."

"Find a clearing," Naz's voice called from somewhere to my left. "They can't be touching you when we shadowwalk and a group of them have already run, most likely going to tell Levana Elara is alive."

Dragging his sword across another's throat as he extended his arm, Zaeth kicked the body into a shallow pool, the blood gushing from the wound and staining the waters like ink spilling onto a page.

"Naz is there," I said sensing the shift in the shadows to our left, just as Silas stepped out from the grove of white oak trees to our right, a dagger flying from his palm.

I twisted, rolling my shoulder just in time. The blade grazed me as it passed, drawing a gasp from my lips and a flash of red to my sleeve—Red streaked with orange.

My pulse raced, alarm and adrenaline temporarily holding off the effects of the toxin. But Silas's blade had been tipped in somnus, and I didn't have any of Lannie's counter salve to help.

"How?" I breathed, hating the satisfied smile stretching across Silas's face?

I thought we'd destroyed the rest of the crop, and if some had survived, surely Veles would have what remained.

"Draven had a container on him," Silas sneered. "Spoils of war, and all that. Levana thought it worthless, but she'll be so pleased when she returns. You're not supposed to be alive, you know."

"El!" Naz yelled, working her way toward me in shadowy bursts.

Despite my best effort, my movements started to slow as Silas pressed his advantage.

Zaeth's roar of rage drowned out the rest of the world. He looked to the streak of red across my shoulder, and the shadows around him exploded. They lashed through everything, shredding muscle and viscera in a brutal rage to create a path leading straight toward me.

My mate was a blur as he flitted forward. The would-be-king raised his arm to block Zaeth's descending sword, providing him the perfect opportunity to thrust his hand into Silas's chest. The crunch of bone echoed through the bog, stunning those nearest. Silas's men stared, horrified as they watched Zaeth's fists draw back and collide with their ruler again. And again.

My vision swam, my knees buckling as I crashed into the muddy earth. Naz had me in her arms moments later while the sound of shattering bones continued.

"The winged fae are almost here," Naz breathed, glancing toward the sky. I could hear them, now, dozens of them flying toward us. She was right, but Zaeth's snarls still filled the air, even after Silas's whimpers had gone quiet. "We need to go before the somnus progresses. Hold on."

We folded into darkness, all sound momentarily halting, until we appeared beside Zaeth. What remained of Silas's men had retreated, but crazed laughter buzzed from above as Levana's winged fae reached us.

"It smells glorious," one said, inhaling deeply.

"Mother said we weren't to eat her other creatures," one snipped.

"A little late for that," another countered.

"I suppose you're right," the cautious one sighed. "We're already in for a lashing. Might as well make the most of it."

"Zaeth!" Naz yelled beside him, but he was lost to his fury, his fist raining savage blows against Silas's already pulverized body.

The first of the winged fae dove toward us.

With a curse and no other choice, Naz gripped Zaeth's leg. The three of us vanished, reappearing on obsidian stone floors, the throne room of Caligo winking into life around us.

The floor was cold against my back, the thick scent of sulfur causing my stomach to clench. I could feel the effects of somnus growing stronger as it worked through my body, every movement taking immense amounts of concentration.

Searching for Zaeth or Naz, I willed myself to rolled over—
And came face to face with Silas.

30

ELARA

"Naz," Zaeth thundered. "Get Jarek."

I felt more than saw the darkness move as Naz vanished. Silas's body was ripped away, tossed across the room like a sack of bloody, unwashed clothes as Zaeth came into view.

"Stay with me, love." Cinnamon eyes ringed in light peered down at me, burning with stubborn determination. He flitted from the room, returning a heartbeat later with a metal tin: Lannie's antidote.

Applying the salve liberally, he pushed strength through the bond, his dark affinities awakening mine despite the somnus's sedating effects. This must be one of the newest batches of the poison. It was more potent than the somnus I'd felt before. *This somnus was not only sedating but weakening me.*

Naz and Jarek appeared in a flash of light, Jarek's gaze darting around the room until he found me. "Gods above, kitten. Can you not go on one scouting mission without getting in trouble?"

My lips twitched, already showing my body's response to Lannie's salve. Jarek pressed a palm to the cut along my shoulder, a faint light flaring beneath. I felt the skin knit back together, the burning from the toxin lessening and then vanishing. But I was still fighting to keep my eyes open.

Jarek's storm blue gaze found mine. "The poison is no longer progressing, and the point of entry has been healed, but I can't undo the effects already circulating in your system."

"You were able to purge somnus previously," Zaeth growled, as he brushed the hair away from my forehead, his gentle touch so at odds with his tone.

"*Previously,*" snapped Jarek. "Somnus wasn't this potent. It's been reformatted somehow. I can get Lannie, if you want. Specific counter toxins are more her specialty. But Elara is safe. She will be tired, and should rest of the evening, but I don't sense anything strong enough to cause permanent damage."

I felt the flare of frustration through the bond before Zaeth gave a tight nod. "Don't leave yet. I have a favor to ask."

The question was on the tip of my tongue, but my eyes had already closed.

"It's okay, love." Zaeth breathed, his scent of cedar mingling with the metallic tang of blood. He pressed a kiss to my brow as his thumb brushed the curve of my cheek. "I have everything under control. Sleep."

Unable to protest, I yielded to the undercurrent and let consciousness fade.

"SHE SHOULD BE WAKING SOON." LANNIE'S VOICE REACHED ME AS if through a thick fog. "I thought we didn't have to worry about somnus anymore."

"So did I," Zaeth muttered, his voice right beside me. "Silas said he took it off Draven's body."

Lannie was silent for a long moment. "He's really dead?"

"He is, but Veles escaped."

"Which is a good thing," Jarek chimed in. "Because we need

him to split Levana's forces and her power. Especially with what you and Naz described. Are you sure they weren't Merged?"

My mind flashed with an image of King Dragcor, the only Merged I knew of. He was ancient and powerful, but still possessed a moral code. Those creatures were something else—something darker.

"I'm sure," Zaeth answered. "They had characteristics of both dark and fire fae but weren't of this world."

"They must have slipped through the rift between realms," Lannie said. "Along with the ice wyvern and probably several other creatures. Did you get a glimpse of what grabbed El in the water?"

"No," Zaeth muttered, his voice low. "There was a faint singing... a call right before the water surged around her."

"And that's not a water fae trait?" Lannie asked.

"None that I've heard of," Zaeth answered. "But you can conduct your own investigation when you and Queen Halcyon request their aid," Jarek said. "When do you leave?"

"Tomorrow," Lannie said, the edge of my bed dipping. I felt the press of her small palm to mine, warmth flooding from her finger tips. "Wake."

It felt like a command, her affinities flowing into me. My breathing increased, the blood in my veins surging forth as my eyes flicked open.

Lannie's hand fell away, her shoulders hunched and sweat on her brow, but there was a smile tilting her lips.

"How?" I asked, slowly pressing up. My body was sore, muscles aching but I could feel the lingering effects of the somnus dissipating.

She shrugged. "I've been practicing. I'm not nearly as powerful as Jarek, but I've made progress."

"That she has," Jarek said, stepping forward. "I hate to cut this short, but I really must be getting back."

My shoulders tensed. "Is Greer okay?"

"Yes, kitten. Greer is fine. Her choice of a wedding dress was not quite what *I* would've chosen, and the decor is seriously lacking, but that's really more Cress's fault, what with upholding the air fae's ridiculous notions of knowledge before ego—"

"Jarek," I interrupted, a headache starting. I looked at him then, realizing how dark the bags under his eyes were, how his normally pristine eye liner was smudged and his hair left loose, lacking its typical product. "What's wrong?"

His shoulders tightened.

"It's Evander, again," Lannie said softly, almost like she didn't want to know the answer. "Isn't it? He hates that I saved him."

"It's complicated," Jarek said, the weariness noted throughout his features seeming to grow worse. "But I don't want him on his own for too long."

My eyes narrowed, unease twisting in my gut. "You're worried he'll do something drastic?"

"I'd rather not take the risk, kitten." Jarek's gaze bounced to Lannie. "Now that you'll all caught up, we can better prepare for your trip tomorrow. I'm assuming Queen Freya arrived in the Earth Kingdom today?"

Lannie glanced toward me before nodding. "Along with Alarik. She thinks it will help to have a man with us, regardless of him being a human."

Jarek lifted a skeptical brow but didn't push the subject. He looked toward Zaeth seated beside me. "I'll relay what happened to Ryuu. With the wedding moved up, I should be able to start mobilizing the troops as soon as I return from the Fire Kingdom."

Zaeth's gaze was dark, his worry about our situation rippling through our bond. Outwardly, he gave Jarek an encouraging nod. "The Fire Kingdom's allegiance is more important than ever. Do your best to win them."

Jarek's blond head dipped.

"I'll see you soon, El." Lannie gave my hand one last squeeze before going to Jarek's side and accepting his outstretched hand. "Please try not to die. Greer's wedding is days away and you know she'd kill you if you missed it."

I laughed, the sound fading into seriousness as I stared at my sister. She wouldn't turn eighteen for little over three months, but she was already standing before me with wisdom beyond her years. I guess war does that to a person.

"Likewise, sister."

"Oh," Jarek said, his eyes meeting Zaeth's. "I took care of that favor you asked for. It was touch and go for a bit, but he's stable and ready for torture. I had the guards string him up in the dungeons for you."

"What?" I asked, eyes wide.

Jarek blinked as Zaeth glared. "Thank you, Jarek. As always, your words know no limit."

A nervous chuckle escaped him. "I assumed she knew. I mean, he did nearly kill her. She'd probably enjoy a good torture, being all scary dark fae like you."

"Torture?" I asked, pinning Zaeth with a glare. "Who are we torturing?"

Zaeth's jaw ticked.

"I'll just leave you to it," Jarek said. Lannie waved, the hint of a smile playing along her lips as the two of them luxed out of sight.

"Zaeth," I said, pushing from the bed. "Who's in our dungeon?"

"Our?" His lips tilted in a lopsided smirk, the tips of his fangs peeking through. Zaeth's arms came around my waist, pulling me close. "I like the idea of this being *our* home."

I lifted a brow, undeterred.

He sighed. "That would be Silas."

31

LANNIE

"I still can't believe Greer's getting married at a time like this." I tipped the large, diamond bowl on its side, pouring a fresh batch of the somnus anti-toxin into tins. El had told me the rest of the crop had been burned, but I should've known better than to rely on another. From what I'd seen, this had to have been a potent batch... not quite strong enough to kill a fae but far too close for my comfort.

"Me either," Halcyon muttered, placing lids on the salves that had cooled. "In just a few days, your sister will marry into the ruling line of the Air Kingdom. With any luck, our trip to the Water Kingdom will be a quick affair and we'll make it back in time for the rehearsal dinner."

Scraping the last of the salve from the bowl, I cleared off my workspace and looked at the clock. Halcyon had wanted to leave this morning, but I'd insisted on completing the anti-toxin, just in case.

I shrugged. "She's already mated."

Halcyon laughed as I pulled off my smock and tossed it in the laundry. She led us out of the lab and up the gem studded road. The great tree palace glimmered ahead, amethyst giving off a purple hue beneath the blanket of silver leaves. "It's for the court. Your sister will become a royal and the next queen."

"It didn't seem like she wanted to be queen."

"Sometimes the responsibility simply needs to be shouldered."

Picking up on the undertones in her reply, I lifted a brow toward her. "Did you not always want to be queen?"

Halcyon glanced around, halting our conversation as we stepped under the black branches and ascended the spiraling staircases crafted from ebony wood. Only once we were secured in her rooms and the servants dismissed, did she answer.

"I've only just started the second decade of my life. Most fae haven't even shifted yet."

My eyes widened. I knew she was young, but not that young... only a few years older than me.

"I was raised to become queen, and so I am." She started pacing the length of the moss covered floors. "But this kingdom has been at war with itself for centuries. I'm trying to enact change for people who are terrified to believe it's possible, and battling those who seek to repress basic human-fae rights."

Despite us having spent most of our days together, I hadn't been inside her rooms often. Plants and jewels were everywhere, the walls a wash of color and vines. There were a pair of closed double doors to the right, most likely leading toward her bedroom. I wondered what it looked like. I wondered if she liked fluffy blankets or simple ones.

"And the oppressors *actually* believe they're being attacked. Like allowing people to choose who they love or allowing body autonomy is somehow an unforgivable atrocity against them."

"I'm sorry," I said, meaning each word. "I can't imagine trying to manage a nation battling itself while also being at war."

"You think the end of the world would put things into perspective. But the hatred in some of my citizen's hearts is unending." She huffed a laugh devoid of humor. After a long moment, she spoke. "I have the upper hand currently... but it feels like I'm always one step away from failing. And failing in the Earth Kingdom doesn't mean exile."

"Gods," I breathed, realizing just how much pressure she was under... just how many lives were depending on her.

Her silver eyes met mine, a stray violet curl falling forward from her half-tied hair. "I understand your sister's position more than you realize. Both of your sisters, if the Dark King's reaction to El is true. It's also why I would never chain you to this life."

I stilled, unable to look away, helpless to feel anything but sincerity through the bond.

"We *are* fated, Melantha. In one way or another, we will be in each other's lives. Our story will unfold when it is time but trust me when I say that we need to be back in time for your sister's official wedding. She needs to make a strong impression on the air royals, especially following Prince Ryuu's vacancy in recent years. The two of them being gifted a mating bond by the goddess will sway many, but they need to maintain an appearance of strength."

"I didn't realize," I said, sounding just as small as I felt.

Halcyon smiled at me, the movement not quite reaching her eyes. "How could you? You were raised to be human."

"Speaking of which, Queen Isla tolerates humans, but I thought the Water King is strictly against fae-human relations."

Halcyon nodded, just as there was a knock at the door.

"Halcyon, are you in there?" Queen Freya's voice sounded from the other side. There was a faint, masculine muttering stilling her hand for a moment, before the pounding against the door resumed even stronger. I recognized Alarik's voice around a curse right before Queen Freya pressed on. "I thought you wanted to get to the Water Kingdom a few hours early to take a look around."

With a sigh, Halcyon flitted to the door and beckoned them inside. "I also wanted it kept a secret."

"Oh," Queen Freya said, straightening up. "Well, you should've said that before I started yelling."

"I would have if I'd known to expect the yelling," Halcyon retorted, shifting her weight. The position drew my eyes to her curves, to the beautiful roundness of her thighs. Her silver eyes were slightly narrowed, her arms crossed, and there was a faint hint of color along her cheeks. Gods, she was stunning, her irritation only serving to improve upon her perfection.

Brushing away her annoyance, Queen Freya moved to the couch, sitting as if she'd been in this room dozens of times. Maybe she had. I swallowed down the lump in my throat as jealously rolled through me. Not that I had anything to be jealous over.

We were just friends—barely friends... but destined to be in each other's lives all the same.

My gaze bounced between the two of them and then to Alarik who followed and sat beside the Wild Queen. No, I didn't think the queens had anything romantic between them... but I didn't like how much that idea bothered me.

"Being that King Kai is a zealot asshole and his wife, Queen Isla, hates confrontation, this mission is sure to be useless." Queen Freya shrugged, her palm coming to rest on Alarik's thigh. He stiffened, his gaze darting to the two of us, but he didn't pull away.

"Thanks for that," Halcyon said, her fingers pinching her brow. "The king may be a lost cause, but I've heard Queen Isla has taken liberties she hadn't previously dared to."

I tilted my head to the side, studying my would be mate. "I thought the plan was to convince them to give us their army."

Halcyon's silver eyes found mine. "That would be ideal."

"Though not at all rational," Queen Freya added.

"You did say Queen Isla has been saving human refugees in

secret," Alarik said, sitting up straighter as all eyes turned to him.

"That's one rumor," Queen Freya countered.

"One strong enough to hang our hopes on?" I asked.

Halcyon's face crumpled, the glimpse at her true emotions shrouded in less than a heartbeat. "We need it to be."

"True," Queen Freya said, pushing to a stand. "We're bringing General Holt, so that will help us with the male issue. But he *is* human, so we'll see if the Water King's hatred for women or humans is stronger."

Alarik scoffed. "Good to know you find my presence reassuring."

Queen Freya flashed him a wicked grin. "I find your reputation on the battlefield to be impressive, but it's your ability to disarm and charm enemies that I wish you to call upon today."

A laugh bubbled from Alarik's chest. "I would hardly call forcing you into a duel to prove my worth 'disarming' or 'charming', though I am glad you accepted. If you hadn't fought me and I not risen to the occasion, I doubt you would've granted me a tour of the Wild Kingdom."

"And *then* where would we be?" Queen Freya asked, shaking her head with a playful glint in her eyes.

"Freya," Halcyon said, and I felt the flutter of surprise down the bond. It seemed the Wild Queen didn't act this way with just anyone.

"Right, a portal." Queen Freya stood, the runes running down her cheeks and beneath her chin illuminating as she raised her hand. And then stopped, her gaze falling on me. "Aren't you going to change first?"

I blinked.

"Freya," Halcyon hissed as Alarik shifted his weight, doing his best to look anywhere but my direction.

"Oh," Freya said, her brows lifting. "Right, the whole mad-scientist thing is an angle we can exploit."

Glancing down, I saw there were a few bright orange stains on my top, despite the smock I'd worn, and a slight scorching along the cup of my long, white sleeve. Mad scientist, indeed.

~

After a quick change into a pair of battle leathers and fitted top, we stepped through Queen Freya's portal and into the Water Kingdom.

Halcyon woven two thin braids framing my face, leaving the rest of my dark hair down, and I found I liked the style. I'd like her doting on me even more.

My heart stuttered as I recalled the way she'd sat me down on the side of her bed, her fingers weaving through my hair, grazing my scalp, my cheeks, my neck as she worked. It had only been a minute. No doubt, she had attributed the thundering of my pulse and the quicken of my breath to our upcoming mission… but it had felt good to allow myself to feel something other than grief.

I knew Ser was gone. Knew that future was no longer an option and there was no reason why I shouldn't allow myself to embrace whatever was forming between Halcyon and I… but it still felt like I was betraying her.

Halcyon reached for my hand as the portal vanished behind us, tugging me toward an up-sloped balcony. My skin tingled at her touch as she beckoned me to look over the tanned railing.

A breath of citrus and salted sea air filled my lungs. Homes dotted the horizon along rolling hills that end in cobalt blue waters. The brightly painted buildings were lined with climbing vines and magenta flowers with interspersed lemon trees throughout.

Sandy coves lined the coast, the houses seeming to come right to their edge. The sea was calm, the clear blue waters kissing rocky shores in gentle waves. Even in the dead of winter, the Water Kingdom remained warm, the wildlife and foliage thriving. It was beautiful.

"I felt the same way seeing it for the first time," Halcyon said.

"If only such a beautiful place wasn't governed by such a hateful king," Alarik added, shattering the small reprieve I'd dipped into. But he was right. We weren't here to marvel at their kingdom, we were here to enlist the water fae's help in defeating Levana and saving Pax.

"The shores are less filled," Queen Freya said, looking toward the coast with contemplative eyes. "Perhaps Queen Isla really has sequestered the royals below."

"Below?"

Halcyon pointed to switchback roads cutting through the hillsides and continuing straight on into the water. Other spots had smoothed staircases leading down, and as I stared at the water longer, I noticed color variations that couldn't have been constructed naturally.

"Many of the water fae live beneath the sea, breathing water just as easily as you and I breathe air."

"I hadn't realized," I said, noting how vacant the beaches were. I knew water fae could breathe water by the patches of scales behind their ears, but I thought most chose to live on land.

"It wasn't always that way," Queen Freya said. "Only in recent years have the royals chosen to return to the sea."

"Which, in turn, forces distance between them and humans," Alarik nodded. "You said Queen Isla is behind this?"

"As far as I can tell," Halcyon said, studying the horizon. There were clumps of rocks in the distance, small islands stretching toward the open ocean. "She has been very vocal about water fae retreating to the heart of their kingdom and leaving the rest of Pax to its own devices."

"Exactly what you want to hear before asking them to join a war," I murmured.

"As I said, hopeless." Queen Freya shrugged. "We should have enough time to scout the nearby villages before proceeding to the meeting point."

"Why are we scouting villages?" Alarik questioned, saving me the trouble of asking. I felt a flicker of unease down the mating line.

"The Water Kingdom has been conspicuously absent from Pax, especially during Veles's attacks."

"They are isolated here," I pointed out. "And if more are choosing to live in the ocean, maybe they think war won't find them."

"War finds everyone," Alarik breathed, his voice going low. "When you have beings like Veles, creatures who believe with every ounce of their corrupted souls that they are better than others, that they *deserve* to shape the world how they see it, their hatred will touch everyone. It's only a matter of time."

"We're here to make sure that doesn't happen," Queen Freya soothed, her words uncharacteristically kind.

I looked between the three of them. "We're going to scout a few of the local village, make sure there are no signs of Veles, his brothers, or Levana, and then meet the Water King and Queen for lunch and beg for their support?"

"Sounds about right," Queen Freya answered with a grin. "And when it all goes to shit, I'll just make us a portal and we'll leave."

"We'll be fine," Halcyon gritted through clenched teeth. "Just behave yourself."

"I always behave myself," Queen Freya answered with an innocent grin.

Halcyon rolled her eyes. "That's what I'm afraid of."

32

LANNIE

We portaled across hillsides, Halcyon and I flitting through towns while Queen Freya and Alarik stood guard. I kept waiting to find atrocities, expecting to discover humans locked in cages or some other sort of depravity, but there was nothing. Only peaceful towns spotted the rocky coastline, the small villages mostly populated by humans. Fae became more frequent as we headed south, with a distinct shift in culture.

Quaint towns gave way to sprawling estates, most with their own access to the ocean. Some mansions were half below the water, with surrounding coral reefs rather than gardens. But amid the beauty, we witnessed the disparity of wealth.

Humans were decidedly in the lower class, found to be working in the citrus fields, or along the docks. They were dirty and weathered, their hands calloused, but they came and went as they pleased.

"It's time," Halcyon said, giving Queen Freya a nod.

The Wild Queen raised her hand, the runes across her face flaring as a portal shimmered into place. I took Halcyon's outstretched hand, my heart fluttering as we made contact. It was a small gesture, nothing but the appearance of unity, but as

I saw Queen Freya reach for Alarik, I wondered if maybe it meant something a little more.

The four of us stepped through to a narrow outcropping overlooking a wide lagoon. In the center was the Water Kingdom's palace. White domed tops sat above high archways. Narrowed bridges connected the shore to the palace, and then the palace to the ocean on the other side. Slender columns shimmered in the descending sun, the pearl sheen made all the more charming by the full blossomed trees and waterfalls cascading from every terrace. The turquoise clear waters tumbled into the lagoon below, the gentle churning crafting a melody that carried up to us.

"Gods," Alarik breathed. "I've been through the Earth Kingdom, and even the northern territories, but I've never seen the Water Palace before."

"It is alluring," Queen Freya said, but her eyes were hard. "Don't let the elegance lure you into a false sense of safety. Water fae can be just as ruthless at dark fae, and just as cunning as light."

"Based on what we saw," I said. "We might not meet many fae on land."

"Yes," Halcyon nodded, her brows furrowing. "But is that a kindness from the Water Queen or a display of the royals power?"

"Even if it was the later, humans are doing better without fae influence," Queen Freya said. "Humans won't care about why the fae with elitists complexes leave, as long as they're left to themselves. Though, I am surprised at the number of humans still residing this far south. Last I heard, most had moved out of the Water Kingdom."

"A lot have," Halcyon agreed. "I've welcomed many from both the Water and Light Kingdoms, but some don't want to leave their homes."

"Even if they wanted to," Alarik said with a somber edge.

"There are many who cannot make the journey. Whether it be for financial or health reasons, there will always be those who can't leave even when war is at their doorstep."

"We should start making our way down," Queen Freya said after a moment, stepping around a patch of thorny bushes and starting toward the winding dirt path. "We're to meet the king and queen in the Welcome Pavilion."

"Part of the palace?" Alarik asked, following closely behind her.

I dipped my head slightly, extending my hand for Halcyon to go first. She gave me a small smile before stepping in front. My stomach fluttered as I trailed after her, not minding the way her rich vanilla scent mingled with the salty sea air.

"See where the palace tapers toward the mainland?" Freya pointed toward the middle of the lagoon and then drew her finger north, tracing the way the terraces lowered as they extended out from the middle. "The Pavilion is surrounded by the cluster of trees."

"Are those cherry trees?" I asked, noting the soft pinks of the blossoms, but they looked larger and fuller than what they should be.

"A variation of them," Halcyon answered with a glance over her shoulder. Her lips twitched. "If you're impressed by that, wait till we get inside."

We made steady progress, the early evening going smoothly, until we reached the shores of the lagoon. Fae stared with their faces scrunched in anger as they focused on Alarik's hand clasped in Queen Freya's. Even the humans were shooting him dirty looks of betrayal.

We'd come so far from this type of blind hatred in the north, it was jarring to see there were places where the vast majority still thought it unnatural for fae and humans to be together.

Alarik glanced around, taking note of the stares and whispers that had gathered strength. "Maybe we shouldn't hold hands here."

"Nonsense," Freya said, looking straight ahead. The narrowed path had widened, lined with sleet rock until it shifted to something finer at the edge of the water. "Us choosing to hold hands or not won't sway the king."

"It might," muttered Halcyon, her brows furrowing as she, too, noticed the group trailing us.

"We're doomed, anyway." Queen Freya shrugged, dragging Alarik with her as she stepped on the white stone leading toward the Welcome Pavilion and the palace beyond.

The sneering fae halted at the edge of the water, their skin shimmering like the path we were walking on—shells, I realized. The entire palace and pathway were made of shells and studded with pearls.

Halcyon reached for my hand, snapping my attention forward.

"At least they stopped," she whispered, but the tightness along her jaw and the flicker of uncertainly down the bond suggested different.

For now.

With a deep breath, we stepped beneath the canopy of large pink blossoms, the off-white wood of the trees complementing the opulence of the shell archway. Columns stretched overhead, allowing for great windows to bathe the room in natural light, each alcove home to a thriving pale-barked, pink-blossomed tree.

The shelled walkway transitioned into brilliant pearl stepping stones set above teal waters that grew deeper the closer we came to the palace. Stairs climbed both into and out of the water's edge, spiraling up to the second floor and stretching down beneath my line of sight, as if one were meant to change from air to sea with little more than a thought.

Sculpted benches were placed throughout the space,

surrounded by wild sea roses. It was huge, allowing for ample sitting areas and small landings for fae to gather. Though the room had been nearly vacant when we'd arrived, it had filled considerably in the few minutes we'd taken to cross toward the palace.

I spotted a familiar looking fae to our right. His clothes were soaked, streams of water trailing from his dark hair. The glimmer to his skin was stronger now, exposing the scaled patches behind his ears and along his neck. It was the same fae who'd been at the front of the pack following us.

He was beautiful, but the coldness of his black eyes had the fine hairs on the back of my neck pricking. Another at his side curled his lip as they watched Queen Freya and Alarik. The leader muttered something to the group behind him, inciting a low murmur of disapproval.

All of them had followed us, choosing to travel through water rather than land.

"I don't like this," whispered Alarik, but being surrounded by fae, everyone could hear.

"Me either," Queen Freya muttered, inconspicuously noting how many had trailed us. She let go of Alarik's hand, her palm taking on a faint glow. "Halcyon?"

Halcyon glared, and I could practically see how badly she wanted to chide Queen Freya for not taking the threat seriously until we were surrounded. Instead, she let out a harsh breath and gave one swift shake of her head. "We need to try. All of Pax is in danger. One battalion—one solider—could be the difference between victory and death."

"And if the four of us are killed before that happens?" gritted Alarik, his palm poised over his sword.

A spike of panic shot through the bond as still more water fae emerged. I moved closer to Halcyon, feeling my light fae affinities rise to the surface. I wasn't a fighter, not by a long shot, but I only needed to survive long enough to get Halcyon through the portal.

"Freya," I breathed, bracing myself for an attack as I pleaded with her to get us out of here. Her palm flared, energy buzzing through the air—

"I hope you're not leaving."

Cold dread trickled down my spine as I turned toward the frigid voice. Shrewd green eyes peered beneath thick lashes, pinning me in place. Her tanned skin was on display, the deep turquoise skirt slit to her hips on either side. Rounded beads made from the finest abalone shells were woven together with golden chains across her chest, matching the intricate belt set low on her waist. Her long, black hair was tied back in dozens of complex braids, the beauty of it untarnished despite her skin still glistening with fresh water droplets. A pearl crown set atop her dark locks, the sleek, narrowed spikes meant to look like coral, but giving off the impression of tipped daggers: Queen Isla.

"Dinner has been prepared." Queen Isla's dusty rose lips parted in what should have been a welcoming smile, but something was off about it. The gesture looked more like a warning, her green eyes seeming to grow darker.

She tilted her head to the side, letting a glimpse of the predator show.

"I insist."

33

ELARA

"I thought you killed him," I breathed as we continued down another flight of stairs. "Silas is dangerous, Zaeth. We can't risk him escaping or worse, rallying others to his cause."

"I agree with all of that, love," Zaeth answered, spine stiff. My gaze snagged on the way his fists continued to clench and un-clench. "But a quick death was too good for him. He hurt you—almost killed you."

"His dagger hardly nicked me. It was only a cut—"

"A cut that leaked poison into your veins and nearly stopped your heart from beating," Zaeth snapped spinning around to face me. I was a few stairs above him, the positioning forcing him to look up. What I saw nearly broke my heart.

It wasn't rage that spurred him on, or even bloodlust. No, the emotion burning through his eyes was far worse… fear. It wasn't an emotion that often plagued Zaeth. Fury, the twisted pleasure that came from justly killing our enemies, even detachment—but never fear.

Swallowing, I moved down one step, bringing us face to face as I leaned into him.

"I'm here," I breathed. "I'm safe."

Zaeth's hand fisted in my hair, his lips crashing into mine. He was branding me, reassuring both of us. So much had gone wrong. Too many people had been taken from us, but we were going to get through this. We had to.

Chains rattled, jerking my attention to the end of the stairs and the faint light beyond.

"Draven may be gone and Veles momentarily serving as an asset in this war, but we need more information on Levana."

My gaze bounced back to Zaeth, the bright rings around his irises glowing for me. I felt my own dark affinities mirrored back at him, the tingle between my shoulder blades indicative of my violet wings urging to break free.

This would not be quick. Zaeth meant to take all his grief and frustrations out on Silas. Not only had Silas announced himself the Dark King, but if what we learned a few weeks ago was true, he'd done unspeakable things to women. He'd allowed his men to commit horrid, degrading acts without repercussions. He'd aided Levana for gods knew how long and had made at attempt at my life.

Zaeth may savor the sounds of his screams, but I intended to bathe in Silas's blood right beside him.

Rolling my shoulders, I allowed my depraved thoughts to surface, imaging the multitude of ways I could inflict pain so severe, that all the people of Pax would be avenged. Zaeth groaned as he felt my affinities swell, his fangs elongating as his fingers dug into my hips. His body pressed against mine, making his desire clear as my wings unfurled in a great arch.

"You are *everything*, love." Quicker than should have been possible, Zaeth fisted my hair, tugging my chestnut curls down as he pressed me against the obsidian wall.

A gasp stole from my lips as his tongue licked along my collar bone, my wings splaying outward. His fangs scraped the curve of my neck as his hips locked me in place.

"These wings..." Zaeth purred, caressing the soft feathers

along my spine. My thighs clenched as heat rolled through me, made all the stronger by the promise of his fangs biting into my flesh. Another stroke of his skilled fingers had me shuddering, my back arching in wanton need. "I wonder if you could come from them alone."

The hard length pressing against my center suggested he was just as willing to find out as I was.

Chains rattled again.

The promise of cruel torture thick in the air only served to further my debased thoughts. Zaeth pulled back, his eyes sparking with challenge.

"You want to punish him?"

I lifted my chin, unashamed of how the idea of spilling the blood of such a terrible creature did nothing but stoke the flames blazing between us. Blood and lust—the two were linked for us, tangled in a wash of our dark fae affinities.

Zaeth let out a low growl as my hips shifted, showing him just what that idea did to me.

"Together," I breathed.

He paused, only for a moment, looking as if he might warn me away, but then gave a small nod. "As you wish, love."

I flitted down the rest of the stairs, anticipation building as I set foot on the rough stone floor. The obsidian walls along the staircase were replaced by course marbled rock, the bricks thick enough to house various bolts and chains. They covered the floor, only breaking to allow for the narrowed drain at the center of the room, too small for anyone to escape through, but large enough to wash away any gore that might be spilled across the wide space.

A small tray filled with a fine, shimmering powder and several polished blades sat to the left of Silas. There was nothing else in the space, save for the stairs at my back.

Perfect.

My eyes landed on the slumped figure dangling by his wrists in the far left corner. There was a bar between them, forcing his suspended arms wide, his toes skimming the ground. Only a tattered, stained strip of cloth covered him, more for our benefit than his. And every surface of his pale skin was covered in slashes, the edges raw and puckered. Unhealed.

"How did you stop his healing affinities?" I asked, my voice drawing Silas to the edge of consciousness, his eyes flying open and fixating on me. The flash of fear in them made me smile.

"I didn't." Zaeth stepped toward him with delight gleaming in his eyes as he surveyed the network of angry cuts. "His body is constantly healing, but the shards of glass powder rubbed into each of them prevents the skin from sealing."

Silas flinched as Zaeth pressed the flat of his dagger to a particularly swollen strip of flesh. Blood welled, oozing around the angry cut.

"It's effective at maintaining a constant level of pain without endangering our guest's life." Zaeth's eyes shifted into a cold darkness, one filled with revenge. "And strikingly similar to the injury he delivered you. I'd meant to inflict every injury he's delivered to others back on him, but the things he admitted to— the priestesses..." Zaeth shook his head, his anger mixing with a wave of repulsion so strong that my own stomach twisted. "The somnus was only the beginning of his plans for you."

My brows lifted as I glanced toward my shoulder where the poison from his blade had sliced the skin. Bile burned the back of my throat at what Silas's intentions had been. For what crimes he must've already confessed to for Zaeth to be this angry, this intent on watching him suffer. "You wish to keep him alive?"

"Please," Silas murmured, his black eyes pleading as if I'd grant him mercy.

Zaeth shrugged as he unleashed the dagger along his

tattooed forearm. "For a time. I needed to make sure that was the last of the somnus."

"Was it?"

"Yes," Zaeth answered. "And now that he's confirmed it, I thought you would like to have a little fun before we disposed of him."

A challenge lit in my Dark King's gaze as he extended a blade. I took it without hesitation, my body humming as my vision sharpened.

"Please," Silas pleaded, as if he hadn't tried to kill me. Hadn't try to do far worse.

"*Please*," I taunted, my lip curling in disgust as I stared at the filth before me.

With a vicious growl, I drew the blade across his chest, deep enough for the steal to scrape bone. He screamed, the agonized sound reverberating off the walls. The deeper parts of the wound started to knit itself back together. I let it, watching until only the faintest traces of blood remained before grabbing a handful of the shimmering glass powder and smearing it across the cut.

Silas wailed, the metallic clang of the chains ringing as he thrashed. If I couldn't see the blackness of his soul, I might have stopped.

"Beautiful," Zaeth purred, his own wings shadowing mine as he leaned forward to draw my chestnut curls to the side and kiss the back of my neck. We stared as the imposter king. At the sniveling mess he'd become.

"What are Levana's plans?" I asked, surprised by how calm I sounded. But Silas had chosen his path when he'd harmed the first priestess. When he'd ruined another's life.

"No plans," Silas rasped.

My eyes narrowed. "She's just relaxing in the Shadowlands? Murdering red-eyed commanders, plotting the end of the world?"

Silas shook his head but clamped his mouth shut.

Another quick flick of the blade, this time along the large vein just above his suspended elbow. He howled as I ground the glass powder into the wound far sooner than the last. The wound had started to heal, but just barely. A steady drip of blood continued down his raised arm, continuing down along the front of his chest.

"Would you like to try again?" Zaeth drawled, his eyes fixed on Silas over my shoulder while his fingers traced patterns along my hip.

"She thinks you're dead," he panted, his black eyes fixed on me. "She said your father's blessing meant she couldn't purge you from your own body, but that her rebirth required your death."

Silas had mentioned something of the sort at the bog, but I'd been too busy fighting for my life to remember. Levana thought I was dead... which would explain why she'd fled the temple, but I was sure my reprieve was short lived as plenty of her creatures had seen be before Naz had shadow walked us to safety.

"And," he pressed.

Silas's chest heaved, sweat gleaming across his brow. "And she's tracking Veles."

"Yes," I snapped, selecting a particularly serrated looking blade. "We know that."

"How?" He sounded genuinely shocked, but it wasn't his place to ask questions.

Slice. Powder. Screams.

I stepped back, assessing the mirrored cut along his other arm. His knees would be next.

"Levana wants the Fractured—"

"We *know*," Zaeth cut in, his voice a warning. "She needs them to defeat us, but how will she attack? When? Is Caligo her target?"

Silas looked at Zaeth for a long moment, the blood running

down his suspended arms to either side of his torso. Silas shook his head as I raised the blade once more—and then started to laugh.

It was the laugh of a man who knew he'd lost everything. Maybe he finally realized he wouldn't be walking out of here, or maybe a slim, resilient part of him knew what he'd done was unforgivable. Knew that this prolonged death full of pain was deserved.

The unhinged cackle ended abruptly, shifting into a rabid scream, until he fell silent.

"Wants," Silas muttered after minutes of nothing but our heartbeats and breaths filling the room.

Zaeth and I glanced at each other, both of us believing he'd finally cracked.

Silas lifted his filthy head, the edge of his cheek smeared with blood from where it had been resting along his arm. He looked stronger in that moment. Less worried about his immediate pain and more determined to deliver us a blow in any way he could.

"She *wants* the Fractured." Silas whispered, forcing us to strain to hear him. "Not *needs*."

Dread pooled in my stomach, the scent of my fear causing Silas to smile.

"More of her children cross every day. Hundreds of creatures. Soon, she'll have no need of Veles's borrowed army."

"Where?" Zaeth repeated, his own dagger slashing across Silas's inner thighs, both cuts coated in glass powder immediately.

Silas's yells were tempered with crazed laughter. "Everywhere. Anywhere she wants. She is a goddess. *The* goddess. She's in you, Dark King, as she is in me."

I could see the questions ignite in Zaeth's eyes, but we needed answers to the impending war, not riddles spoken by a dying man. And judging by the volume of blood now pooling on the floor and flowing down the drain, Silas *was* dying.

"Does she mean to attack from the air with her dark fae hybrids or land?"

"Land, air, water. All are her domain. But her night children are hungry. Always hungry. *They* will be Caligo's undoing."

"What of the other kingdoms?" I asked, the urgency in my voice betraying me. Caligo was nowhere near water. Sure, an air strike could happen, but then why make a point of listing water? "Silas, does she intend to attack the coast as well? The Air Kingdom?"

His smile widened, his complexion bone white. "This is her world, Dark Phoenix. You may be a tool derived by the light goddess, one blessed by the God of Night, but Levana *is* darkness. She is shadow. She is the shameful, corrupt truths of our souls. No kingdom is safe from her wrath. All will be conquered. All are forsaken."

He coughed before his eyes drooped shut and his head lulled to the side.

"Even me."

The last words were a whisper, muttered half consciously.

Zaeth moved forward, his dagger carving out the slash across Silas's chest to remove a sizable chunk of flesh. It hit the floor with a wet slap as he moved to his arms.

"What are you doing?" I asked, watching as he worked.

"Cutting out the glass. He's lost a lot of blood." Zaeth moved to his other arm, doing the same thing, cutting out the glass powder—and allowing the muscle and skin to heal.

"You're saving him," I breathed.

Zaeth's spine stiffened as another slab of muscle splatted in the puddle of blood. "I'd hardly call it *saving*. Silas will heal and we can question him again."

"You think he has more to offer?"

Slowly turning to face me, Zaeth shook his head. "No. I think he finally broke."

"Let him die," I said, glancing past Zaeth to the two large wounds still bleeding from his thighs. Zaeth lifted a brow, the unspoken question reverberating through our bond. "I'm sure. We got what we came for. I'm done wasting time."

"As you wish, love."

34

GREER

"Is he speaking about things yet?" I asked, being sure to keep my voice low as Jarek and I dropped behind Ryuu and Evander. The air whipped through the Jagged Mountains, flurries swirling across thick snowbanks. Tugging the edges of my clock further around me, I leaned into Jarek, greedily taking whatever source of warmth I could. If I wasn't so worried about Evander, I'd insist Ryuu's dragon heat the air around me.

"It comes in bursts," Jarek said, the fatigue underlying his voice twisting my stomach. "I can't reach him. I've tried, but he only retreats further."

"I wish he would talk to me," I grumbled, knowing my would-be brother was hurting. "If anyone understands losing Jem, my sisters and I would... Evander got through it once. He can get through it again."

Jarek nodded, but I saw the way his shoulders hunched as if he didn't really believe it.

My stomach twisted, pained by being so incapable of helping Evander when he needed it most. I'd tried talking to him, tried distracting him with wedding talk, boy talk, war talk—which had been a stretch for me. I'd even gone as far as reading him poetry from his favorite, worn out book.

Nothing helped.

We'd left for the Fire Kingdom early this morning, with assurances from Ryuu that things would work themselves out in time.

In time.

Like I was supposed to wait patiently and just let Evander feel terrible until it passed. My teeth ground together as I watched Ryuu and Evander flitting ahead of us. Evander's shoulders looked less hunched than they had been just yesterday, and his gait appeared a little less heavy.

All Ryuu had done was walk with him. In silence. *I* could've walked with him. I'd tried just a few hours ago, and it'd gotten me nowhere. Though the silence part hadn't gone too well for me.

The edges of my cloak were wretched open with a burst of wind, drawing a chilled shriek from me.

"Isn't this supposed to be the Fire Kingdom?" I grumbled, closing the distance to Ryuu. I'd leave Evander alone, if that's what he wanted, but I couldn't stand another moment in the cold.

Ryuu's lips quirked as he opened his cloak, allowing me to cozy up to him as we continued. Warmth instantly enveloped me, melting the bits of ice that had started to form along the tips of my silver curls.

"No wonder most fire fae chose to live beneath the ground. It must be warmer than this."

"It is," Jarek answered, catching up to the three of us. "Underground rivers of fire are said to heat their cities."

Evander scoffed, the first indication he'd been listening at all.

"If not fire, then what?" I asked.

It took a long moment, but Evander eventually slowed,

allowing the four of us to join in conversation. "Magma. It's molten rock that remains in liquid form far beneath the earth's surface. Most of the Fire Kingdom resides miles above great pools of it. The churning heat is powerful enough to keep them warm, but there are areas where it breaks free."

"You speak as if you've been there," Ryuu remarked, his tone carefully neutral.

Evander shrugged. "After Jem died, I wandered."

I blinked, my throat going dry. I knew he'd been to the Fire Kingdom before, but I'd assumed it was above ground. And on the order of the Legion of the Light or order from Alarik—something that had *forced* him to come.

"You wandered. By yourself. Into the Fire Kingdom?"

He shrugged again. "The Fire Kingdom is just like any other. There are those who choose a life of acceptance and those who cling to prejudices supported by their own fear and hatred. The fact they're immune to fire is comparable to water fae breathing under the sea or air fae flying along the wind."

"They're immune to fire?" I shook my head. "Gods, that would be helpful."

"And some of them can fly," Evander added. "Though their wings are leathery, no feathers. Think bats verse birds."

"We are not like birds," Ryuu growled, his wings bristling.

I cocked my head to the side. "No, Evander is right. I can see it."

Ryuu's eyes narrowed.

"Like a giant owl," I added after a moment.

Evander's lips twitched.

"A strong, intimidating owl with great hair," Jarek added, his gaze darting toward Evander as the faintest of smiles appeared. Some of the tension constricting my heart released.

Ryuu rolled his eyes. "Yes, fire fae are powerful and versatile, which is why this meeting needs to go well."

"We're all aware what's at stake," I said, the words coming

out harsher than I'd meant, but the frown was firmly in place again across Evander's face with Ryuu's talk of war. "Levana is a scary goddess."

"That she is." Jarek sighed. "It's just a little further through here. I didn't want to alarm the guard."

We crested the hill, coming to the mouth of a hidden cave. It was enormous, the opening taller than it was wide and bordered by rocks shaped into large spikes along the top and bottom. Snow and bushy pine trees covered most of the mountain and a good portion of the cave's opening, but as we drew near I saw the spikes had distinct groves in them.

I blinked, scrutinizing the odd shape as we stopped just before it.

"Oh my gods, are those teeth?"

My heart hammered as a flickering orange light flared from deep within the cave, further illuminating the serrated edges of the sharp fangs surrounding us.

"They are," Evander answered, as relaxed as ever. "The entire entrance is made from a dragon skeleton. Great fire dragons used to fly through these skies. Some say they live still, beyond the continent and across the sea."

"I've heard there are entire worlds beyond our continent," Jarek said, his voice low and contemplative as he gazed upon the skull we'd stepped into. "I confess I've never sought to confirm the truth of those rumors myself. Ryuu? Any discoveries out your way?"

He shook his head. "As air fae, we enjoy stretching our wings but want to make sure we have a safe place to land. I know there were once great islands east of the air kingdom, home to dragons of a sort."

Heat licked up my cheeks as I remembered the island Ryuu's dragon had brought me to. The palace had been beautiful even with the wearing of time. I could only imagine what it must have looked like with an entire kingdom sprawled around it.

"But they're all gone now," I answered, letting the melancholy of that statement ring through me.

Ryuu's pupils shifted as the green embers within flared. He lifted a hand, pressing his palm to the soft part of my belly. "The ancient dragon line is not lost to us yet, my darling."

Jarek's brows lifted before he cleared his throat and started a light-hearted conversation with Evander. For once, it seemed Evander was willing to talk, if only to avoid the awkward tension brewing between me, Ryuu, and his dragon.

The dragon within had been making remarks alluding to children more often than not. I'd taken my tonic only a few weeks ago, deciding that bringing a child into this bloodthirsty world at war with itself was crazy. Sure, I loved kids. And when I pictured the future, I guess I did see a bunch of little winged terrors running around us. They'd have Ryuu's dark colors and my curls, our two personalities shaping fierce, outspoken little princelings. It would be exhausting and consuming. Terrifying and... wonderful.

In some distant, far off, centuries-from-now-world, having children would be a great adventure.

But the world *now* was quite literally about the end. Levana had already fractured the realm. Even if we found a way to defeat her—which was a very large *if*—her creatures would continue spilling into ours.

Unless...

"Jarek, your aunts were mated?"

The light fae turned, halting mid-sentence to lift a quizzical brow at me. "Yes."

"Were they able to share power?"

Ryuu shrugged as Jarek and him locked eyes. "Each mating bond is different."

"I can sense your light affinities but cannot wield them," Ryuu answered my unspoken question as the deep voice of his dragon vibrated beneath.

Tugging my cloak tighter around myself, I shot him a glare. "You tried to take my power?"

A sheepish grin tilted his lips. "Not take, darling. Borrow. I even tried pushing some of my fire into you. Nothing happened. Our gifts remain our own."

I turned inward as Ryuu's dragon eyes search my face. Our bond was strong. Searing. It was fire and passion, two souls melded into one. I knew he'd never hurt me, or his dragon. He inhaled sharply, pupils dilating, as a wash of love consumed me. With a smirk, I sent a bolt of heat down it, loving the pleasurable torment I could inflict on him.

But the bond I shared with my sisters... those felt different. They were cool, calming even. A steady force. Testing them, I tried to draw on their affinities. The connection flared in welcome recognition, but no transfer was made.

On a whim, I sent a ripple of my power down their lines, feeling the force of the energy leave me.

"Greer," Ryuu rumbled, his thick arms coming to my waist. It felt like I'd just constructed an impenetrable ward spanning an entire city. I swayed, my knees buckling, but he was there to catch me. As he always was.

"What happened?" Jarek asked, his palms illuminating as he sought an injury.

"I couldn't draw on their power any more than I could take from you," I answered, my eyes fluttering shut as I leaned into Ryuu's warm chest. I loved his scent—like wild winds and embers. "So, I sent them each some of mine."

The light along Jarek's palms dimmed and then extinguished as he drew away, allowing an irritated Evander into view. It was the most emotion I'd seen from him in weeks. His auburn eyes were blazing, worry and fear pinching his brow.

"We are moments away from being escorted to the Fire Palace to secure an army because a mad goddess has decided to destroy our world, and you think it's a good idea to experiment with blasting your power across invisible bonds? Without even warning your sisters first?"

Swallowing, I pushed from Ryuu's arms, proud that my legs held. "When you say it like that, it sounds a little reckless."

The vein along Evander's neck bulged as he fought to control his breathing. All four of us were aware of the footsteps ascending from within the cave—dragon skeleton—and we wanted to give off a good, respectable first impression.

We needed to be welcomed inside and taken directly to the king. There was no time for anything else. The four of us had to appear united if we had any hope of earning the fire fae's respect. They were a notoriously secluded group—one known for being exceedingly definitive. If we messed this up, we wouldn't get another chance.

Evander stepped near, his voice dropping so only the four of us could hear. "Do not show weakness. A certain level of daring is admired, but weakness—*foolishness*—is not tolerated."

Before I could reply, a torch illuminated the descending slope of the skeleton dragon's throat, followed closely by a tall, muscular woman with dark skin and even darker hair. Her sleek locks were left unbound, the torch highlighting blue undertones. Bronze eyes peered out beneath thick lashes, seeming to miss nothing as they swept through our group. The dagger strapped along her thigh over her battle leathers was made from bright shimmering stone, the same stone used for the arrows stored in the quiver along her back: fire opal.

Jarek had warned us they had an abundance of fire opal, the one stone he couldn't lux through.

Two guards appeared behind her, positioning themselves at her sides. Each had swords fashioned from fire opal, the alluring rock seeming to shift like the flames of a torch.

"Evander," the woman beamed, stepping forward to draw him into an easy embrace.

"It's good to see you too, Cyra." Evander's spine was stiff and the pats on Cyra's back anything but comfortable, but she didn't appear to notice.

"King Dante sent me to toss intruders into the magma pits, but he'll be delighted it's you."

Ryuu and Jarek tensed, their stances mimicked by the guards at Cyra's back.

"Now, now, boys," she chided with a playful edge. "There's no need for that. Any friend of Evander's is a friend of ours. Our king has been waiting on a visit for years. We shouldn't delay him any longer."

The three fire fae turned, striding down the dragon cave without a glance behind. Jarek's gaze cut to Evander, willing him to explain what his relationship with the Fire King was or had been, but Evander refused to look back, choosing instead to follow Cyra and the guards into the tunnel.

"We just… go?" I whispered low enough for only Ryuu and Jarek to hear.

"I don't like it." Ryuu tugged me closer, his warmth chasing away the cold as my breath puffed in the air around us.

"I don't like it, either," Jarek muttered. "But Evander's already started down, and we don't really have a choice. You know as well as I do how likely it is to get backing from the Water Kingdom. We need them."

With serious doubts still swirling in my mind, I gripped Ryuu's hand and followed Jarek into the belly of the beast.

35

LANNIE

Insist.

Queen Isla's command rolled through the room, the four of us taking a collective breath as the water fae surrounding us stilled. If we left now, it would be an insult to the queen, and therefore the entire Water Kingdom. We'd lose any chance at gaining an army. An ally. But the glares and low murmurings of the crowd suggested that was a long shot, anyway.

I glanced toward Alarik and Queen Freya, waiting to see if she would complete the portal and take us out of here, but the Wild Queen was staring at Halcyon. The entire room seemed to be poised on the tip of a blade, waiting for her verdict.

Halcyon smiled brightly, stepping out of the safety of our group to embrace Queen Isla in the typical water fae fashion. Only I felt the flicker of fear lick up her spine as Halcyon pressed her cheek to the Water Queen's, repeating the gesture on the other side.

The water fae hovering along the edges seemed to retreat. There were still glares thrown our way, but most of the immediate crowd had slipping beneath the water as Halcyon engaged with Queen Isla.

It was flawless, the way Halcyon assured her of our eagerness for refreshments and hope for productive conversation. If I didn't know any better, I'd swear Halcyon was an old acquaintance of Queen Isla, the two of them coming together for a casual meal among close friends.

"This is Queen Freya of the Wild Kingdom," Halcyon said after the small talk had concluded and the tension in the room had lifted. Queen Freya gave a simple nod in acknowledgement but didn't move forward to embrace Queen Isla as Halcyon had.

Rather than be offended, the Water Queen's eyes seemed to spark. "Pleasure. And this is your human?"

"General Alarik Holt, Your Highness," he answered, his spine stiffening as her emerald gaze swept over him. One dark brow lifted, curiosity flickering across the Water Queen's face as Queen Freya slipped her hand into his.

"I see." Queen Isla glanced between the four of us, her eyes narrowing as she took inventory. "Right. My husband is waiting. We are to meet him for dinner to discuss the fate of our world."

"We are grateful for your hospitality, Queen Isla." Halcyon nodded, slipping into the role of a friend with little effort.

Amusement flickered through the Water Queen's gaze, but she only nodded. "This way."

We followed her to the end of the pavilion, turning up a set of spiral steps which took us to the second floor and across a narrow bridge suspended above the ocean. We were forced to go one-by-one as we crossed, each step drawing us further away from the shore.

From this vantage point, I could clearly see shadows moving beneath the water—the rest of the water fae, if I had to guess. Probably off to tell the king we'd arrived and were being led toward him.

"Your palace is lovely," Halcyon said. "This will be my first time past the pavilion."

"Yes." Queen Isla waved her hand over her shoulder. "Beauty stretches as far as the eye can see here. But remember, you see only the surface. Imagine how remarkable our palace is beneath the waters. What wondrous lives my husband and his royals live."

"You don't live below?" I asked, hearing a trace of something almost like a warning underlying her words.

Queen Isla didn't answer.

We stepped into the palace one after the other. The tall arches seen in the pavilion continued through the white halls with the scent of salt thick in the air. Rather than trees, alcoves were home to intricate fountains sculpted from pearls and shimmering shells, each a depiction from the sea. Water tumbled down carvings of great sea monsters, and lavish coral, pooling in wide basins before tumbling over the edges and joining the ocean on the floor below us.

The sounds of churning water would have been soothing had it not been for the shifting shapes that seemed to track our every movement beneath us.

We turned down another hall, entering a large foyer that split into an imperial staircase. Queen Isla led the way down, bringing us back to the first floor and the grand dining room at the water's edge.

White stepping stones led to a long table set on an island of stone raised a foot out of the water. It was donned with the finest cutlery overlying white lace. Golden candelabras flickered, their soft light barely managing to starve off the dark as the sun descended and clumps of shells and coral decorated the table in place of flowers.

Again, it was beautiful, but the proximity to the water and the inability for any of us to see below the surface was unnerving. And I wasn't the only one feeling uneasy.

Alarik's entire body was tense as we were ushered across stepping stones and toward the head of the table where a middle aged man sat. An ornate crown of thick spikes set with dozens of pearls sat atop his closely cropped reddish-blond hair. His toned bronzed chest glimmered with water, reminding us there was an entire network of paths below us that we couldn't access.

"Queen Halcyon of the Earth Kingdom and Queen Freya of the Wild Kingdom are here to speak with us, Your Grace." Queen Isla bowed to her husband, gesturing for us to do the same. Alarik and I dropped our heads, but neither Halcyon nor Freya moved. To bow would have been admitting his superiority, and I couldn't blame them for not wanting to get close enough to follow water fae custom like Halcyon had done with Queen Isla.

It seemed the Water King didn't agree.

King Kai's black eyes appeared to harden as we watched, his fury whisked away the next moment by a mask of politeness. "My wife tells me you wish to discuss the goddess Levana."

I felt Halcyon's unease spike down our bond. The tightening along Queen Freya's jaw and the twitch of Alarik's hand toward the dagger hidden in his boot suggested they felt the same, but we did our best to remained composed.

"We wish to discuss how best to keep our people safe, Your Highness," Halcyon smiled. "A topic I'm sure you're all too familiar with."

"Yes," he drawled. "Though our views on how that is to be achieved I fear are vastly different."

"I hope to find a common ground that will work for all of our kingdoms," Halcyon said, the three of us happy to let her do the talking.

King Kai looked at her, his dark eyes narrowing as if he were examining a specimen under a microscope. "We shall see."

"Should I show them to the study, Your Grace?" Queen Isla asked, already motioning for us to follow.

"No," the Water King cut in, freezing her movements. "We'll discuss matters here after refreshments are served."

Queen Isla's pulse picked up, the faint humming only standing out to me because of her nearness. I lifted a brow toward Halcyon, curious if she felt it too. She sent me the faintest shake of her head.

Not yet, she seemed to stay. *We don't need to run, yet.*

"Have a seat," King Kai grinned, yellow teeth showing beneath his sanguine smile. "The human can wait along the wall until we're finished."

"I prefer to sit with Queen Freya," Alarik stated, his tone flat but brokering no argument.

"Is that so," King Kai asked, his amusement clear. "And what does our Wild Queen have to say about such a clingy pet?"

Queen Freya's lip curled back in distaste as Alarik stiffened, but Halcyon interceded before either spoke.

"The four of us have traveled a great distance and have grown fond of one another. We don't wish to be parted. Perhaps we can retire to the study as Queen Isla first suggested."

Yes, I thought, noting how the shadows lurking beneath the water had grown. We needed to get out of this place, to put some distance between whatever King Kai has waiting beneath the sea.

"Queen Isla misspoke."

The tension in the air coiled tighter and I could see Queen Freya's hand start to shimmer as guards emerged from the water at the far side of the room. They continued marching in the opposite direction, but my stomach twisted at the sight of them.

"One must always offer their guests refreshments," King Kai continued. "As you said, you've traveled a great distance."

"We're not hungry," Queen Freya countered. "And I prefer a study to a dining hall."

"Tea then." The smirk vanished from King Kai's face as a

dozen servants swept into the hall, each setting down a steaming mug at the table. "Or do you insult me by denying my gracious offer?"

Alarm shot down the bond, and I could practically see Halcyon trying to figure out what she could say to get us out of taking tea. It was clear Queen Freya wouldn't sit. I didn't trust King Kai either, but another dozen guards rose from the water, lining the edges of the room as he waited for an answer.

"We have time for a glass," I offered, knowing the silence had stretched too long. I pinned Queen Freya with a plea in my eyes, needing her to realize this was the only option. "One glass seated together before we all retire to the study."

It was a risk, but it was the only compromise I could see that didn't end in us being slaughtered right here. Queen Freya could generate a portal, but it took a few seconds to manifest. We had a handful of weapons on our persons, but no shield. Nothing to block an attack that could so easily be delivered by the Water King and his men. We needed time.

"Agreed," King Kai said, waving an impatient hand toward the steaming cups.

Begrudgingly, we sat, the four of us as close to each other as we could get without raising suspicion.

Queen Isla released a long, tired sigh. "I tire of tea, Your Grace. Should we not retire immediately?"

"Enough," he reprimanded, the thick vein in his neck pulsing. "This is why I host dinner, *dear*. Your fragile countenance doesn't understand guest etiquette."

"Yes," she said with resignation, taking a seat on Halcyon's other side. "One of my many faults."

My brows furrowed as I blew on the steaming mug before me and sipped, trying to puzzle out why she sounded so sad. Halcyon said they had a strained relationship with the Water Kingdom since her reign began, but it was still civil. Why would they agree to meet us if not to discuss war? Surely, the water royals weren't arrogant enough to think they could attack us without repercussion.

I took another sip, the slightly bitter taste stronger this time, despite the overly sweet honeysuckle added to the mix. My mouth went dry, terror climbing up the back of my throat as I glanced down at my cup, swirling the contents at an angle so the light gleamed across its surface. The flames from the candelabras cast just enough light for me to see the red hue —hemlock.

Gods, they *were* trying to kill us.

"Don't," I breathed, knocking Halcyon's cup from her hands, grateful that Alarik and Queen Freya had yet to touch their glasses. The tea spilled across the table, the red stain seeming to launch everyone into action.

Alarik flipped the table, the few blades thrown toward us narrowly missing as the room exploded. Halcyon aimed her tea at the king, the porcelain shattering upon contact to slice the skin across his chest.

The king howled, falling behind a curtain of guards before diving for the water surrounding us. Halcyon ducked behind the table, raising her chair over head for additional cover. The thunk of blades impaling the cushion sounded a moment later, but I forced my sleepy gaze to focus on Queen Freya.

"I need half a minute," she called, launching daggers and throwing metal diamonds into the onslaught of water fae with her free hand.

"Done," Halcyon panted, using the decorative trees overhear to her advantage. They grew, stretching over us in a giant shield, while others lashed out to knock emerging fae back into the ocean.

"Kill them," King Kai bellowed, his black eyes blazing as a great tail thrashed beneath the water. He'd shifted, his legs transforming into a powerful, scaled tail.

"We're trying to, Your Grace," Queen Isla said just on the

other side of the woven branches offering us protection. I could see her through the hasty lattice, and for one brief moment, her green eyes met mine. "The wall is impenetrable on this side. I'm completely cut off. Can't see a thing."

"Freya," Alarik warned, gripping his sword, but we all knew we were done for if they broke through the branches covering us.

"Ten seconds," she gritted.

"No time," I breathed, already feeling my lungs slow. Hemlock typically took minutes to take effect, sometimes hours if the poisoner was clever. King Kai must have significantly concentrated it—so much so, my fae affinities were losing the battle to counter its effects.

I sent a wave of love toward Halcyon, filling her with peace. She hadn't chosen me as her partner, had been every bit thrown into being my fated mate as I was hers, but she'd never made me feel anything but welcomed. I wasn't an obligation. Had never been a burden to her. She looked at our situation and found a way we could both benefit. No pressure, no expectations, just patience.

Something I'd practiced every day of my life for others, but hardly was given the same gift. Being a healer, people sought a cure immediately. There was a constant urging to move quicker. Sow faster. Find a cure now. It was an endless uphill battle—one I realized wasn't something I could win... only ever weather.

Halcyon had gifted me an island of peace among the infinite storms.

"Done," Freya called, the portal shimmering a brilliant silver as the final piece locked in place.

"Go," Alarik called as Halcyon lifted me in her arms. The sound of wood splintering chased me as we dove toward freedom.

"Stop with all of the mushy thoughts, Melantha," Halcyon

chided as Alarik and Queen Freya followed us through the portal. "You aren't dying."

"It was concentrated," I countered.

"I don't care," she snapped with a little too much edge to her voice.

I sensed the rush of her earth fae affinities ripple down our bond in the next breath, felt the way her essence flowed so easily with mine. My innate healing abilities sped up with Halcyon's essence, the two working in tandem to find all traces of the poison and purge it from my body.

The last of the tea's effects were nearly gone when I felt a pulse of energy barreled into me. I gasped at the force of it, my eyes flying open to find Halcyon's bowed forward under its weight. With our affinities combined, she must have felt the power through our bond.

I sat up with little effort, gathering Halcyon in my lap as my fingers tingling with the need to heal. I brushed the pad of my thumb over her cheek sealing the scratch there but everything else felt whole.

There was so much. The rush of air in and out of her lungs, the dilation of the small vessels beneath her cheeks that drew a faint blush as we stared into each other's eyes. I knew the rate of her heart, sensed the strength contained in her arms. Her thighs.

And gods, the earth. I could feel the pull toward different gem stones. Appreciate the thousands of years it took to forge such beauty.

Halcyon's silver eyes sparked as a sliver of bloodstone beckoned her.

She pushed to stand, the amethyst crystals of her personal garden shimmering all around us. I hardly saw them. With the way we were still connected, her affinities intertwining with mine, I felt the call just as strongly as she did.

We turned toward a narrowed path leading into the darkness, one I hadn't realized was there until this moment.

"Where are you going?" Queen Freya called after us, but we were already gone, following the silent urging as it led us through cracks and around walls.

Our bodies fought to keep up with the internal call, slipping down forgotten spiraling staircases of the inner most portion of the Earth Kingdom. It was a blur of black and red, until the scene grew darker, our path leading us deeper.

This way.

Down we went, flitting as fast as our feet could carry until the small path opened.

A vast cavern pulsed with dark green and black hues with spots of red. There were variations throughout the rock, shades of grey and blue, but there was no mistaking it for what it was: an entire chamber made of bloodstone.

It was similar to the one housing the victims of the sleeping sickness, but this cavern was far older, the stone rough. By the sharp slashes of crystal along the edges, it had formed naturally.

The gentle sounds of a rolling underground stream reached me, drawing my attention to the far corner. Black sand met the water's edge, the tiny stones smooth from years of the water lapping at them.

I blinked as the faint silver light in the chamber flickered. It seemed to drain away the last of the power that had blast into me—into us. My connection to Halcyon cooled, returning to the normal mating bond, but I felt the spike of dread coming from her as if it were my own.

"Look," she breathed as I turned to face her, finding her silver eyes staring across the dark space.

Following her line of sight toward the source of the dimming light, I saw a temple crafted entirely from bloodstone. Faint silver script pulsed along its columns in an unfamiliar language, but a chill ran down my spine as if sensing a threat.

"What is that?" I asked, my voice only a whisper but still seeming too loud.

"I don't know," Halcyon breathed as she took a step nearer.

I grabbed her hand in warning, only to realize that I'd stepped forward too. We were only a few paces away from the temple now, the silver seeming to feed off our proximity.

"I don't think we should be here," I said, my grip tightening in hers.

"Me either," Halcyon said.

Both of us inched closer as if in a daze. My pulse was racing, Halcyon's chest heaving, but we peered through the shadows, catching a glimpse between the opened bloodstone doors. Whatever led us down here wanted us to look inside, needed us to see what lay within.

Our toes were so close to the base of the primal temple. One step, and it would be over. I didn't know what this place was, but every second spent here drained more of my affinities, weakening my body, along with my resolve to flee.

"Lannie," Halcyon cautioned, her voice pitching as panic swelled between us.

I ground my toes in the earth, halting our movement with the last of my strength. The silver script pulsed, the flare of light catching speckles of red and green from the bloodstone and illuminating the chamber within. And the sealed tomb that sat at its center.

My foot lifted, hovering over the cursed stone. I reached for Halcyon, for my sisters, for every ounce of will power I possessed as I fought the temptation to step forward.

The silver script flashed and then extinguished, plunging us into complete darkness.

36

ELARA

"Again," Zaeth called, helping me to stand before dropping into a fighting stance once more. The nearly full moon illuminated the top of the castle, the smooth obsidian stone reflecting the beauty of the stars. The scent of pine and snow drifted on the air, but the battle leathers I wore kept most of the chill at bay.

Heeding Zaeth's command, I repositioned and lunged.

I couldn't sleep after what Silas had said. He was dead, nothing more than a memory, but his ghost whispered in my ears.

All will be conquered. All are forsaken.

We'd been prepared for an attack on Caligo. Had transported refugees, the young, the old, and those too sick to fight through the portals into the Wild Kingdom. All who remained were prepared to fight for their lives. For their world. The capitol of the Dark Kingdom had essentially been turned into a fortress, but if Levana meant to attack other locations, if this was to be a coordinated strike throughout all of Pax…

Zaeth's fist found my ribs, the blow softened but still

impactful. "Keep your hands up, love. As distracted as you might feel, you need to focus when facing an opponent."

I spun, swinging my leg toward his head.

A dark chuckle rumbled through him as he caught my ankle, tugging me closer as I fought for balance. "Or we could create a distraction of our own."

Allowing him to place the weight of my extended leg on his shoulder, I leaned in as if for a kiss before throwing my off-balance weight into a jab to his side.

"You know violence only adds to your allure, love," Zaeth grunted with a wicked smile on his lips as I snatched my leg back. He feigned right, delivering two strikes to my left. I deflected both, my heart hammering with the speed at which we were moving.

"Levana thinks I'm dead," I panted, offering counterstrikes. "Silas implied Erebus's blessing saved me, but Levana knew Erebus was my father."

Zaeth intercepted the punch I'd aimed at his face, twisting me until my back was flushed with his chest. His breathing was just as heavy as my own, and his body just as hot.

"The term 'father' is loosely applied regarding gods. Being that they aren't in physical form, it's considered more a great blessing of their power that overwhelms the genetic input from another."

"Then I *should* be dead," I muttered. "According to Levana. She's a goddess. I'm sure she knows how these things work."

Zaeth seemed to weigh his next words carefully. "Maybe. Or maybe the gods aren't as lost as we thought them to be."

My spine stiffened, Zaeth's grip loosing around my waist. Using the distraction, I slammed my head back, catching him in the nose.

He grunted as he snapped the bones back in place, offering me a blood-tinged smile a second later. "Good job, love."

I raised my hands, dropping into a defensive stance automatically. "You think Erebus is still here?"

Zaeth's fists shot out, but the blows were easily deflected. "It would seem he'd have to be, and powerful enough to go to your mother."

My hands dropped to my sides and all thoughts of sparring were forgotten as flashes of memory ran through my mind.

"What is it?" Zaeth asked when the silence stretched.

"When I visited my mother in the after, she showed me glimpses of her past. There was so much going on. I'd thought I was dead, and then I came back. And Levana had been reborn..." I shook my head, swallowing back the wave of disbelief. "There was a memory of Mother accepting Erebus's hand."

Zaeth lifted a brow, his voice carefully controlled. "As in Erebus had a corporal form?"

"It had to be him." I nodded slowly as the pieces fit together. "Do you think he might be my father—and not just from a blessing of his dark power but my *biological* father?"

Zaeth leaned in, the warmth of his breath sending shivers down my body as his hands came around my waist. When he spoke, it felt more like a question offered up to the moon rather than me. "How else would you have survived her flames?"

I tilted my head forward, allowing Zaeth's scent of cedar and darkness to calm me. There were so many thoughts swirling in my mind. If Erebus was somehow my father more so than a blessing, would that make me part god?

"My sisters and I are blessed by Eunoia," I breathed into Zaeth's chest. "Maybe that's why I survived Levana's fire."

"No, love." Zaeth pressed a kiss to my brow before tilting my chin up. "The power in those flames was pure shadows. A blessing wouldn't have saved you."

I read the ghosts of grief in his eyes and hated that I'd been the cause—even if it had been temporary and out of my control.

Needing to stop his thoughts before they spiraled, I pressed up on my toes and captured his lips.

The light around his cinnamon eyes flaring at my challenge. His tongue swept the entrance of my mouth, and I groaned as my lips parted, allowing him to sweep inside. My thighs clenched as his fangs extended, his hunger for me blasting down our bond.

His fangs were at my throat, his hand fisted in my curls as he yanked my neck to the side. I gasped, staring up at the stars. A flash of silver-blue streaked across the sky, a reminded that the sphere of protection around Pax had been shattered.

"We need to close the rift between worlds," I breathed, my neck tilting further despite myself. Levana won't seek Veles for long, not with her creatures spilling into our world.

"If we could, love," Zaeth murmured against my throat, inhaling deeply as he licked the pulse at my collar bone. I arched into him, my breasts pressing against the hard planes of his chest. "To seal the rift would require stitching together the atmosphere itself."

"Like a ward?" I questioned, somehow following this line of thought despite my body yearning to give into Zaeth.

"The ultimate ward, one that would take a force beyond our power." His hand trailed down to my hip, curving around the swell of my ass to grip me tighter. "Something like that could only be crafted by..."

"A god?" I asked. Zaeth stilled, drawing back to look me in the eyes. "What about the daughter of a god?"

Cool air swirled around us, causing a shiver to race down my spine.

"Even if you did have the amount of power needed, your affinities don't include constructing wards." Zaeth's cinnamon eyes sparked, emotions flashing too quickly for me to pin down.

My shoulders slumped as the tenuous blossom of hope wilted. He was right, as he always was. I was dark fae. Even if I did have more of Erebus in me than I previously thought, I was no closer to suddenly being able to craft wards. That talent resided with Greer.

The reality of the situation slammed into me as flurries fell around us, the light snowflakes catching in my hair and along my lashes. For every enemy we struck down, twenty more slipped through from the rift. We'd be locked in battle forever with no hope of a future.

An endless war.

"Stop it, love." Zaeth's voice was a gentle warning as he took hold of my body once more. "We're together."

"The world is literally falling apart—"

His lips found mine, silencing the worries poised on my lips.

"But we *are* together. If this realm needs to be reshaped to fit our needs, we'll find a way."

I wanted to disagree, to demand how he knew we'd make it through the end of the world, but his lips were on mine in the next breath, distracting. Disarming.

The snow started picking up, but the wind had stilled. There hadn't been much of a Yule celebration this year. Too much was at stake to let down our guard, but in this moment with the gentle drifting of snow from the clouds above, each snowflake sparkling under the bright light of the stars, it felt like a small glimpse of what home could feel like.

"You're beautiful, love." Zaeth's thumb traced the curve of my cheek. "Captivating in every way."

I looked at my mate. My Dark King. He would never give up on us—on me. Even death hadn't kept us apart.

Just then, I felt a surge of power well within me, crashing through my body with the force of a hurricane. I gasped as my fangs descended, my wings bursting free. Zaeth must have been hit with it too or felt the effects through our bond because his own wings were thrown wide a heartbeat later.

He was enthralling. I could see my own dark rings reflected

in his eyes. My own longing and desire thrown into overdrive by the power coursing through my veins.

"I need to—to," I started to say but could finished. I needed to do *something*.

Everything.

I wanted to run for miles. To push my fae affinities to the test and see how powerful Erebus's daughter could be. I wanted to race back to the dungeons and resurrect Silas just so I could torture and kill him all over again.

"I feel it too, love." Zaeth threw his head back with a groan. "Gods, it feels incredible."

Heat flooded through me at the sound of his desire spiraling out of control. Without another thought, I launched myself at him.

Zaeth barely managed to avoid my fists, his body reacting as if on instinct. He growled in warning, and I snarled back, the primal part of us taking over. I was dark fae. I was the daughter of the God of Night, half of the Dark Phoenix. My mate needed to be able to withstand all of me. Every debauched thought, each immoral impulse.

Zaeth chuckled as I lashed out. "Do your worst, love. I want all of you. Every broken, corrupt little piece. You are *mine*. From now until the end of days and even then, I won't let you go."

With a challenging smirk that did wicked things to my body, Zaeth launched himself into the air.

I forced my own violet wings to beat, my coordination far less fluid than Zaeth's, but the uncertainty faded away as I gave into the thrill of power humming through me.

The two of us hovered in the cold night air with nothing but the moon and stars above. Nothing but freedom.

"You promised me a night to remember once I could fly."

"Do you think your wings can hold?" Zaeth's pupils dilated, looking as if he wanted to devour me.

"There's one way to find out," I taunted as his nostrils flared, no doubt scenting my desire.

He flew forward before I finished speaking, my back pressed against his chest as he yanked my neck to the side.

There was no hesitation, no gentle preparation.

Zaeth sang his fangs into my neck with a savageness that had my body shuddering. He sucked as his other hand stroke the soft feathers just beside my shoulder blade. My body ignited, waves of pleasure rocking through me—climbing higher—as his fae affinities linked with mine.

Just when I was on the edge of euphoria, Zaeth's hand was there, working the button of my pants free. The pads of his fingers trailed lower, teasing and taunting as I writhed against him.

"Gods, Zaeth," I breathed, rocking my hips against his fingers, begging for more. For the release he held just out of reach.

I arched my back, slipping my hand between us as I grasped the hard length pressing against my ass.

He gasped as I freed him, wrapping my fingers around his cock and matching my strokes to his. I was so close—the tension coiling tighter and tighter. I sent each pulse of want he created back toward him, demanding he feel every second of the tantalizing torture he forced me to endure.

A wild growl reverberated through him as I squeezed tighter, my body clenching around his fingers as he pumped.

Yes, I thought, knowing he could feel everything. *Take me.*

Zaeth gripped my hips, yanking my pants down. Cool night air caressed my skin, but I lifted my ass, knowing what we needed. I was too lost in pleasure to keep flying, my violet wings fluttering but doing nothing to keep us aloft.

Zaeth's ebony wings beat the air in great strokes as I worked the rest of my legs free. One of his palms pressed against the small of my back, bending me over as his other looped around my waist, holing me aloft as he lined himself up.

"Mine," he promised as he thrust into me with one powerful stroke.

"Yes," I panted, loving the painful stretch as he filled me. My body clenched around him, the two of us spurring the other on. Each thrust sent waves of ecstasy through our bodies, rippling down the bond at a punishing pace. Until we both exploded.

Zaeth groaned as he pumped, emptying himself inside me as my body hummed with the force of our combined bliss. Gods, did he know how to make every inch of me feel alive.

It wasn't until we'd showered and were lying entwined in each other's arm between pillows and soft sheets did I wonder where that burst of power had come from.

37

GREER

We walked through the skeleton of the dragon and down into the earth for nearly an hour before we reached the heart of the Fire Kingdom. I removed my coat and gloves as we descended, the temperature steadily growing warmer until the worn dirt path opened into what could only be described as gardens.

"Whoa," I said, staring out at the valley before us. A river of fire snaked along the outskirts. I would have thought it inhabitable, but there were red poppies with black leaves growing along the winding banks, stretching across clumps of volcanic ash and porous stone. Sharp spire buildings with gothic arches reached high in the underground cavern, their tips still miles below the earth's edge.

Fires were everywhere, their flames and the slowly moving lava creating a sauna that was nearly unbearable.

"How long are we expected to stay down here?" I asked, shooting a worried glance toward Ryuu. He may have been part dragon, but I most certainly was not. Jarek's damp brow and cautious glance toward Evander told me he was thinking the same thing.

"Opps," Cyra called, flitting back toward us and extending a small bag secured on a twine necklace. "I forgot."

"Thanks," I said, lifting a brow as I took the necklace. "It's not really my style, but I appreciate the gesture."

"It's to help regulate your temperature." Cyra laughed, her bronze eyes gleaming. She squeezed the sack until there was a loud pop before draping it around my neck. Cold blossomed across my chest as it settled between my breasts right over the dragon pendant. "Water is held in a small bubble surrounded by crystals of ammonium nitrate. When the two interact, ice forms, or nearly forms. As you can see, the cooling effect of the process serves our guests quite well."

"Gods, that feels incredible," Jarek muttered, trailing the necklace across his brow and down the sides of his cheeks. "Can I have a spare one in case this one wears out?"

Cyra grinned again but extended us each an extra three necklaces. Ryuu declined, and I noticed the vertical slits of the dragon within staring at the kingdom before us. He was relishing this atmosphere, noting the arching bridge connecting our path to what had to be the Fire Palace.

The pointed arches were framed by extensive designs carved into pale stone and filled with large stained glass windows creating colorful depictions of lovers.

A tall fae with long black hair and light skin exited the building, his red robes flowing out around him to expose his sculpted chest. Loose black pants hung low on his hips and, if the two women half-dressed and chasing after him were any indication, he'd just left something very intimate.

"When I didn't hear the sound of bodies screaming as they splashed into the river of magma, I knew Cyra must have found a friend." The fae's golden eyes were fixed on Evander, the same shade as the gilded crown on his head.

"It is good to see you again, King Dante," Evander bowed.

"It's been too long, Evander," King Dante said, searching his face. "I trust all is well?"

Evander tensed, a lie poised on his lips, but he shook his head at the last moment. "No, actually."

The Fire King nodded, staring at Evander for a moment longer before acknowledging Jarek, Ryuu and I for the first time. King Dante visibly stiffened as he met Ryuu's dragon gaze.

"Prince Ryuu. This is a surprise. I can see we have matters to discuss." King Dante glanced toward Evander once more, his brows pinched in worry for a beat longer before he turned toward the palace. "Cyra, prepare the war room for us."

"The war room is currently occupied, Your Grace," Cyra said, tilting her head toward the two waiting women. "As you are aware."

"Right." The Fire King cleared his throat as Evander raised a brow in his direction. "The banquet hall, then. I'm famished."

I watched as the king tore into a chicken leg, the juice dripping down his perfectly pointed chin. It was unrefined and a little gross, but Evander didn't seem to mind. I finished off the rest of the food, feeling decidedly better with a full belly.

Cyra had cleared the banquet hall for us, the spacious room surrounded by high-arched windows and two long tables. A meal heavy in meat and wine was offered to us and the half-a-dozen other fire fae who'd been welcomed to join. Based on the uniforms, they were most likely guards or perhaps even generals. They helped themselves to the feast, ripping through roasted birds and seasoned slabs while gorging themselves on drink—all except Cyra.

Evander sat at King Dante's side with Cyra on the other, her bronze eyes missing nothing.

"Last time I saw Evander was nearly eight years ago," King

Dante said, swallowing a large gulp of spiced red wine. "He was fearless."

"Fearless?" I asked, eyes narrowing on my would-be brother a few seats down. "Evander?"

Evander's cheeks blazed, but King Dante shook his head as if Evander being anything other was ridiculous.

"He joined us during our Litha celebrations, the long sunny days allowing most of my court time above ground. Without any hesitation, Evander walked right up to me and demanded he be allowed to participate in the games."

Jarek shifted, his light blue eyes bouncing between Evander and the king. There was a distance between the two of them I hadn't noticed before. I knew Evander was dealing with a lot with losing Jem all over again, but I hadn't realized how detached he'd grown from everyone—especially Jarek.

The two of them had become close this last year. They weren't overtly affectionate in public, but they were always near one another. This display was all wrong.

Evander had taken a seat next to the king—one across from Jarek—and hadn't done anything to deflect King Dante's attention.

Servants made rounds through the banquet hall, swiping away dishes and depositing shallow bowls with warm cloths. The Fire King washed and dried his hands, flashing a smile down at Evander as he rested his palm on his thigh.

My eyes widened as Evander leaned into the touch. I knew Jarek hadn't insisted on anything exclusive. In fact, the two of them were open to exploring things with others. But always together. And what Evander was doing most certainly had not been discussed with Jarek previously.

"I don't know much about the Fire Kingdom's games, but I can imagine they were challenging." Jarek's tone was forced politeness as he crafted a hollow smile, but his gaze bored into King Dante. "Please, share the details."

The king laughed, the fire in his eyes smoldering as he looked back at Evander. "There are many aspects to the celebrations. Sparring with fire fae in shifted form, charming a dragon long enough to place a feather in her nest, even free falling toward the River of Fire. And then there are the parties afterward that require their own type of courage." The king's hand drifted up, the not-so-subtle movement drawing Jarek's attention. "Evander never came across a challenge he couldn't tackle."

"I required your help on more than one occasion," Evander grinned. It was genuine, the smile he offered—hollow, but still given freely.

Jarek noticed, too. "That sounds dangerous."

"It was," King Dante laughed. "All the best things are. Always on the edge of annihilation—there's not a better way to live."

I opened my mouth to interjection, but Ryuu grasped my hand, the gentle squeeze a reminder to keep my opinion to myself.

Okay, okay, I squeezed back. Overprotective dragon.

"Risking death *would* remind you your heart is still beating," agreed Jarek with a particularly long swig of his wine. "Nearly eight years since Evander has been here, you said Would that be right after the storm?"

"It was," answered King Dante with a far off look on his face. "So much uncertainty at that time. Each day could have been our last."

"And that's a good thing to you?" I asked, ignoring Ryuu's nudge. "As in, you enjoy danger, the possibility of death, even?"

"We do," the Fire King nodded. "There are subtle changes in the earth that suggest such a time is coming, again."

"That day is already upon us," I countered.

A few of the men looked up with narrowed eyes, wine goblets still clasped in their hands, but Cyra's bronze gaze was locked with mine.

"Please," she said. "Continue."

With a deep breath, I explained. "Levana has broken the wards protecting our world. More of her creatures are spilling through it each day."

The king took his time chewing, his golden eyes turning to Evander. "This isn't a trip of pleasure, then?"

I felt Jarek stiffen beside me, his grip in the wine goblet tightening the longer Evander took to answer.

"No," Evander finally said, pointedly avoiding Jarek's gaze. "We seek your aid against the enchantress, Levana."

"Enchantress." King Dante mulled over the word. "Rumor has it, she's a goddess, the *rightful* goddess of Pax. There are whispers claiming that it is *her* darkness—not Erebus's—that spawned the fae."

"Among other creations," Cyra added, her gaze sharp as a hawk's.

Ryuu stilled, his skin increasing in temperature as the green flecks of his eyes sparked with the unspoken challenge hovering in the air.

My Dragon Prince had immense power, I could craft a shield in seconds, Jarek could lux all of us to safety in a flash, and Evander... well, he would just have to hang on. So, there was no reason to feel threatened when we held all the cards.

I placed my hand on Ryuu's thigh with a smile, reminding him we wanted to try to charm the fire fae first.

"We've heard that theory, as well," Evander replied formally, setting his wine down. "Creator or not, she means to destroy us."

"To make way for her other creations," one of the guards added. I assumed the shiny badge on his chest of batwings and flames marked him as someone important in the army, maybe a general.

"Does the reason matter?" I asked, focusing my attention on King Dante. "She's plotted for thousands of years and sacrificed countless lives to earn her release."

"Why was she imprisoned in the first place?" King Dante asked. "Because her sister born of light thought her shadows were too dark? To corrupting? Tell me, Daughter of Light, mate of Prince Ryuu, who decides which beings get to live?"

"This isn't the same as your situation," Evander said, cutting through the conversation and earning a glare from King Dante. His voice lowered, growing softer as if speaking to someone far closer than a friend. "You know my views on kingdom elitism. I support you and your people, Dante. Levana doesn't simply wish to bring her creatures over. She means to destroy *everyone*."

"How do you know?" the general asked.

"She possessed my sister." I lifted my chin as my declaration rang through the hall, all eyes turning to me. "Levana may have been a victim once, but she has no compassion. No sympathy for any living creatures—her own creations included. She's sent thousands of Fractured to die under Veles's command, her black army murdering plenty of fae, dark and otherwise, in her quest for freedom."

After another moment, Cyra turned from me to face the king. "There *have* been fatalities in every kingdom. If this were about breaking the chains of oppression, would she not have spared her dark children?"

"What of the creatures who have already crossed?" The general asked. "Are they not innocent?"

"Our aim is to stop Levana before Pax is destroyed," Ryuu said, the accent of his dragon bleeding through. "Those who have aligned with her decided their fate."

"And if they don't fight with her?" King Dante asked, his golden eyes hard.

Ryuu shrugged as if it were of no consequence. "All other matters can wait."

I lifted a brow in his direction, feeling his brush of reassurance through the bond despite his mask of control. The creatures from the otherworld may not be our priority right now, but that didn't mean they'd be allowed to kill freely across the seven kingdoms. Still... I guess we needed to take this one step at a time.

"Come now, Fire King," Evander purred, his playful tone not unnoticed. "You've faced monsters of flame and ash. Would squaring off with a Goddess of Shadows not be the battle of a lifetime?"

Murmuring broke out among the guards at Evander's challenge, but King Dante turned to Cyra with a somber expression.

"I believe they're correct, Your Highness." Cyra gestured toward us. "If Levana meant only to gain her freedom, she has done that. It's not my place to decide if her vengeance is justified, but the death of thousands of children across Pax suggests no price is too great for her. Siding with her is a risk we cannot take."

The room seemed to hold its breath as King Dante considered her input.

"We cannot risk losing any more fae children." He looked between Jarek and Evander, his gaze passing over me to settle on Ryuu. "The Fire Kingdom's Dragon Warriors will join you, Prince Ryuu."

Ryuu inclined his head in respect, accepting his pledge before the Fire King pushed back from the table and addressed his men with his glass raised. "And I can think of no greater challenge than going to war with a goddess."

The generals cheered, throwing back their own goblets and glasses.

"Dragon warriors?" I asked, looking to the fire fae slamming empty glasses on the table.

All of them grinned.

"Now, that business is settled, we can get back to the evening," King Dante said with a wicked grin as he extended a hand toward Evander. "Please, join me."

Evander hesitated, his auburn gaze—finally—sweeping toward Jarek, who had just pushed from the table.

"Lead the way, King Dante," Jarek said, flashing a dazzling smile that had the king lifting an intrigued brow. "I've heard fire fae know how to have a good time."

38

GREER

STRINGED INSTRUMENTS BLENDED WITH BOISTEROUS DRUMS AS fae danced around the giant flames positioned in the center of the palace grounds. The red poppies blooming on blacken ground thrived in the heat, some daring to grow right alongside the fire pit. Spiced wine flowed freely, and everywhere I looked fae shifted into their flight forms.

Where air fae's wings were a constant part of themselves, fire fae were able to call upon their wings at will—similar to how my sister's wings worked. But that's where the similarities ended.

"It's incredible, isn't it?" Ryuu asked, his arm around my shoulder as we leaned against a stone bench. He tilted his wine goblet back savoring the rich flavor as we took in our surroundings. "They look so similar to dragon wings."

I nodded as I drank from my own newly filled goblet, feeling the effects of the alcohol already. Cyra had been right when she warned it was strong. "But theirs appear leathery, while yours have a golden shimmer to them."

"True," he signed, those vertical-slit eyes meeting mine. "Some believe thousands of years ago, when fae dragons flew through the skies in abundance, our kind were once the same. Even before the Merged. Soaring over endless oceans used to be nothing but an adventure. Some believe dragons may have flow across the seas, appearing on the far side of the world."

Taking another sip, I studied the fire fae, watching how they moved. The king was sandwiched between Jarek and Evander, the three of them writhing to the beat of the music. The generals who'd joined us for dinner were lost to their own partners, flexing their bat-like wings, launching into the air at random intervals in some type of competition. Bodies were everywhere, women and men filling every bit of space as the drums beat.

Jarek moved Evander's hands from the king's waist down, guiding him lower as King Dante's head fell back with a moan on his lips. His leathery wings expanded, the back of them pressed against Evander's chest, the light from the fire highlighting dark red hues within.

"Maybe the stories are right," I considered, taking another sip of my wine. It tasted like sweet berries and warm spices. "Do any of them have family that have dragons like you?"

Ryuu shook his head, averting his gaze from where King Dante had dropped to his knees in front of Jarek. At some point, Jarek had pushed his pants down, his tanned ass on full display. Jarek fisted his hand in the king's dark hair, slamming his cock into his mouth before pulling the king off him. The king's lips were swollen, his cheeks damp with tears from his red-rimmed eyes, but his gaze swam with carnal hunger. Jarek pinched the king's chin between his fingers and whispered something in his ear.

The music was too loud to hear, but it must have been a command, because the next moment Evander was stripping, withdrawing himself as Jarek turned the king, forcing his royal mouth open.

"Oh my gods," I breathed, downing the rest of my wine. "I could've lived my entire life never seeing that much of Evander."

Ryuu's deep chuckled rumbled against me as I buried my face in his chest. "Should we retire to our suite, my darling?"

I peered up at Ryuu with heavy-lidded eyes. The liberating effects of the wine and the deep rumble of his voice had me licking my lips. "I'd like that."

Tucking me close, Ryuu's feathered wings beat, launching us up above the fire and surrounding fae. Cheers sounded from below, urging us on, daring us to go higher, but Ryuu banked right, landing on the upper floors of the palace along the open alcove leading to our room.

It was all sharp points and cutting edges, the room softened only by the large, downy bed in the center and the stained glass above.

"I wish you could unleash your wings," I breathed, tracing my fingers through his feathers and making him shiver. "Show them what true dragon wings look like."

A low growl escaped him as Ryuu's eyes smoldered. "Someday, my darling, when you are seated on the throne, all bowing before you, it will be safe to show the world who I am."

My fingers stilled on the buttons of his tunic, the top three already undone. "You hide your form for me?"

"Yes and no." Ryuu's dragon dragged the tip of his nose up the length of my neck, yanking off the cooling necklace and tugging the strings keeping my dress bound. The fabric along my breasts eased, the rest of the material falling off my shoulders until it pooled at my feet. "Dragons—true fae dragons—have faded into myth. Fae fear what they don't know. You are fae, blessed by the goddess, her chosen cursebreaker, and powerful beyond my kingdom's understanding... but you do not have wings of your own, which is a weakness in the eyes of my people. Once we show them you are strong enough to lead, I will reveal myself."

I focused on undoing the last of his buttons until I pushed the material from his chest. My hands explored the hard planes of his torso, all tapering perfectly into that 'vee' shape I loved so much. As if his body was begging me to continue further south.

"Our wedding is in three days," I said, kneeling before him, unbinding his ties. My silver curls had already adjusted to the heat, tumbling around me like a wild mane, but Ryuu was as pristine as ever. If anything, his dragon seemed to be closer to the surface, his shoulders broader, his thighs thicker. "Would you have me be your queen, then?"

Before he could answer, I drew his length into my mouth, swirling my tongue along his crown. The veins along his neck strained as his back arched, a hiss of pleasure escaping him.

"You are my queen, Greer. You will *always* be my queen." The last 'r' of my name rolled with his accent as I opened my jaw wider. I blinked up at him, taking him deeper as I stared into his eyes. "It is your choice if you wish to be theirs."

Unable to give him an answer, I drew him forward, swallowing around his length until my nose was pressed against his stomach. He groaned, making use of my curls as he guided me up and down, thrusting the length of himself down my throat with growing ruthlessness.

I wasn't sure if I was ready to be queen of a nation right now, but I knew I would gladly spend the rest of my days worshiping my Dragon Prince.

I loosened the muscles around my mouth, my hands gripping the back of Ryuu's thighs as he fucked my face. Tears streaked down my cheeks as I gagged around him, and I swear his dick grew larger.

With a groan, Ryuu yanked on my hair, popping me off of him to look down at me, my chin clasped between his fingers.

"You're so beautiful, my darling." My breasts were heaving as I fought to catch my breath, but my thighs clenched as he praised me. "Now go to the bed and lie down."

Licking the taste of him from my lips, I stood, swaying my ass slowly as I made my way across the room, knowing my leisurely pace would drive him crazy. A low rumble sounded behind me as Ryuu's dragon emerged further, my lips twitching as I reclined on the soft pillows.

The deep green in Ryuu's dragon eyes smoldered as he lingered by the edge of the bed. He had grown taller, the defined muscles spanning his chest and shoulders shifting slightly as he gripped his hard length in his hand and stroked.

"Spread your legs for me, darling."

I let my knees fall open, my breath hitching as his dragon wings snapped wide.

"So wet for me already," Ryuu's dragon rumbled, flitting forward. The bed dipped as his knees pressed my legs further apart, the scent of embers and untamed winds swirling around me.

"You are mine. My mate. My goddess." His mouth closed around my nipple, drawing a moan from my lips as his palm cupped my core.

"I will be the only one to touch you."

His fingers dipped, sliding through my slickness. He pumped once, twice, before his hands were at my knees, pushing them wider as he shifted lower.

"I will be the only one to taste you."

I gasped as he bent, lapping at my entrance with a tongue that seemed impossibly longer, reaching that sensitive spot within as he buried his face between my thighs. Too soon, he pulled away, poising the head of his cock at my entrance.

"The only one to fuck you."

He buried himself with one deep stroke, my body bowing as he split me. I gazed up into vertical slits, carnal desire blazing down at me as he slowed, allowing me a few moments to adjust to his size.

I'd had Ryuu before, even pieces of his dragon, but it was

clear Ryuu had always remained in control. This time was different.

He must have seen doubt flash through my gaze, because he shifted his weight onto one hand, tilting my chin up with the other.

"You can take me, darling. You were made for me."

Ryuu's dragon captured my lips with his as his pace increased, the gasp tearing from my lips shifting into a guttural moan as our bodies synced.

His mouth was everywhere, nipping my bottom lip, trailing kissing and tender bites along my neck. Everywhere he touched was on fire, my body humming from the inside out as he wound me tighter and tighter, taking me to the edge but never letting me fall.

"Ryuu," I panted, my nails digging into his back as he wound me up for the third time. Everything was heightened, pulsing with a need just out of reach.

"Beg me," Ryuu's dragon purred as he leaned back, careful to keep the same pace. To keep me teetering on the edge of oblivion. He watched as I writhed under his touch, loving the needy sounds spilling from my lips. "I want to hear how that pretty mouth of yours sounds when you're desperate for me."

"Please," I whimpered, bucking my hips as his fingers teased my clit. "I need you."

My hand came to my breast, only just brushing my nipple before it was pinned above my head. A protest was poised on the tip of my tongue, but then Ryuu's dragon was moving, every stroke hitting the sensitive spot within.

My chest heaved as my body tensed, fearful that he'd stop again.

"Come for me, darling."

His skilled fingers stroked my clit, sending me soaring into the beyond. Electricity raced through my body, every nerve ending on fire with pure ecstasy as I convulsed around him, feeling his body shudder in time with mine.

When I finally blinked my eyes open, it was to a warm towel between my thighs, cleaning me before he tucked in beside me and pulled me close. I noticed his claws had retracted, my mate shifting back into his normal glorious self, as his arm came around my middle. I allowed my eyes to close, listening to the sounds of our hearts beatings, the feel of his chest against my back.

"I love you, Greer."

My lips twitched at his accent, knowing that I'd never get sick of hearing it. "I love you too, my Dragon Prince."

39

ELARA

"We were wrong," I said as Naz paced the length of the dark war room. "Silas confirmed Levana means this to be a coordinated attack."

"Which explains why she's pursuing Veles and the Fractured," Zaeth added, his eyes tracking his sister. "There will be no battles in this war. No second or third chances to regroup and strategize. Levana means to obliterate all the seven kingdoms at once."

"Even if Caligo survives the first wave, we'll be surrounded before the battle is over," breathed Naz, her boots clacking across the obsidian floor of the war room as she processed everything. She stopped, her eyes going wide. "But she won't attack *all* kingdoms."

My brows furrowed, understanding dawning a moment later. "Not those who've aligned themselves with her."

Zaeth shook his head. "Even the Light Kingdom are enemies now, what with Veles on the run."

"Are they, though?" I countered. "Vesna was clearly loyal to him, but there were light fae in the Shadowlands."

"True," Zaeth said. "It's a stretch, but that could be one less area to defend against."

"One more point of entry for her army, as well," Naz countered.

"Any word on Lannie from the Earth Kingdom or Greer from the Fire?" I asked, meeting Naz's dark gaze. She shook her head.

"I haven't had time, what with scouting the Shadowlands."

"How has that been going?" Zaeth asked. "Any casualties?"

"No," Naz answered, finally taking a seat across from us. "We've kept to the shadows and are always down wind. Levana's winged fae are still eating members of her army. So often, in fact, that she's recently separated them from the rest. They grow more agitated by the day, and with Silas gone, there's a struggle for power."

"Good," Zaeth said. "A squabbling army won't attack, and we need as much time as we can get."

Naz nodded. "The shadow wraiths have formed their own group, the goblins and the cú sídhe, as well. They only listen to Levana's commands, despite the light fae attempting to assert dominance. The ice wyvern keeps to herself in the thickest part of the silver-blue mist. I can't be sure, but I think another might have joined her."

"And Veles?" I asked, addressing the hovering question in the room. We all wanted to see him pay for his crimes, to witness his suffering, but his death would seal our own.

"No sign of him," Naz said.

"How is that possible?" I asked. "He has thousands of Fractured with him."

"Fractured who are controlled by him," Zaeth said. "Governed by his will completely. Without hunger or rest required, he could command them to transport him in his sleep."

"Surely, Levana would've found them by now," I said, not understanding how Veles escaped.

"I would've seen her return," Naz said, shaking her head. "She searches still."

"But she's a goddess, one of the goddesses who helped create this land."

"Create, yes," Zaeth said, and I could practically see the wheels turning in his mind. "But she's been caged for thousands and thousands of years. Much has changed since the start. Pax—the earth—it's been shaped by storms and volcanoes, by water and rains and fae. Think of how different it must appear to her. Consider all the roads and passages she's unaware of."

"You think Veles knew an escape route?"

"His army has been roaming the countryside for nearly eight years." Naz tilted her head. "It's not impossible. I'll shift gears and see if we can find anything in the west, but I don't want to risk encountering Levana."

"Agreed," Zaeth said, considering the situation. "Inquiries only. I don't want anyone near the Jagged Mountains while Levana is poking around—not even you, Naz."

She lifted a brow at him but nodded. "I'll update the army and send word to our outposts to prepare. Everything will be reconfigured, but we need to know where the rest of the kingdoms stand."

"We need to know who we can trust."

I looked between the two of them, knowing they felt the weight of our decisions just as strongly as I did. One wrong move, and we were done for. My sisters and their mates, Alarik and the Select Guard, and all the people like Liam, Lucy, and their young daughter. Humans and fae. Old and so very young. It all could be gone in a moment.

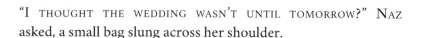

"I THOUGHT THE WEDDING WASN'T UNTIL TOMORROW?" NAZ asked, a small bag slung across her shoulder.

"That's right," I said, finishing gathering my own things. "The ceremony is at dawn. Zaeth and I thought this would give us a chance to catch up with my sisters."

She held her palms out for Zaeth and I to take, a yawn escaping her.

"Everything okay?" Zaeth asked.

She huffed a forced laugh, the sound one of exhaustion rather than any actual amusement. "Just peachy, brother. I've distributed all updated information. Soter is seeing that the adjustments are made."

I liked how transparent the Dark Kingdom was with its people. They trusted their citizens and their warriors to handle information. Nothing was withheld.

"Let's go," Naz said, reaching for us once more. "I'll need to check in with Soter after we discuss matters with your sisters."

Shadows folded around us, opening to reveal burnt-sienna rock walls and large windows open to the starry night sky beyond.

"Oh, good," Greer's voice reached me, causing me to turn toward the sound of eight heartbeats. "You're here."

I was surprised to find everyone surrounding a large table with a map strung across. Greer and Ryuu were at the center, the Air Prince's gaze still focusing on a point on the map. Lannie and Queen Halcyon stood near the head of the table behind Queen Freya and Alarik. The Wild Queen was hunched forward, clearly having been in the middle of describing something. Evander and Jarek were on the other side of Greer, both with grim expressions across their faces.

"They were just discussing the Water Kingdom's betrayal and attempts on their lives," Greer said, causing Queen Halcyon to stiffen.

"It wasn't the entire Water Kingdom," Lannie countered. "The queen covered for us."

"*The queen* clearly knew she was outmatched and didn't want us to kill her," Queen Freya countered.

"That's not true, Freya." Queen Halcyon met the Wild Queen's glare without flinching. "She could've killed you a dozen times before the portal was finished. She didn't."

"She didn't help us, either," Alarik said, coming to Queen Freya's defense.

Queen Freya nodded, sliding closer to him. I doubted she even knew she did it, but it was clear her trust in Alarik was quickly growing to rival the level of faith she placed in the Earth Queen.

"If she had, the king would've killed her," Lannie said. "I was looking right at her, and she lied for us. She said there was no way to reach us through Halcyon's shield, but water could easily have slipped through and finished us off."

Halcyon.

It seemed Alarik wasn't the only one growing more comfortable around a queen.

"Say the Water Queen is with you," I interrupted, joining the center of the table with Zaeth and Naz at my back. "You said yourself the king could kill her. Even if Queen Isla was on your side, you still have no real power with her backing."

Lannie frowned, her gaze drifting to Queen Halcyon, but neither argued.

"So, the Water Kingdom is out," Naz said. "Meaning it's one less area to protect but it can also be a weak point in our defenses."

"One less area to protect?" Ryuu asked, his gaze darting between Naz and Zaeth. "I thought all troops were to gather around Caligo."

"Silas thought differently," I said. "And he wasn't in a position to lie."

"Silas, as in the asshole who allowed Blackwell to abuse

women?" Greer asked, an angry growl rasping beneath her words.

"Yes. He's dead."

"Good," Greer breathed, looking like she needed a bit of good news. "Any word on Veles?"

I shook my head, turning my gaze toward Evander. The dark shadows under his eyes had lessened and there was a small amount of color returned to his cheeks despite the chill of winter.

"What about the Fire Kingdom?"

Jarek and Evander shared a glance, both deferring to Ryuu.

"They've joined us," Greer answered as Ryuu opened his mouth to speak. "Bat-like wings and all. They're sort of adrenaline junkies and think this war will be the ultimate rush, but at least we've got their army. Well, the Dragon Prince does."

Ryuu opened his mouth once more, but Greer pressed on, oblivious.

"Though I guess I have their army, too, in just a few hours. Isn't that right, husband?"

My lips twitched as Ryuu nodded. "Right, indeed, wife."

"Meaning," Zaeth said, finger sweeping across the map, "that the north is secure except for the Shadowlands."

"Good," Naz breathed. "We need to keep them away from the Wild Kingdom at all costs."

"The mist should hold," Queen Freya said. "It extends above and below. Any who try to cross with ill intent will be harmed."

"Harmed," Lannie repeated, her dark eyes swirling with thoughts. "But not killed. Could it be overwhelmed?"

Queen Freya shook her head. "It's an ancient power, one tied to Pax."

"But if Pax were changed?" Lannie said. "If this land was shifting to reflect a new era, the mist would have to reflect that change."

Queen Freya shook her head. "The only other way to manipulate the essence of Pax would be if the creatures from the otherworld outnumbered us."

"Or if their dark powers gifted from Levana diluted Pax's current system," Lannie murmured, more to herself than to us as her mind worked. "Essentially altering Pax's core chemistry."

"Let's hope it holds," Zaeth said. I didn't like the main point of our battle strategy resting on hope, but there was no way around it. Either the mist would hold, or it wouldn't. The best thing we could do now was plan for war.

"Queen Halcyon, can we count on the Earth Kingdom to protect the Wild Kingdom's southern border?"

She nodded in my direction. "Yes, though the number of warriors we can spare depends on how the sleeping sickness progresses."

"Fair enough," Zaeth said. "Likewise, the Air, Dark, and Fire Kingdoms will need to defend against the Shadowlands but also possible attacks from the Light Kingdom."

"It's unlikely Levana will expend much of her forces in the Fire Kingdom," Naz added, going to Zaeth's side to stare at the map. "Only Fire Fae can survive temperatures underground for an extended period, and there isn't much of an army above. She could make a ploy for the Earth Kingdom, though being underground does have its advantages there as well." Naz's dark eyes landed on Queen Halcyon. "Are you able to seal off all entrances?"

Queen Halcyon shook her head. "I can close some, but there are hundreds of tunnels connecting to my kingdom, some of which are still unknown. We're constantly finding new paths."

Naz frowned. "We could try to relocate some of your people to the Wild Kingdom…"

"No," Queen Halcyon countered. "We still have the strongest chance of defending our city below ground. At least some of Levana's creatures will be hesitant to delve beneath the earth, and others will be weakened by it."

"We'll need to send scouts to the Borderlands," Alarik said, his voice measured. "It's little more than rubble, but we need to make sure Veles or Levana aren't hiding troops there waiting to pounce."

"Agreed."

The eight of us stared at the map, gazing at all the unknowns. We could prepare for an army, could scout and plan like we would for any battle, but none of us had gone to war against a goddess before.

Veles was a good distraction. A vital one, at this point. But what happened when Levana grew tired of waiting? How long would we last if she decided to try her chances against us without the Fractured?

Looking down at the wash of gaps between our defensives, I prayed we'd never find out.

40

GREER

The world was ending. At least, that's what I'd gotten from our little discussion late last night. We were surrounded, a rampaging goddess was stationed in the northern Dark Kingdom, and the wards surrounding our realm were quite literally cracked.

Gods, we were so fucked.

"You look beautiful," Jarek said, adding another pin to the braids looping my hair back.

I'd decided on the gold lacy dress, the one with yards and yards of fabric that had once looked like it would swallow me whole. Now, the lace was redesigned, sown and draped across the back of my gown to give the appearance of gilded wings. The silk paneling beneath remained, except for the added slit up to my waist along my left thigh to showcase my dragon brand. Because I was me, I also had the neckline lowered, my sapphire dragon pendant now visible.

"Despite the fact that I'm supposed to be sleeping this early in the morning, I do think it turned our nicely." I grinned at Jarek in the mirror, finding my sisters' face just behind him. "I know this isn't exactly good timing for a wedding, but if we are this close to fighting for our lives, I'm glad we get one more day together."

Lannie nodded, her gaze growing distant. "One more day of fun."

"Stop it," El chided. "The both of you. We're going to win this."

"How?" Lannie asked, shaking her head.

"I want to believe the best, too, El," I said. "But I can't see a way out of this. Maybe if we could restore the wards around Pax, we'd at least have a chance. I tried, you know. I'd hoped we'd be able to share power through our sister bond, but even that didn't work."

El blinked, her mouth opening like I'd just slapped her.

"Wait," Lannie said, her gaze narrowing. "You shared your power with us?"

"I tried, but nothing happened."

"Something happened," Jarek corrected. "You were drained, and right as we entered the Fire Kingdom, too."

El gasped as Lannie stared, her eyes wide. "That was you?"

"You felt it?" I asked, inhaling sharply. "Were you able to construct a ward?"

"No wards," Lannie said. "Halcyon and I were linked at the time it hit. It sort of spiraled through me into both of us and heightened her affinities. Actually, I need to speak with both of you about what we found but didn't want to take the attention away from your big day—"

"What about you, El?" I cut in, needing to know if we had a chance. If El could construct wards, she might be powerful enough to fix the rift.

El shook her head, her cheeks pinking. "I felt your power. It amplified my own, but it didn't gift any of your affinities."

"You thought they'd be able to generate wards like you?" Jarek asked.

"Yep," I sighed, feeling the barb of failure prick. "I'm not strong enough to seal the fissure between the otherworld and Pax, but I thought it was worth a try to see if one of them could."

"Our own affinities were magnified by you," Lannie said, expectation growing in her voice. "What we need to do is feed *our* power into *you*."

My gaze swung to Elara, mind whirling with the possibilities. "I don't know if I could contain that much power."

"It would be a lot..." Lannie breathed, her mind working through possibilities. "But what if the energy transfer was more of a flow than an exchange."

"That would fix the little issue of me combusting, but how would that be possible?"

Lannie's gaze swept from my sister and I, hovering a beat longer on Jarek. "Halcyon and I were waiting until after the wedding to say anything, especially because we still don't know what it means. It could be nothing. Then again, it could be everything—"

"Lannie," El cut in gently. "It's just us."

"And Jarek," I added.

"Thanks for that," he mumbled. "I can leave if you want—"

"No," Lannie said, exacerbated. "It's nothing like that. Just—we found a tomb."

"Okay..." I said after a few seconds had gone by in silence. "Was there something off about the tomb?"

"Yes, but I'm not sure what." Lannie let out a long breath. "My point is, when I connected with Halcyon, I felt the exchange of power with Pax itself. It was more like a river than a flame, the waters something we could access when needed, but never overwhelming."

"You want Halcyon to help in this?" Jarek asked, uncertainty pitching his tone.

"Yes," I answered for Lannie, my mind catching up to hers. "Halcyon could help ground Lannie, and therefore ground all three of us. And El, you're scary powerful. You could be the force that drives this while I construct."

El's lips pressed thin, but it was Jarek who gave voice to her fears.

"You'll need Zaeth, kitten." Her hazel-blue eyes glanced up, meeting his storm blue ones. "If not for power, then to remind you of who you are when the blood haze starts to take over."

"If you two get your mates there, I want mine, too," I grinned.

"I think you'll need him," Lannie said, and I could see the final pieces of the puzzle lock together. "You'll need a guiding tool for that type of power."

"Like a talisman?" El asked.

"Like a spear," Jarek breathed, eyes side. "Gods. This could really work."

My stomach flipped as I turned toward the door.

"Where are you going?" Jarek called as I reached for the handle. "You can't mean to test out our theory *now*. You're getting married."

"It's more a formality than anything," I said, trying to step around him.

"I mean, she is already mated," Lannie added.

"Exactly," I breathed, my hands coming to my hips as Jarek blocked me again.

"No, he's right," El said. I lifted a brow in her direction, waiting for her to continue. "We need the Air Kingdom's backing to defeat Levana and that will only happen once you are queen. Even if King Dragcor agreed to aid us, the warriors wouldn't follow without your marriage, mated or otherwise," she added with a glance toward Lannie who'd been about to speak.

"Okay," I said, deflating. The truth was, I was more nervous for this ceremony than I'd thought I would be. "Wedding first, then we'll convince our mates to help us repair the wards of the world and hopefully not die in the process."

A knock sounded from the other side of the door.

"I'm not expecting anyone," I breathed.

Jarek cocked his head to the side as if telling me to hurry up and open it. With only a slight eyeroll, I did, coming face-to-face with King Dragcor.

My sisters and Jarek left as the Air King entered. I plastered something that looked like a smile on my face, the edges only a little strained, and guided us toward the table covered in the rejected gowns. Try as I might, I couldn't hide the fact that King Dragcor appearing at my door moments before my wedding to his one and only son made me uncomfortable.

"Let me just make some space for you," I said, scooping the rejected dresses up and tossing them onto my bed in the other room. "There."

He didn't sit.

My false smile wavered. "What can I do for you, King Dragcor?"

"Ryuu has made it clear this war cannot be avoided, but he has faith the goddess will provide for us, as she has done in the past."

I swallowed, unsure what he wanted me to say, and instead chose to wait for him to continue.

"I would have to see her, but if Levana is who I think, she *is* a goddess. And every bit as powerful as Eunoia—possibly more so."

"Do you know her? I mean, personally?" Because it was starting to sound like he was confessing something.

"I have lived for a very long time. Most of that time, I've

spent alone." Dark eyes with vertical slits speckled with orange embers met my gaze. "Merged do not feel the way humans do."

"I'm not human," I breathed, lifting my chin.

His eyes traveled to the tips of my pointed ears. "No, but you were raised as one. Even fae feel emotions more acutely than Merged do. You must understand, that when years turn into decades and decades into centuries, creatures such as myself seek a reason to continue."

He swallowed as he wings twitched. "At the time, whispers of the dark goddess were enthralling. They were stimulation in an existence that had become stagnant."

"You worshiped her," I whispered as my eyes widened. "That's why you think we are going to lose. You've met her before."

"Not met," King Dragcor shook his head, but there was guilt twisting his features as he spoke. "Not exactly. Before the seven kingdoms were established, this was all one land. One could travel for days, just following the wind to unknown locations. I first stumbled upon her at an oasis. You know it as The Seven Sacred Pools."

"Gods," I breathed, sitting in the chair I'd offered to him. "You really *do* know her."

"Ryuu's mother and I met there. She felt it to... Levana's pull."

My voice turned to steel as I pushed from the chair, holding the Air King's gaze. "Did you help her? With the otherworld, with Veles and his brothers. With the storm. Were you a part of it?"

His eyes widened, sorrow flowing in a moment later. "No, cursebreaker. Though, there are some who would consider my crimes worse."

"Worse than the blood of thousands?"

"She shared her plans. Levana even showed me what our life

would look like ruling over a world uninhibited by fae morals. A life of freedom."

"A life of chaos," I countered.

"Yes." King Dragcor's voice was clear, but I didn't like the hint of longing beneath it. "In the end, I fled."

"You denied Levana?"

"I did, but just barely." A long, weary sigh left the Air King's lips, his gaze swinging toward the still-dark horizon. Dawn was coming, but for now, we were surrounded by the last glimmers of night. "I knew what was to come, and I did nothing. People often think doing nothing is passive. They're wrong. The choice to *not* act is powerful. It can be the difference between life and death."

Dark eyes swirling with brilliant orange embers stared down at me, searching for something. "You love my son."

It wasn't a question, but I answered anyway. "Very much."

"You love his dragon."

"Yes," I breathed, unsure where this was going. King Dragcor knew Levana from a different time, but we were still no closer to defeating her. If he knew of anything that would've helped us, I was sure King Dragcor would've already shared it.

The Air King's brows furrowed as if trying to stare through murky waters to see the pebbled riverbank beneath. "I can sense your love for the people, perhaps indirectly, but it's there. You would make a fair queen, one ruled by compassion."

I swallowed, twisting my fingers. "Thank you—"

"Why do you reject it?" His voice was calm, the question asked without malice, only a resounding uncertainty.

"I'm not rejecting it," I countered, irritation bleeding into my voice as my temper flared. "But I wanted time to live my life before I took on the responsibility of thousands of others. Is that so terrible?"

King Dragcor only stared, his shrewd gaze seeing too much. "He will renounce all that he is for you."

My stomach twisted, because I knew Ryuu would.

"The weight of the crown can be heavy, but who better to bare it than someone who understands the cost?"

I shook my head, holding back the tears that pricked the edges of my eyes. Because I knew he was right. Being queen didn't scare me as it once had. A part of me had a been excited for the future, but the timeline was all off.

"Ryuu feels deeply," King Dragcor said, dragging a finger across the wooden chair. "He has spent a great portion of his life thinking himself unfit to rule, only embracing his past, and therefore his dragon, in the recent months. The concept of being worthy is new to him, but it is something he desires, whether he is ready to admit it or not."

Those ember eyes found mine again, staring straight through me.

"I have a feeling it is something you desire, as well."

I didn't *not* desire it. Ryuu's plans for the wedding and postponing the coronation ran through my mind. We wouldn't have to accept the throne today, and we could probably continue to find ways of avoiding its responsibilities for a while, but to what end?

My fingers grazed over the silky golden fabric of my gown, tracing the slit up my thigh to run along the dragon brand. My brand. My own set of wings.

"What is stopping you from accepting your destiny, cursebreaker?"

Cursebreaker. Not Mate to the Dragon, or sister to the Dark Phoenix. Just Cursebeaker. Just me.

"Nothing."

41

GREER

Evander and I hovered just outside the gilded doors of The Great Library. I'm not sure what I'd been expecting. Maybe a picturesque union atop the cliffs above the clouds, but Cress had made it clear Ryuu and I needed to have the official ceremony in the library, proving our dedication to learning above all else. For air fae, learning meant the ability to grow. Adapt. It signified a resilient leader capable of not only bending but reshaping completely rather than breaking.

"You look beautiful," Evander said, tears welling in his eyes. "Jem would've been crying the moment he saw you."

I snorted a laugh, the sound muffled by the hiccup of emotion clogging my throat.

"They are here with us," he said, rubbing a soothing hand along my shoulder.

"You really think so?" I asked, dabbing away the damp spots at the corners of my eyes. It had taken me *way* too long to look this perfect.

A sad grin tiled Evander's lips, the gold of The Great Library doors set before us highlighting specks of yellow in his auburn gaze. "I know. I've returned from the dead, remember?"

"Half-dead," I corrected, adjusting my dress as I listened to our guests finding their seats. "Lannie can't resurrect people."

"Are you ready?" Cress asked, her heels clicking through the halls. "Everyone is waiting."

I took a shuddering breath, trying and failing to let it out smoothly.

"It's normal to be nervous," Evander said, offering his arm. I took it.

"He's right," Cress said, her long legs and red lips looking stunning in a white silk gown.

All our guests would be in white today, representing the clouds in the sky—all except Ryuu and me who were dressed in gold. We were to be the dawning of a new era, two suns joining as one to illuminate the world around them.

"Cleaver idea with the lace wings, by the way." Cress looked over my dress, everything seeming to meet her standards. "The royals will love it."

"You think?" I asked, wanting them to like me despite myself.

"I'm sure of it," Cress said reaching for the doors. "You've done everything. All that is left is to walk down the aisle toward your prince and bind your souls together before the goddess and all the air court."

"Is that all," I glared, feeling my palms start to sweat.

Cress lifted a perfectly sculpted brow in my direction, waiting for me to get all my nerves out.

"It's not the binding part," I sighed, wanting to wipe my palms but worried I'd ruin my dress. "I've already done that. It's the court aspect. The crown."

Cress's fingers hovered along the golden handles as she held my gaze. "You're the fated mate to the Dragon Prince, sister to the Dark Phoenix, and you have an abundance of power of your own, cursebreaker. You are our queen. Believe it, and they will, too."

"She's right, you know," Evander chimed in with a half smirk.

I shot him an exacerbated glare, some of the fluttering in my stomach quieting, before looking back to Cress. "Thank you, Cress."

"Just do everything right and you won't let me down," she grinned as she pressed the doors open.

With a deep breath, I stepped forward, the dark colors of night lingering a moment longer before the sun crested the horizon. The light of dawn streaked through the windows as I took my first step, landing on my golden dress. The shimmering material illuminated the space around me, making it look like I was walking on sunshine.

Fae were lined on either side of the aisle, their feathered wings dipping as they bowed. Gentle murmurings started, and my chest heaved under their attention—but then I saw Ryuu.

And everything quieted.

He looked glorious. His dark hair had been half bound, showing off his sharp cheekbones and green-flecked eyes. The golden tunic was trimmed perfectly, hugging the planes of his defined chest. The sun was at his back, silhouetting his beautiful white wings and the golden barbs within. Ryuu looked every bit the fae prince he was meant to be.

I practically floated toward him, everyone else in the room fading away. Ryuu's lips stretched into an elated smile, for once, unencumbered with the worries of the world. In this moment, we were simply two fae who loved each other.

Evander slipped my hand into Ryuu's as we reached the dais, the two of us staring into each other's eyes as King Dragcor stood before us.

"Today, we celebrate the binding of two souls, their hearts melding as one under the first light of dawn…"

Are you okay? Ryuu sent a flicker of uncertainty down our bond, the feeling almost clear enough for words.

Yes. The truth of my answer hummed through me, causing his beautiful smile to grow. Gods, he was perfect. My prince. My Dragon King.

King Dragcor had been right. Ryuu would give everything up for me. I felt it each time we touched. He'd shown it countless times in the way he waited for my decision before committing us to something—the throne, the war, this kingdom. Ryuu was my mate in so many ways, had taken care of me without me ever having to ask.

It was finally time for me to take care of him.

"I do," I said, voice ringing clear throughout the room. Excited murmurings from the air fae started, growing louder as Ryuu echoed my answer.

"I proclaim you husband and wife, souls sealed together until the after claims you," King Dragcor's voice rumbled, the scent of embers flaring as his eyes glowed. I could've sworn there was a sheen of tears in them, but then Ryuu's hands were at my jaw, tilting my lips up to his.

The air royals cheered as Ryuu branded himself against my lips before the kingdom.

I was a little breathless by the time we broke, but the shaking of the floor drew my attention. I blinked up, feeling the crisp, cool breeze of winter steel through the room.

"Are they opening the windows?" I asked, drawing closer to Ryuu and the warmth he held.

He chuckled. "They are opening the glass doors for us to take our first flight together. It's tradition."

Glancing around, I met Lannie's small, encouraging smile and El's surprisingly loud calls for us to jump. Her hazel-blue eyes gleamed with love and a slight sheen of tears as she waved.

We'd grown up together, the two of us raising Will and Lannie as partners. Had lied about how much food was left so Lannie and Will wouldn't feel bad about eating their share. We'd grieved together. Had dug graves for our parents and elder brothers.

Gods, did I miss my brothers. My parents.

It was in moments like this, when my soul felt so happy it could burst that the dagger of loss sliced the deepest. My eyes snagged on the hollowed crystal clutched in El's hands, the one containing our little brother's ashes. Waves of sorrow for the past mingled with the joy of the present, the contrasting emotions nearly unbearable in their potency. But I looked to my sisters, feeling their beating, bleeding hearts alongside mine through our bond and knew were going to be okay.

A large gust of cool morning air blew in as the last of the large paneling was lowered, an entire face of The Great Library open to the bright clouds and swirling mists below.

"It is my honor to present your next King and Queen of the Air Kingdom." King Dragcor's voice boomed, and his proclamation was quickly drowned out by the excited cheers of the court —our court.

Ryuu's eyes widened, the pupils shifting into vertical slits as they met my waiting gaze. "I can deny it," Ryuu whispered in my ear. "If this is not what you want—"

"It is," I breathed, a relieved smile breaking across my face. He looked confused. "Sorry to spring it on you, *husband*. Your father only just spoke with me before the ceremony, but I think this is the right step for us."

Ryuu cocked a brow, his hands still gripping mine.

"I want to be queen—your queen and theirs."

A flicker of want hummed down the bond, Ryuu tamping it down a second later as if he were afraid to believe this was really happening.

"Don't," I said, pressing his palm to my chest, to the heart beating below. My pulse was steady. "This isn't something I've been forced into. I want to rule this kingdom with you, Ryuu."

It was a future I'd hardly let myself think of, knowing all that we needed to accomplish to make it even a possibility. But our moment was here, and I wasn't going to keep running from it.

"Goddess above," Ryuu said, gathering me up in a fierce kiss. He pulled away, all too aware of the flush to my cheeks and the rush of heat pooling lower.

"In this life and all others," I breathed, low enough for only him to hear. "We will be."

He led us toward the open expanse of the room, a few of my silver curls stirring in the wind. We turned as our toes hit the edge, standing tall as all those at court bent their knees and bowed. Even Cress poised at the edge of the room, offered me a triumphant smile as she dipped her head.

There was no going back. I was the Air Queen. For better or worse.

With one last smile for my sisters, I took Ryuu's hand in mine and jumped.

42

ELARA

"It could work." Zaeth's cinnamon eyes stared back at me, the intensity in them unnerving. Choosing not to leave the Air Kingdom, we'd met with my sisters, their mates, Freya, and Alarik in Zaeth's rooms. They were just as lavish as Ryuu's were, but distinctly less occupied with wedding gifts. Evander and Jarek had also arrived, meaning we'd caught everyone up on our plans to seal the rifts between Pax and the otherworld.

I could feel Zaeth's hesitation through the bond, but on the surface he looked calm. "Especially if Erebus being your father means more than just his blessing."

"That's still weird," Greer said.

The rest of the room continued talking, our three mates bouncing ideas off each other. Jarek, Evander, Queen Freya, and even Alarik chimed in, as well, each with decidedly different opinions. The only thing they could agree on was that our plan was too risky.

"Tell me about it," I muttered.

"Does that mean she… like…got with a god."

"Greer," chided Lannie as she shook her head. "Do you really want to think of Mother that way?"

"Eww," Greer shot back, looking appalled. "No. I meant it more conceptually. She had to have slept with someone. I just thought it was some random dark fae blessed by Erebus's dark power, but the memory shared with El makes it seem like Erebus *was* the dark fae."

Lannie cocked her head to the side, her gaze sliding from Greer to me. "Meaning Erebus would've had to been on Pax twenty years ago."

"Twenty-one," I corrected.

"And why would he pop on down just to bed Mother," Greer pushed. "Isn't he supposed to love Eunoia? It doesn't make sense."

"You don't think I'm really his daughter?"

Greer's light blue eyes focused on me with a look of incredulousness. "You survived a goddess literally possessing you and then dousing you in flames, El. Power like that has to be more than a blessing."

"Then, what?" I asked.

"Things between Erebus and Eunoia must not have been as perfect as legends convey, but more importantly, Erebus must be here. On Pax." Lannie looked at me, the spark in her eyes burning bright each time she discovered something new. "He must be bound, like Levana was. And if both him and Levana are here..."

"Maybe Eunoia is, too," I finished, realizing what they were getting at. "We need to find them, or we don't have a chance of winning this war. Not really. Even if we could seal the crack Levana punched through our world, she'll just do it again when she's gathered enough strength."

"But if we had actual gods on our side," Greer nodded, "they'd be able to get her out of here."

The room had gone unusually silent, the three of us turning to find everyone staring.

"Have you all finally realized the three of us are more

capable than you gave us credit for?" Greer asked, addressing the crowd.

Sheepish looks flashed in our direction before Alarik cleared his throat. "They do seem to have things figured out."

"Thank you, general." I shot Alarik a grateful smile, happy to have his support without any lingering entanglements.

"I trust you, love." My gaze settled on Zaeth, warmth spreading along our bond. Gods, I didn't deserve him. Zaeth's lips twitched as he felt my flicker of gratitude. "If you say this is how we seal the rift between worlds, then I believe you..."

"*But,*" Greer prompted, hearing the word lodged in Zaeth's throat. And I swear Ryuu almost rolled his eyes.

"*But,*" Ryuu glowered. "We want to ensure your safety."

She flashed him a grin. "You will be. By lending *us*—your beautiful, brilliant, and powerful mates—your unending support. And power. We'll probably need to draw on that, too."

"Actually, we're going to need a lot more than that if I'm correct in how this is going to happen," Lannie said, her gaze flicking to Queen Halcyon. "As the grounding force, I'll need your ability to connect directly to Pax's core."

Queen Halcyon nodded. "Like when we followed the bloodstone."

"Yes," Lannie said, her eyes turning to Zaeth. "El is the power source—or at least the main one. I think we're also going to need her darkness to balance out Greer's overwhelming use of light affinities in patching the wards—because it's not a ward at all. It's a shield; one never meant to be broken."

"A light ward would ultimately need to be recast, or at least strengthened when they started to weaken," Jarek nodded. "But the barriers between realms need to be permanent."

"If I'm right," Lannie started.

"Which you always are," Greer grinned.

"Dark affinities melded with light and forged by a curse-breaker into a net of protection—one that links seamlessly to the edges of the intact barrier—should last. But it will require a great deal of power."

I nodded, knowing I'd have to give myself fully to the darkness in my veins. My stomach fluttered, and I wasn't sure if it was from fear or anticipation.

"I'll be here, love." Zaeth's steadying pulse synced with mine, his presence soothing the cyclone of worries before they could take hold.

"Meaning, all I have to do is construct the impenetrable wards perfectly," Greer finished.

"With Ryuu's help," Lannie added. "Ryuu is the only one we've found who can wield the Spear of Empyrean. Without it, you won't be able to craft the intricate network."

"And we'll just be standing around?" Queen Freya asked, looking decidedly upset at the thought.

"We're going to need protection," I said, conceding that point. "It will fall to you four."

Evander and Jarek shared a look, one of mutual understanding before Evander nodded. "We can do that."

"Okay," Alarik said as Queen Freya narrowed her eyes. "Say we do this and you six are successful as restoring the realm. A force like that will be felt in every corner of Pax."

"Levana will sense it," I breathed, eyes darting to Zaeth. Grim resignation was staring back at me.

"Yes," he acknowledged. "But without breaking the link between our world and Levana's, we've already lost."

"We are not only referring to Levana," Queen Freya persisted, eyes turning to Lannie. "If what you said is true, Erebus and Eunoia could be out there. You three were speaking as if they're on our side, but you forget they're gods—the three of them. How are we to know they won't *support* Levana?"

"They won't," I said with certainty. "She hates them. The entire time she was possessing me, her thoughts were consumed with anger directed toward her sister, but also toward Erebus. I thought it was because he was protecting me, but now I'm wondering if there was something more between them. Either way, she wouldn't align with them."

Queen Freya didn't look convinced.

"A concern for another night," Alarik said, taking her hand. The small gesture drew her attention to him, her eyes finally breaking from mine.

"What about Naz?" I asked, as couples started pairing off, low murmurings of what was to come.

"She and Soter are doing their best to maintain faith, but our troops are rattled." Zaeth drew me near, the scent of cedar and spice its own balm of comfort. "We'll have to do this alone and update them later."

I nodded, knowing every second we wasted more monsters came through. The other couples seemed to have similar thoughts because when I turned back to face them, there was a resonating consensus of our group primed for action.

"We need to be at top strength, and today has been a long day," I said, meeting the eyes of everyone before me. "Tomorrow, we heal the world."

And hopefully don't die in the process.

43

LANNIE

QUEEN FREYA PORTALED US TO A PLATEAUED SUMMIT FAR ENOUGH away from the Air Kingdom's capital of Serene to not be interrupted, but close enough not to alert any of Levana's forces hovering in the north. We weren't sure if her monsters had locations other than the base at the Shadowlands, but we'd all agreed this was a risk we needed to take.

"Places," I said, directing my sisters and their mates.

Halcyon was at my side, her hand firmly clasped in mine. She was generous with sharing her affinities, and I could feel the earth's subtle draw already humming through me. I closed my eyes, feeling the ebb and flow of life.

It was incredible.

Pax was like a body, composed of vast networks of connecting veins and arteries that provided life—essence—to thousands of creatures.

There were pits and patches of corrosion where the Fractured had been, where the ground was forever stained by blood. There was a great cloud of darkness in the north—the Shadowlands—and a pulse of light loaded somewhere in the ocean far into the southeast—the Sea of Dreams and a surprisingly strong one in the heart of the Wild Kingdom. The fine hairs on the back of my neck pricked as I traced the connections, nearly missing the void set in the center of the Earth Kingdom.

Gods, it was huge, a blot on the otherwise pristine capitol... and it was shrouded, as if the shadows were keeping the drain of Pax's power from detection. But the greatest injury was the massive hole punched through the vast shield stretching over our world. Pax was hemorrhaging.

"I'm linked," I breathed, making sure my sisters and their mates were positioned just right. We stood in a triangle with our mates beside us, but all I could focus on was my sisters. The three of us had been through so much and had lost even more. But we were here. We'd kept fighting, despite the hundreds of times when it would've been easier to give up.

"Thank you," I muttered, feeling their flood of understanding meet mine.

"I love you both," Greer whispered.

"We've got this," El said.

"Yes," rumbled Zaeth, his hand firmly in El's. "You do."

With a nod, I stepped forward, my sisters doing the same, as we joined hands. Ryuu raised the Spear, his other hand pressing to the small of Greer's back, as Zaeth and Halcyon shifted their hands to our waists.

I could feel El's affinities build, the darkness swirling higher. It caressed my mind, infiltrating my bones. Gods, it was intoxicating. It felt like power and adrenaline wrapped up with the unwavering knowledge that I could destroyed fae in a blink of an eye. I could shatter bones and tear vessels with hardly a second thought, knowing my dark power would deliver victory on the battlefield.

Wait. Not *my* dark power.

Taking a deep breath and with the help of Halcyon, I pushed my own calming energy out, seeking a balance. It twined with El's, tempering it into something manageable.

Greer tapped into the swirling power, gasping under the force of it.

Millions of particles flared to life before her. She raised her hand, crafting a gleaming blanket of power, until the light particles started pushing back, scattering along the edges.

"Now," Greer breathed, guiding Ryuu's hand and the Spear of Empyrean where she needed them. The golden diamond along the tip of the spear glowed as it bent to Greer's thoughts.

It was working.

Electricity was thick in the air, buzzing all around us and then circling back to the earth. I could feel everything my sisters were feeling. See what they saw. We were ourselves and not. Connected while remaining distinct.

Such power. Unstoppable power.

Shadows spooled around Zaeth and El as she sent wave after wave toward Greer and me. More of her affinities slipped through, causing her thoughts to tangle with mine.

Levana was just the beginning. With power like this, nothing could stand in my way. There would be no need to conceal my true self. No fear of being seen as a monster, one cast down and slaughtered by the very people I was trying to save. I could take anything. Destroy anyone.

I shook my head, focusing on Halcyon's hand on my waist as I forced El's throughs from my mind.

"Zaeth!" I called, glancing to my right to find him gritting his teeth, his great, black wings expanded and glinting with silver barbs.

"I know," he panted, hands tight around my sister.

El's violet wings unfurled, silver barbs slashing against Zaeth's forearms as they did. He grunted against the pain, pushing more of his affinities into El, calling her back to him.

It felt like a flood of warmth after standing in the snow for hours. The first warm ray of sunshine after an endless winter. El gasped, some of the blood haze clearing as her eyes met mine.

I'm here, she said through the bond, the darkness flowing through her but no longer wrestling control of her mind. It felt like a deep ocean directed by the currents, one storm away from everything being blown off course. But El leaned into Zaeth, allowing him to sail the waves of with her.

Halcyon's grip along my hip tightened as her power dug into the earth, bracing for the building transfer of power sure to come from El.

I looked to Greer, the prisms of light already sparking around her, a wide transparent blanket stretching high overhead. She nodded, Ryuu mirroring her as he readied the spear to lift the blanket of light toward the gap.

El met my gaze next, her eyes clear despite the sweat gleaming across her brow. Zaeth's concentration was fixed on her heart, as if ensuring it was untouched by the surge of dark powers.

With a deep breath, El and I turned toward Greer and opened the floodgates.

44

GREER

Gods, this was a lot of power. I felt like I was lightening, a brilliant, charged particle floating through space.

My body hummed as my sisters' full might was unchained— all of it funneled into me. If it hadn't been for Ryuu's arm around my waist, the feel of his warm, broad chest against my back, I may have given into it. To freedom. To the infinite nothingness and life all around me.

As it was, I let myself breathe in his scent, let the mating bond tether me, driving our souls closer together, and channeling the power up.

The net of light I'd crafted ignited, flaring as power was guided through the Spear of Empyrean and up into the atmosphere.

I saw everything. The shield spanning Pax was massive and intricate, a masterpiece of balance and strength. I'd thought I needed to construct a ward, one strong enough to act as a shield, but this was different.

Pax was surrounded by a complicated lattice, like branches braided together and then layered a hundred times. There was flexibility, like the surface of water, but unified into one cohesive swathe of energy.

This was what Will had been maintaining. I could see it in the way the network of light rippled, sense the hint of his essence, long since passed. My little brother had given everything for us. For this world. He'd asked me to stop the brothers, and intern, stop Levana. If we managed this, if my sisters and I truly repaired what had been broken, we'd be one step closer to upholding our oath.

More power siphoned into to me, wrenching a gasp from my lips.

"Focus," Ryuu growled, the spear raised beside me.

"There," I breathed, guiding him through our bond.

The golden tip swirled in the air, like a brilliant wick forging a primal shield. We worked, raising the lattice until the edges brushed the crack in Pax's expansive realm. It was close but I'd missed a few layers.

I pulled energy from my sisters, but where their essence had once been a tidal wave, it felt more like a dwindling stream.

"I need more," I gritted, feeling the strain of wielding the spear through Ryuu.

A heartbeat passed. And then another, but I was unable to check on my sisters, too focused on maintaining the fragile lattice. Once it was complete, it would solidify, but right now, the edges were left open and unanchored.

"El," I breathed as I felt the strain of maintaining such a thing.

A ripple of shadow washed into me, darker than any before. It felt ancient, primal—like a tendril of night itself.

With forced concentration, I directed it through the spear, as I had done to every other spark of essence before. But it didn't follow my command.

Instead, the shadow stretched over the entire framework, seeping into vacancies I hadn't known were there on its own volition. It trickled through hollows and gaps, filling in the imperfections, until every inch was melded with the darkness.

The lattice tugged, the edges brushing the jagged remains of the broken shield left behind from Levana's damage.

Screeching sounded from the other side as my shield started to fuse with the original—Levana's children in the other world.

"Greer," Ryuu called, the spear's tip brightening, burning a hot blue.

"I know," I stammered, the weight of the shield sucking more and more energy from us as the pieces sealed. It was like the tides had turned. Instead of forcing our essence up, the shield was drawing from us, siphoning as it pleased. "But it's working."

Another coil of darkness slithered through me, whisked away by the shield a moment later. The nearest edge blazed and then cooled, the edges whole once more. It rippled outward, the screams of the otherworld creatures deafening as they felt the power shift. The heat bleeding from our world and into theirs pulled away.

"Almost," I panted through clenched teeth.

A massive claw reached through the remaining gap, black talons puncturing the incomplete portion of the shield.

"El," I heard Lannie gasp as our elder sister let out an animalistic snarl, her dark essence coming in a burst a heartbeat later.

It seared through me, into the spear clutched in Ryuu's hand. The spearhead flashed from blue to a scorching white, the golden tip more power than mental. El's shadow essence shot toward the talons invading our world, cauterizing the lattice closed despite the intruder.

A thundering roar was heard for a split-second before the shield sealed completely, the bloody claws falling from the sky to the earth below.

My knees buckled as the bond to my sisters was cut. I felt the Spear of Empyrean thumped to the earth beside me, Ryuu's hunched form following a moment later. His chest heaved in time with mine, both our brows damp and our affinities spent, but the shield protecting Pax from the otherworld had been reforged.

We'd done it.

A disbelieving smile broke across my face. Brushing silver curls away from my eyes, I glanced up, seeking my sisters' faces.

Horror shot down my spine as El came into focus, her back was arched as a twisted smile played across her lips. Zaeth was on his knees, eyes gritted in pain, his black wings bent and flared out behind him. He looked half unconscious, but he reached for El again, brushing her waist as she yanked on Lannie's arm.

"El, please!" Lannie pleaded, trying desperately to free her hand from El's grip, but our elder sister's smile only grew, her sharp fangs lengthening, the black ring around her eyes stretching until no color remained.

45

ELARA

THIS WAS POWER.

This was life.

What else had consumed my thoughts before? There *was* no right and wrong. No good or evil. There was simply power. And I was its wielder.

The cursebreaker had taken from me, urging the weakness of my consciousness to relinquish all that we were, but the one tethered to the earth—she was the connection to everything.

Such a forthcoming conduit.

All of Pax was at my fingertips, and now that this world was once again its own, all I needed to do was purge it of my competitors. There were three who posed a threat, all of them gods connected to this place—this world's creators.

But I knew them, now. Could sense each flash of pain and longing, every flare of jealousy and misplaced vengeance cycling through them.

And hatred.

Gods, they were all swimming in hatred for each other. This would be easy. I'd dismantle them, setting them up to take each other down, all without lifting a finger of my own. Then, this realm would bow to me.

"Elara!"

My eyes closed, a flicker of recognition breaking through the surrounding shadows. I shook my head trying to clear it, but it was like the first pebble of a failing dam had broken free.

Light flooded through the darkness of my mind, the rays illuminating black wings.

"Come back to me, love."

I gripped the sides of my head, dropping my sister's hand as the warm of his touch wrapped around my waist. I wanted to stay in the primal darkness. This life was too messy, too convoluted. In the darkness, there was simplicity. There was power and... peace.

"You don't want that," the deep voice rumbled, sending a flood of warmth and love through my body.

I gasped as the force of his passion wrapped around me, forcing my heart to beat in a thrumming rhythm that wasn't entirely my own. Glimpses of skilled fingers and sharp fangs flashed through my mind, leaving memories of loving caresses in their wake. Of a euphoria only achievable with another—with my mate.

The scent of cedar and spice lingered on my skin, my fangs throbbing, my body aching with a need I didn't quite understand.

"I'm here, love."

The metallic tang of blood joined the tantalizing aroma, forcing my eyes open. Bright rings of light surrounded cinnamon-colored irises, commanding my attention. He tilted his head to the side, one hand firmly holding my waist to his as his other traced the outline of a pulsing vessel along the slope of his neck and the thin trickle of blood his nail had produced.

"Bite."

My mouth watered as my thighs clenched, the darkness

retreating further, coaxing me closer toward him with the light of his eyes. Toward the wicked pleasure I knew his blood promised.

I pounced, sinking my fangs into his neck with savage hunger. I drank greedily, savoring the moan that rumbled through him, his body igniting in time with mine. Every nerve ending was alive. Blood streamed down my throat, the taste invigorating as flashes of bodies joining poured into my mind—my body and the fae before me offering me his life.

I would have it, too. Another few pulls on his neck and he would be mine.

I drank again, but this time the flashes shifted, gifting me with smaller moments. Gentler ones.

He was watching me cut through a group of Fractured, standing against them with just a handful of humans and a half-fae at my back. Another showed us dancing at a ball, twirling around while others looked on in shock, but he only had eyes for me. The scene changed and we were soaring above the forest, me asleep and tucked tightly against his chest. Flickers of a burial shroud, much too small for an adult came next, causing a stab of pain through my chest, one that was soothed as a hollow crystal with ashes was placed around my neck.

Each memory brought with it waves of emotion, each more powerful than the next. Each awakening a gnawing chasm of longing and want inside me. An awareness of something missing.

We were in a dimly lit hot spring, the purple-blue stones shimmering as my head was thrown back in pleasure, Zaeth poised between my thighs. But it wasn't just a physical feeling. We'd joined at this moment, our two consciouses linking.

My draw on his blood lessened as he sent more images. More feelings. Until I was telling him I loved him. Promising that I would always be by his side. And he at mine.

I ripped my fangs away from his neck, faintly registering the screams of others around us. Their pleas with me to stop.

Zaeth's gaze found mine as he slumped forward, his skin a sickly pale. "Come back to me, love."

Something in my chest cracked as his eyes fluttered shut, his essence twining with mine to send a last flutter of feeling: forgiveness.

"No," I breathed, memories flooding back—all that I was, all that *we* still were.

Ripping the vessels along my wrist open with my teeth, I pressed the serrated flesh to Zaeth's lips, the red streaming down his chin, his neck.

Please, I pleaded, reaching for our bond. For my mate. His heart was beating too slow—much too slow—but it was there. He was still here, and fate couldn't be this cruel.

I tilted his neck up, forcing more of my blood down his throat. His pulse increased, giving my own a flutter. And then his eyes opened, the rings of light blazing. Zaeth's fangs snapped down, piercing the flesh around my healing wound, as he drank.

Each pull strengthened our bond, Zaeth's heartbeat syncing with mine, until his cinnamon eyes fixed on mine.

"What were you thinking?" I screamed, tears spilling down my cheeks as I knelt beside him. Zaeth righted himself, his palm coming to my cheek. "Why didn't you stop me? The wards were fixed—Pax was fixed—and you still offered me your neck when I was drunk off power."

Zaeth's lips twitched, him tanned complexion nearly back to normal. "I would offer you everything, love. My essence, my blood, if you asked me to rip out my heart and feed it to you, I would."

A whimper rocked through my chest as I saw the sincerity of his words, felt them ripple through our bond.

"I could have killed you," I breathed, horrified to know how close I'd come.

"I know." Zaeth's black wings furled out, brushing against the undersides of mine as he pressed a sweet, slow kiss to my lips. "Death would've been kinder than living in a world without you."

"You don't get to make that decision," I snarled, more anguish than anger. "Did you ever stop to think that I can't live without you? If I hadn't stopped—If I'd killed you—"

"But you didn't."

"I could have," I insisted, eyes wide with fear. Gods, a few more seconds and I would've sealed both our fates. Because I knew I couldn't survive in a world without him.

"Shh," he breathed, wrapping his arms around me as my wings shook. I was spent, both emotionally and physically. All I wanted to do was collapse, to rest my head on his chest and hear his heart beating in time with mine.

"You can let go now, love." Zaeth pressed a kiss to my brow, his hand rubbing soothing circles along my back. My wings shimmered and then vanished as I let go of the last tendrils of darkness I'd been clinging to.

Ryuu, Greer, Lannie, Queen Halcyon, Evander, Jarek, even Alarik and Queen Freya were surrounding us, panic etched across their faces.

"Your wings," Greer stammered, eyes wide as she looked at me cradled in Zaeth's arms. She swallowed and started again. "We couldn't get past them, El."

"I could feel it wasn't you," Lannie stammered. "But I couldn't break through. You kept pulling…"

"It was like you were able to reach into the earth and draw directly from Pax," Queen Halcyon added.

Queen Freya cocked her head to the side, her lips pressed into a hard line. "Is that what I felt? The aftershock of power spiraling out?"

"Yes," Queen Halcyon said. "And no. It was El, but there was something else tapping into the exchange."

"A darkness," I said as Queen Halcyon's silver eyes turned toward me. "But stronger. More like a void."

She nodded, her brows pinching as her gazed darted between Lannie and me.

"It was centered beneath the Earth Kingdom," Queen Freya confirmed. "With dark branches snaking out, but it felt conscious... like it was alive."

"Levana?" Jarek asked with Evander by his side.

"No," I answered. "She's more shadows than darkness. This was black. Like the night without a moon or stars."

"Night?" Zaeth asked, his voice humming through his chest. I drew back meeting the question looming in his eyes.

"Yes," I breathed, dread coiling in my stomach. "Erebus."

46

LANNIE

We hadn't updated the group on the sleeping sickness. Halcyon wanted to keep the information as quiet as possible, and up until now, there hadn't been much to say. She didn't trust many in her court, relying mostly on Queen Freya and General Xavier. Halcyon and I knew the bloodstone was storing power, draining essence from the fae fallen ill by the sleeping sickness, but we'd assumed it was Levana. When all this time... it had been Erebus.

"We don't know it's Erebus," I repeated as El and Zaeth stepped through Queen Freya's portal, Evander and Jarek following shortly after. Greer and Ryuu were obligated to remain behind, what with their court turning to the new king and queen after all of Pax felt the after effects of us sealing the rift between worlds. They couldn't run away at the first test of their rule.

"We don't," nodded Alarik, "But we must assume it *is* Erebus. El is the only one who has felt the power of both Levana and Erebus. If she thinks it's the later, it probably is."

"It's not Levana," El confirmed, her eyes meeting mine as

Halcyon and I shared a look. My sister lifted a brow, catching the silent exchange. "What aren't you telling us?"

I fidgeted with the edge of my coat, the heavy material feeling oppressive now that we were back in the ever-warm Earth Kingdom. Slipping out of it, I tossed it across the back of the main couch in Halcyon's sitting rooms. I loved this room, the dark bark offsetting the rich greens of the vines growing from the ceilings, the walls. The scent of fresh spring water and subtle vanilla emanated through Halcyon's quarters, mingling with gentle blossoms in the amethyst garden below and the moss-covered floors.

We'd spent little time here in the beginning, working through what the sleeping sickness could mean, debating if we should worry the others. But we hadn't had any proof. We still didn't—

"Lannie," El said, drawing my attention back to the present.

My gaze flicked to Halcyon again, her own feelings of unease tinged with dread coming through the bond. She lifted a shoulder, her silver eyes peering into mine.

Your call.

"The sickness plaguing the Earth Kingdom's people is comprised of them falling into a deep slumber. Their vitals are stable, for the most part, but their bodies continue to deteriorate." I took a deep breath, forcing my gaze to El's and ignoring everyone else's. It was the only way I'd get through this. "We discovered a correlation, possibly a causation, but we couldn't be sure."

"We both hoped to find more information before we worried anyone," Halcyon supplied.

"About what," El cut in, her tone growing clipped.

"There are dozens of earth fae in a state of slumber, all of whom were found next to bloodstone. More than that, we think their essence is being stored."

"We'd thought Levana was behind it as there was a surge of fae claimed on the day she was reborn, but..."

"But now that El is sensing Erebus," I continued, watching my sister's eyes flash. "Maybe he's been gathering their power all this time."

"Which can mean only one thing," Halcyon said, her hand slipping into mine and offering me strength.

"He's been trapped on Pax all this time—"

"And wishes for his own freedom," El breathed, her eyes going wide.

"Gods above," Evander muttered, shaking his head.

"More like gods below," Jarek smiled. Evander shot him a glare. "Too soon?"

"You should have told us," Queen Freya snapped, her eyes flashing with hurt as she stared at Halcyon.

I didn't like the way she looked at her, like the thought of the two of them not sharing something was unthinkable. Halcyon frowned, but lifted her chin, her hand flexing in mine.

"It wasn't a secret. We just didn't have anything concrete enough to worry everyone."

"And now we do," Zaeth cut in. "We need to explore those claimed by the sleeping sickness right away."

"And the tomb," I added, my stomach twisting with the possibility that Erebus, God of Night, could be the one housed within, only meters below.

"Tomb?" Jarek and El said at the same time.

"This just keeps getting better," muttered Alarik. Queen Freya's eyes narrowed, but she didn't speak.

A rush of power shuddered through the earth, causing Halcyon to gasp. I caught her as her back bowed, her breaths coming in short, staggering bursts.

"We need to go. Now," she said, her silver eyes looking up at me.

I nodded, helping her to her feet.

The others fell in behind us as we flitted through the Earth Kingdom, following the pulsing surge of power along veins of bloodstone, going deeper and deeper beneath the earth as we followed the dark void.

"Something's wrong," El breathed as our speed dropped into a light jog. We slowed further, Zaeth's gaze locked on her. Her spine stiffened as she inhaled deeply, the dark rings around her eyes flaring.

Zaeth cocked his head to the side, great shadows stretching out and solidifying behind him into ebony wings. Rings of light blazed around his irises as his eyes searched the path before us. "There are heartbeats up ahead."

"A lot of them," El added.

Alarik and Evander unsheathed their blades as Jarek and Zaeth exchanged a loaded look.

"Any sign of trouble and I'll lux everyone out," Jarek promised.

"And I'll be ready with a portal," Queen Freya added, meeting Halcyon's gaze with a nod.

Zaeth started forward, El bringing up the rear as Halcyon and I directed our group through the last of the turns, drawing nearer to the thrum of beating hearts. Bloodstone glinted from every wall, the reds, blacks, and greens tangling together around the last curve before opening.

Just as before the cavern we'd discovered comprised entirely of bloodstone stretched before us, complete with the gentle sounds of the underground river flowing along black sands in the back and the temple set in the center.

And every inch of the floor was covered in bodies.

Black unseeing eyes, grey decomposing corpses—hundreds of them leading up to the pillars of the temple: the Fractured.

Stepping closer, I peered through the columns, finding the tomb in the center. But the bloodstone lid was shoved back, exposing the empty chamber within. My pulsed raced, a chill slinking down my spine as I realized what that meant.

"How did they get here?" Alarik asked, his head swinging side to side as he searched for any clue. "The last I heard, the Fractured were with Veles—"

"And on the run from Levana," breathed Jarek. "Being that the God of Night was supposedly in that tomb, which is now empty, and there are hundreds of sleeping Fractured linked to Veles, I say we leave immediately and regroup above with an army of warriors. Who's with me?"

The ground rumbled before anyone could respond, several bodies toppling over one another as streaks of darkness pooled in the far recesses of the cavern.

"There's a river back there," I whispered, hardly daring to speak. "Just beyond the slope."

El's need for action flashed down our bond, her hazel-blue eyes meeting mine before she gave a quick nod and started forward. Zaeth pulled ahead, Jarek luxing to his side in a flash. He staggered as he reemerged, brows furrowing as he stepped away from the dark shadow before him.

"I can't lux through that," he muttered, eyes widening. "It's pure darkness. There are no light molecules for me to latch onto."

"You'll just have to go around," Evander said, catching up to them.

Jarek swallowed, still looking shaken, but nodded as we crept forward. I saw the others stiffen up ahead, and I strained to hear what they did.

"My life, my army, my loyalty—all is yours."

Zaeth's wings tucked in, the grip on his sword tightening.

"I ask only that you spare me and grant me long enough on this earth to see my brothers avenged and Levana destroyed."

The earth shook, the strands of darkness wicking forward. I

followed the tendrils of night behind Zaeth, Jarek, and Evander with Halcyon trailing me by a few paces, peering around the bloodstone temple to find, a hulking body rising near the river's edge.

Hard planes and thick muscles banded across a long, chiseled torso rose from the darkness along with a pair of eyes that seemed to glow. I felt the breath in my lungs leave, as if his darkness were consuming it, dragging pieces of me toward him like gravity. This must be Erebus.

I stumbled back, gasping for air. Halcyon was beside me in a heartbeat, her skin taking on a pale sheen as she fought to control her own breathing. But it was too late.

The shadows wrapped around us, ushering us forward along with the others as Veles snapped his head in our direction. Hollowed eyes narrowed into slits as we were thrust forward toward the black pebbled banks.

Halcyon, Jarek, Zaeth, and Evander sprang to their feet in front of us, creating a wall of protection as El helped me stand. Queen Freya's palm was flashing with Alarik by her side, but no portal came.

I stared at my sister, taking her hand as I got to my feet, but there was something off about the way she held her sword—and something different about our bond, like a numbness had started to creep in. A dark haze.

"El," I said, gripping her hand as panic rocked through me. She couldn't be possessed. Not again.

Her lips twitched, the slight smile not reaching her eyes. "It's just my affinities, Lannie. They're stronger here, in his presence, but I'm still me."

"Please, Erebus," Veles said. "They're enemies of Levana, God of Gods."

El's head whipped toward the sound of Veles's voice, her eyes narrowing. It almost sounded like Veles had defended us—the creature responsible for our brother's death, for the death of thousands of brothers, and sisters, and loved ones across Pax.

"They have power. More than expected," Veles continued, turning back to the dark figure, whose glowing eyes were fixed on our group. "You know all, God of Gods, but I believe they could be useful."

With that, Veles dropped to his knees, bowing his head as he waited for Erebus to make his decision.

"We'll never work with you, Veles," El seethed, her violet wings snapping free. "You'll die at my hands. It will be slow and painful, and I will relish every second of it."

"I'll welcome death with open arms." Veles's dark eyes flared as he bared his teeth. "As long as that bitch, Levana is put to ash first."

I felt the shock rippled down El's line, but her face stayed hard as stone.

"Enough," Erebus boomed, the shadows through the room seeming to grow even darker. It was pitch black, the seed of darkness that every other shadow grew from. "I will speak with my daughter."

Zaeth stepped in front of El just as the shadows condensed, but even his wielding of darkness couldn't contend with the tendrils of night governed by Erebus. They wound through our group and then parted, like two great arms throwing us aside. All but one.

El stood, her violet wings stretched wide, sword poised for battle as she stepped forward to meet the God of Night.

47

GREER

We had actually done it. We sealed the realm and cut off Levana from her corrupted creatures in the otherworld. I'd thought most of that process would've been mine alone to shoulder, but it had taken more out of my sisters than I'd thought possible.

El had tapped into something primal. Something dangerous. I'd always known she had darkness in her, but none of us could've predicted just how absolute that darkness was—including El. She'd looked horrified when she'd returned to herself. And Lannie… well she'd nearly been drained by El.

Swallowing against the dryness of my throat, I remembered the way Lannie's face had paled, her knees going weak as Queen Halcyon refused to let her go, sending wave after wave of her own essence into my little sister.

I knew Lannie was still grieving Ser but thank the gods Queen Halcyon was here looking after her.

"Your Majesty?" Cress asked, and judging by the sharp pitch of her voice, it hadn't been the first time.

I blinked, not yet finding the will to turn away from the balcony overlooking the valley of Serein. A thick blanket of snow covered the plateau tops, the burnt sienna color of the rock beneath contrasting with the sheer purity of the white. The crisp air was calm, as if the world was holding its breath for our next step, waiting to see if it would survive.

At least we had a chance now. A small, microscopic chance, but a chance none the less.

I'd wanted to go with my sisters, but Ryuu was right in assuming we'd be needed here. The aftershock of sealing the realm created a tidal wave of panic among the royals, all of whom looked to us for guidance.

All yesterday had been spent in countless meetings and public appearances, assuring everyone that the Air Kingdom was safe and reiterating that their new king and queen had already taken huge strides toward their protection.

"Greer," Cress called again, losing all pretense of composure. I blinked, tearing my gaze away from the peaceful scene to meet her narrowed eyes.

"Yes?"

"King Dragcor will be here any moment. I need to finish getting you ready."

"Why is he coming? I thought Ryuu and I were to visit the Eastern Islands and survey the Sky Warriors." Although Ryuu and I had accepted our place as the new rulers of the Air Kingdom, we'd yet to complete a coronation, meaning we were sort of tied for power with King Dragcor.

"Yes, Your Highness," Cress gritted out, looking like she might burst a blood vessel. "But King Dragcor wished to complete the blessing ceremony before you left."

Seriously, there was more?

"Didn't we do that with the whole marriage thing?"

Cress shot me a glare, not bothering to hide her frustration as she tugged me toward the closet with a huff. "You are our queen. As such, you're expected to be on the frontlines with our army. I've taken the liberty in ordering your battle attire. Being that you are still within the first year of marriage and rulership, you are expected to always wear some form of gold—"

For an entire year? Gods, I really needed to catch up on air fae traditions.

"So," Cress pressed on, revealing dozens of gilded outfits as she stepped into the large, walk-in closet. "I've had all of your black battle leathers adjusted."

My eyes widened as she withdrew a new set. Fine, golden thread had been woven throughout the chest, spanning the shoulders in a pattern that could only be described as dragon's hide. It shimmered in the light, the contrasting colors looking just as menacing as they were refined.

"It's perfect," I breathed, knowing that I wanted to impress the Sky Warriors and that pretty dresses weren't going to win me support.

Cress smirked, the small movement seeming to say, 'I know,' but she held her tongue and helped me dress. Somehow, she managed to tame my silver curls into a braid wrapping around the side of my head and over my shoulder, weaving in the fine, golden crown as if it were a part of me.

I looked at myself in the mirror, both impressed with her skills and surprised to find that the sight of the crown across my head didn't unnerve me as much as I thought it would.

A knock sounded from the door, and Ryuu entered a moment later. His own dark locks had been tied back in a half knot with a matching golden crown set atop his head. His battle leathers were gilded to match mine, but where mine held delicate touches, his were brutal. The dragon scales were accented by rich greens and dark reds to give the appearance of impenetrable armor.

My Dragon King.

"Hello, my husband," I said, letting my eyes wander over his muscles. Cress rolled her eyes.

"King Dragcor will be here any moment," Cress sighed,

heading for the door as Ryuu's pupils stretched into vertical slits. "Try to behave."

The door clicked behind her as Ryuu gathered me to him, his lips pressing against mine. "How are you feeling?"

"Better but still a little drained," I answered truthfully. Reaching for particles of light, I let them shimmer around us, subtlety linking into a transparent shield before falling away. "I can still call on it, but I won't be fully recovered for another day or two."

"We'll be safe," Ryuu promised. "The Sky Warriors are unbeatable in the air and fierce contenders on the ground."

I nodded, knowing how important this trip was. We were expected to lead them in battle—*we*, not just Ryuu. He'd been their general for years, checking in even while they'd been at peace, even while he'd scoured the seven kingdoms with Zaeth at his side hunting down Veles.

But me. I was completely new. I had no wings, no royal lineage, and was half-human to boot. This trip would be my introduction to the fighters of our kingdom, and I couldn't help but feel that it would prove more vital than any wedding day or coronation.

Ryuu stiffened, his ears picking up King Dragcor's arrival a moment before mine.

"Son," Dragcor said as he entered, his deep voice rumbling before he turned his reptilian eyes on me. "Daughter. Today marks the day you solidify your rank. I have no doubt you'll win the hearts of the people, and the royals are now firmly under your control with how you've handled the last day-and-a-half of panic. They've been lulled into a feeling of security despite Levana roaming our world."

I dared a glance up, but Ryuu's eyes were fixed on his father.

"But to keep the crowns firmly on your heads, you need the loyalty of the Sky Warriors. They will test you, my daughter. You must meet their strikes with counterattacks of your own."

"She'll be with me," Ryuu nearly growled.

"Yes," his father's lips twitched. "But she must prove she doesn't *need* to be with you."

"I can take care of myself," I said, tipping my chin up.

"*I* know you can." The orange in Dragcor's eyes flared brighter. "You must show them beyond any doubt that you are their queen."

"I will," I swore, and the pride swelling in King Dragcor's eyes had the lost little girl in me wishing my father was here to see this day.

My sisters and I had been forced to face the horrors of the world much too young. We'd lost our brothers, our parents, and through it all, we'd somehow managed to grow closer. El would call me foolish, but I knew we could get through anything. I *had* to believe it, because if this was all there was in life, if we were destined to lose and keep losing...

No. I refused to believe it. And maybe that only proved I was naive, but I didn't think I could find the will to keep going if I let that last bit of hope die.

"You're the greatest son a father could ask for. I'm honored to see you rise as king to our people with a fierce mate at your side." Dragcor placed a heavy palm on Ryuu's shoulder, his eyes flickering with an unnamed emotion.

Ryuu's throat bobbed, a pulse of trepidation coming through the bond. There was a question swirling in his eyes as he stared at his father, but he couldn't find the words to give it life.

"Let the winds guide you, my son."

With one last breath, King Dragcor flitted from the room.

48

GREER

The chill of the wind lessened as we flew toward the sun, sweeping over a vast stretch of ocean. I'd grown accustomed to the heights of Serein, but there was nothing like the feel of the sun warming my skin as the scent of salt caught on a breeze brushed through my hair. It reminded me of the first time Ryuu had flown us across the ocean, taking us to the birthplace of dragons—to my mating night.

This time, we angled south, passing small patches of islands as we went. The sun was high in the sky by the time a large island came into view, the winged fae in the clouds indicating that this was home to the Sky Warriors.

"Are you sure that's an island?" I asked, trying to see the end of land and failing.

"It's an island," Ryuu grinned. "A very large island, but an island all the same."

"It's not on any map I've seen."

Ryuu shook his head. "It was safer to hide the bulk of the Sky Warriors from the knowledge of other kingdoms. Under my father's early rule, kingdoms would invade for no other reason than to prove they maintained the strongest army. The

Sky Warriors were a constant target due to their strength both in the sky and on land. Only the Fire Kingdom rivaled us, but we were constantly at war."

"So, you hid them," I said, watching transfixed as the warriors completed synchronized maneuvers through the clouds. "Does Zaeth know?"

"Yes," Ryuu said as we swept closer, the small group bowing its head as we passed. "I trust Zaeth and Naz with my life and the lives of my people."

"So, the base among the closer islands, the one Cress mentioned—"

"A real base with real warriors," Ryuu said. "But substantially less warriors. It helps others underestimate us. *This* is our real base."

My stomach fluttered as we dipped, Ryuu's great wings tucking in tight as we dove for a grassy field bordering a stretch of sand. Wind rushed through white feathers, his wings expanding moments before we hit the ground to level us out.

It would've already been impressive had it just been Ryuu, but then he lifted me in his arms, as if I were a goddess descending from the heavens. My toes hit the ground as Ryuu gently set me down, his hands around my waist falling away as he took a step back.

A large crowd had gathered around, a tense wavering pause hanging in the air as they watched their king step back and kneel.

"My queen," Ryuu rumbled, the vertical slits fixed on me as the green embers of his eyes smoldered. "I give you the Sky Warriors, the most skilled winged soldiers of the seven kingdoms. We will be your protectors in the air, your shield, your guardians."

The largest of them stepped forward. Stark white wings expanded and then tucked in tight against his back. Brilliant green eyes stared at me, as he dropped to his knees beside Ryuu.

"I am General Bane, leader of the Sky Warriors, second only to our king. We will serve you until death, Your Highness."

The others fell in a wave rippling out, each professing their fidelity, until the entire army bowed at my feet.

Ryuu stood, coming to my side. His chest pressing against my back as we watched the Sky Warriors slowly rise. His breath fanned my ear as his hand wrapped around my waist, holding me close.

"My queen."

We toured the island, going through formations and defense strategies for a hundred different senecios. It was thoroughly impressive how coordinated they were, their wings almost locking to form an impenetrable shield with the sharp barbs lining them. There were archers, swordsmen armed with curved blades, and those wielding long spears tipped with vicious points. Ryuu had boasted of their skill, and I couldn't help but agree.

"As you know," Ryuu addressed the Sky Warriors. "We're no longer mobilizing to Caligo but will be reenforcing our own defenses throughout the kingdom. An attack on Serein is unlikely due to the terrain serving as a barrier to all non-winged fae, but we can't rule it out."

"Levana has creatures, a dark and air fae hybrid from what we can tell," I added, sure to match Ryuu's steeled tone. "A small contingency of warriors will go to our capitol, but most of you will be deployed to the borders."

Ryuu and I had discussed this with the others at length, but I couldn't shake the feeling that we were missing something.

"The most likely strikes will be along our northwest border with the Dark Kingdom. We can also reasonably expect a strike from the Light Kingdom to the south—"

The earth shook, tall trees swaying and causing more than one warrior to stumble as we searched for the cause. Shouts erupted from the beach, two air fae pumping their wings furiously to reach us.

"The sea!" one of them screamed as another crash sounded. Ryuu had me in his arms, his wings thrusting down as we shot skyward. Sky Warriors launched into the air, automatically falling into formation as those on watch reached us.

"We're under attack," the second one panted, a long spear clasped in his hands as he whirled around to join ranks. "There."

All eyes followed his outstretched hand, finding the section of rocky cove that looked as if a bomb had struck. Heart racing, I scoured the horizon, finding nothing. No one.

"Who—"

A gasp pulled from my lips as a great tentacle rose from the sea. Thick, grey puckers stretched as saltwater tumbled down, the massive limb growing until it tipped forward and fell into the watch tower.

Stone exploded. The towering outpost crumbled into the sea as other tentacles lashed out, pummeling the coast with blows.

"Kraken!" Ryuu bellowed, angling us toward the monster. "Archers!"

The archers drew their bows, letting loose a hail of arrows under Ryuu's command. They sliced into the grey flesh, rivets of black blood streaming down to stain the ocean in a dark cloud.

The creature shrieked as more and more arrows sunk into its writhing limbs, the pain sending it retreating into deeper waters.

"How are we supposed to fight against the ocean?" I breathed, low enough for only Ryuu to hear.

He shook his head, jaw clenched. "We can't. These islands are low, much too low."

With my chest heaving, I glanced over his shoulder, peering between his pumping wings. The island was, indeed, low set and sprawling. So were the smaller ones positioned to the side.

"Ryuu," I said, my voice pitching as my breathing hitched.

Dark figures moved beneath the water, heading straight for the other islands—the ones mostly composed of the Sky Warriors' homes. And families.

"They're targeting the residential islands," Ryuu called to the others, a curse leaving his lips. "Save your families. Then retreat to the sea cliffs. We need to get out of range."

The fae with the stark white wings and tanned skin met my gaze, his green eyes hard before he dove.

My stomach twisted, feeling like I had just been weighed and come up wanting. I was their queen, sworn to protect them and all I was doing was watching as they fought to save their families. Worse—Ryuu needed to carry me, meaning I was keeping their king from joining the battle.

The first of the sea monsters neared the small island, its bulbous body climbing through shallow waters as it sought to reach its target. Its head billowed out behind it, covered in barnacles and sharp spikes as two black eyes seemed to focus on the homes along the water's edge. There was far too much intelligence held within their ink-black depths, the creature's cleverness proven as it maneuvered with the speed of a monster used to seeking prey.

Ryuu shouted orders, orchestrating attacks from the archers while the others flew with all their might toward their families. But they weren't going to make it.

I fixed my attention back on the nearest kraken, my heart thundering as it reared up before the unsuspecting homes, its front tentacles stretching high.

I thrust my hands out, the particles of light flaring to life as I wove them into a hasty net. The tentacles slapped against it, great suckers sliding down as I fought against the weight of their attack. Against the power humming in the creature's body.

Taking a deep breath, I forced another hasty shield around the next island. And then another until each were covered. The wards were flimsy and full of holes, but I only needed to hold the beasts off until all fae were in the air.

A wave of power crested down the mating bond as Ryuu's arms held me closer.

"Greer," he warned, feeling the toll of this display. I was still weakened from sealing the realm, my affinities not yet replenished, but I couldn't yield. Not on this.

"I know," I gritted out, feeling sweat bead across my brow. I focused on keeping my meager shields intact, on bracing for the impact of the other sea beasts as each of them launched toward families now screaming and fleeing for their lives.

I was their queen. Their protector just as much as Ryuu was. I couldn't soar through the skies or wield a weapon like he could, but I could do this. "Just a little longer."

The Sky Warriors swept through the buildings, young children and families flooding the sky shortly after. All those who couldn't fly were carried, each of them helping each other until the entirely of the homes were empty and the air was filled.

Tentacles thrashed against my shield as we lifted higher into the clouds, the usually sunny day so at odds with the heaviness of the fae around us. Only once the Sky Warriors had done another sweep, did I allow my shields to flicker and then fade.

The krakens surged forth, renewed in their onslaught. Wreckage battered the water's surface, pristine homes and buildings reduced to rubble settling on the ocean floor.

"For all of our planning, we never considered an attack from the sea."

"Queen Halcyon and your sister told us Levana held their allegiance." Ryuu's fingers flexed around me, his arm cradling my shoulders and knees. "I never considered they'd travel this far north, or that they knew of our base."

"You think it was Levana's doing?" I asked, leaning into him as the exhaustion of the day caught up with me.

His head gave a small dip, his gaze angling down until it met mine. A prickling sense of foreboding trickled down my spine as I felt Ryuu's emotions churning. Because we both knew what this meant.

"Levana is no longer waiting."

49

ELARA

It had been nearly two days since Erebus accepted Veles into his fold. Two days of me having to resist slitting his throat every time I saw him. Even now, my fingers twitched with the need for a blade as I stared at him across the field of burning funeral pyres.

There was no smugness in his gaze. No triumph as he watched Queen Halcyon lean forward and put the torch to dried wood, the flames catching and racing upward toward another corpse. After Erebus had awoken, all those affected by the sleeping sickness died. Most of the earth fae had said their goodbyes when their loved ones fell ill, but this—the gentle words, the burning at dusk—it was the sliver of closure they'd been missing.

The remainder of the earth fae retreated below as the last burial shroud was consumed by fire.

"Why aren't you rejoicing?" I snapped, glaring at Veles. "This is what you wanted, right? All of us dead except your precious light fae."

"El," Lannie sighed, the shadows under her eyes revealing

she'd had difficulty sleeping since Veles arrived as well. "Can we not do this?"

"Not do what?" I continued, unable to let my anger go.

The need for vengeance hummed through my veins, causing my fangs to elongate and my vision to sharpen. I spotted the tick in Veles's jaw. I could hear the way his pulse sped up, could sense his own darkness rising. Good. I wanted a fight.

"He should be on one of those pyres joining his brothers and whatever endless torment awaits them."

"You think I don't know what's coming for me?" Veles snapped, flitting so fast I nearly flinched. His lip was pulled back in a snarl, one that Zaeth matched by my side. "My brothers and I sacrificed *everything* to make the world better for our people."

"Yes, the poor little light fae—"

"You don't know what it was like," Veles countered, his fists clenching. "We were the objects of constant ridicule. Easy targets for the brutish northern fae. Never mind the physical pain we suffered, but the mental anguish that occurs after centuries of derision."

I didn't like the pang of sympathy that rocked through me or the blatant hurt flashing in his black eyes. But then I remembered the thousands of innocents he'd slain. The families he and his wretched brothers had destroyed.

"You may have been the hero once, Veles, but the world changed while you were away. Everything you've gone through, the sacrifice of your brothers—your soul—it was all for nothing. You're the monster, now. The villain. The beast we need saving *from*. Nothing more."

His throat bobbed, and I swear there was a flicker of remorse mixing with the violent pools of anger staring back at me, but he flitted away before I could be sure.

"Speaking of villains," Queen Freya said. "We need to discuss Erebus."

I stared at the burning bodies and the ash swirling in the air above for another moment before I was calm enough to face the group at my back. Zaeth sent a wash of love through the mating bond, seeming to say that he understood where my fury was coming from and wouldn't try to stifle it. I slipped my hand into his, needing his grounding presence, his unabashed comprehension of who I was in a life where even those I cared about constantly misunderstood me.

Lannie lifted a brow in my direction but held her tongue. It was clear she hated Veles as much as I, but she was able to let logic override her personal feelings. If Veles died, the Fractured would shift back to Levana, and though we were preparing for war as much as possible, we were still greatly outmatched.

Queen Halcyon stood beside my little sister, her silver eyes hard as she watched the bodies of her people burn. Alarik was behind Queen Freya, the two of them hardly separated for more than a few moments, with Jarek and Evander hovering close by.

"Erebus is a problem." Evander met my gaze, his auburn eyes cutting through me. "If not yet, he will be."

Queen Freya nodded in agreement, Alarik mirroring her. Glancing over my shoulder at the smoke thickening in the sky, I could only agree. Erebus had been unleashed from his prison at the cost of dozens of earth fae and hundreds of Fractured.

Lannie had been right in her assumption of a force slowly siphoning their fae essence while they'd been trapped in slumber, but with the horde of Fractured willingly giving up what remained of their souls, he didn't need to be careful with the bodies he drained. No, he simply took what he wanted, leaving husks of what they'd once been.

After he confirmed as much without even a flicker of remorse, I'd refused to talk to him. I was pretty sure he could've forced me, but it seemed I was the only thing on this planet he cared about. At least for now.

"We need him to defeat Levana," I reminded them.

"We need both him and Eunoia if the legends are true," Zaeth said, his gaze finding mine. "You need to speak with him."

"I updated Naz and Soter about our hunt for the light goddess," Jarek added, "but they're just as lost as we are."

As if summoned, pitch black tendrils stretched from the nearest cluster of trees, the ferns and moss at their base eclipsed as if plunged into the darkest night. Erebus emerged from the center, his body stretching until his form settled.

He was tall, taller than Zaeth, with tanned skin and hair that looked as if it were made of the center of the galaxy, the black strands glinting with hues of dark purples and blues. The brightness of his eyes dimmed, giving way to white irises contoured by glints of cerulean and ringed in black.

"We have much to discuss, Daughter."

The urge to reject him as my father was poised on the edge of my tongue, but he had the same high cheekbones, the same sharp nose and upturned eyes.

"I've given you time to acclimate, but we cannot afford to squander another day waiting for your emotions to quiet."

Blood coated my tongue as I bit my lip against a thousand curses.

"Levana is sure to have felt my emergence. We must work quickly if we are to free Eunoia and rebind Levana before war comes."

"Rebind?" Lannie asked, flitting to my side in a show of solidarity. She may not like my temper at times, but I knew she would always stand by me. "Your initial binding failed. Why would a second prove any different?"

Erebus's eyes flashed. "Despite Levana's many transgressions, Eunoia wanted her sister close, bound to the planet the two of them created. It was a risk I will not allow again. This time, I'll ensure she is separated from her source of power."

"The two of them created?" echoed Jarek. "As in Levana and Eunoia?"

Erebus's piercing gaze settled on him. "Yes. I was drawn to the dichotomy the two of them possessed: one sister born of order and light, the other of chaos and shadows. They should have destroyed one another, but the two forces worked in tandem, creating lifeforms never before seen. A world of both dawn and dusk, one rich with creatures."

I blinked, realizing what he was saying.

"Levana said she was setting things right," I breathed, looking for any sign from Erebus that would confirm her allegations. "She said that Eunoia had interfered with the type of world she wished for—the world you and her intended."

Erebus stilled, the subtle pull of his darkness the only indication he remained listening. After a while, he spoke.

"Her chaos was alluring. Beautiful and deadly. There was a time I indulged in her cultivated pandemonium, but there was no end. Levana's creations were uninhibited, unleashed despite the havoc they wrought. She was always pushing. Seeking more, desperate for the next adventure."

"So, you locked her up?" I wasn't sure why that knowledge pricked, but it did.

"I contained her madness." Erebus drew himself up, the stretches of darkness swirling. "She knew no bounds. Some of her creations were tolerable, but most consumed. Eunoia and I pleaded with her to control the monsters she unleashed, but she refused. If we hadn't stepped in, Levana would have lain waste to more than just this world."

I stared at the god before me, keenly aware of the lack of emotion underlying his words. Nothing he said was wrong... but there was something missing.

"You don't care if this world falls."

Erebus didn't speak.

A hoarse, unamused laugh left my lips. "This whole time, binding her, giving up your own freedom, it wasn't for some honorable desire to protect innocent lives or even because you fell for Eunoia. It was so Levana wouldn't mess up other worlds —*Your* worlds."

"Yes," Erebus hissed. "Following my curiosity to this miserable world was the biggest regret of my existence. If I could simply destroy it and be done with Levana and her sister, I would. But Levana had already proven she's skilled at evasion as well as her ability to move between realms."

"Why not destroy it?" I asked, hating that I was related to him. Wishing I could scrub away every molecule in my body inherited from the God of Night.

"El," Lannie muttered, fear flashing in her eyes, but I pressed on.

"When you realized Levana was dangerous, why not crush this world in its infancy while she was bound?"

Erebus glanced toward the horizon, toward the last rays of the setting sun.

"Eunoia," Evander breathed, wonder dripping from the goddess's name. "The legends are true. You wouldn't leave her, couldn't shatter this world because to do so would have crushed her. And you couldn't harm the one being—in all your existence —that you'd come to love."

"As I said," Erebus responded, his voice clipped. "I've made mistakes. This time, I'll bind Levana to a realm of my making, knowing she'll corrupt and destroy it slowly, but she'll be unable to gather the power to slip between worlds when she is isolated so completely from her own essence."

"Even at the expense of Eunoia?" I asked, thinking of Zaeth and the lengths he would go to keep me. There would be no stopping for him.

Erebus watched the sun sink beneath the trees, waiting until the violet light of dusk faded into a deep blue before he spoke.

"Unless we find and free Eunoia, there won't be a choice. This world will fall, and all others after it."

"Where is Eunoia?" Zaeth asked. "How do we free her?"

The others shifted, waiting for the God of Night's response.

"We were separated when we first bound Levana. I don't know the specific location, but I know it's in the north, beyond what you refer to as the Shadowlands—"

Erebus's head snapped to the east, my ears picking up on a sharp whistling sounds a split-second later.

I turned, finding the tip of an arrow inches from my head. A blanket of darkness ensnared it, consuming it until only the brittle, decayed remains of the wooden shaft were left. It crumpled into ash as it hit the ground, the metal tip gleaming in the moonlight.

My pulse beat frantically, my eyes wide with the knowledge that I would be on my way to the after had Erebus not intervened. I met his gaze, staring at the creature that was my father. His eyes grew hard, the dark rings at the edges thickening.

"We have company."

50

LANNIE

Jarek dove as arrows shot. He managed to grab hold of El and I and luxed us to safety beneath the earth before any of us were harmed. He flashed out of existence again, returning a few moments later with a perturbed looking Evander alongside Halcyon, Zaeth, Alarik, and even Queen Freya.

Halcyon immediately flitted from the room searching for General Xavier. She didn't say as much, but I'd been more aware of her since we repaired the crack in the wards, picking up on emotions and even fleeting thoughts the longer we spent together.

"She's gone to mobilize the Earth Army," I said, meeting the other's gazes.

The Wild Queen lifted her chin, as if daring me to question why she hadn't created a portal, but I'd been with her at the Water Kingdom. In the half-a-minute it would have taken her to construct, we could have been killed.

"Who was it?" I asked, instead.

"Light fae," Zaeth growled, looking as if he might demand Jarek return him to the surface just so he could get his hands bloody.

"I thought Levana was waiting until she had Veles's army?" I glanced around the familiar space, as if expecting to find Veles but recognized Halcyon's sitting room instead.

The space was well lit, but darkness pooled among the lush vines, the blackness stretching until Erebus appeared.

"It would seem Levana is done waiting." The God of Night looked to El. "The light fae above are sworn to her, their essence corrupted by her chaos."

"Great," Jarek muttered as he paced the length of the room.

"We can't hide down here," Alarik said, having unsheathed his sword. There was a hard glint in his eyes, a determination to stand a fight rather than hide. The general had been beaten, his base decimated, and still he found the strength to rise again.

I glanced to Queen Freya next to him, catching a softness to her features when she looked at him. Another moment and all tenderness vanished, sealed behind a mask of impatient waiting. The others had the same pent-up energy, and it was clear none of them liked running from a fight.

"Join me," Halcyon said, flitting into the room in a silver armored gown. Panels of it hugged her shoulders, her waist, before splitting along the outsides of her thighs. Her legs were protected beneath the intricate fabric with battle leathers while also allowing for freedom of movement.

Zaeth stepped forward, the bright rings around his eyes glowing as ebony wings crafted from shadows solidified. El was at his side, her own violet wings expanding.

"We are at your service."

Halcyon looked between the Dark King and my sister and nodded. I hadn't allowed myself to fully comprehend what being Zaeth's mate meant for El, but looking at her now, I realized she would be the Dark Queen. And, in many ways, she already was.

"Leave them," Erebus commanded, his dark-ringed eyes fixed on my eldest sister. "Our priority is finding Eunoia."

El gritted her teeth. "We can't abandon the Earth Kingdom."

"You can," Erebus countered.

"This is Levana's first attack," El pressed, unfazed by the way the darkness around Erebus flickered. "If we don't stand together, we'll all fall. Maybe not today, but Levana will win if we remain divided."

"She'll conquer more than this world if we don't bind her," Erebus snapped, the swirls of night around him growing.

"Then help us defeat them. Quickly." El practically snarled at the God of Night, refusing to back down.

The sound of boots pounding against earth and the clanging of metal resonated beyond the room.

"It is time," Halcyon said, her silver eyes blazing as her gaze sweet through all of us. Daring to meet Erebus's cold stare. "This would be easier with you by our side."

Without another word, she flitted from the room, leaving the door open as she went.

I found myself moving after her, along with Alarik and Queen Freya.

"Care to test your skills in battler, healer?" The Wild Queen's lips quirked, but I shook my head, my lips pressing thin.

"There'll be plenty of fae on the verge of death for me to tend to soon enough."

The smirk vanished from her face, her honey eyes growing hard. "That there will."

"What do you need?" Jarek asked, his hand opened in invitation.

"Supplies," I breathed as Evander joined us. "Can you take me to the infirmary first?"

Jarek nodded.

"We'll be along shortly," El added, still glaring at Erebus with Zaeth at her side. A frowned tugged at my lips as I watched them stand off, but I could feel Halcyon moving quickly, moments away from breaching the surface with her army.

"See you under the stars," Jarek said, nodding toward my sister as I placed my hand in his.

～

Crisp evening air pricked my skin, the warmth of the Earth Kingdom finally giving way to winter.

Earth fae rushed from the ground in various locations, taking a few of the light fae by surprise. But they were vicious in their attacks, lashing out as if they knew they wouldn't walk away from this fight, and were determined to drag as many of us into death along with them.

Blood sprayed, the terrible familiar screams of agony drawing me forward. I flitted through the fray, Evander close to my side offering protection, as we found broken bodies.

The first was an earth fae with thick, brown ram horns spiraling back from his head. Viscera spilled from the wide gash across his abdomen, blood seeping from the wound as he desperately tried to hold pressure across the torn flesh.

"This is going to hurt," I warned him, dropping to my knees and forcing the intestine back inside. He howled in pain, the wound spurting fresh blood, but then my palms were pressed over the raw tissue, forcing broken vessels and split muscles to knit back together.

My palms eased as his intrinsic fae affinities took over, and I was happy to see his breathing even out. He'd be weakened with the loss of blood, but at least he'd survive.

Cries rang through the air, each needing my attention. A streak of blond hair flitted among those on the opposite end of the field, flares of light flickering as Jarek alternated between saving and slaying.

I concentrated on those before me, relying on Evander to keep me safe as I worked. His sword sliced through the air, relieving a light fae of his head as I secured an IV along the crook of a wounded fae's elbow. The mating bond gave a tug as the last few drops of luminescent fluid drained into the fae's arm. Her chest heaved, proving that the newly expanded lung was as good as new.

I barely heard her thanks as she flitted back into battle, my gaze searching for violet hair and silver eyes. She was flanked by Alarik and Queen Freya, with a small trickle of blood dripping from the shallow gash along her shoulder. It wasn't anything to worry about. Her fae affinities were nearly finished repairing it, but I still felt the urge to tend to it myself.

Darkness flashed, tendrils of night snaking out from between the trees. Erebus leaned against a large trunk with his arms folded across his chest as the battle raged. He only watched, doing nothing to stop the bloodshed as his eyes fixed on the two blurs flitting among the light fae: El and Zaeth

Bodies fell where they went, some light fae still swinging blades before they realized their lives had already been claimed. El and Zaeth were ruthless in their slaughter, the bond connecting me to my sister vibrating with exhilaration and an insatiable thirst for more.

More blood. More death.

My eyes widen as I saw archers regrouping in the shadows of the forest. There were dozens of them, all arching their backs as they drew back arrows and aimed—All of them pointed at El.

Horror twisted my gut as the arrows loosened, another volley flying through the air. Zaeth's blade deflected the first wave, but he couldn't move fast enough to stop the ones coming from behind the first. Or the third.

A scream lodged in my throat as I watched Zaeth flit, his shadows snaking out in front of him, despite knowing it wouldn't be enough.

Darkness reared up, eclipsing Zaeth's shadows to snatch the arrows out of the sky, just as he had done before.

El cursed, shooting Erebus a glare as he lowered his hand, the dark rings around her eyes blazing just as strongly as his.

"The trees," Halcyon commanded, sending a team into the forest. They wove through vines and lush ferns as they hunted down every last archer.

El and Zaeth joined the rest of the army in finishing off the surrounded light fae while Jarek sheathed his blade and helped me tend to the injured.

"That would've gone a lot quicker if you bothered to lift a finger," El seethed, the grip on her dagger tightening as Erebus looked down with a bored expression on his face.

"I did," he shrugged. "When it mattered."

"Each life holds the same value," Alarik growled as he wiped the gore coating his blade against a blanket of moss.

"You don't really believe that." Erebus's lips twitched. "None of you do. The light fae lying at your feet meant very little. The lives of all the creatures Levana created, they mean nothing. You hold yourself and your world in higher regard."

"They're *invading* our world," Queen Freya countered.

Erebus fixed his cool gaze on her. "If you had been born in the otherworld, a place filled with darkness and mayhem, and there was a chance you could forge a life in the light, would you not do everything in your power to seize that chance?"

Alarik frowned as Queen Freya glared.

"Levana and her creatures are not seeking refuge," I said, speaking into the ringing silence. All turned to face me, and I felt a flicker of pride down the mating bond as the Earth Army paused to hear what I had to say. "If her monsters sought sanctuary, we would welcome them."

"Is that so," Erebus mused, pushing off the tree and striding toward me. "If the horde of Levana's creations came to you this very moment seeking peace, you would grant it, despite past transgressions?"

"Yes," I answered honestly, but Erebus smiled like I was a mouse caught in a cat's claws.

"If Veles sought your mercy, would you grant it?"

"*Veles* has earned his place in the endless fires," El snarled, her wings snapping wide.

"Enough," Zaeth growled, glaring as Erebus's grin stretched. "We need to focus on the task at hand, not hypotheticals that will never come to pass."

"Agreed," Halcyon said, coming to my side. "Do a sweep of the forest and report back every hundred miles until we have clear borders." The army peeled off, heeding her orders as she glanced between the rest of us. "Jarek, can you get word to King Ryuu and Queen Greer? We should take the morning to rest, but then we need to alert the other kingdoms to the possibility of an attack."

"Sure thing," he answered after sharing a look with Zaeth. The Dark King nodded, and Jarek was gone.

"This doesn't feel right," Zaeth muttered, turning his back on Erebus to face us. The God of Night stiffened but glanced to El, to his daughter a moment longer, before he faded into the night.

Her shoulders slumped around an exhale. "I know but we can't exactly go up against both him and Levana."

"No, I mean the light fae attack." Zaeth glanced at the bodies littering the ground. "There were little less than three hundred fae here. Enough to cause a problem if left unchecked, but not nearly enough to have a chance of winning."

My brow furrowed as I ran the numbers. "Even if they'd had direct access underground and surprised us, the Earth Kingdom still would've won."

"Then why attack at all?" Alarik asked.

My gut twisted. "Why, indeed."

GREER

We were now working with gods—well, a god with plans to find, free, and align ourselves with another.

Jarek luxed to the Air Kingdom, appearing the day after the attack on the Sky Warriors. I'd thought it was perfect timing, despite it being early evening, until he relayed all that had happened in the Earth Kingdom.

Ryuu and I luxed back with him the next day to Queen Halcyon's domain, joining Queen Freya, El, and Zaeth in order to figure out our next move.

"We only have an hour before we need to return," Ryuu said, taking a seat around the round, wooden table.

We'd followed Halcyon and Lannie into the top of the canopy, the war room surrounded by arched clear windows and small balconies to reveal the beauty of the Earth Kingdom. I'd thought being underground would feel oppressive compared to the open skies I'd come to care for, but the glimmering stones and precious jewels sparkling along every surface were dazzling.

Not sparing any details, I gave a rundown on our own encounter with Levana's forces.

"Another ambush with far too weak of an offense," Zaeth said.

"I wouldn't say that," I countered. "Many families would've been killed had we not acted quickly."

"But the moment the air fae were sky borne, the battle was over," Lannie breathed, shaking her head. "Is Levana toying with us?"

The shadows overhead darkened, stretching and condensing at the same time until a large, muscular figure emerged. His skin and hair were a few shades darker than El's, but the slope of his nose and the dark rings around his eyes left very little doubt as to who he was.

"Erebus I presume?"

He lifted a thick, dark brow in my direction.

"I'm Greer, El's other sister."

Erebus nodded, his gaze darting to Ryuu and back. "Perhaps you can help her see reason."

El stiffened, but I didn't take my eyes off him. "There are many things I'd like to help El with. Her inability to stay away from danger, her short temper, her aversion to wearing anything other than black."

Indignation flickered down our sister bond as El rolled her eyes.

Erebus's jaw clenched. "All of this is pointless. We need to find Eunoia and free her before Levana destroys everything."

"He's right," Lannie said, cutting off El and what was promising to be a snarky reply based on the viciousness of her glare.

"What?" El asked, clear astonishment on her face. "We need to secure the borders before we can afford to start on some quest."

"On the contrary," Queen Freya said, looking decidedly unhappy about agreeing with Erebus. "If we don't find and awaken Eunoia, there will be no stopping Levana."

El's eyes narrowed as Erebus dipped his head in thanks to the Wild Queen.

"I'm not saying this for your benefit," Queen Freya snapped. "You've made it clear containing Levana is your only goal. That and keeping Elara safe, apparently. The only reason I'm agreeing with you is because Eunoia is the best chance we have of making it through this alive."

"Erebus doesn't care about me," El countered, but I could see the lie of those words written across her face.

"Where is Eunoia?" I asked.

"We don't know," Lannie answered with a sigh. "Somewhere in the north, according to Erebus."

"There's not some magical way to track her?" I pressed. "Levana had those silver-blue stones. Erebus felt like a void in the earth. Eunoia must have something."

"She has a point," Ryuu agreed, his gaze swinging to Zaeth. "You've traveled the north extensively. Anything stand out?"

Zaeth started to shake his head and then stopped, his warm brown eyes finding El.

"You think?" she whispered, the two of them seeming to have a full conversation without speaking.

"You felt it when we flew over, the same as I did." Zaeth tilted her chin up, bringing her gaze to his. "The rush of life, death, power. The infinite expanse. The feeling of being everywhere and nowhere all at once. It must be her."

The longer the silence stretched, the more Erebus looked like he was getting ready to string Zaeth up and demand answers.

"Where" I nudged.

"The foothills of the Jagged Mountains," El said.

Erebus stood, looking as if he would sink into the shadows that very moment to find the goddess.

"How do we release her?" I asked. "Levana took thousands of

years to store the power and I'd really like to avoid sacrificing a few hundred fae if we can help it."

Erebus narrowed his eyes. "The tethers binding Levana, Eunoia, and myself were linked, much in the way you, your sisters, and brother were linked. When one breaks, the others are weakened. She will not require nearly the same sacrifice as I did."

"Still," I pressed. "We'd prefer not sacrificing *anyone*."

Erebus looked from me to his daughter, the stubborn set of his jaw the same expression I'd seen a hundred times on El's face. "There is always a cost."

"Then let your pet, Veles, pay it," El said, pushing to stand and pacing the length of the room. "He has plenty of Fractured puppets at his disposal."

"That's not a bad idea," Ryuu murmured meeting Zaeth's gaze across the wooden table. "We can bring back the goddess and dispose of Levana's army at the same time."

Erebus's face twisted as if tasting something sour. "I'd prefer the offering be pure. Their essence left a lingering aura of grime that is only now dissipating."

"*I* would've liked to never have witnessed humans dying by the hundreds as Veles tore through my base," Alarik said, his temper flaring as he stood.

"I would have preferred my people never succumbed to the sleeping sickness," Queen Halcyon said, her voice soft but firm as she stared at the God of Night responsible for their deaths. She too moved to stand.

"To have had the chance at knowing my parents," Lannie breathed, joining her fated mate.

"To have lived a long, happy life with the man I love," Evander added, resting his hand on the back of Jarek's chair.

I lifted a brow at the present tense, daring a glance to Jarek who looked as if he'd been slapped.

"If it had not been for Levana and her scheming, our lives

would've been vastly different." Zaeth said, joining El as she stared daggers at her father.

"Okay," Erebus said, and I swear he was close to rolling his eyes. "I get it. Veles and the Fractured will join me."

"We're not letting you go alone," El chimed in. "The Jagged Mountains are Zaeth's territory. We'll accompany you and pinpoint the region most likely to house Eunoia."

"Naz will need to be informed," Zaeth said, his gaze sliding to Jarek with the unasked question.

Jarek gave a nod, still seeming to be replaying Evander's last statement. "I'll drop in after I return Ryuu and Greer to the Air Kingdom."

"We should be going," I said, feeling the weight of the Air Kingdom on my shoulders. "We need to meet with the Sky Warriors to discuss postings as well as come up with evacuation plans. We won't be taken by surprise again."

"Any word from the Water Queen?" Ryuu asked, looking toward Queen Halcyon. She shook her head.

"Not yet. I've sent a message, but I fear it'll be intercepted by King Kai. For now, we must assume they're against us."

Ryuu's eyes shifted into vertical slits, the promise of war and violence hanging heavy in the air. "We're moving all people residing on low-lying islands to the mainland."

"I'll portal back here once I know my kingdom is secured." Queen Freya said, shooting Erebus one last glare as she and Alarik retired to the back of the room, a portal flashing into being.

"Lannie?" I asked, wanting to make sure she intended to stay in the Earth Kingdom. "Your obligation to the sleeping sickness has been fulfilled."

Her brown eyes widened, her gaze immediately turning to Queen Halcyon at her side. To her credit, the Earth Queen offered her a small smile with no traces of pressure slipping through.

"You're free to go where you wish, but I would be lying if I said I didn't hope you would stay."

Uncertainly flashed through our sister bond, Lannie's tangle of emotions too muddled to understand. Something seemed to shift between the two of them as they stared into each other's eyes. Not quite electricity, but a warmth. Maybe the start of a friendship that could grow into something more.

"I wish to stay," Lannie breathed. An unrestrained grin stretched across Queen Halcyon's face, coaxing one from my little sister. The two of them breathed each other in for another moment before remembering we were there.

"Just checking," I said, my lips twitched as a faint blush worked across Lannie's cheeks.

"I'll stay here," Evander said, drawing my attention back to Jarek. "I like the gardens."

Jarek looked like he wanted to protest but thought better of it. "If that's what you want."

"It is," Evander nodded, placing a chaste kiss on Jarek's cheek before flitting through the door.

For one unguarded second, anguish twisted Jarek's features, but I blinked, and the moment had passed. He fixed his light blue eyes on me.

"Ready to go?"

52

ELARA

Erebus, Zaeth, and I waited for Jarek to return from the Air Kingdom. Erebus could fade into the night whenever he wished, but he said our weak fae bodies wouldn't survive the way he traveled. Something about the pressure squishing us as easily as a boot stomping on a bug.

So, we were stuck waiting.

We'd remained in the war room set in the canopy of the Earth Palace, and despite the dire circumstances and even worse company, the views were breathtaking. From the small balcony, I could see precious stones glimmering in every direction.

The road before me was studded with diamonds. They were everywhere, crafted into hanging ornaments, inlaid along benches or buildings as they led up to the amethyst palace grounds. The plants were just as captivating, the dark hues giving the kingdom a much needed contrast to the glamour all around.

The scent of cedar and spice surrounded me as Zaeth's hands came to rest on either side of the balcony rail, boxing me in. His breath fanned my ear, and I pressed my back against him, craving his grounding presence.

"It's beautiful," I said, letting my head fall back against his chest. "If Lannie does choose to stay here, and in some distant future her and Halcyon decide to embrace their mating bond, I wouldn't mind visiting."

Zaeth's chest rumbled as a chuckled rocked through him. "A distant future?"

"Mhmm," I nodded, allowing myself to think about what that future might be like. "We could tour the kingdoms. Greer and Ryuu would be the most loved rulers the Air Kingdom has ever seen."

Despite her worries, Greer was made for life at court. People were drawn to her. She'd even won over Cress, though I doubted she realized it yet.

"Lannie will stay here, expanding her knowledge and affinities for healing. Halcyon will support her through it, their friendship building as my little sister's heart becomes less guarded."

I chewed my lip, letting my heart lead me on this beautiful daydream. If we could shape the perfect world, what would it hold?

"Once we defeat Levana and Veles, there will be a vacancy in the Light Kingdom. Jarek will fill it. He'll turn things around, bring diversity and love, acceptance and knowledge to the east. Evander will realize Jem would've wanted him to live. To be happy. Evander will finally see how crazy Jarek is about him, and he for Jarek. Maybe there will even be another royal wedding."

Zaeth pressed a kiss to my head as we gazed at the underground world.

"And us?" he asked, voice soft. "What does that wondrous mind of yours see for our future?"

"We'll be the happiest of them all." My lips pulled into a grin as I envisioned the adventures we'd have. "We'll give Naz a much needed vacation. Then, we'll rebuild."

Zaeth nuzzled my neck, the subtle scrape of his trimmed beard causing me to shudder. "Just like that?"

"Just like that," I grinned, spinning in his arms and pressing my lips to his. "One good thing that has come from Levana, is that the dark fae realize you've been defending them, despite being the Dark Phoenix. You've spent your entire life—given every ounce of your being—to protecting *them*. It's about time we showed the Dark Kingdom the incredible king you are."

Zaeth swallowed, gathering me into a fierce kiss before pulling back, our foreheads pressed together. "Gods, I don't deserve you."

"No, you don't." Erebus agreed, his voice like a bucket of ice water spilling over us.

"Says the god who wouldn't care if the entire world burned," I snapped, hating the way Zaeth's jaw ticked, as if he might actually believe Erebus.

"I won't claim to understand what fae emotions are like," Erebus said, the dark rings around his eyes blazing. "But I know you are far more powerful than him. Eunoia may have bestowed her blessing on the Dark King, but you have a part of my being. My essence. You are more powerful than you know."

"Blessing?" Zaeth asked, the right of light around his eyes igniting. I could feel the shock rocking through him, but also the nagging feeling that this was true "What blessing?"

"Speed, strength." Erebus's eyes trailed over him. "Your wings. The runes coating your skin designate you as Eunoia's chosen defender in a time of great peril. But all of it fails in comparison to my lineage."

"Your 'lineage' did very little when I needed it most," I seethed, thinking of Will. Of our bound powers.

As if hearing my thoughts, Erebus narrowed his eyes. "Your mother knew who I was when she chose to lay with me. She was clever and cunning. Brilliant and beautiful. Everything a goddess should be, despite her being fae."

My brows furrowed, taking in the god before me. "You... loved her?"

His lips curled back as a flustered grimace twisted his lips. "'Love' is not a concept familiar to gods. I was captivated by her strength. Most trembled before me, or offer me their lives in supplication, but your mother looked at me as a challenge. She wanted to birth the savior of this realm. So, she did."

"Savior?" Zaeth said, knowing my mind was reeling too much to give voice to the questions tumbling around in my mind. "Did Adara know of Levana, even then?"

"Eunoia sensed a disturbance. We both did, though neither of us understood what it meant. Eunoia's light is connected to this planet in more ways than I understood. She would've been content to let us all sit in our bindings forever."

I lifted a brow at the bitterness lacing his worlds. "Eunoia professed the prophecy. The one that caused Mother to bind our powers."

Erebus nodded. "When Adara sought me, she believed she was creating a being strong enough to stop the prophecy. When she discovered *you* were the very thing she was fighting against, she did everything in her power to stop fate."

Because of Levana. Because the Goddess of Shadows wanted revenge on her sister. All this boiled down to fae dying in a war we had nothing to do with.

"We will stop Levana, my daughter," Erebus said, his voice rumbling as the doors to the war room opened. "And you will complete the future your mother intended."

I wanted to ask why he cared, why he thought he could ever claim me as his daughter when he'd been nothing more than a one-night stand planned by my mother. But in that moment, all of my self-control went to not flinging a dagger toward the door.

Veles entered, his silver hair and pale skin looking a little grey. The dark rings under his eyes had grown, the hollowness of his gaze even more so. He was wearing the same armor he'd had on when Draven stabbed me in the stomach. I noted the blooming peony set before a rising sun, remembering the havoc Aldridge had caused, the families in Sonder who had suffered before of Veles and his brothers, and all traces of empathy vanished.

"The Fractured are ready to go, God of Gods." Ignoring Zaeth and I, Veles turned toward Erebus and bowed.

"Great," I muttered to Zaeth, not bothering to lower my voice. "I hope Jarek gets back soon, because despite knowing it would only serve Levana, I really want to put a blade through his neck—"

Jarek flashed into being, chest heaving and eyes wide.

"Caligo, it's under attack."

53

ELARA

"Mobilize the Fractured to the Jagged Mountains," Zaeth commanded Veles, knowing we had no viable way of transporting that many beings. "We'll find you once Caligo is safe."

I expected Veles to sneer or curse, but he only gave Zaeth a tight nod before flitting from the room.

Erebus met my gaze with a promise in his eyes.

"I don't need your protection," I snapped, willing him to stay away as I accepted Jarek's outstretched hand and let him whisk me away.

He didn't listen.

Pitch black shadows condensed across cobblestoned streets as the sounds of war rose. The sun was sinking behind The Dark Palace at our backs with the bulk of the battle appearing along Caligo's northwestern section. Dark fae warriors flooded the streets, rushing toward the sounds of pain and not too distant snarls.

"Shadow wraiths and cú sídhe," Jarek said, his sword whirling through the air and slicing through a wraith's neck. The thin grey skin stretched tight over bones gave way beneath his blade, the skeletal head rolling as it toppled from its bony shoulders.

I unleashed the sword along my spine as a howl sounded to my right. Giving into my fae affinities, I let the longing for bloodshed fill me. My vision sharpened, my hearing snagging on the hundreds of heartbeats thundering around me, the whooshing of blood through veins.

The metallic tang of blood and grime and fear filled the air as Zaeth and I joined the fray, spreading the word that the shadow wraiths could only be disposed of through beheading as we dodged the talons and teeth of the cú sídhe. The massive wolves had descended on Caligo in packs, the alphas seeming to work together to dismantle our warriors.

"We need to take out their alphas," Zaeth called, yanking his sword from the belly of a beast. My gaze zeroed in on the black taint of its blood.

"Agreed," I shouted over the howls erupting from the cluster of cú sídhe in the north. They were growing closer. With a quick jerk of my chin, I referenced the beast at Zaeth's feet. "They've evolved with the help of Levana's meddling. The black tint in their blood is evidence to that."

"Meaning, they'll be harder to kill," Zaeth finished, dodging a scythe and ending the shadow wraith's life with a quick flick of his wrist.

A chorus of howls rang through the blood-filled streets, echoing around us as a wide shadow on the horizon grew darker. The buzzing cloud grew thicker, the collective form splitting into hundreds of snarling, winged fae with sharp fangs.

"Levana's creatures," I said, narrowly avoiding the sharp edge of a scythe. I rolled, coming up behind the shadow wraith with a swing of my sword.

Shadows condensed just behind Zaeth, my heart stuttering for a moment before Naz appeared.

"Those are the fae we saw in the north," she panted. Her tight curls were secured back in a knot at the base of her neck, and her black battle leathers coated in a wash of blood and fur. "The ones that eat fae."

Her eyes widened as the first of them reached the outskirts of battle, diving into the crowded streets. A half-a-dozen followed, sinking their fangs into the hide of a cú sídhe. It roared, thrashing and clawing as they drank. The wolf managed to rip a few throats out, but three more descended for each it killed. Soon, the wolf was just another body to add to the growing piles.

"Apparently, they eat cú sídhe as well," I said, my hard gaze fixed on the frenzy erupting on the edge of battle.

"They're attacking their own troops," Jarek uttered, whirling with his blade.

"They did the same thing at the Shadowlands," Naz said, fading into the shadows and then reappearing moments later behind the nearest shadow wraith, her blade removing its head with a few quick strokes.

The dark swarm continued their destruction, eating and killing as they neared. Soon, cries of dark fae joined the screams of Levana's creatures as the plague reached the point of our two armies clashing.

"They have no allegiance to Levana?" Jarek asked, dipping down as a wolf leapt for him, his blade finding a soft patch of belly.

Zaeth shook his head after dispatching the cluster of wraiths nearest him. "Their hunger rules them. I'd wager they are too ravenous to follow orders."

Naz shared a look with Jarek before focusing on Zaeth. "We need your wings, brother. We are no longer children and our father's hatred has been gone for some time. Our people will understand."

My stomach twisted as I felt Zaeth's trepidation. Zaeth had hidden his identity for so long, shame forcing him to keep his wings out of sight. But Naz was right. Despite the Dark Kingdom's hatred and fear of The Dark Phoenix, we needed him.

More winged fae dove from the sky, some picking up bodies and ripping them apart in the air.

"They're hunters looking for prey," I said, watching as they tore through bodies like swarming locusts set to a field. Even the shadow wraiths weren't spared, though most of the flying fae avoided them after the first bite. "We need to show them we're predators, just as they are."

I focused on the swarm, on the beating of their hearts and the faint glow around them. It wasn't black, like most of Levana's creatures were—not golden like Eunoia's children either—but a swirling of indigo and deep violet with flares of cobalt, as if pieces of the otherworld were contained within.

"Levana may have created them, but she doesn't own them. Not like the others," I said, finding Zaeth's cinnamon glaze lock on mine. He sensed my vision through our bond, feeling my conflicting urges of wanting to destroy them, while also realizing they weren't doomed. But everywhere they went blood sprayed.

"Let your viciousness out, love. The hunger, the hatred, the insatiable need for revenge. We'll show them this kingdom—our kingdom—is home to monsters just as ruthless as they are."

Zaeth's fangs elongated as his wings unfurled, his dark affinities triggering my own. Whatever traces of hesitation that had been there moments before were gone. My Dark King was ready to fight for this nation, to lay down his life, if need be.

But we wouldn't be the ones dying today.

"The ultimate monsters," I breathed as my violet wings stretched. I wasn't as graceful as he was with flying maneuvers, but I could handle the basics.

We rose in the air, blades in hand, and charged.

The battle of wolves and wraiths was still waging below, our dark fae warriors not giving an inch of ground, but for all our planning, we were still unprepared for an attack from the sky. For the savageness of their assault.

A few glanced up from their feast, their mouths coated in red and black rivulets moments before we were upon them. We dropped from the sky, our wings going wide as we arched over the bloodied ground where they were gorging themselves. Our blades cut a path, splitting open necks, bellies, and limbs—slicing right through their leathery wings.

"Their wings don't have barbs or bones!" I called as Zaeth and I soared into the clouds, preparing for our next strike. Even fire fae had spindles snaking through their webbed bat-like wings, serving as points of contact that could withstand strikes. They weren't nearly as effective as the air-fae's barbed wings, but Levana's creatures were left with nothing—a vulnerability.

Zaeth nodded as streams of blood sprayed across him, dripping off his tunic as the cool winter air whipped around us.

"And they are distracted easily," Zaeth breathed as a group of Levana's creatures split from the pack and headed right for us. "Another pass."

I nodded, diving toward the snarling fae. Tucking my wings in, I slipped to the side of the group, watching from the corner of my vision as Zaeth did the same. Our blades cut through the group wedged between us, broken, mangled chunks of flesh falling as we worked.

Bodies tumbled to the group, landing on their brothers and sisters with sickening splats.

We hovered over them, wings pumping, our swords dripping with blood. And waited.

"Are you ready, love?"

Zaeth's voice was low, calm even, but I could feel the mounting excitement humming through his veins as a great portion of the group turned toward us. Every nerve ending in my body was aware of Zaeth's, of his own wicked delight of battle—nearly as strong as mine.

My lips twitched as I held his gaze, the sharp points of my fangs peeking out beneath my lips. "They've no idea who they're up against."

Zaeth captured me in a fierce kiss, the taste of his tongue mingling with the blood of our enemies. "Let's show them."

We split apart just as they reached us, a laugh tearing through my throat as we dodged attack after attack. They were half mad with rage and ruled by hunger, the group of them fighting like wild beasts on the verge of starvation.

More and more bodies fell, and soon the whole swarm was upon us. We hacked and sliced, flying among them as they swiped at us with fangs and pointed nails. Curses mingled with shrieks of pain as Zaeth and I moved faster, managing to avoid the worst of them thanks to the protective barbs throughout our feathers.

I glanced to my mate, aware that my body was tapping into the darkness gifted to me by Erebus and surprised to find Zaeth keeping pace. My eyes widen as I noted the control in which he wielded shadows like a lasso, flinging and breaking fae without a second through. A faint glow had started along his skin, the brands igniting into a blinding light.

The rings around his eyes flared the same hue as his brands, the silver barbs in his beautiful onyx wings glinting against the setting sun. For a moment, he looked suspending with his great wings stretched, fangs gleaming, and blood splattered across every inch of his skin.

Light gathered, illuminating Zaeth further as if he wielded the wrath of the gods. And maybe he did, because a collective shudder swept through Levana's dark creatures as he stilled, looking down at the collective group of winged fae before us.

"We don't have to be at odds," Zaeth boomed. "You have my blessing to feast on all those who serve Levana. But make no mistake, if you harm one of my people, there will be consequences."

Low murmurings broke out, their leathery wings beating in place as they glanced at one another—And then fled. A few returned to the north, reporting back to Levana, no doubt. But a great number of them split from the others.

"They're headed south."

Zaeth nodded as the light gathered around him dimmed. "Perhaps Levana has another base."

"Maybe," I conceded. "Or maybe they're heeding your advice."

Cheers rose from the city beneath, drawing our attention away from the retreating cloud of creatures. From here, we could see the battle on the ground had been won. The corpses of shadow wraiths and cú sídhe were strung about the streets as fae pounded their chests and raised their blades into the sky.

Zaeth and I descended to the sounds of their exhilaration. We'd won, but to do so also meant Zaeth had exposed who he truly was.

I could see the tension in his jaw, the way his wings snapped in close as we landed, but there was no hiding, now. Everyone had seen him. Everyone knew he was The Dark Phoenix.

It didn't matter I was the other half of the prophetic creature, the one with the God of Night's blood running through my veins. Zaeth was the figurehead, the disowned and feared Dark Prince who'd avoided gossip when possible but had never denounce the rumors.

Zaeth's ruins chose that moment to pulse, igniting as the last rays of light stretched over the Jagged Mountains to cast him in a silhouette.

"Eunoia's blessing," a deep voice rumbled as a hush fell over the crowd—the voice of the God of Night, himself. Darkness gathered where Erebus was leaning against the building at the edge of the street, tucking into the shadows as the sun descended.

"The Dark King rises!" Naz shouted from the front, her eyes shining with the hint of tears.

"And all will fall!" Soter answered beside her, dropping to his knees.

"And all will fall," echoed the crowd, bowing before their king.

Overwhelming warmth flooded through the bond. It was the feeling of finally coming home after a long journey, one filled with pitfalls and dead ends. Of death and immeasurable pain. But Zaeth had returned. Welcomed by his people.

It should've been perfect. Zaeth had sacrificed years of his life, his family, the feeling of having a home. He was finally seen for the protector he was, but a nagging in my gut drew my eyes back to Erebus.

His arms were crossed over his chest, the dark stretches of night pulled in tight. Erebus met my gaze unflinchingly, the look conveying everything and nothing all at once. It almost felt like he was relieved, proud I'd fought so well, and yet…

"Don't," I breathed, much too soft for him to hear.

Erebus dipped his head across the boisterous crown as if to say, 'I must,' before the black tendrils of night rose and he was gone.

54

ELARA

"Erebus has gone to free Eunoia," I shouted. I looked to Naz, to Soter at her side but they couldn't hear me over the crowd's cheering.

Zaeth's hand came around my waist, following my line of vision to where Erebus had been a moment ago. "There's no way Veles has even crossed the border."

"He's going to choose his own sacrifices."

Panic clawed up my throat as the dark fae surged forward, ushering us toward the castle as all called for a celebration.

"What is it, kitten?" Jarek appeared next to me, his blue eyes searching mine. His light blond hair was in disarray, dirt and blood clinging to his person, but his tone was gentle. Ready to help.

"Erebus," I breathed. "He's gone."

Jarek stiffened, searching the boisterous crowd until he found Soter and Naz. He luxed to their side, reappearing by us with them in tow a moment later. "Let's go somewhere we can talk."

Zaeth and I accepted his outstretched hand, the five of us trusting Jarek to take us somewhere safe.

The clamor of the city was heard even from the upper towers of the Dark Palace. Dozens of bonfires were being erected as fae flitted through the streets. Somewhere in the distance, the beat of drums had started, but all I could think about was who Erebus would deem 'pure' enough to sacrifice.

"You're sure it's just beyond the cottage, at the foothills of the Jagged Mountains?" Naz asked, wiping away the worst of the blood from her face.

"Yes," Zaeth answered, scrubbing a towel over his forearms. "No other place on Pax has called to me. El felt it, too."

"Felt what?" Soter asked, his molten gold eyes swirling. There were dark stains on the tips of his thick ram horns, and I wondered if he'd gored someone with them.

"Like all of Pax was connected to that one spot," I said, my eyes drifting to my own hands as I reached for a damp towel. Dried streaks of black and burnt umber flaked across my knuckles, collecting in the groves of my hands—evidence of the battle we'd just won. "Like the origin of life itself. I'll answer any questions on the way, but we need to go if we have any chance of stopping Erebus."

"We *don't* want to stop him," Soter argued. "We only want to decide the cost of Eunoia's freedom."

"There's no way Veles or the Fractured are anywhere close to the border, let alone the Jagged Mountains," Jarek said, meeting my gaze. "El's right. If we don't move quickly, innocents will die."

Naz frowned, looking toward the windows and the growing night beyond. "I'm still drained. I'll be able to shadowwalk by myself but traveling with others will be a last resort until I'm recovered. Jarek?"

"I should be able to lux the five of us, but my healing will be restricted."

"Let's make sure we don't need it, then," I said, holding my hand out. The worst of the blood had been wiped away, and I knew we needed to act quickly, but I couldn't shake the feeling that we were heading into another battle we were unprepared for.

～

The sharply slated roof and wrap-around porch of Zaeth's cottage were the same as I remembered, but the clusters of mushrooms and lush moss coating the base of thick birch trees had gone, replaced by deep snowdrifts. The forest was cast in shades of black and white under the early evening moonlight, and I caught more than a few fleeting pixies darting overhead before fleeing into the forest.

Memories of my short time here with Zaeth flashed through my mind, momentarily halting the mounting panic swirling through me. It was before we knew about Levana, before the Spear of Empyrean was reformed, back when we were still hopeful.

Zaeth had taken me to the pools, showing me the beauty of the underground hot springs and then we'd opened ourselves to each other. It had been the first time I'd felt whole. He'd seen me—all of me—and had loved me all the more for it.

Zaeth's lips quirked as he sensed where my thoughts had gone. I leaned into his touch as his wings slipped around us, drawing me close to hold off the cold.

"We *will* have those moments again, love," he promised as the gentle caress of his lips heated the shell of my ear.

It was a vow spoken to my soul. We'd have an entire future full of sweet kisses and tantalizing touches. We'd have time to enjoy each other, explore every inch of each other's bodies, learn each other's minds in the most intimate ways. We *would* stop Levana and bring Erebus to heel.

"It's just south of here," I breathed, unable to look away from

Zaeth. His smiled hitched, the tips of his fangs peering from beneath his lips.

"We will lead the way," Zaeth promised, shifting my hand in his.

We flitted through the trees, dodging the worst of the snow and sticking to paths carved by deer and the like. My heart gave a lurch as we reached the blessed area, the two of us brushing against an unknown pull, trusting Eunoia's blessing to aid us.

We wove through thickets of trees until we came to the edge of a shallow brook, the waters tumbling over slick stones. The nearest bank was lined with snow, the slow-moving pools in the shallows covered with a thin layer of ice. Just before the water's edge sat a small field of snow drop flowers clustered around a slab of silver stone.

There wasn't a pulsing glow around it like Levana's altar had. No hidden steps, or underground chamber, but I could feel the earth come alive as we neared.

Levana had a tomb—a prison—but this felt like Eunoia had chosen a bed within the earth, unencumbered by pillars. She was simply beneath the ground, surrounded by everything she'd created.

Zaeth's affinities intensified as power rose toward us, as if in greeting.

"She's here," I said, awe coating my words.

"But where's Erebus?" Soter asked, his golden eyes scanning the trees.

I frowned, seeing the pristine snow and the clusters of flowers that had shot up through the undisturbed frost. There were no tracks or footprints.

"Is this the place?" Naz asked, her gaze bouncing between the slab of stone and Zaeth.

"Yes," he muttered, his head jerking toward the trees as shrieks caught on the air.

We turned as one, drawing blades and preparing for a fight

as the ground beneath our feet shuddered. A wave of power crested over us, reaching. Seeking. Hunting for its next meal.

My jaw clenched as streaks of night condensed, so absolute that even the white of the snow was eclipsed.

"Erebus," I said, foregoing the sword along my spine and unsheathing the dagger strapped to my forearm.

He manifested, tendrils of night stretching out behind him to reveal his prize. Three fae women were crying and clawing at the darkness that bound them, great wisps of it wrapping around their necks. They wore long tunics, the faint hint of earth and heated waters still clinging to them.

"Let the priestesses go," Zaeth said, his low voice rumbling as his runes ignited. But I could feel the hunger beneath our feet, the connection flowing into me through our mating bond, just as Zaeth could.

Eunoia wanted this. She yearned to be set free, to have the blood of her most beloved followers offered up to her.

"The sacrifice of those who have proven their love, their loyalty, is worth more than a hundred mindless, broken souls." Erebus's darkness flexed, sending a wave of panicked whimpers through his prisoners.

"Take as many Fractured as you need," I said, inching closer to draw his attention while Naz stepped back. "But the priestesses are off limits."

Erebus laughed, the sound causing the fine hairs on the back of my neck to stand as the harshness of it rang through the frost-covered clearing. "Nothing is 'off limits' for me, daughter. It's time you learned what true power means."

Naz faded into the shadows, reappearing beside the three captured women. She reached for the first, her fingers brushing the back of her hand just as Erebus sent another swath of night behind him.

It wrapped around her, binding her arms to her sides as she was forced to join the others.

"No," I shouted as Zaeth and Soter darted forward, blades raised.

Jarek attempted to lux, but a wave of darkness washed over him, forcing him to reappear right where he'd left, panting and gasping for air.

Erebus's eyes flashed, the dark rings around his irises glowing as he batted Zaeth and Soter away with a flick of his wrist. Their bodies smacked against trees as they flew through the forest, knocking snow from branches as they disappeared into the distance.

"Stop!" I shouted as Erebus took another step toward the stone slab. "There's no need to kill them. Veles—"

"*Veles,*" snarled Erebus, pitch black plums billowing around him. And I realized I'd yet to see even a fraction of his power. "Veles is a vile creature desperate for revenge and craving the blissful peace of death. He would give me everything, do anything I asked if it meant seeing his brothers again."

Snow crunched beneath his feet, Naz's curses joining the pleas of the others. Another step closer to the stone. Another second to stop him gone.

"I don't *want* Veles or his Fractured. I have been lenient with you, daughter. Patient, when I would've rather pushed, and *still* you defy me. You may be my blood, my one true child in a millennium of solitude, but there are somethings even you can't sway me from."

My mind whirled as his words rushed over me. *One true child.* In all his existence.

"You must make a choice," Erebus continued, his shadows rushing forward. I could hear Zaeth and Soter rise, flitting through the trees back toward us. There was a hitch to Soter's step and a faint gurgling sound emanating from Zaeth's lungs, but they'd heal completely in a few more minutes.

My gaze snapped to Naz. She gritted her teeth as her fingers searched for a way to pry the cord of night from her throat. As much as I hated to admit it, I knew there was nothing she could do to stop this. Nothing any of us could do.

"You can save the Dark King's sister *or* the three innocents. I will have my sacrifice this night, daughter. Which do you choose."

The priestesses renewed their pleas for mercy, one of them listing off all the ways in which she had served Eunoia. Of the sisters and family she would leave behind.

"El," Zaeth panted from the edge of the small clearing. Erebus's shadows had stretched into a circle, blocking anything from entering. My eyes bounced to Soter as he came to Zaeth's side, his molten gold eyes fixed on Naz. She stopped struggling, her dark eyes flashing with a resounding sorrow that looked like it broke something in Soter.

"No," Soter shook his head as her lips tilted into the ghost of a soft, sad smile. "No, Naz. You don't get to give up."

"We can't fight two gods, kitten," Jarek breathed, his voice raw as he stepped to my side, the only person still encased in this ring of death with me. "What choice can you live with?"

I forced myself to look at three priestesses. They were young, even by fae standards. Probably in their first few decades of life. Scared gazes met mine, begging me to save them. Knowing I was the only thing stopping them from joining the after.

"I'm growing impatient, daughter," Erebus called. "Perhaps I should offer all of them to the goddess, despite the dark fae's resentment. Such hatred for Eunoia, for the life bestowed on her."

Naz stiffened as Erebus dragged her forward, her features twisting in hatred as she stared into his eyes. "Fuck you."

Erebus chuckled. "A pity you weren't there for my release."

"Stop," I cried as the tendrils of darkness twisted tighter around her neck. I took one last moment to look at the others, to memorize the priestesses' faces, their hope. "Take the others," I breathed, watching their hope crumble. "I choose to save Naz."

Erebus's malicious gaze turned to me, the shadow holding Naz lashing out and throwing her at my feet. The others started anew, their cries embedding themselves on my soul forever. I've killed plenty, but never an innocent. Never someone who deserved to live.

"So be it, daughter."

Erebus closed the distance to the stone, his three prized sacrifices held aloft by the streams of darkness behind him. He knelt, knees crushing the fragile white blossoms along the stone's edge as he withdrew a bloodstone dagger.

"Goddess of Light, take these offerings and be awakened once more."

The first of the three was thrust forward, her blond hair splaying against the silver stone. "Stop! Please!"

Erebus dragged the dagger across her throat, the tip of the blade scraping the stone beneath. Scarlet splattered white petals as blood flowed over the sides of the stone, steam rising where it met the snow beneath.

"Gods," the second priestess breathed, her eyes wide as she stared at her future. Erebus shoved the still warm body to the edge of the silver slab, making way for his next sacrifice.

"*Gods*," Erebus mimicked. "We never quite match up to our reputations, do we?"

He grinned as his shadows slammed her head down, his blade slicing across her neck in the next moment with ruthless efficiency.

A horrid gurgling sound bubbled from her throat, her chest heaving as she fought for breath through the blood. Each failed attempt sent another gush from the gaping wound of her neck as her mouth opened and closed around silent screams.

Erebus waited until her body stilled, his manic gaze settling on the last of the priestesses. Jarek took my hand, steadying me as I was forced to watch, but the priestess's gaze was fixed on Naz.

"For you, my princess, I give my life freely." Her vivid green eyes bored into hers, resigned understanding swirling in their depths.

"I'm not your princess," Naz cried, tears tumbling down her cheeks as she thrashed against Erebus's hold. "I'm not worthy of your sacrifice. El, change your mind. Choose me!"

My stomach twisted, bile burning the back of my throat, but my decision was made. Zaeth couldn't lose Naz. So much had been taken from him. Even if Naz hated me forever, she'd be here. Alive.

So, I watched, chin raised as the tears tumbled down my cheeks. As Naz's pleas turned to cries.

Erebus offered the bloodstone dagger toward the priestess, his brow quirking as if this were an interesting turn of events.

"Don't," Naz shouted, fighting against the band of darkness around her waist, but there was little effort in it. The priestess's fate was already sealed.

"It's okay," the priestess smiled as she turned the dagger in her palm and sank the blade into her chest.

55

ELARA

The third priestess slumped forward as the red stain grew in the moonlight. The silver stone pulsed as it was coated in blood, the third and final body joining Eunoia's alter.

"Tsk," Erebus chided, tiling Naz's chin up so that she was forced to look at him. "Such a burden you've had to bear. Princess to a kingdom in need of a king. Postponing all your dreams. Your future."

"Get your hands off her!" Soter shouted, flitting forward to where Jarek and I were.

Zaeth was there at his side, but Erebus's shadows rose again. Naz was just out of reach. Erebus had kept her beside him, trapped in a cloud of night with the three dead priestesses, forcing us to watch.

Forcing us to realize we were helpless against him.

Erebus turned Naz's chin toward us as he leaned in. "Does your brother know how you yearn for a quiet life, one in the countryside with a home filled with children? Do you think it's even crossed his mind that you hate the crown, but you continue shouldering its burdens for him?"

Shock shot down the mating bond, Zaeth's cinnamon eyes

wide as Naz shook her head against the truth.

"What would he say if he knew you desired his friend, the one being he entrusted with your safety?"

Zaeth's head snapped to Soter who was still beating against the darkness, shouting for Naz.

Erebus drew himself up, looking down his sharp nose at her. "You would've made a terrible sacrifice."

Naz was thrown from the ring of shadows, a cry ripping from her chest. Soter caught her before she hit the ground, murmuring soothing words as he pressed kisses to her brow, her hair, holding her tight.

Zaeth's throat bobbed as he fought for words, trying to figure out where we go from here.

"We should leave," Jarek breathed, his blue eyes bouncing between us. "Give me your hands."

"No," I muttered, hardly believing what I was saying. "You said yourself we can't fight two gods."

"Yes," Jarek snapped, his gaze slipping back to the silver slab where Erebus waited, watching the pools of blood mix. "And now there are three. We need to leave before Eunoia awakens."

The ground shook, two thundering booms vibrating beneath our feet as if two great fists were beating on a door.

"Almost, Eunoia." The darkness around Erebus shimmered with the color of a thousand galaxies. "Soon, the last of their blood will drain and you will be free."

"She's right," Naz said, pushing to stand, her voice surprisingly steady. "If we don't work with Erebus and Eunoia to bind Levana, all of this was for nothing."

Boom. Boom.

The stone split, a porcelain hand reaching up through the scarlet soaked snow. Another punched through beside it, both clawing their way through soil and blood and bodies until a being stood before us.

Long silver hair tumbled around her in gentle waves, the

blood from her sacrifices having dripped down to add ruby streaks. Black eyes ringed in silver looked out beneath thick, white lashes, her full pale lips tilting up in a fanged smile as she spotted Erebus.

Erebus's tendrils of night wrapped around her, shrouding her in a dress of darkness, stark against the white of her skin.

"Thank you, Erebus," Eunoia said. Her voice had a gentle cadence, but the sharpness of her smile stripped any warmth from it. "The blood was delectable, as always."

A chill run up my spine, and the others visibility stiffened.

Eunoia turned her striking gaze toward us, looking at each before she settled on Zaeth. "You have done wonderfully, my blessed child. And you, daughter of Erebus, you've heeded my prophecy and played your part well. I have long sensed my sister growing stronger. The time is upon us to reforge her prison."

"That's it?" I asked, trying and failing to keep my anger in check. I'd just been forced to condemn three innocents to death, watch as my bastard of a father murdered them, and all she was going to do was put Levana in time-out? "You're not planning on killing her?"

Eunoia's eyes narrowed as Erebus's shadows flickered around her. "She will be imprisoned."

"In bindings that she's already broken free from," I countered. "You can't be serious."

"El," Zaeth cautioned, his wings twitching as Eunoia's upper lip curled back.

The Goddess of Light stepped forward, the snow crunching beneath her bare feet as she approached. Moonlight gathered around her, illuminating her hair, her skin, sending the dark blues and violets of Erebus's shadows shimmering.

"She's the cause of thousands of humans and fae dying—thousands of *your* children. Even Erebus admitted binding her was a mistake."

Eunoia whipped around, her fingers lengthening into sharp, black-tipped talons.

Erebus drew himself up, his shadows condensing, thickening around Eunoia. And her movements halted. Erebus's shadows held her in place, her dress crafted from night shifting into restraints.

"Risks were taken last time, Eunoia," Erebus spoke, his voice clipped. "She was able to break her bindings, travel in the space between realms—all while we slept. It's only her hubris that has kept her from already decimating this world."

"Hubris?" Soter asked. "She's killed thousands."

"Yes," Eunoia snapped, not taking her eyes off the God of Night. "She could've killed thousands more, but my sister relishes in the destruction. In the pandemonium her plans conjure. Her goal is not to rule this world, but to unleash its chaos."

"Exactly," Erebus said, the streaks of night easing. "She can't be left to wreak havoc on worlds unchecked."

"She's my sister," Eunoia countered, her rays of light blasting through the tendrils of night keeping her bound. Her black-tips talons were at Erebus's throat in an instant.

"Kill me if you like." Erebus lifted his chin, exposing more of his neck for her. "When the dust from this form has collected as millennium pass and my essence is reformed, I will find you, Eunoia, knowing she left you with nothing."

"The void didn't cure her of her madness last time." Eunoia whispered, her chest heaving. For a moment, her grip tightened, the prick of her black talons nearly puncturing the soft flesh of Erebus's neck. I wasn't sure if I wanted her to stop or to keep going, but Eunoia released him with the next breath. "I won't betray her again."

Erebus held her gaze a long moment, the dark rings around his eyes deepening before he nodded. "Then we bind her to one of my worlds—"

"No," Eunoia countered.

"Her power must be contained and the two of you separated," he insisted. "Any realm born of you or her is too easily manipulated."

"You would cast her from our world?" Zaeth asked. "Bind her to another place and time and ensure she could never return?"

"Yes," Erebus confirmed.

Eunoia was silent for a long moment before she dipped her head, yielding on this one point. Brushing away the last tendrils of night clinging to her, Eunoia gathered the soft light of the stars and wove them into a translucent, shimmering gown. Her talons shifted back into slim fingers, the rings around her irises dimming, as her breathing steadied.

"First, we need to find my sister." Eunoia lifted her chin, turning her back on Erebus as she focused on the five of us. "Where are her forces?"

"Multiple kingdoms," Naz answered, all of that agony there a moment ago buried beneath a tight mask of control. "There have been reports of attacks along the Earth Kingdom's eastern border, the Air Kingdom's islands in the east, Caligo, even the fire fae were intercepted."

Zaeth lifted a brow at that, but Naz shook her head. *Later.*

Eunoia cocked her head to the side. "Were any of these real attacks?"

"People died," Sorter snapped, his molten eyes swirling.

"But not many," I breathed, my gaze flicking to Zaeth and Naz before landing on Jarek. "There weren't nearly as many casualties or injured as there could have been, not even in Caligo."

Jarek frowned. "It's true. Previous strikes have been worse."

"Strikes under Veles," Naz said. "Maybe not having the Fractured weakened Levana."

"Unlikely," Erebus countered smoothly. "The creatures you

call the Fractured are deadly due to their numbers, but Levana doesn't win wars with brute strength. She is clever, planning her moves centuries before she makes them."

"Chaos and disorder—that's what Levana craves?" I asked, my gut twisting as a pulse of trepidation rocked through me. I could feel it mirrored in Zaeth, his own suspicions spurring my thoughts.

"Above all else," Eunoia nodded. "Her creatures are born from a primal wildness. It's not that she seeks to destroy life, only she believes in natural consequences."

"If one cannot survive in brutality, they are destined to die," Erebus added.

"She doesn't care who lives or dies," Jarek translated. "I guess it's not quite murderous intent, but it's definitely the ultimate level of apathy."

"The attacks weren't attacks at all," I said, my pulse quickening as pieces slotted into place. "They were distractions."

"Possibly," Erebus said. "Or a game."

"No," Eunoia countered, her dark eyes fixed on me. "Your daughter is right. We're missing the point. Killing fae, leveling cities, it passes the time, chipping away towards her ultimate goal, but Pax has changed since the storm born of her essence was unleashed. Inching ever closer to the time when her and I first created this realm together."

My eyes widened.

"A time before humans," Zaeth breathed, his cinnamon eyes flaring.

"Very good, my blessed one." Eunoia smiled. "Her true mission must be to rid Pax of humans and tip the balance between control and chaos in her direction."

"Where are most of your humans kept?" Erebus asked, his darkness swirling in the air around us.

I swallowed, fighting back the urge to flit all the way there.

"The Wild Kingdom."

56

LANNIE

"Our entire coast is effected now, Your Highness," General Xavier said. Strands of his dark hair fell forward around umber colored ram horns as he leaned over the map spanning the black wooden table. There was a line of red marks peppering the Earth Kingdom's eastern shore, all coming from the water.

We sat in the same war room my sisters and I had occupied a few days ago, the silver leaves of the Earth Palace shimmering up above. I remember thinking how bleak things had looked at the time, but the situation had only grown more dire.

Evander refused to leave the gardens of the Emerald Provence, despite my persistent urging. I'd thought he was coming out of this after the Fire Kingdom. He and Jarek had almost looked happy for a few days, but this seemed like a downward spiral, one I was helpless to stop.

"They're claiming we stole the queen," General Xavier said, his gaze hard.

Halcyon sat up, her violet hair falling over her shoulders. "Queen Isla is missing?"

The general nodded, the others behind him shifting uncomfortably. "A woman in town claimed a water fae with the king's crest delivered this."

"Why not bring this to me immediately, Xavier?" Halcyon accepted the letter he held out, her eyes darting across the yellow-stained page. The seal was broken but a three pronged trident was still clearly visible.

"We didn't take it seriously, Your Highness. Not until the attacks started."

Halcyon's silver gaze snapped up. "When was this?"

Xavier swallowed, the other generals behind him stiffening. "A day after your return from the Water Kingdom."

The room seemed to hold its breath as fury flashed through Halcyon's gaze.

"Send a messenger to King Kai immediately in an attempt to clear this up."

"Yes, Your Highness."

Two guards broke away as Halcyon's silver eyes roved across the map.

"You are seeking reinforcements for the west, but there have been no ground attacks. Only monsters ravaging the coast. Is that correct?"

"Yes, Your Highness," General Xavier answered. "We thought it best to be prepared for a land assault."

I wasn't sure when I'd started thinking of the Earth Kingdom as my home, but I realized I wanted to keep this land and its people safe just as much as Halcyon. There was a certain peace that came from being surrounded by earth constantly... it was a comfort I hadn't realized I'd been missing.

"Evacuate all citizens along the coast," Halcyon said. "Relocation facilities will be established within five hundred leagues of the capitol. All are welcome. Those who wish to remain will need to go underground."

"Your Highness—"

"Tell our army to fall back to the designated perimeter."

"But that would leave us vulnerable—" another general spoke from the door, his upturned nose and condescending glare making it clear he had nothing helpful to say.

"Within a fortnight, we have been attacked along opposite ends of the kingdom with minimal casualties. The Water Kingdom shares our southern border. If they wished to invade—truly invade—they would've attacked by both land and sea at the same time."

General Xavier shifted on his feet but nodded after a few seconds. "You think this is a ploy to draw us out?"

"I think that evacuating the coastal villages prevents causalities from sea attacks, while also allowing our troops to stay together. I'd rather prepare for a battle on land, one where our army isn't stretched thin, then guess where King Kai might attack."

"Yes, Your Highness," General Xavier said, bowing his head. The others dipped their heads, though it was clear more than one didn't agree with her ruling.

"Go," Halcyon commanded, dismissing her generals with a wave of her hand. The door clicked shut a heartbeat later, leaving us alone.

"You're expecting an attack from the south?"

"Perhaps," she said, her silver eyes returning to the map. "But why not start there? The Water Kingdom could've deployed fae to the south and water creatures to the east, but they didn't."

"You think they're otherwise occupied?"

Halcyon shook her head. "I don't know, but they *are* working for Levana. That much was clear. We need to be prepared."

I nodded, my brows furrowing as I tried to figure out what we were missing. The fine hairs on the back of my neck pricked as my worry grew. The same foreboding sense of unease had been present since Greer left, heightening shortly after when El and Zaeth had vanished a little later.

I knew Greer had a kingdom to run and that El and Zaeth

needed to investigate Eunoia's resting place, but normally El would've said goodbye before leaving.

"Did you feel the disturbance last night?" I asked, lowering my voice despite us being the only ones in the room.

Halcyon shot a look toward the door before answering. "It felt similar to when Erebus's binds broke. And it felt like it was coming from the base of the Jagged Mountains."

My lips pulled down in a frown as my initial concerns were confirmed.

"Eunoia," I breathed.

"We must assume she's been released, intentional or not. But I'm surprised Freya hasn't portaled in to see what's happening. She suspicious of everyone, let alone Eunoia awakening without her being present."

"I'm sure Jarek or Naz will be along for an update as soon as possible."

She nodded, but both of us still felt a chill in the air.

The budding silence was broken by hurried footsteps as half-a-dozen soldiers flitted toward us.

"Your Highness!" General Xavier panted as he burst through the doors. "Queen Isla—she's here."

WE FLITTED THROUGH THE EARTH KINGDOM, FOLLOWING THE generals as they led the way up the winding stairs and toward the surface.

Crips winter air stirred as the sun reached the midpoint in the sky, shining upon hundreds of water fae clad in blue scaled armor. The armor shimmered in the light, giving the appearance of waves cresting through the surrounding forest. The warriors parted to reveal a tall figure with green eyes and dusty rose lips. A crown crafted to look like coral sat upon her head, woven into the top of her dark hair before the long strands were braided down her spine.

"Queen Isla," Halcyon said, bowing her head slightly. "Your husband is looking for you."

The queen gestured for her troops to stand down as she stepped out of their protection toward Halcyon. Daggers were strapped to her hip and along her forearm, but I got the feeling the true danger was her mind.

"Yes," Queen Isla answered her lips pressing thin. "He's attacked under the guise of my capture, though we both know that's not the truth."

Queen Halcyon lifted a brow, waiting for her to elaborate.

"As you've seen, my husband has aligned with Levana. The attack along your western coast was meant to draw your forces out. The same with the attack to the east from the Light Kingdom."

"How do you know this?" Halcyon asked, the generals at her back stiffening. Half of them had gone to relay Halcyon's orders and proceed with evacuations.

"I heard him before I left," Queen Isla said as she leveled her gaze with Halcyon. "You've achieved much on your own. The youngest queen to ever take a throne and keep it. And with no male counterpart by your side."

My shoulders pulled back at the mention of Halcyon with a man—with anyone other than me. It shouldn't have bothered me. We weren't together, but somewhere between Ser's death and the world ending, I'd begun to let go of what I should and shouldn't feel.

Greer had asked me point blank if I wanted to stay in the Earth Kingdom with my obligations fulfilled. It had been an easy answer. I would stay by Halcyon's side as long as she would have me... not that I'd ever tell her that.

"You've proven a woman can be strong," Queen Isla continued. "Can revolutionize a kingdom all on her own. I want that.

It's time I stepped out from beneath my husband's shadow and took a stand."

Halcyon's silver eyes stayed closed off, but I could feel how much she wanted to believe she had an ally in the Water Queen.

"I take it these men are loyal to you?" I asked, feeling that Halcyon wished for more time in weighing her decision.

"And women," she nodded, her green eyes swinging to mine. "We've come north along the southern border and are here to offer our aid."

"We don't require assistance in defending our kingdom," Halcyon said, and my heart fluttered at the use of the word 'our'. I wasn't sure if she'd meant it, but a warmth spread through me at the thought of her intending that plural for us. "The strikes have been mild—"

"Because their intention is not to take your kingdom, but to distract your focus from the north."

"We've had no signs of an attack from the north," General Xavier stated. "The Wild Kingdom remains our allies."

But Queen Isla was shaking her head before he finished. "Not from them, *for* them. King Kai spoke of an attack at the heart of Pax to purge the world of its human infestation. Rumors have circulated that the Wild Kingdom has become a refuge to all those who need it, including humans."

Halcyon's silver eyes found mine, our fears from earlier given life. She turned, meeting General Xavier's dark eyes. "Report."

His spine stiffened as he drew to attention. "Four generals have fled to the borders on your orders. They should be able to relocate all citizens within a fortnight."

"The Wild Kingdom won't last a fortnight." Queen Isla stepped forward. "Levana intends it to be her primary target. I know water fae aren't known for their skills on the battlefield, but we can defend your capitol while you lead your army north."

"We can't abandon the city—" General Xavier started, but Halcyon cut him off with a sharp look. They been friends for years, and I knew she trusted him. He'd been one of her only confidants beside Queen Freya, but I couldn't help but feel like he would watch the other kingdoms fall if it meant the Earth Kingdom was left standing.

Halcyon turned back to Queen Isla, her voice steady. "I won't yield my kingdom."

"I would never think to take it." Queen Isla stared at Halcyon unflinchingly. She swallowed. "I've watched my husband do unspeakable things, turned my back when I should've stopped him. I have much to atone for, Queen Halcyon. If we don't stop Levana, I fear I'll never get the chance."

Halcyon stared at her, studying the posture of her shoulders, the slight frown marring her full lips, searching for a lie. After another moment, she spoke.

"I'm choosing to trust you, Queen Isla. Don't make me regret it."

"Your Highness—"

"Prepare the troops, General Xavier. We leave at dawn."

57

GREER

"The last of the islands have been secured," Ryuu said, the two of us standing across from King Dragcor. He was seated on the throne, his dark wings tucked in close as morning light streamed through large windows.

"And our troops?" Ryuu's father asked. His gaze was fixed on the clouds beyond, watching as the light of the sun grew strong, bathing the sky in oranges and yellows.

"Positioned throughout our borders with the majority prepared for a strike from the Dark Kingdom."

Dragcor nodded, his reptilian eyes turning to us at last. "The Shadowlands."

"Yes, but we believe Levana's focus will be drawn further south near the Jagged Mountains, what with the power surge a few nights ago."

Three nights.

It has been three nights since Eunoia was released and I could practically feel the tension in the air as we waited for an attack.

"We've bolstered our troops to reflect this," Ryuu added.

"So you've mentioned." Dragcor lifted a brow, considering. "How confident are you that the shift in power was Eunoia?"

Light particles around us electrified, their energy dimming when Jarek appeared a moment later, sparing me the need to reiterate *yet again* how confident we were.

"Oh, good. You're here." His light blue eyes swept the throne room, his usually well-kept blond hair rumpled and wind-swept.

"What happened?" Ryuu asked, wings twitching.

"My sisters," I started. "Are they okay?"

"The Earth Kingdom is my next stop, but El is safe." Jarek walked to a cushioned chair facing the window and threw himself down. "Levana's creatures attacked Caligo."

Ryuu inhaled a sharp breath, his fists clenching.

"Then Erebus did his fade-to-black thing and gathered priestesses from Eunoia's temple." Jarek drew a hand across his face, weariness seeming to grip him tighter. "We couldn't stop him."

"Priestesses?" Dragcor asked, the orange in his eyes flaring.

Jarek nodded. "Now, we have three murderous gods roaming free."

"I thought Erebus and Eunoia were on our side."

"I thought so, too." Jarek sighed. "But after what I saw, I don't believe they're on anyone's side but their own. Eunoia *thanked* him for the blood offering and Erebus doesn't care who dies, except for Elara."

My eyes narrowed. "He's confirmed she's his blood daughter?"

"One and only," Jarek said. "Apparently, being the God of Night doesn't afford a lot of opportunities for reproduction." Jarek's brows furrowed. "Though I am surprised at that. He's an unfeeling, murderous asshole, to be sure, but he's delicious to look at."

"Jarek," I chided. "That's my stepfather... ish. No ogling."

"Gods can create, but very few are able to reproduce," Dragcor said, our heads turning toward him. "It's thought to be a cost of power. The way the universe maintains balance. If Elara is his blood daughter, I would imagine her safety is very important to him."

"Good to know." Jarek frowned but nodded. "Eunoia and Erebus believe Levana's main target is humans, meaning the Wild Kingdom. They're arguing over the best way to stop her."

"The same agenda Veles had," I sighed. "It makes sense. He was working for her. How is Veles behaving?"

Jarek shrugged. "He's supposed to be on route from the Earth Kingdom to the Jagged Mountains with the Fractured, but we haven't seen him."

"Do you think he's rejoined her?" King Dragcor asked. "Hatred for human kind has proven a powerful motivator in the past."

Jarek shook his head. "He had the same goal as Levana but different motives. Veles really believed he and his brothers were superior while Levana wanted her freedom. Now, she's accomplished that, she wishes to stoke the fires of chaos. Humans are simply a sacrifice to achieve that."

"Levana plans on destroying the Wild Kingdom and all the humans within?" I asked.

"That's what we think."

"It makes sense," Ryuu said as King Dragcor stepped from the throne and joined us. "All of Pax's creatures are joined together, our essences are a great collective flowing through the earth. Without humanity to temper our ruthlessness, fae will revert to a primal period, one in which Levana ruled beside her sister."

"We need to go," I breathed. "We need to send troops as soon as possible."

"That's the thing," Jarek said. "I've been attempting to breech the mist surrounding the Wild Kingdom for the past three days, but it's changed. It's thicker, more hostile. I flitted and luxed all around it but couldn't find a way in to warn Queen Freya."

"Any signs of an attack?" Ryuu asked.

"Maybe. I couldn't see through the mist. There were flashes of light, sometimes shouts and screams on the thickest parts." Jarek shook his head. "Something must've triggered it."

"Then we set up our warriors around the mist," I said. "Construct a perimeter of protection while El and the gods work on killing Levana."

Jarek grimaced. "About that. Eunoia has made it clear she won't kill her sister."

I blinked.

"What are they expecting to do?" Ryuu gritted out.

"Re-bind her," Jarek said. "But on one of Erebus's planets or realms or something. I don't really care as long as it's far away from here."

"Surely, they can see repeating the same thing isn't the best option," King Dragcor said, his brows furrowing. "Levana must die to ensure our safety."

"Our sentiments, exactly, King Dragcor. But Eunoia wouldn't hear of it."

"And we need Erebus and Eunoia if we're to stand a chance," Ryuu said, pacing the length of the throne room.

"You've got to be joking," I grumbled, rubbing the side of my temple.

"We'll deal with that when it comes." King Dragcor waved his hand as if letting Levana live was a problem that could wait for another day. "First, we need to stop Levana from conquering the Wild Kingdom."

"Agreed," Ryuu said. "With the wind in our favor and the men well rested, we should be able to make it to the Wild Kingdom in two days, less if we rush."

Jarek nodded, pushing to stand. "I'll tell The Dark Army to look to the east at dawn in two days' time."

King Dragcor let his dark wings flex, the sun illuminating his silhouette as he stood before the windows. "Levana had been unfinished business of mine for quite some time. I will do everything in my power to protect this realm."

Ryuu looked like he wanted to say something, but I could see the steeled resolve settle across King Dragcor's face just as he could. He'd be joining us in this fight.

"Rest tonight," Ryuu said, looking to each of us. "Tomorrow we prepare for war."

58

ELARA

Eunoia was just as bad as the others. A part of me held on to the myths, the ideas passed down for generations about the great light goddess who loved and protected her people. I should've known.

The legends were wrong. They always were.

Eunoia didn't like the idea of Levana killing her creations, of the disorder thrust upon her perfectly balanced realm, but it was clear the loss of control bothered her more than the loss of lives.

Since she'd been freed, we'd started our trek south, stopping often for her... *feedings*.

"Please! I have a brother. He's going to be looking for me—"

My stomach twisted as the woman's pleas turned into screams, Eunoia's fangs ripping into her neck to silence them all together. Eunoia insisted on blood sacrifices, on drinking her fill as often as she wanted.

My fingers itched for a blade, and I wished more than anything at that moment to drive the sharped tip between Eunoia's eyes.

This had been a mistake. A huge mistake that we couldn't undo.

"Stay with me, love," Zaeth whispered. "We'll get through this."

"But they won't," I breathed, hating the way the goddess's throat bobbed as she swallowed. "We're just supposed to stand back and watch her kill? How many more, Zaeth?"

His jaw clenched. "As many as it takes, love. If Levana goes unchecked, we're all dead anyway."

"And once Levana is gone?" I asked, needing to know he was with me all the way.

A fire flickered through our mating bond, one filled with anger and pent-up fury.

"Then," Zaeth said, leaning forward, his lips grazing the shell of my ear. "There'll be nothing to stop us sending her into the void. And her sister along with her."

I nodded, swallowing down my anger for another day.

"Mouthwatering," Eunoia called, letting the body tumble onto the snow-covered ground. "Erebus, I believe she said there was a brother around here."

~

WE WOKE EARLY THE NEXT DAY, CONTINUING OUR JOURNEY SOUTH along the foothills of the Jagged Mountains toward the Wild Kingdom. I'd learned to block out the screams, focusing on the things I could control.

At least Naz and Soter had been allowed to stay behind, the two of them promising to send the Dark Kingdom's army south as soon as possible. Even Jarek had been granted freedom. My instinct was to thank the gods for him being able to warn my sisters, but a glance over my shoulder at the gods behind me had me biting my tongue.

I would never offer them a prayer again.

"Are you three the only gods?" I asked, needing a break from the sounds of cracking twigs beneath our feet.

"There are more," Erebus answered cautiously. "But Eunoia and Levana created this world."

"And you," I added, gesturing toward the frosted world around us and then to myself. "You contributed, too."

Eunoia stiffened. "Erebus added a few last minute touches, but my sister and I are responsible for Pax. We fashioned all of this out of nothing, granted life to thousands of creatures."

"Is that why you feel entitled to kill whenever it pleases you?" I asked, unable to hold my tongue.

Zaeth shot a warning down the bond, urging me to be cautious, at least until they accomplished what we needed.

"Yes," Eunoia answered, her voice clipped. "I've granted them life, expended my own essence to bring them into this world. I am owed their thanks, and at times, their sacrifices."

"You are owed *nothing*." I spun, pinning the light goddess, the mother to us all with a glare fierce enough to make grown fae cower. "We didn't ask to be created. Once we were given an existence as something separate from yourself, our obligations ended. We are our own beings with our own thoughts."

The light around Eunoia's eyes flared and I swear Erebus's tendrils of night thickened between us, as if he were preparing to intervene.

"You're lucky Erebus is fond of you, girl." Eunoia let her fangs lengthen as her full pale-pink lips tilted into a smile, the sharp tips gleaming. "If you were purely my creation, I'd already have silenced that mouth of yours forever."

"Enough," Zaeth snapped, stepping before me.

Shock flashed across Eunoia's face, as if she couldn't believe her blessed child would choose me over her. "Careful, Dark King. Another move like that and I'd think you weren't grateful for my blessing.

Zaeth held her gaze. "She is my mate. Surely, you intended for us to grow close."

Eunoia lifted a brow, her gaze moving toward Erebus before she spoke. "The mating bond is... peculiar."

Erebus shifted, the darkness around him swirling.

"Wait," I said, looking between the two of them. "Isn't the mating bond given from the gods?"

"No," Erebus answered, the one word causing Eunoia to flinch. She regrouped quickly; all signs of discomfort hidden behind a stoic mask. "Even we are unsure where the connection originates from."

"Though we think it has something to do with which particles of the universe are in your genetic make-up," Erebus added. "Fated mates are thought to be complimentary to one another but aren't guaranteed to be perfect."

I let that idea take root in me, imaging Zaeth and I born from the same star, the same soul, thousands of years before Pax was created. The idea that we would continue finding each other in any life, in any world, settled something in my chest.

A pulse of love hummed down the bond, enveloping me completely, but Zaeth was careful not to move toward me, not to look back with Eunoia before us.

"Can you still sense Levana?" Zaeth pressed, forcing the change in topic.

Eunoia's gaze narrowed, but she nodded. "She's made it to the Wild Kingdom, but I'm bolstering the mist to keep her creatures from reaching its center."

"Another reason not to delay," Erebus cut in.

He'd been compliant with Eunoia's every whim these last few days, but there were moments where he looked as disgusted by her as I was. Curious, seeing as how he'd given up his freedom to remain with her, tethered to this world. I wondered if the past few thousand years had changed his mind. Something must have shifted, because he'd manifested in a mortal form for my mother. And was attracted to her enough to sire me, so...

"Come," he commanded, flitting into the trees. His tendrils of night wrapped around my waist, dragging me after him before I had time to follow.

~

WE REACHED THE MIST QUICKER THAN ANTICIPATED, MY FATHER guiding us through the last of the trees.

"It's expanded," I breathed, halting before the edge of the silver fog. Even from the north, I could tell the mist was different. More aware.

"I told you I had it covered," Eunoia said, reaching a hand out as if to stroke it. The mist swirled beneath her touch, the silver clouds flashing with light as energy rumbled through it.

"Is it... alive?" I forced the question out, eyes wide as I watched the mist curl around Eunoia's fingers.

"In a sense." The tips of her fingers shifted into talons as she mimicked scratching a dog's head. "Mother is here, now. You can rest."

The mist shuddered, the sound like a beast relenting to sleep after a long day. Slowly, it faded, the mist evaporating in billowing waves fanning out from Eunoia's touch.

Dark shapes frozen in time came into view, their features clarifying as the rest of the fog vanished.

"Gods," I breathed, drawing my blade. Zaeth did the same, both of us horror struck at what was before us.

Wild fae and humans fought side-by-side, frozen in the throes of battle against shadow wraiths, light fae, and other monstrous beasts I didn't recognize. Cú sídhe were slinking along the edges, joined by other snarling wolves who looked like they were part bear. Their front paws were huge, great claws digging into the earth before them as they faced off against flickers of black.

My eyes widened as I recognized the small, foxlike creatures battling against them. Ebony fur erupted into black flamed tales, the feline creatures looking to be just as ruthless as the monsters before them—Vulplings.

There, in the center of the mayhem was Queen Freya and Alarik. The Select Guard was arranged around them with Vidarr at Alarik's back. He was thinner than I remember, the silver in his hair much more pronounced. They were surrounded by dozens of light fae, outmatched and looking as if they desperately needed help.

"Zaeth," I breathed, but he was already starting forward.

I flitted after him, my pulse spiking as bodies came alive.

59

ELARA

The screams of the injured mingled with bloodthirsty battle cries, urging us to move quicker as the forest came alive around us.

My sword blocked the edge of a fae blade aiming for Queen Freya's neck as she blinked back to consciousness. I kicked the light fae square in the chest, my boot cracking ribs, before I swung my sword across his neck.

"Sorry it took us so long," I said, taking advantage of the momentary break as Zaeth killed the last of the fae surrounding the Wild Queen and the Select Guard. "We didn't know the Wild Kingdom was the target until now."

"The mist," Queen Freya fought for words as, some of the panic in her eyes ebbing as she spotted Alarik near Vidarr, unharmed and ready for the next attack. "It changed. It expanded and then caged us in."

My gaze darted toward where I'd left Erebus and Eunoia—finding them in the exact same spot. The two of them were lounging near a large pine tree, Eunoia basking in the sun while Erebus clung to the modest shadows, both looking bored.

They would flick a wrist whenever one of Levana's monsters

came too close, sending the creature careening away, but other than that, they did nothing to help.

"Cowards," I said.

Queen Freya's gaze followed mine as she dodged the scythe of a shadow wraith. Its head tumbled into the muddy ground a beat later, but her eyes were fixed on the pair of gods behind me. "Let me guess, the mist was a curtesy of Eunoia?"

"Yeah," I said, sending two more light fae into the after. "She said she strengthened the mist as a form of protection. I should've known there'd be a catch."

"I'd say so," Queen Freya growled, her sword swiping through the neck of a light fae before plunging into the belly of another. The runes along her cheeks flared as she tapped in to more of her wild fae affinities. "Where is The Dark Army?"

"Caligo with Naz and Soter."

She cursed, the sentiments echoed by Alarik at her back.

"Naz is due to check in tomorrow night if we're not back," Zaeth added. "But we have no way of reaching them."

"Jarek knows of Eunoia," I said, grunting as I withdrew my sword from the hide of a wolf. "He'll reach them."

"It will still take time to mobilize," Queen Freya shook her head.

"We need reinforcements," Alarik called, brushing sandy blond hair back from his face.

"What about Queen Halcyon?" I asked. "You could portal—"

"I can't portal," Queen Freya answered. "I siphoned my affinities into the mist to protect the summit. I'll need time to recover."

"How much time?" Vidarr asked, appearing beside Alarik. The creases at the corners of his eyes had grown deeper, the silver flecks throughout his braided and knotted hair giving way to grey, but his storm-grey eyes still held warmth. "It's good to see you, lass."

"It's good to see you, too," I breathed, my heart squeezing

with the pain I knew he still felt for Ahmya. "Though, I do wish it were under better circumstances."

"Then let's make sure we have the chance to catch up at another time." Vidarr looked beyond my shoulder to Queen Freya. "How long till you recharge, Your Highness?"

"Morning," she said, her frown deepening as her blade leveled another wraith.

Grim understanding dawned as I realized we'd have to face the bulk of this attack on our own.

Even if Jarek had luxed straight to my sisters, and if their troops had been ready to mobilize immediately, he'd need time to recharge before diving into battle or luxing again. We would still have another day or more before they reached us.

"Establish a perimeter," Zaeth called. "A line of protection around the humans."

"We had that with the mist," Queen Freya snapped, shooting a glare toward Erebus and Eunoia. "Can we get a little help?"

Erebus swatted another light fae away, the body exploding as it crashed into a large truck. "We need to save our strength for Levana."

"There'll be nothing left for you to save if you don't help us," I countered, letting my anger and frustration ring through.

For years—years—I'd survived. Hade somehow managed to get through those awful, lonely periods. I'd never admit it to another, but some nights when the world was quiet and my thoughts took a turn for the worst, I would think about what it would be like to end things. To escape the only way I knew how.

But I kept going.

I'd clawed my way up from that hopeless place, that endless grave I'd let myself sink into, and found the strength to keep fighting. Not because I'd discovered a new outlook on life, but because I refused to believe this was all I got.

The world was shitty and terrible and unspeakable things happened, but this was my life. My *life*.

I *would* find a piece of untarnished happiness to cling onto. Even if I had to carve it from the flesh of my enemies myself.

And there Eunoia and Erebus sat, letting the world descend into chaos.

"You misunderstand," Eunoia said, waving her hand to snap the necks of the wolves foolish enough to come near her. "Our goal is to bind my sister. Nothing else."

"And if all of humanity falls?" Alarik called. "If the foundation of Pax—your world—is thrown off-kilter, what then?"

Eunoia looked down her nose as Alarik side-stepped a swipe of claws, his sword diving into the beast's spine. "Then I'll rebalance it."

"You are our goddess, our mother," Vidarr said, something in his voice breaking. "You're meant to care for us. To guide us from this world into the after. Do you not hold your creations dear?"

Eunoia's gaze found Zaeth flitting through the trees near us, leaving nothing but death in his wake. "There are those I find more valuable than others, but nothing will sway me from Levana."

"We're on our own," I seethed, turning away. "Zaeth's right. We need to establish a perimeter we can defend, while giving you time to recover your strength."

Queen Freya nodded, echoing the plan to her people as we ascended the mountain.

I shot a glare over my shoulder toward Eunoia and Erebus, realizing I blamed them most of all. These were our creators, the gods meant to look after us... and they were useless.

"I *will* kill Levana," I promised, memorizing the way Eunoia's eyes narrowed, feeding off the look of hatred she shot my way.

"You'll never get the chance," she countered. "Your destiny is to die on this planet serving me."

For a moment, I thought I felt Erebus's tendrils of night thickened around the goddess, but one look into his cold eyes had me banishing the thought. He's chosen his side. And it wasn't mine.

I'd get no help from the gods, but when had I ever? Today wouldn't be a day for miracles or sunset endings. It would be bloody and brutal, a battle of the mind as well as the body... a perfect day to defy destiny.

60

LANNIE

"Is Queen Halcyon really trusting the Water Queen to guard the capitol?" Evander asked as the horses carried us over the Earth Kingdom's northern border and into the Wild Kingdom. We'd left El's horse, Ember, behind. She'd grown to be just as savvy as any warrior and I had no doubt she'd lead the other horses to freedom if it came down to a battle. Not to mention, she wouldn't let any person—fae or human—ride her besides El.

At least there was one being I trusted remaining at the Earth Kingdom.

The journey had been hard, with us stopping only long enough to sleep and eat before continuing. Based on the way El's connection was humming, I knew the battle had started sometime in the night, and I didn't like the idea of her fighting without Greer and I there. The sun was already high in the sky. If she was north of the Western Woods, it would take us until night fall—at least—before we reached her.

"Yes," I breathed, trying not to sound irritated. I knew Evander was being practical, but he couldn't feel the urgency I felt vibrating through my body as El's fae affinities continued to spike. Closing my eyes, I focus on sending her grounding reminders, connecting her fae essence back to Pax while also giving her affinities a boost.

"I guess we'll see if we survive the battle of the gods first," Evander said softy. "Then we'll worry about ambitious queens."

"El's in trouble," I said, my eyes snapping to Evander's and then beyond him to Halcyon. She stiffened, feeling the flood of worry through our bond. "How much further?"

Screams pierced the air as the wind shifted, bringing with it the metallic scent of blood and destruction. I knew it well. And had grown to dread it.

It meant warriors torn apart, holding ropes of their intestines in their hands as their bodies tried and failed to heal quick enough. It meant broken families and orphaned children and a nearly overwhelming amount of pressure to save as many lives as I could.

Evander looked at me, the world seeming to stand still for a moment as he realized this was it. This would be the battle that determined our future... That determined if we *had* a future.

He didn't speak, but it felt like so much was being said. Years of love and pain and hope for a better future all twisted together with the grim reality of this moment.

Something in my chest twisted as his throat bobbed, bringing with it a fresh wave of guilt for forcing him to feel Jem's loss all over again. But I didn't regret saving him. I couldn't.

"Evander, I..." *I needed you here. I couldn't lose you.* But each phrase sounded more selfish than the last.

"It's okay," he murmured. "You're a healer, Lannie. That's what you do."

Holding his gaze, I felt the weight of the silence grow.

"But..."

There it was. My stomach flipped as I waited for his scorn, his hatred.

Evander took a deep breath, meeting my eyes as he let it out slowly. "There *are* those you can't save."

"I know," I replied bitterly, thinking of Ahmya and the way Vidarr broke as her essence bled away. Of Ser and her unfailing optimism ending in the blink of an eye. I thought of the dozens upon dozens of men and women, of the burnt homes and children toys littering the streets of the base as smoke and flames and screams filled the air... of the bodies I'd spent hours sowing together, forearms covered in their blood and *still* I had to watch as they passed from this world.

"And there are those you *shouldn't* save," Evander said, his voice much too soft.

My brows furrowed, searching his face, but finding only a carefully neutral expression. "If I can save a life, I will. I always will."

His lips tilted into a sad grin, one that housed centuries of knowledge that I couldn't yet understand.

"Lannie!" Halcyon yelled, snapping my attention to the front of our warriors. "We need you."

I glanced back to Evander, hoping to find clarity before this started, but he'd already slipped from his horse, along with most of the warriors and flitted toward the sounds of battle.

With a curse, I made to do the same, slinging my pack of healing supplies over my shoulder before turning my horse free with the others. I caught a glimpse of Evander cutting through a group of goblins, his auburn hair unique even among fae. It felt like there was a thousand things he'd wanted me to understand... and I hadn't been able to hear any of them.

Shaking my head, I forced myself to put that conversation away for another time—because there *would* be another time—and find Halcyon.

Goblins slinked through bare trees, their unnaturally black eyes and clothes stark against the snow covered forest. As I ran, my gaze lingered on the ground where bodies already littered the ground. There had been a battle here before we arrived. Some of the bodies looked like they'd been here for days...

I took my place in the heart of the warriors, knowing Halcyon would find me. We'd already discussed my skills with any type of weapon to be more a hindrance than a help. I was to remain in the center of our troops, ready to heal. So, that's where I was.

Steel clashed as the first of the goblins reached the group, the warriors dodging and dancing around me. Barely avoiding a thrown dagger, I tripped over a bloated, rotting corpse, the stomach splitting open as I rolled.

Rancid odor filled the air, bile singing my throat as I fought down the urge to vomit. I pressed to stand, scrambling back as I stared at the black unseeing eyes of a Fractured.

My stomach twisted for an entirely different reason.

"The Fractured are here!" I shouted, pulse racing.

"I know," Halcyon said, her voice right beside me.

Her blade came up, poised to defend us as a goblin charged, but one of the Fractured intervened. Its movements were sloppy, but in the end, the goblin was the one to join the others lying on the muddy forest floor.

"They're helping us. It seems Veles kept his word," I said, still adjusting to the Fractured being on our side.

"For now," Halcyon ground out, clearly not trusting the arrangement. I glanced around, finding the group of warriors has shifted, stretching north to join the Fractured against the horde of goblins slinking through the trees. "Stay alert. I'll cover you."

We were off, Halcyon hacking through goblins while I searched for wounded fae. They were a few of our warriors with shallow cuts and minor injuries, but all the bodies we passed were either goblins or the Fractured.

The sound of dried branches snapping jerked my attention to the right as a cluster of goblins rushed toward us. Halcyon was already there, sword whirling as sprays of black blood splattered her violet hair and great, arching ram horns. Her silver eyes blazed with fury as her full lips pulled back in a snarl.

She was beautiful. Somehow the bodies left bleeding in the snow around her only added to her charm.

"The Fractured continue north toward the Western Woods," Evander panted, flitting to our side. "But the bodies thin out. If Levana did send creatures that way, they're gone now."

He dodged a swipe of a goblin, the rusted blade swinging wide. Evander had the creature on the ground in the next heartbeat, looking as if he'd been brought back to life with the adrenaline of battle. His skin was flushed and marked in sprays of blood, and his chest was heaving, but there was a spark in his eyes that I hadn't seen in weeks.

"Push north toward the Western Woods." Halcyon nodded her thanks, before relaying the news to her generals. "Any sign of Veles, report back immediately. Do not engage but be cautious."

Howls sounded in the distance as more goblins rushed through the trees. A pack echoed the call just a few leagues beyond our point, the noise growing louder as we pressed on.

"Incoming!" Evander called, darting forward as the first of the wolves broke through the trees.

The beasts were huge, larger than I remembered and even more ruthless. Claws sank into flesh, ripping torsos apart quicker than I could reach them. Everywhere I looked, monsters struck, like sharks in chum-infested waters.

Red sprayed against patches of white, the warm fluid melting snow, creating shallow pools of muddied blood. I forced a deep breath into my lungs, letting the roar of war wash through me.

One body. That's all I could do. Just focus on one broken, bleeding being—and save them.

I dropped to my knees beside an earth fae struggling to

stand. A large gash marred his outer thigh, the shaft of bone showing beneath the chunk of missing tissue.

He hissed as I pressed my palm to the wound, twisting away from my touch a moment later to sink his blade into the belly of a goblin.

"Try to hold still," I called, grabbing the powder I knew would stop the bleeding long enough for his fae affinities to take control.

"If I did that, I wouldn't be alive for you to heal," he said, tipping his storm-grey ram horns down to watch as the I applied the powder. I'd discovered a blend of herbs that, when concentrated, aided the body's natural clotting factors. It didn't work against internal injuries, but with my added fae affinities, It had proven effective for even the largest of gashes.

The bleeding slowed as I willed the flesh to mend.

"Thank you," he called over his shoulder, flitting into the fray before I could apply a bandage.

A familiar cry pierced through the cacophony of war, jerking my head up.

Evander was bleeding, red streaming down his arm as he pressed his back against the wide base of a tree, fighting to catch his breath.

I flitted toward him, watching as he flexed his fingers one, twice. His chest heaved as he sheathed his sword, exchanging it for the lighter dagger along his thigh. He gripped the hilt, raising it high as he spun around the trunk and launched himself forward into the open jaws of a beast.

Sharp teeth started to close, but Evander thrust his dagger up. There was a sickening crunch as the sharp points of the wolf's teeth pierced Evander forearm. But its jaw grew slack in the next heartbeat, and the beast slumped to the ground.

Before I could so much as blink, a goblin dove toward me. I cried out as its claws dug into my thigh, its bloodied dagger swiping for my chest as I flitted back, barely managing to escape. I felt Halcyon's panic shoot down the mating bond, responding to my own, but she was yards away, caught up in the pandemonium of battle with dozens of monsters between us.

I had a blade tucked into my boot, one El insisted I wear every day.

Just in case, she always said. Thank the gods for overprotective sisters.

The goblin snarled, bounding forward as I fumbled with the laces. A scream built in my chest as I watched the dirty edge of its blade draw near, but a Fractured threw itself in my path, catching the dagger below the ribs. Its sword arched through the air, severing the goblin's head from its body as my fingers grasped the hilt of my dagger and pulled it free.

My heart raced, my chest heaving as I watched the two fell. The Fractured twitched as if still fighting to stand, despite the mortal wound it had received. It was still alive.

Catching the straps of my bag, I spun it around, reaching for the healing powder. But Halcyon was there, her hand stilling mine before I could use it.

"Leave it," she commanded.

"But he just—"

"*It* followed orders." Halcyon's silver eyes were hard, needing me to understand. "The Fracture have no souls to save, Lannie. It wasn't altruism that saved your life, but blind obedience."

The Fractured who'd intervened on my behalf twitched once more before stilling. It had sacrificed itself for me… but maybe Halcyon had a point. Did the act of saving a life mean anything when the one doing the saving didn't care? I wondered if those who believed in the after thought it was a series of positives and negatives, like a scale of your soul—the good having to weight more than the bad. Or was it what resided in your mind that decided your fate? If a being only did 'good' things for others because it was instructed to or from a perspective of self-benefit, would it still count as a 'good' deed?

Looking at the bodies surrounding us, marring the beauty of the earth, knowing their muscle and fat would bloat in a few days' time with rotting tissue erupting to spread decay, it was a wonder people believed in an after at all.

"Lannie," Halcyon called, yanking her sword from a chest cavity. "We need to keep moving."

With a deep breath, I secured my pack and followed the pull toward my sister.

61

ELARA

The night was long. Wave after wave of light fae, wraiths, cú sídhe and their bear-like cousins, tested our boundaries with unrelenting determination. Vulplings fought alongside us, the foxlike creatures proving to be quick and nimble, and just as deadly as any wolf. Queen Freya had drawn most of her army back, the wild fae forming a ring around the summit and the humans beyond.

Zaeth and I had pushed through the night, but the others had set up a rotation to afford each a few hours' sleep, including Queen Freya. If luck was on our side, she'd be recovered soon and portaling to the Earth Kingdom for reinforcements.

What was left of Alarik's men joined ranks, Vidarr being one of the most active among them. He was eager for a fight, seeking an outlet for his hatred against the cruel twist of fate that brought us to this place.

"How are you feeling?" Alarik asked as Queen Freya joined, her blade already slicing across a wolf's hide. Vidarr, Zaeth, and I stepped forward, taking the brunt of the attacks while they talked.

"Ready," she said, her palm glowing as a portal took shape.

"Queen Halcyon always has a small contingency ready for battle. I'll portal them first—"

"You can't go by yourself," Alarik cut in, stepping in front of her as the portal finished. "You don't know the state of the Earth Kingdom."

"I'll keep the portal open," she insisted. "Honestly, it's adorable how you worry for me. Maintain the lines, General Alarik. I'll be back with an army before you know it."

Alarik frowned but didn't stop Queen Freya as she pressed a kiss to his cheek and moved around him and through the portal.

"She's more than capable of taking care of herself," Vidarr said, delivering the killing blow to a light fae Zaeth had wounded. "You need to trust her."

"I do," Alarik muttered, sword catching a light fae through the stomach. "I know Freya is trained. I know she's not... her."

Brushing the strands of hair that had come free from my braid back, I dared a glance at Alarik. His lips were pressed thin, grip tightening on the hilt of his sword as he stared at the portal, waiting for Queen Freya to return.

"Rhosyn is at rest," Vidarr soothed, joining Zaeth against a bear-wolf hybrid. "It's long past time you let your fears of fate repeating go."

Rhosyn.

The memory of her parents murdering her before Alarik's eyes still twisted something in my chest. He'd been so young at the time, far too young to witness his fiancée's death. A small part of me wondered if things might have ended differently between us had he let that pain go.

To my surprise, Alarik turned away from the portal.

"You're right," he said, shaking his head and turning toward the cú sídhe stalking us through the trees. "She's the queen of the wild fae for gods' sakes."

The portal flashed and then vanished—without Queen Freya.

A string of curses left Alarik's lips, his shoulders flexing as he lashed out at the nearest unlucky light fae.

Zaeth glanced toward me, questions in his gaze.

"She knows what she's doing," I said in answer, loud enough for Alarik to hear me. "If the Wild Kingdom falls, so will all of Pax."

Though it felt like hours, a portal shimmered into place a few minutes later.

"Gods, Freya. Don't ever do that to me again." Alarik rushed forward, gathering her in his arms and punished her with a brutal kiss. Queen Freya's ruins flared under the onslaught, before Alarik pulled away. "What happened?"

Before she could answer, a woman with long dark hair and piercing green eyes stepped forward. Her battle leathers were composed of a material that looked almost like blue scales, and her tanned skin held a slight shimmer. All lingering questions as to her identity were answered when I spotted the coral crown atop her head.

"Queen Isla," Zaeth dipped his head in greeting as wolves prowled on the horizon. "What a pleasant surprise."

"Queen Halcyon is already on her way," the Water Queen answered. "I'd planned to stay and defend the capitol, but Queen Freya said our aid was needed."

"Our?" I asked, grateful for the lull in battle. Zaeth flitted to my side, his chest warming my back. I inhaled deeply, relishing the way his scent of cedar and spice overwhelmed even the worst of the gore surrounding us.

"Ours," Queen Isla answered, stepping aside as water fae warriors poured through the open portal.

Each wore the same blue-scaled armor Queen Isla did, carrying a variety of weapons including curved blades, three-pronged tridents, and arrows.

"A few hundred remain to defend Xyla, but most have come."

"And the water fae with you?" Zaeth asked, his gaze watching every movement she made. "Are they loyal to you or King Kai?"

Queen Isla lifted her chin. "Each fae here agrees Levana must be stopped. Not only have our shores been changed, but the seas are being invaded by monstrous beings, creatures with speed and cunning, devoid of empathy. Hundreds below the waves are dying every day. And then for my husband to pledge our help—our *lives*—in service to the very being responsible for their deaths." She shook her head, those nearest her mirroring her disgust. "It ends today."

"Thank you for your help, Queen Isla," Zaeth said, his gaze snapping toward the gathering wolves. Light fae clustered between the trees, seeming to wait for the wolves to make the first move. There were a few remaining shadow wraiths, but the long scythes hadn't fared well among the trees.

Zaeth dropped into a fighting position, turning away from the Water Queen as we braced for the next attack.

"We look forward to establishing a better world with you at our side," Queen Freya said, raising her sword.

"We're not well trained for land battle," Queen Isla confessed, as the last of them poured from the portal. "But I'm glad there are enough of us skilled at generating mist to help you, Queen Freya."

My head snapped toward the Wild Queen.

"That's right," she said with a smirk. "I mean to regenerate the mist, securing my kingdom and therefore Pax's chance at outliving this, *without* the aid of the gods. We'll start with a ring around the summit. Once in place, I'll be able to bolster it like I did before."

The thrumming of heartbeats cut through discussions, jerking mine and Zaeth's attention northward. My eyes strained as I peered through the forest already piled high with bodies. A humming started soon after, my brows furrowing as I tried to place it.

"Is that…"

"Wings," Queen Freya answered, unsheathing her blade as she turned toward Queen Isla. "How are your archers?"

"Some of the best," Queen Isla replied evenly.

"Good, because we're going to need them."

62

GREER

We flew as fast as we could, racing the rising moon. If the sister connection between us was right, El had been fighting for nearly twenty-four hours, and I was more than a little aware of her growing fatigue. While I knew dark fae were more resilient than others in times of war, I wasn't sure how much longer she could last.

King Dragcor and half of our army was ahead, while the rest of the Sky Warriors flanked Ryuu. We'd left one fleet behind, just enough to cover the capitol in case this was another one of Levana's deceptions. But something in my bones told me this was it.

Our final stand.

The Wild Kingdom came into view, but the thick mist I'd grown up around had vanished.

"Gods," I breathed as we neared. Snowy mountain slopes were painted in red and black, the layers of bodies so thick it was impossible to see the ground in parts.

Above all the mayhem of war sat picturesque long wooden homes nestles across the mountain's peak. It was clear most had taken shelter within, but fae soldiers created a ring around the summit. Wild fae were easy to discern, even under the cover of night, but there were others with cobalt armor and a slight shimmer to their skin interspersed throughout. It looked as if they were working together to generate small clouds of silver mist, highlighted by the light of the moon.

"The south looks calm," Ryuu called to the others, the Spear of Empyrean held tight in his free hand. "The current battle is centered along the northern section, spilling out around the sides of the mountain."

"Your Highness," General Bane called, drawing our attention toward the west. I'd come to know the largest of the Sky Warriors was nimble in the clouds and had the ability to see further than any other fae I'd know. He'd been the first to bow before me, and for that, I'd be forever grateful. "Fae spotted cresting the sky along the Jagged Mountains."

My eyes narrowed as I fought to make out their features. "Are those Levana's creatures?"

"No," rumbled Ryuu, but there was an elated ring to the word. "Those are fire fae. They've adjusted course to hit the western side of the mountain. We'll descend from the east—"

A great screech blasted through the night sky as a creature of ice and darkness ascended. Its hide looked like it was crafted from diamonds, the sharp planes glinting in the starlight. Thick, leathery grey wings pumped as it rose, its colossal frame blotting out most of the moon as rows of pointed fangs flashed with another ear-piercing scream.

"The ice wyvern," I breathed, more in awe than actual panic.

Five more wyverns rose behind it, only half as big as the first, but the barbs along their tails and the talons at the knuckles of their wings promised to be just as deadly—And seated on the smallest was Levana.

"Shit." *There* was the panic. My anxiety only grew as I watched her, dark hair billowing out behind her as her scarlet lips parted on a crazed laugh.

General Bane lifted a brow as if surprised by my language before his gaze returned to the band of ice wyverns heading our way.

"'Shit' is right, Your Highness. What are your orders?"

"Those gods better be protecting my sisters." I spared one glance down at the battle on the ground, hoping they could hold on a little longer. "We need to stop the wyverns from reaching the summit. If Levana manages to get within striking distance, she could destroy what's left of the humans without even setting foot on the ground."

I'd hoped that Queen Freya would have other defenses in place, and by the look of the small area still surrounded by a thin layer of mist, I assumed she did. There was a small village atop the mountain, but *all* our refugees had been transported here. They were either underground, or the summit was a portal of sorts. Either way, we couldn't let it fall to Levana.

Ryuu nodded, his feathered wings lengthening as his vertical-slit eyes studied the skies. "The fire fae have seen the wyverns and are redirecting their attentions. We will join them in this but be wary of the wyvern with the rider. The Goddess of Chaos rides upon it. And she is mine for the taking."

"Yes, Your Highness," General Bane said.

They peeled off, arching into the stars with howls of determination. The fire fae across the skies echoed the battle cry as their leathery wings joined our feathered ones. The two group merged, circling above the wyverns once to sync with one another, before diving.

The largest of the ice wyverns drew in a breath, a sot blue glow emanating from its chest before it blasted shards of ice at the attacking fae. Those hit were frozen instantaneously, their bodies plummeting to the earth below and shattering among the trees.

The remaining fae split into smaller groups, dodging blasts from the other wyverns as each creature screeched.

Some of the fire fae were able to cast what appeared to be shields of heat before them, warming the deadly cold air, but most were forced to rely on their skills of flying.

"We need to help," I said, shooting a few barbs of light toward the massive creatures. They struck against wings, tails, hides, but none of my light spears pierced fleshed.

Ryuu's shoulders broadened, the golden barbs of his wings stretching into dragon's hide as his wings shifted. There was a slight dip as the change overcame him, the grip around my core tightening as his talons appeared, but we remained aloft searching for Levana in the clouds.

"There's a very real possibility we won't make it out of this, my darling," Ryuu's dragon rumbled. "I won't disrespect you by asking you to sit this out—"

"Good, because that's not going to happen."

"But," his dragon continued with a slight growl. "Be smart about using your affinities. Wars like this aren't over in a matter of minutes."

"Noted," I said, realizing I wouldn't be of help against the wyverns. The smallest of them darted away from the cluster of wyverns, exposing Levana.

Ryuu's dragon wings pumped, picking up speed as we raced toward her. Chaos descended all around us, the cries from the ground carrying up on the wind as we neared, but I couldn't afford to split my concentration.

My gaze was fixed on the paled-skinned, dark haired, bitch-of-a-goddess who was determined to destroy my world. Who thought she was *owed* the sacrifice of anyone and anything she pleased.

"She's ours," I seethed, hungry for a fight. I'd promised Will all those months ago that I'd see him avenged, that we'd save this world. It was finally here, the battle that decided the fate of an entire realm.

"Yes, my brave, fierce mate," Ryuu's dragon rumbled. "She's our target. Her wyvern may be the smallest, but it's the nimblest and I would bet the deadliest. See the slight coloration difference?"

Sharp crystals coated its body like the others, but rather than the whites, and soft blues of the others, Levana's wyvern had streaks of black interspersed throughout.

"Black diamond wyverns possess neurotoxins in their bite."

"As if anyone would survive a bite that big," I muttered, the distance between them and us growing shorter.

Fire fae and Sky Warriors swarmed the largest wyvern, another chunk of our warriors caught in the monster's icy blast. Not only that, but the creature was easily ten times the size of a full grown fae with a diamond-covered hide of armor to boot. And its tail, the shards along it could skewer three fae at once.

"How are we supposed to kill them?" I asked, realizing I'd been so focused on Levana, I hadn't stopped to think how we'd defeat the wyverns. "Their hides are impenetrable—"

A blur of dark feathers and golden armor shot up from the ground beneath the largest creature, his wings beating furiously as he raced up, up.

King Dragcor's sword pierced the soft patch of scales along then largest of the ice wyvern's chest, his wings snapping in as the force of his ascent propelled him through the creature and out the other side between its shoulder blades.

An agonized shriek tore through the night air as the wyvern arched, its pale blue wings flapping once more across the moon, before its shimmering body started to fall.

I knew it was a monster from Levana's otherworld, born of a place without warmth or kindness and that it probably had no other desire than to kill everyone here, but I couldn't help but think of how beautiful it was. Even as its neck lulled and the life left its eyes, the light of the stars glinted off its diamond-studded hide, and I wondered if in another reality, in another time, we might not have needed to kill such a creature.

The remaining five wyverns dated forward in a flurry of ice and fury, crushing fae in their jaws and gulping them down whole. Spiked tails whirled through the frosted air, delivering many unsuspecting fae fatal blows.

Bodies rained from the sky. Dark droplets of fae blood sprayed the night air, the macabre rain tangling with torn feathers and strips of shredded leather wings as death covered the skies. I did my best to shield where I could. Beckoning the hovering light particles to move, I crafted hasty nets, throwing them between fae and attacking wyverns. My simple wards shattered under the force of the wyverns attacks but were able to slow the creatures down enough for fae to escape.

"Hold on," Ryuu's dragon called as we twisted through the sky, tracking Levana's movements. She had dropped beneath the clouds when the remaining wyverns attacked, using the distraction to slip behind most of the army.

"She's heading toward the mountain," I called as Ryuu spun, avoiding the bloodied spikes of a wyvern's tail. "There."

Heeding my words, Ryuu's dragon picked up speed, twisting through snapping jaws and sharp crystal hides until we were trailing Levana. She might have been riding the smallest of the bunch, but even in his shifted state, Ryuu was but a fraction of its size.

I glanced behind us, realizing that fae were losing ground, the wyverns forcing us back toward their goal—toward the summit.

King Dragcor managed to punch through the wing of a second wyvern, sending the poor beast spiraling. Fire fae and Sky Warrior pounced, finishing off the creature before it had a chance to recover.

The remain four were guarding their weak points, swiping with their tails or fangs, sending icy blasts into the air, the moment a fae got close. Some of our warriors were saved by my light shields, but I couldn't defend against all the wyverns at once, especially as we flew after Levana.

My stomach twisted. Those were our people. Our warriors, and I was leaving them on their own.

"If we don't stop Levana now, there will be no one to protect," Ryuu's dragon rumbled, his wings pumping, as we gave chase.

"Where are the gods?" I yelled, knowing he was right, but hating that Levana still went unchecked when we'd done everything possible to free Eunoia and Erebus. They were released to bring Levana to heel, but I'd seen nothing of their infinite power. Nothing of their aid.

A pulse of bloodlust rocked through me, causing me to gasp as the force of El's emotions shot through our sister bond. She was tapping into a lot of power, opening that dark place within and letting Erebus's affinities rise to the surface.

I let her anger, her hunger fuel me, steeling my resolve to take as many of Levana's monsters down as I could—starting with the Goddess of Chaos, herself.

"Hold on, El. I'm coming."

ELARA

BIRDS OF PREY WITH SHARP, BLACK-TIPPED TALONS AND translucent wings streaked with icy-blue veins swarmed with the setting sun. They circled above as light fae rushed from the sides of the mountain.

"Archers!" Queen Isla called, sending the water fae scrambling for formation. Arrows were poised a moment before the winged beasts reached us. "Fire!"

Arrows tipped with sharped shells flew through the air, piercing pale feathers as fae rushed to our line of defense with their shields raised.

A sickening crash sounded throughout the mountain, talons clashing with metal. Fae screamed as the birds of prey ripped through skin and tissue, coating the muddy ground in fresh sprays of blood.

Vulplings continued fighting beside us, but they were no match for the wicked birds.

I lifted my blade, dodging hooked beaks and flitting through the mess of wraiths, light fae, and beasts.

Each pass left bodies in my wake, but there were more.

Always more.

Shadows darkened my path, smothering creatures before they reached me. It had happened a few times now, when the monsters were closing in, and it looked as if I'd be cornered. At first, I'd thought it was Zaeth, but he was yards away cutting through his own group of monsters.

I had a prickling sensation that Erebus was responsible—was aiding me. He and Eunoia hadn't joined us at the summit, choosing instead to remain near the base of the mountain as they waited. Maybe he could see me from there. Maybe he and the goddess would help when Levana showed up, but I couldn't count on them.

I had decided to end this war on my own terms—gods or not.

My arms ached and my muscles burned as I forced my body to keep moving, tapping into that dark place deep within. Zaeth's warmth flooded down our bond, joining a grounding force I knew came from Lannie. I hadn't understood what it was earlier, but I did now.

My sister was coming and bringing the might of the Earth Kingdom with her. *Sisters* if the nervous buzzing flowing through Greer's bond was any indication. She must have been close, closer than I thought possible.

"Just a little longer."

I spoke to the stars, to all the other gods on other planets who might not have been as cruel as the ones we were given. And hoped beyond reason, one of them would answer.

Zaeth whirled behind a light fae, wrenching his head back as he dragged a blade across his throat. Blood gushed from the wound and Zaeth's eyes brightened.

"We can defeat anything," he said, fangs gleaming in the moonlight as the high of battle took hold. "Gods—the stars themselves. Nothing can part us."

"Nothing," I echoed as he flitted toward me. His fingers were in my hair, the ragged braid matted in swaths of dried blood and dirt, but I savored the feel of his lips pressing against mine, the scent of cedar and spice warring with the metallic tang of blood.

It was a stolen kiss on a field of death. We were nothing more than monsters fighting other monsters, but we would prove to be the worst of them.

Zaeth's lips twitched as he felt my affinities spark. "Let's show them who we are, love."

My eyes went wide as the shadows behind him parted. Zaeth spun, sword poised, but lowered it a moment later with a sigh of relief.

"Naz. How did you find us?"

"Never mind that," she answered as Jarek luxed into view beside her.

"You found them. Thank the gods—well, not those gods. They've proven to be a pair of assholes, but you know what I mean." Jarek waved his hand, looking back to Naz. "Here looks as good a place as any."

"For what?" Zaeth asked, his eyes focused on the rustling of the trees around us as our enemies drew near.

"For our army," Naz smiled, before her and Jarek vanished.

Naz and Jarek worked delivering The Dark Army in clusters along the mountainside, relieving our exhausted forces. Alarik and Vidarr were taking a much needed rest, along with most of the wild fae, as they arrived.

"Rest," Jarek insisted, but I could see the dark circles under his eyes.

"You luxed an entire army to the Wild Kingdom?" I asked, ignoring his advice while I clipped one of the birds of prey's wings with a well-placed thrust of my sword. Zaeth finished it off behind me, snapping the bird's neck with his hands.

"Half an army," Jarek corrected, flitting between two wraiths and severing their heads with a single blow. His eyes darted to the trees. "We moved in small spurts, going back and gathering others as those we just transported flitted ahead. It was a team effort, really."

"You should rest," I countered, noting how he hadn't bothered to try to heal the shallow cut along Vidarr's shoulder when he'd first arrived. Normally, Jarek was all about healing things before they worsened. The fact that he hadn't offered meant his affinities must be running low.

"All in due time, kitten," he said, searching the forest as if hoping to find someone—Evander, I realized. The moon was high in the sky bathing pine trees in white light. With our fae sight, it was nearly the same as fighting beneath the sun, but it was clear the humans weren't faring as well.

"Evander isn't here," I said as his light blue eyes raked the horizon once more. "But Queen Isla said the Earth Kingdom is moving north. I'm sure he'll be with Lannie."

A great screech blasted through the night, sending a chill down my spine.

"What was that?" I asked as another shriek reverberated through the trees.

"Icy wyvern," Zaeth called, withdrawing his sword from the chest of a small creature. He stared at the body he'd just impaled, the slightly tipped ears filled with rings and jagged teeth. "And goblins."

"Prepare for a swarm," Jarek breathed, staring at the point in the shadows the creature had come from.

Fae near us drew close together, forming small clusters as they heeded his warning just as the rush of goblins came into view. The dashed up the mountainside, followed closely by throngs of the Fractured—and the only creature who could wield them: Veles.

My pulse spiked, the drive of battle and fury zeroing my

focus on him—only Veles. If this was to be my last day, I'd make sure he was dead—

"El," Zaeth said, flitting in front to stop me. "Look at the Fractured. They're *helping* us."

My chest heaved as I fought to tear my eyes away from their leader, the held responsible for Will's death. When I finally did, I saw that Zaeth was right. The Fractured chased after the goblins, turning against the wraiths and cú sídhe as well. Even the light fae—Veles's precious light fae—were under attack.

"I only want Levana's head," Veles said, his black eyes meeting mine. The moonlight increased the contrast of his features, his pale skin and bone-white hair bleached further and his eyes—they were two pits of unending darkness.

"Didn't you hear?" I taunted, unable to help myself. "Your god, Erebus, has agreed not to kill her."

Ire ignited in those depthless pits, his sword lashing out quick as a flash to catch two goblins in the stomach. "We had an agreement."

I shrugged, slashing through the neck of a wraith.

"Take it up with Erebus," Zaeth gritted out. "He's probably still at the base of the mountain with Eunoia, relaxing against a tree."

An agonized shriek snapped my attention back to the sky.

"There," I said, pointing in the distance. The two fae armies merged in the sky, circling the wyverns from above. "The Sky Warriors have arrived," I breathed, knowing that mean Greer and Ryuu were somewhere above us.

"The fire fae, as well," Veles said, pointing to the fae with the bat-like wings, flying just as skillfully as any of the air fae.

"It looks like King Dragcor flew right through the largest ice wyvern," I said, watching as the great, diamond-covered creature fell through the air. Gods, it was huge.

"Maybe we have a shot after all," Jarek smiled.

I let hope flare bright for a heartbeat longer—until I saw the five other wyverns behind it.

Jarek's smile faltered. "Or maybe not."

"Don't give up that easily," Evander said, flitting toward us as Zaeth slashed through three more goblins.

Jarek was on him seconds, wrapping Evander in a fierce hug.

"Next time, stay with me," Jarek breathed, resting his forehead against Evander's.

Flashes of light flickered in the sky, illuminating the remaining wyvern and the fae fighting against them—shields interspersed throughout blasts of ice. Feathers and bat-like wings mixed blurring around the larger creatures but there was one among them who stood out.

"Greer," I breathed, focusing on Ryuu's dragon. He was flying toward us chasing the swiftest, smallest wyvern. My brows furrows as I fought to make out details, the animal's speed and dark hide making it difficult to focus.

Zaeth followed my line of sight, distracted with the one Greer was chasing as much as I was.

Shadows wrapped around it, but I caught a glimpse of pale skin and dark hair, realizing who sat upon its back.

I reached deeper within myself, allowing that dark monsters within to stretch her legs. My dark fae affinities rose to the surface, burning through all feeling of fatigue as the need for vengeance consumed me.

"Were you serious about taking Levana's head, Veles?" I asked, keeping my gaze locked on the wyvern covered in shadows, watching as Ryuu's dragon gave chase. Greer launched light shards through the air, but all were disintegrated by the shadows surrounding her.

"I'm owed her life," he growled and from the corner of my eye, I saw his attention had shifted from the battle on the ground to the Goddess of Chaos.

"Then perhaps we can call a truce until there's one less goddess in this world."

64

LANNIE

We followed the bodies of the Fractured north through the Western Woods, fighting our way through the troves of goblins and cú sídhe, until finally the prized mountain of the Wild Kingdom was found.

The moon was high in the sky, casting a spot light on the great beasts flying through the night—and Greer chasing one.

It had to be her. No one else could cast net wards as they were hurtling toward a vicious monster while clutched in the arms of her own shifted dragon-fae. Of course, Greer would be reckless in chasing after a wyvern—

My eyes widened as two sets of wings rose from the forest, one black and the other a deep violet. They launched into the sky, like an arrow intent on claiming the stars, until they banked north, heading off the small wyvern while Greer and Ryuu's dragon came up from behind.

"No," I breathed, straining my eyes to focus on the shifting shadows wrapped around the rider on the dark wyvern. "They wouldn't."

But that twisting in my gut told me that they would. My sisters were flying right toward the Goddess of Chaos.

"Lannie," Halcyon called, snapping my attention back to the ground.

One of the cú sídhe were sprinting right at me, it's snout curled in a sharp-fanged snarl. But its face was shorter, the jaw thicker, and its paws were huge. The bear like creature reared back on its hind legs, claws swiping for me.

I stumbled back, flitting just fast enough for the tips to catch the side of my thigh. I let the stinging wound focus me as I raced toward the cluster of earth fae, knowing Halcyon was fighting her way toward me.

Her troops opened, forming a ring around me as the bear-like beast closed in. It was faster than its weight should've allowed, but I reached the safety of Halcyon's warriors before it could finish me, the slashes along my thigh already healed.

Half-a-dozen other beasts joined, swiping at the fae protecting me. I healed while they fought, applying salves and suturing as fast as I could to those who needed it, taking care of the worst of the injuries, and trusting their fae essences to do the rest. Infections could be tended to on the morrow.

Soon, the last of the beasts were put down with minimal causalities from the earth fae. I wondered what type of creatures lurked in the wilds of the Earth Kingdom to afford them such skill. It was something I needed to learn if I remained by Halcyon's side—if we survived this.

"There are other creatures here." Halcyon's voice washed over me, calming my frantic heart. "Shadow wraiths, light fae, ice hawks, even ursa lupine have joined Levana's forces, as you saw."

A grim understanding swept through our cluster, reverberating throughout the rest of the earth fae and a few dark fae who'd come to aid us. We must be close to El.

"Be prepared for anything."

They raised their sword, rushing into the trees with a roar.

"I need to reach my sisters," I said, staring into her silver eyes, knowing she felt my panic but not sure if she understood why. "The connection between us—I can feel El tapping into the darkness again. Last time, I thought she wouldn't return."

Halcyon nodded, her blade rising to intercept a scythe aimed at her neck. She spun, kicking the wraith back just enough to lift her blade and drag it across the creature's throat.

A blood-chilling screech rang through the air.

Greer had thrown a shield before the wyvern, one large enough to force it into a vertical climb. Levana's shadows snapped back to her side, steadying her on the beast's back while Zaeth and El gave chase.

Ryuu's dragon anticipated the wyvern's move, his powerful leather wings beating as he lashed out with the Spear of Empyrean. It pierced the wyvern's left flank, its tail whipping toward them. Shards of black-streaked diamonds were set to impale Greer, but her hands came up piecing a shield together right before it struck.

El and Zaeth nearly had Levana, the Dark King's shadows doing battle with the goddess's as El leveled her blade. Before either could catch her, great claws of night rose from the earth, snapping closed around Levana and tugging her free from the injured wyvern.

The battle of the remaining wyverns against the air and fire fae continued, bellowing cries piercing the night air as icy blasts came. The night was filled with fae dying and monsters snarling, but all I could focus on was the way the dark rings around El's eyes seemed to grow, her fae affinities vibrating down our bond as she tucked her violet wings in and dove after the Levana.

65

GREER

The black-diamond wyvern shrieked as it was thrown back, caught between the force of Levana's shadows and what looked like night itself, before it steadied itself and fled toward the Jagged Mountains.

Erebus.

It had to be him, the God of Night coming to destroy Levana. My gaze connected with El's, the black rings around her irises, too large, her fangs too prominent.

"Erebus won't save us," she said.

Her violet wings snapped closed in the second it took me to process what she was saying, sending her into a free fall after Levana and the God of Night below.

Zaeth dove after her with a look that said he'd explain later, but that she wasn't wrong.

"What should we do?" I asked, glancing over my shoulder to see wyverns fighting against the Sky Warriors and fire fae, both kingdoms led by King Dragcor. One of his feathered wings were bent and blood covered his battle leathers, but there was a fire in his eyes that I hadn't seen before.

A smile split his lips as he thrust his sword up, aiming for the soft spot along the chest of one of the remaining wyverns. The Sky Warriors around him did their best to distract the monster, but its tail whipped around, catching Dragcor in the thigh just as his sword pierced its chest.

The great beast howled as it fell, the prominent talons along the knuckle of its wings goring King Dragcor in his side with its last burst of life.

Ryuu's dragon tensed, fear rippling down our bond, but his father gave a crazed laugh as the beast crashed to the earth, raising his sword high.

"We battle the gods," Ryuu's dragon rumbled. With the Spear of Empyrean gripped in his hand, we dove after my sister.

The earth shuddered as we landed near the summit, the two of us thrown into a storm of mists and monsters.

The edges of silver mist rolled through the forest, coming from the wall at our backs encompassing the small village. Queen Freya was kneeling, her palm pulsing with silver light as her essence gravitated toward the swirling mist. Alarik was at her side, flanked by Vidarr and the other Select Guard, finishing off any creatures who made it through the outer circle of wild fae.

Their cluster was the only sign of order. Everything else was mayhem.

Pixies and fairies warred with one another, the foxlike vulplins' black-flamed tails darting among the cú sídhe and their bear-like cousins. Earth and wild fae fought side-by-side against goblins and wraiths. Even Veles was flitting among the masses, slaughtering light fae at an alarming rate as if each had personally wronged him. The water fae archers were locked in a stale mate against the savage birds, picking off just as many of them as they were of us.

And there, in the center of it all was Levana.

Erebus stood a few paces away, the night rising around him in the form of two claw-tipped hands. They tried repeatedly to grip the goddess, but she was too nimble, seeming to know exactly where and how he would strike.

"Come now, sister," Eunoia called, stalking out from the forest as if we were in a tranquil garden rather than a mountain full of death. "You know we can't let you roam free after what you've done."

"What *I've* done?" Levana snarled. "You bound my power and locked me away for eons, forcing me to watch as my children were purged from our world, as Erebus turned from me and fell into *your* lap."

Erebus's control of the night flickered, his eyes darting between the sisters. "That's not exactly how it happened—"

"Please," Levana interrupted as she threw off the remains of his darkness. "You saw the beauty in my creations, basked in the rawness of their emotions, their brutality, until *she* convinced you I was dangerous."

"You *are* dangerous," Erebus thundered, the darkness around us thickening until the stars themselves were blotted out. "You managed to turn this entire world into a power source, crossed realms, even found a way to be reborn—"

"To be free," Levana roared. Shadows lashed out, hammering Eunoia and Erebus in a vicious onslaught, forcing them to shield.

Seeing an opening, El dove in. She lashed out with her sword, but each of her strikes were intercepted by either Levana's blade or her tendrils of shadows. Zaeth added his own control over the darkness to strip some of her deflections, but El's blade never pierced Levana's skin.

"You're supposed to be dead," Levana seethed, focusing her attention on El.

Her boot collided with El's chest, my shield of light appearing a moment too late. El was thrust back, sailing through the trees with Zaeth racing after her.

I expected Levana to set her sights on Erebus, to chase after the gods who'd bound her, but she flitted away, slipping into the tangle of bodies and trees opposite of where she'd sent El. Erebus and Eunoia followed, pulses of light and streaks of shadows lashing after her.

I needed to find my sisters—both of them—and keep them safe. Crafting a shield around myself, I worked through the worst of the battle, the Spear of Empyrean sinking into monsters at my side as Ryuu's dragon stayed close.

A flash of red hair caught my attention. It was Evander flitting toward the large cluster of Fractured and the grounded wyvern they fought against. Though its wings were shredded, and it looked too exhausted to breath ice, its tail continued to lash out in deadly strokes.

For a moment, I considered protecting it. It was already injured. Surely, if we stopped attacking, it would do the same. But then its cold, black eyes met mine. They weren't like the black-diamond wyvern's intelligent gaze. There was no fear or pain or any emotion other than rage peering back at me.

Levana's monsters were all different, I realized. Not so much on the outside, but their internal make up was unique. Some had the ability to feel empathy, while others lived for the chaos they were born from.

This creature was one that would fight until its last breath. And while there was a certain brutal beauty to that, I knew I couldn't save it.

Evander sliced at the creature as the Fractured surged forward, throwing their bodies and blades at the wyvern under the command of their leader. Veles was at their center, his pristine pale hair matted with grime. The wyvern fell, Evander's bright red hair standing out among the sea of black.

"There you are." Levana's voice carried through the air, her body moving nearly too fast to see.

And much too fast for Veles to react.

Shadows billowed out around Levana in a protective cocoon as her fingers gripped Veles's neck, lifting him off the ground.

"You've been annoyingly hard to find, Veles. Had I known you were that capable, I might've let your brothers live."

Veles's sword clattered to the ground as his fingers scratched at Levana's grip.

"As it were," the goddess continued. "It's only fitting I reunite the three of you."

Her fingers dug into the soft flesh of Veles's neck with ruthless speed, ripping away the soft tissue of his throat to reveal the white of his spine beneath. Blood spurted from the gaping hole as Veles thudded to the forest floor, the Fractured all around us stilling as the beating of his heart stopped.

A dark shadow rose from Veles's broken body. Levana inhaled it deeply, her head thrown back, eyes closing as it washed through her. A low moan sounded from her throat as her head rolled forward, the blacks of her eyes igniting with power as she grinned.

"Destroy them," Levana commanded, before flitting into the night.

As if connected to her mind, the Fractured turned, raising their blades against everyone they'd been protecting—including Evander.

He realized what was happening a second before their allegiance shifted, his blade hacking through bodies as he flitted for an opening. But there were so many—too many. And with the speed he was moving, any shield I crafted would trap him rather than protect.

"Ryuu," I breathed, not able to take my eyes off Evander as the Fractured lashed out. I sent pulse after pulse of light spears, but it was like trying to hold back the ocean with a single stone.

Without another word, Ryuu's great leather wings slashed through monsters as he fought his way toward the only brother

I had left in this world. I stayed close by him, tucked into the small path he created for us with my shield firmly in place.

Evander's body was riddled with wounds as he neared the edge of the swarm. But he was slowing. *Gods*, and Ryuu wouldn't be fast enough.

Electricity pricked in the air as a flash of light appeared at Evander's side. He was gone in the next moment.

The two of them appeared near the wall of mist, the silver swirls billowing up around them as Jarek and Evander luxed into view.

With my shield firmly in place, I ran toward them, the throng of Fractured much easier to maneuver now that their attention was split. The swarm fanned out, turning their sights on the rest of our army now that Evander was out of view.

Ryuu was nearly done with this group anyway, the Fractured in his path little more than broken limbs as his feet. He'd be turning to the skies next.

"I didn't need you to save me," Evander growled, shoving Jarek's chest.

Jarek's stormy eyes blazed as he stumbled back, his chest heaving as every line of his beautiful face slackened with fatigue. "You would be dead right now if I hadn't."

"Then I would be dead," Evander roared.

"Do I mean so little to you?" Jarek whispered, flinching back. "Can you not love us both?"

Evander hovered there, poised on the edge of the battlefield, before turning away.

My heart clenched as I watched hurt twist Jarek's features, his shoulders seeming to slump under the weight of it. I was nearly to them, and then I'd force Evander to get his shit together, apocalypse or not.

Evander threw himself into battle, cutting down goblins and Fractured as he went, but his movements were rash, born of pain and loss and unshed grief. He didn't see the bear-like beast crouching in the shadows until it had already sprung.

"Evander!" I screamed, throwing a shield in front of the monster. Claws scraped against the hurried network of light, but it held long enough for Evander to slip around and end the creature.

"Thanks—"

Another launched from the behind, the beast moving quicker than the light molecules moving beneath my touch.

It happened as if in slow motion, the horror of the scene before me in stark clarity to the everything else. The thick pads of the beast stretched, sharp claws extending toward Evander's chest. His eyes were wide, mouth dropping open as if he couldn't really believe this was the end.

As if *maybe*, he didn't want it to be.

The particles I'd been arranging solidified into a shield around Evander just as Jarek luxed into view his spine arching as the beast tore through him.

66

LANNIE

Evander's flare of red hair had drawn me to the edge of the mist, Halcyon and I working our way through the mess of the mountain toward my family. I'd watch him turn away from Jarek, diving back into battle with Greer flitting toward him. She'd shielded him from the beast she could see, but there was another lying in wait.

I screamed a warning to the wind, flitting through blades and bodies as fast as my fae limbs would carry me, but they hadn't heard.

A part of me was relieved when Jarek luxed—that horrible, selfish part of me that looked upon the shredded muscle and skin of Jarek's back and thought, 'at least it's not Evander.'

Guilt burned at the back of my throat as I neared. Jarek was just as valuable as Evander. He had a purpose, a light to offer this world... but I—gods, I couldn't lose another person I loved.

Evander's screams filled the air as his sword hacked at the beast with reckless abandon.

It was nothing but clumps of bloodied fur when I finally reached them, confined in the shielded area with Greer, Evander, and Jarek. My sister saw me before the others, opening a section of the wards to allow me in before sealing it shut.

"Roll him on his side," I instructed, tugged my pack off my shoulder and yanking the tin of powder free.

Evander did, maneuvering Jarek's shaking body until his head was resting in his lap. The battle leathers were in tatters, deep gash marks glaring up between the dark material. I used the last of the powder on them, the blood slowing but still seeping through. With a curse, I pulled a bag of fluids out, maneuvering his arm until it was attached and draining into his vein.

"Why?" Evander repeated the word, tears streaming down his cheeks as he brushed back the hair along Jarek's brow. "I told you I didn't need you to save me. You shouldn't have saved me."

Light glowed beneath Jarek's skin as the fluid spread through the network of vessels, attempting to stitch the muscle back together. The soft glow oozed through the gashes on either side of Jarek's spine, the white of his ribs still visible through the shredded flesh.

"You changed your mind," Jarek chocked out, each syllable jarring his chest and sending a spike of pain through him. "I saw it in your face, right before."

Evander swallowed, unable to deny it.

Jared stared into Evander's eyes, the hint of a smile tilting the edge of his lips. "You die, I die."

"That is the most ridiculous thing you've ever said." Evander shook his head, doing his best not to move him. "But it works both ways. If you die, I die."

A sob rocked through Jarek's chest as I squeezed the last of the fluid into him, tossing the empty bag away as I reached for another.

The vehemence of Evander's words took me by surprise. All this time, I thought his struggle stemmed from unending grief.

While I was sure that was part of it, I wondered if all of this hadn't been due to guilt. Guilt for finding happiness with another when he swore to love Jem forever.

"No one is dying today," I growled, watching as the trickle of glowing liquid slowed and the deepest layers of muscle and fascia knit back together.

"How's he looking, Lannie?" Greer asked, the shield around us flickering.

I glanced up, hands coated in blood as I met my sister's gaze. Her brows were pinched in concentration as darkness swarmed around us, obscuring everything from sight.

"Another minute or two and he should be stable enough to move." Even now, Jarek was pushing to a sitting position, letting Evander cry into his chest as the rest of the skin sealed in a pink scar. "What's going on out there?"

"I don't know," she breathed, sweat beading on her brow. "But El's involved."

Taking a steadying breath, I focused on El's connection. It was sheathed in darkness, the pull to give into it nearly overwhelming. I reached for Halcyon, instantly flooded by fear—fear for me. She must have been out there, watching Greer's shield covered in a swath of night with me trapped within.

I sent a wash of calm down my mating bond, letting her know I was safe, before I connected to El, anchoring the three of us to Pax. The earth hummed beneath my feet, our essences forming a circuit of sorts. El's fae side may be overwhelmed by her god blood but connecting her to Pax would ensure she remembered her humanity.

Greer eased our connection open as well, letting the energy flow through the earth. It helped maintain the shield a little longer, giving Jarek and Evander enough time to stand beside us.

Spots of light flickered in the vast darkness, like stars swirling through clouds. Every few seconds we'd see fierce blots of lightening crack and clash with whips of shadows, but then the darkness would take hold and nearly all the light would vanish.

"We need to get out of this," Greer said, her eyes snagging on the light of the moon that flickered into view. "I'll keep the shield around us as we move up the mountain. We should be close to the mist around the summit. Once we reach that, let's hope we'll be able to work our way out of this."

Leaving my empty pack behind, the four of us kept pace with Greer. We flitted through the darkness, slamming into lifeless bodies and large streaks of cratered earth as we went. I didn't want to think what would've happened had Greer not been here to cast wards around us.

Not until silver mist rose before us and the whole of the night sky winked into view did Greer's shield drop. Her chest heaved as we glanced behind, looking down the mountain to finally catch a glimpse of what was happening.

Erebus and Levana were locked in battle, the area we'd been moments ago caught in their crossfire of violent, warring powers. Erebus was stronger, his lashes of night obliterating the ground where they struck, but Levana was faster. She managed to dodge each of Erebus's and Eunoia's attempts at capture. I could just make out El and Zaeth darting among them, doing their best to dodge while attempting to catch Levana unprepared with their blades.

"Thanks to the two of you, I've had nothing to do but plot and plan." Levana sent a blast of energy that sent Eunoia stumbling back. The light goddess's dark eyes ringed with light blazed as Levana shot her a cocky smirk. "Do you think I wouldn't have anticipated this?"

Corpses and earth exploded into the air as another of Erebus's shadow claws missed the Goddess of Chaos. El brought her sword down, the tip digging into the ground where Levana had been moments ago.

"Levana is too quick," I said. "She's anticipating everything they do."

"She's had thousands of years to prepare for this moment," Greer agreed.

El pulled from us as she recovered, drawing strength for the earth but also our affinities. I could feel Halcyon tapping in, helping to shoulder the burden of tethering us to Pax. I knew it was the only way I maintained the connection. El was drawing too much, burning through essence too quickly for me to keep the connection open on my own.

"We can't keep going like this," I muttered, searching for a solution, but the battle of the monstrous gods still raged without an end in sight.

The mountainside was filled with fae, humans, and dark creatures. It looked like every being of Pax had turned out for this battle, all of them fighting for their lives. There was nowhere else to turn to. No one else to help.

"I have an idea," Greer said, her eyes turning up to the night sky and the heavy clouds coating it. "He's coming."

A screech from far above was abruptly cut off, the body of the last wyvern crashing through the trees moments later. Fire and air fae swooped down, picking off creatures as they joined the turmoil all around us. There, flying toward us was Ryuu, his white, feather-like wings pumping, and the golden tipped Spear of Empyrean gripped in his hand.

GREER

I'D KNOWN RYUU WOULD FIND ME, BUT I HADN'T ANTICIPATED he'd bring back up. The Sky Warriors and fire fae had cleared the night of Levana's monsters, birds, wyverns, even the smallest creatures like the pixies. All had been dealt with. It was a good thing, too, because I was pretty sure we only had a few more minutes before our side lost.

El pulled from our connection again, nearly draining me. Lannie bowed forward under the strain, and I wanted nothing more than to lie down and rest with her, but I couldn't. Not yet. Ryuu had taken one glance my way, the burning green embers of his eyes ensuring I was all right, before he dove into the battle of the gods.

King Dragcor was close behind, looking much worse for wear. His dark wings had shifted to black leather, the orange specks of his eyes fully saturated around vertical slits. His hands had transitioned into claws, and there was a sharp row of fangs where his teeth had once been. It was a wonder he hadn't sprouted a tail.

"Stay here and anchor us, Lannie." My little sister looked up at me, her chest heaving as she did what I instructed. I met Jarek and Evander's eyes. "You two better not let anything happen her. She stays safe, no matter what."

"What would happen, Greer?" Lannie asked her dark, intelligent eyes meeting mine. But I didn't need to explain. She already knew what I was going to do—What I *needed* to do if there was any chance of stopping Levana.

"I love you, little sis." I allowed myself one last look into her eyes, promising I'd do whatever it took to ensure I'd never lose another sibling, before hurling myself into the darkness.

68

ELARA

I could feel myself weakening as the sun rose. Zaeth as well.

We'd been locked in endless battle for two nights, and it was starting to show. Levana and Erebus clashed over and over again, the God of Night growing more aggressive as the battle waged. We would've had her if Eunoia threw her weight behind him, if the two of them stopped trying to subdue Levana and actually attacked.

Shadows collided with tendrils of night as I slipped behind Levana. She somehow knew where I was, crafting a sliver of her power into a whip that slashed across my gut. Zaeth flitted behind me, jerking me back to avoid most of the damage.

I sucked in a sharp breath as blood stained my stomach, but the wound was shallow and already healing.

"We can't get through," I panted, forcing myself to stand, to raise my sword once more. "It's like she knows our next move before we do."

"Maybe she does," Zaeth breathed, his light-ringed eyes studying the three gods. "She was inside your mind. She knew all your thoughts. Your fighting style. And she's connected to Eunoia."

"Meaning she might be connected to you, as well, what with her extra blessing."

"That or it could be my shadows are derived from Levana, as most of the dark creatures of Pax are." Zaeth's jaw ticked before his eyes snagged on Ryuu and Dragcor flitting toward us. "We need something she won't see coming."

I felt Lannie's tether lodge deeper into the earth, as if preparing for my next pull. Pulses of light flashed, drawing my attention toward the familiar pull. Erebus's darkness was dense but directed at Levana. I managed to spot a shield derived from light, finding Greer at its center.

"Three fated mates," I breathed, glancing back to Zaeth. His exhaustion mirrored my own, the look in his gaze telling me he'd realized the same thing I had: this battle was going to take everything from us. There could be no holding back. No thoughts of self-preservation.

"Together, love," he said, pressing a swift, desperate kiss to my lips.

"Together."

We flitted forward, slipping between Levana's shadows as both of us tapped into the powers gifted to us from the very gods we fought with. My affinities consumed me, Erebus's darkness stripping the despair that had gripped me only moments ago. I let it, feeling only my undying need for vengeance roar within as I reached the Goddess of Chaos.

She snarled at me, her blade slashing across Eunoia's chest as her shadows threw Erebus through the trees. Flitting back, she avoided by sword, rebounding with a snake of her own dark essence.

I braced for the blow, but light flared before me, Greer's shield intercepting Levana's power. It split apart, the two powers seeming to cancel each other out, but the shield had served its purpose.

With that split second distraction, I dropped to the ground, my sword slashing across the back of Levana's knees.

She roared as her legs buckled, a pulse of her shadows hurling outward in a violent blast.

Greer was before me, layering light as quickly as she could as Levana's shadows ate through her protection. Zaeth was at her side, diverting tendrils of darkness that broke through away from us with his own control of shadows.

Seizing on her weakness, Erebus flitted forward, tendrils of night wrapping around Levana's ankles and wrists, holding her down just as the ground thundered.

King Dragcor and Ryuu landed, flitted forward. Ryuu reached her first, raising the Spear of Empyrean high above his chest. But Levana broke through Erebus's restraints before Ryuu could finish her, jerking up and slamming Ryuu with a wall of blistering shadows.

Greer screamed as Ryuu's skin and feathers sizzled, the shadows disintegrating all they touched. Half his face was coated in dark burns, the skin oozing as the golden barbs of his wings peaked through ash, his wing looking like a skeletal limb.

King Dragcor's roar filled the air as he flitted to his son's side. An animalistic snarl came from deep within the Air King's chest, his reptilian features shifting further into a dragon as he looked upon his only son unconscious and wounded.

Erebus doubled his efforts as he fought to keep hold of Levana, waves of night regaining control to secure her wrists and ankles. But it was taking too much effort. We needed more help.

Levana's cold, black eyes locked with mine, hatred searing through their depths as she spoke. "Target the sisters. Break their connection."

I blinked, not understanding what she meant, until I heard Lannie scream.

Panic reared inside me as I searched the area for my sisters, finding Greer first. She was kneeling, her face splotchy with tears as she cradled Ryuu's limp form in her hands. I reached for her through our bond, feeling how spent she was, but her emotions were too jumbled for anything else.

Looking past her, I looked for our little sister.

There.

Lannie's heart was hammering, her eyes closed as the toll of maintaining our connection with Pax weighed on her. It was noble and selfless, but gods did I want her to think of herself for once. Just once.

Instead, she was kneeling in the middle of a war zone, entrusting her safety to Jarek and Evander as a wave of Fractured descended.

"Greer," I pleaded, needing her by my side for this. She must have felt the desperation through our bond, because her eyes meet mine, understanding flashing in their depths. We needed to stay strong for a little long, and then we could rest—just long enough to save Lannie.

With a small dip of her head, Greer forced a shield to flare to life around our little sister, doing her best to maintain it across the distance.

Levana growled as Eunoia slammed her hands down, Erebus shifting his power to holding her ankles as the Goddess of Light started chanting.

Erebus took up the words, murmuring in an ancient language I couldn't understand, but I could feel the air prick as their powers grew. Their affinities blended, snaking across Levana's chest to form glowing ropes crafted from darkness— the tendrils of night mixing with Eunoia's light.

A mirthless laugh rocked through Levana as the bindings solidified. She'd stopped struggling, allowing Erebus and

Eunoia to continue to siphon more of their power into her prison.

"So predictable," Levana sneered. "The best part about chaos, one that neither of you understood, is that it's ever changing. It's constantly prodding, searching for weak points in order's constructs. The universe was not meant to be controlled. It *wants* to be free."

Levana arched her neck, meeting Eunoia's gaze poised above her.

The fine hairs on the back of my neck pricked as I raced forward, trusting Greer, Evander, and Jarek to keep Lannie safe as I helped secure Levana's wrists.

Zaeth had the same idea, pressing against her ankles—but she wasn't fighting. Levana's gaze slid to me, the look more amused than anything, before she turned toward her sister once more.

"You should have listened to Erebus."

Levana's hands snapped up, wrapping around Eunoia's wrists as the bindings around her torso flared. The Goddess of Light gasped, eyes going wide as Levana siphoned her power, drawing more and more into herself.

"I can't break the connection," Erebus yelled, trying to withdraw his darkness, but it was intertwined with Eunoia's rays of light across Levana's bindings, the two now inseparable.

Zaeth grunted with the effort it took to hold the Goddess of Chaos down, his shoulders bowing as Levana grew stronger. I still had hold of her arms, forcing them into the ground as she held her sister's wrists, but I had a sinking feeling Levana was allowing me to restrain her, taking this time to focus on her connection with Eunoia.

King Dragcor's head snapped toward us as he tore away from Ryuu's side. His claws reverted into hands just enough to retrieve the Spear of Empyrean before he flitted forward.

He was little more than a blur of leather wings and sharp

fangs, until he raised the spear over Levana's chest—and thrust it down.

I felt the reverberation of the gold diamond tip hit the ground, the shaft impaled between her ribs as the Levana screamed.

"No!" Eunoia shouted. Levana's grip on her wrists weakened, allowing her to hurl a blast of power toward King Dragcor, the wave of light crashing into him with a sickening crunch.

King Dragcor rolled across the ground, crashing to the floor feet from Ryuu. Bile burned my throat as I looked upon, finding half of his skull misshaped, and one of his arms torn off below the shoulder.

Nobody could've survived that, but his leathery wings twitched as he forced himself to crawl, leaving a pool of scarlet in his wake as he reached for his son.

I wasn't sure how he was moving. How he could've survived with injuries that severe, but then his fingers brushed Ryuu's. Gentle murmurings that sounded like blessings rose on the air with the morning sun, the dragon king somehow finding peace in all the pain.

And then he was still.

"Hold her steady," Eunoia panted, snapping my attention back to the writhing Levana.

"What are you doing?" Erebus called, his streaks of night billowing around him.

"Healing her," Eunoia breathed. "Hold her, Erebus. Your blood daughter won't be able to keep her restrained, even with my blessed son helping."

There was a long moment when the God of Night and the Goddess of Light stared at each other. Erebus broke first, his eyes darting to me for a short, fleeting second, before he nodded.

He watched as Eunoia ripped the spear from Levana's chest,

as her hands pressed against the wound, before swaths of night covered them both.

"Back away, daughter," he rumbled, the dark rings around his eyes flaring. "Tell your mate to draw his shadows in."

I was inclined to argue, but something about his tone had me complying. Zaeth and I stumbled back, too exhausted to do much of anything, other than watch as Eunoia poured her essence into her sister.

The bindings around Levana's torso ignited as Eunoia worked, the goddess seeming too occupied with saving her sister's life to notice how the tendrils of night grew stronger. Erebus's night rose around us, blotting out the sun to cocoon us in a shroud of darkness.

Levana's heartbeat was slowing, her chest rising with short, shallow breaths.

"It's not working," Eunoia gasped, panting for air. Her luminescent skin was pale, the ring of light around her eyes dimming as she looked up into Erebus's dark gaze. Shock and something dangerously close to hurt flashed across her face. "Erebus?"

"I'm sorry," he said, his grip on her power tightening.

Eunoia snarled, a last flare of a power igniting within her as she thrashed against his control.

As her sister's heart stopped beating.

"I'll be back for you, Erebus. I don't care how long it takes me to claw my way out of the void, I'll never forgive you for this."

Not swayed by her threat, Erebus commanded his darkness forward. Eunoia screamed as great claws of night dug into her chest, pulling every last spark of power from her being, until her lifeless corpse tumbled forward to join her sister's.

I held on to Zaeth, clinging to the one thing I knew was real. A part of me couldn't believe what I was seeing, Eunoia and Levana... both dead.

Their bodies were splayed across the earth, the Spear of Empyrean like a twisted grave marker, proving that even goddesses could fall. They stayed like that a litter longer, just until all their essence was absorbed by Erebus. And then they crumpled into dust.

Erebus inhaled deeply, the black rings of his eyes expanding to eclipse the white. Power hung heavy in the air; the electric charge nearly tangible in the cocoon of night he maintained.

With a wave of his hand, the darkness receded, and light returned.

I waited for the sounds of battle. For the clash of steal and the snarls of wolves. For the endless assaults from the Fractured —But there was only silence.

"El," Greer whispered, the broken sound of her voice shattering something in my soul. "I couldn't hold the shield. Not when the night expanded."

The rest of her words were lost to uncontrollable sobs as great tears streaked down her cheeks.

My brows furrowed, not understanding as I followed her gaze, staring across the hillside of bodies and blood to the mound of fallen Fractured surrounding a small clearing.

And the unmoving bodies within.

69

ELARA

Zaeth helped me stand. Helped drag my spent body and broken soul across the battlefield and through the circle of corpses—the unmoving Fractured. My stomach twisted as I gazed down at the patch of earth undisturbed by the blacken, decaying bodies.

Jarek and Evander were draped over Lannie's small form, their still bodies riddled with wounds. Their hands were clasped, their heads leaning toward one another, protecting my little sister even in death.

My knees buckled at their feet as a chasm of agony ripped through my chest. I couldn't feel. Couldn't think. There was only pain. Inconsolable, unending misery. It was the tip of a very long blade that would never stop hacking away at my bleeding, battered soul.

Zaeth was across from me, his face streaked with tears as he whispered prayers over Jarek's body, pleading that the gods in the after were kinder than the gods of this world.

I watched in a daze as he moved on to Evander... my brother. My friend. He was the only reason we'd survived after the storm. After Levana's first attack. He taught me how to hunt, how to fight. My entire childhood was filled with memories of him. My adult life too, and now he was just... gone.

Too soon, Zaeth shifted his position, reaching between the two of them toward the small figure within.

"I'm sorry," Greer whimpered next to me, somehow finding the strength to leave her mate's side and cross the mountain of war to reach us. I was vaguely aware of Naz and Queen Freya maneuvering a still unconscious Ryuu, of the distant shouts of Queen Halcyon flitting nearer, but I couldn't look away from the soles of Lannie's shoes peeking out beneath Evander's body.

She shouldn't have been here. We should have insisted she remain away from battle. Remain safe—

Her shoe twitched.

My breathing stopped as I blinked away tears, straining to listen, forcing myself to focus on one body, begging the universe there would be a heartbeat.

Greer's gaze snapped up, following my line of sight.

Thump. Thump.

"Help me move them," I gasped, hardly daring to hope.

Zaeth and nearby dark fae gently lifted and moved Evander and Jarek, setting them in a patch of earth that had been cleared, revealing my little sister.

Lannie was curled on her side, eyes closed. But her chest gave a steady rise and fall.

The tight band lodged around my heart loosened just enough for me to stay present in this moment.

"She's alive," Greer cried, brushing back the hair from Lannie's brow as our little sister stirred.

Halcyon burst through the ring of fae who had gathered around us, eyes wild with worry as they landed on Lannie. She flitted to her side, pressing her palm to Lannie's chest.

"She gave too much of herself," Halcyon breathed, her voice cracking. "I was surrounded by wraiths, and she siphoned her essence into me, regardless of her own safety. Even after all she was giving to you two."

I swallowed the lump in my throat, silent tears falling on my already damp cheeks. It was just like Lannie to give all of herself, more than she should ever sacrifice, to save the life of another.

Halcyon slumped, looking like she might be next to pass out, but a relieved cry rocked through her as Lannie blinked her eyes open.

Gods, she was alive. My little sister was breathing and awake. Greer and I wrapped her in a hug, the three of us clinging on to one another as we wept.

The relief at seeing my little sister wake was tempered by the bodies lying next to her. By Evander and Jarek who'd given all of themselves to ensure she saw another sunrise.

I knew there were thousands more who'd succumbed to death. An entire mountain of pyres would need to be constructed, but my sisters were alive, and I knew that made all the difference.

70

GREER

THE GREATER PART OF THE MORNING HAD BEEN DEDICATED TO tending wounds to those who survived and building pyres for all the rest. Fae from each of the seven kingdoms had fought and died to ensure Pax remained. It was a battle that would never be forgotten... one that I would never stop grieving.

Smoke from hundreds of pyres rose as the sun began her descent. The scent of ash was thick in the air, and there were still hundreds more who needed to be put to rest. The survivors had come together to ensure the fallen were honored, blessed words spoken over each in turn, before the torch was put to kindle.

No such kindness was shown to Levana's creatures. The corpses of the Fractured, goblins, and other monsters were piled in great mounds and set ablaze at random. I took joy in watching their bodies blacken, their flesh rendered to ash, knowing they would never hurt another living soul again.

Soft feathers grazed my shoulders as I stared at the smoldering remains of one such pile. Ryuu's scent of fresh rain and embers was a welcomed change to the surrounding death. I leaned into him as his arm wrapped around my waist, savoring the feel of his body against mine.

I'd been far too close to losing him forever.

The skin along his face and body had started to heal, but the bits of charred tissue and imbedded ash would have to be scraped away before it would seal properly. Lannie informed us it was a slow, brutal process, one that would undoubtedly leave scars marring Ryuu's beautiful body. But he would live.

We weren't sure about his wing. The feathers burned by Levana's darkness had yet to grow back, leaving the golden barbs bare and gleaming in the setting sun. I didn't want to think about what that would mean. What it would be like for Ryuu, the Air King, if he couldn't fly.

Problems for another day.

Today, I was determined to linger only on the good. On how I still had my brilliant, strong, beautiful sisters to turn the pages of life with. We'd survived the prophetic war with the three pairs of fated mates somehow intact.

But there was so much bad mixed in with our victory.

"It's time," El said, her voice heavy with sorrow. Zaeth was beside her, his arm wrapped firmly around her waist, and I wondered if she was just as close as I was to falling apart.

Ryuu stiffened, the movement sending a sharp gasp of pain through him as we made our way toward the summit. It wouldn't just be Evander and Jarek we put to rest there, but King Dragcor as well.

The four walked up the mountainside at a human's pace, none of us in a rush to say our final goodbyes. Because once we did, once we spoke over their graves and sent their essence off into the after... then they'd really be gone.

We crested the top all too soon, meeting Halcyon and Lannie before the pyres. Queen Freya allowed us to build Evander and Jarek a joint pyre set before a large oak tree. King Dragcor's was a few paces away, under the open sky.

Branches were woven together, intricate in their design. Such time had been spent on the pyres, a final acknowledgment of their sacrifice. It must've taken the humans all morning.

The humans of the Wild Kingdom, those who'd been protected during the war, were doing anything and everything to help the survivors. Small trinkets and tokens of a peaceful crossing were added at the base of pyres and along the sides of the burial shrouds.

The scene too familiar, the weight of my previous grief colliding with the present.

Another pyre.

Another brother.

I gripped Ryuu's hand, lending him what strength I could as he gazed upon the body of his father.

Grief was a fickle foe, infinite in her torment. The raw, blistering pain of initial loss would pass, transitioning into something almost tolerable, but I knew there would be times when it felt just as miserable and agonizing as it did now.

Ryuu hadn't lost many loved ones—there hadn't been many to start with. I knew we were going to have to face this together, lean on each other when the moments seemed too big, too dark, to handle on our own. It was the only way to keep breathing.

Pressing his shoulders back, Ryuu stepped forward with the Spear of Empyrean in his hand as the last rays of sun dipped beneath the horizon.

"King Dragcor was a great leader. He cared for his people, protecting them in times of need and tending to them with a kind heart in times of peace. He sacrificed his life—" Ryuu's pupils shifted to vertical slits, the green embers flaring as he fought to control the shaking of his voice. With a deep breath, he pressed on. "I am honored to be his son and heir. As his essence passes from this world and into the next, I will do my best to honor his memory."

Zaeth managed to say some pretty words for Evander and

Jarek, speaking to the gathered crowd on our behalf, even the Fire King contributed to it, but my sister's and I couldn't speak.

The three of us could barely breathe, hardly stand, but somehow we made it through the ceremony.

The flames climbed higher as the moon slowly rose and it felt like a chasm had yawned open in my soul.

I tried so hard to focus on the good, knowing Evander and Jarek had left this world together. Evander would be reunited with Jem, and I had no doubt Jarek would be welcomed with open arms by the both of them, but *gods* did I want them here.

Lannie sniffled, her cheeks and tip of her nose pink.

"They were incredible," she breathed, voice cracking. "I was focused on anchoring us, but the two of them didn't let a single one of those monsters through. And when the shield failed—" She swallowed, gripping tight to Queen Halcyon's hand as she fought to get the words out. "They threw themselves over me."

My heart squeezed as Lannie was consumed by tears. One glance toward El showed me she wasn't much better. Her fingers fidgeted with the grey crystal dangling around her neck, probably remembering how our little brother had looked so much smaller on his pyre than they did.

Guilt twisted through me as a dozen different what-if senecios played through my mind. If I'd only shielded Ryuu. If I'd been able to maintain the wards around Lannie. If Erebus's shadows hadn't been all consuming.

If. If. If.

But there was no use in thinking about what could have been.

The world as we knew it had ended. And we'd have to figure out a way to continue in this one.

The six of us stayed there for what felt like hours, the stars overhead shifting slowly through the night, until fatigue outweighed grief. I swayed on my feet, Ryuu catching me with an arm beneath my knees. He carried me toward our makeshift tent, despite the injuries still plaguing him.

Pyres burned throughout the mountain, the patches of flames seeming to keep the worse of the night away. They would be burning throughout until morning, and a tiny, wretched part of myself was grateful the darkness wouldn't be absolute.

"Do gods grieve?" I asked, as my view of the burning pyres was lost behind the thin tent material.

No one had seen Erebus since he'd drained the goddesses of their strength. El hadn't spoken of him, of her blood father, and I hadn't wanted to ask. Despite him having saved us in the end, I hoped we would never see him again.

"Don't think about him," Ryuu rumbled, turning down the sheets for us.

He slipped off my shoes before removing his own. Both of us had already changed and washed as best as we could from the buckets of fresh water passed among the armies. My mind drifted to the large bath in Ryuu's room back in the Air Kingdom, longing for a time when soaking my body in warm water and oils was enough to relax my soul.

Ryuu slipped in beside me, propping himself up on his forearm. The golden barbs of his wing fanned out, as if there were still feathers overlying them. Some of the soft, downy feathers remained close to his back, but nothing that he could fly with.

I hadn't realized before, but the gleaming, exposed barbs looked like they sprouted directly from his bones.

Ryuu flinched if anything other than a gentle breezed brushed against them, but beside Lannie's healing tonics, he refused treatment for the pain. He said he wanted to be present for today when saying his final goodbyes, and while I understood, it was still nearly unbearable to watch him in pain.

"We'll be home soon," he rumbled.

Home.

The world felt foreign and oddly right. I wasn't sure if I'd ever had a home. Not really. Home had been a concept I craved but had never felt comfortable enough to claim. The house I grew up in was haunted by my missing family, and the base had served as a temporary reprieve, but Ryuu... he *was* my home.

I gazed up at him, at my Dragon King. His left eye was still darkened by the lingering effects of Levana's shadows, all of the white consumed in black, but if I looked closely I could still see small specks of smoldering green near the center. A patch of his long, dark hair had been burned away, the skin raw and embedded with ash. He would have scars covering the whole left side of his body—a testament to his strength.

"Do they bother you?"

The vulnerability in his voice nearly broke me. I propped myself up to his level, letting my fingers trace the pink ridges.

"These show the world how brave you are." I leaned forward pressing a soft kiss to the scarred edge of his brow. "They prove your resilience." My lips trained down along his cheek in a string of gentle touches. "And if anything, they make you look even more deadly."

Ryuu's lips twitched as he kissed me back. "I love you, Greer."

Another part of me settled as he rolled the last 'r' of my name. "I love you, too," I breathed.

The worst had happened, and we were still here.

I slipped into the crook of his arm as we did our best to find peace. The sun would soon be up. Our problems would still be there, but for now, we listened to the rhythm of our heartbeats as burning wood crackled in the distance.

71

LANNIE

IT TOOK DAYS BEFORE ALL THE BODIES WERE DEALT WITH. WEEKS before the blood faded from the earth. But the forest was forever changed. Many trees had been damaged, still more cut down for the needed pyres. Even the trees that had survived were slowly dying, corrupted by the unchecked power of the gods unleashed on this place.

Through it all, the summit of the Wild Kingdom remained untouched. Halcyon and I had returned frequently from the Earth Kingdom, helping the surviving humans settle throughout Pax. Many villages and cities had been attacked by smaller groups of Levana's monsters while the war raged here. There was much to rebuild and lingering creatures to deal with, but we'd started on the long road to recovery.

The leaders of the kingdoms had decided to meet every month to touch base. The first two months had been all about recovery and reestablishing a human settlement along the Borderlands, but I hoped today we could look to the future.

Naz collected El, Zaeth, and the Fire King, while Queen Freya transported Halcyon, me, Queen Isla, and Alarik to the Air Kingdom, the same as it had been last month. Only the light fae were unaccounted for, though I supposed that was another topic for conversation.

"Vidarr and Kavan have established a perimeter where the base once was," Alarik said. The three of them were all that remained of the Select Guard, though Alarik already had plans on changing that. "With the help of the earth and wild fae, we've been able to clear most of the rubble as well as repair the stables and the outer buildings."

"How are the horses doing?" El asked.

A soft smile stretched across Alarik's face. "Ember and Colt are doing well. The other horses are still restless, but it's been less than a week and the two of them seem to be right at home."

El had debated long and hard about relocating Ember to the Dark Kingdom now that Levana was gone, but many of the unchecked monsters remaining in our world resided in the north. It wouldn't be safe for a horse. Still, El had insisted on visiting Halcyon and me in the Earth Kingdom just to ride Ember north and deliver her to the Borderlands in person.

"I anticipate welcoming another wave of humans and fae within the week," Alarik finished, taking a seat next to Queen Freya. We'd only just begun relocating human refugees to the Earth Kingdom, but they'd already made significant progress on reestablishing the base.

The King Kai attacked while we'd been fighting for the future of our world. But the water fae under his command hadn't been expecting the battalion of warriors left by Queen Isla. Her forces defended our capitol, keeping the casualties to a minimum and because of that, we'd been able to construct homes and establish new villages in record time.

It had been three months since the Battle of the Gods and I'd spent most of that time by Halcyon's side. El had returned to Caligo with Zaeth, the two of them taking over the ruling positions of the Dark Kingdom and giving Naz and Soter a much needed break.

El had been worried at first with the transition, but she and Zaeth were welcomed with open arms by the dark fae. All apprehension associated with The Dark Phoenix had burned away like the kindling on pyres. Now, they were seen as a symbol of power, the two strongest beings in this realm—apart from Ryuu.

Ryuu's body had scarred despite my best effort. The network of burns had smoothed out a little with the combination of his fae affinities and my healing, but his left eye remained black. And his wings... his right one suffered very little damage and was good as new, but the left had only just begun to recover.

Small tuffs of feathers along the golden barbs had started to grow. It was patchy at best and there would be no telling if the wing would be capable of flying until it fully healed, but it was a start.

"The Water King has retreated to the ocean..." Halcyon gave our own run down on events.

King Kai's presence hadn't been destructive in the physical sense so much as dangerous in mentality. He wished us to return to a time when humans were little more than slaves and females considered important for breeding purposes only. We'd been transparent with our people and the other kingdoms about it, but a small portion of earth fae had still chosen to move south, joining a large volume of light fae in the Water Kingdom.

I hoped it was nothing more than a few bitter, self-loathing fae causing a commotion, but that flicker of disquiet in my gut had me paying attention to all that went on with the Water Kingdom, Queen Isla included.

"Warriors loyal to me have confirmed he's retreated to the sea palace," Queen Isla said. "All reports agree he is content, despite the swell of support on land. I don't anticipate an attack anytime soon."

"Good," Zaeth said. "I'd prefer not to jump into another war."

"Speaking of war," Ryuu said, his mismatched eyes bouncing between Zaeth and King Dante. "Have thing quieted in the north?"

The Fire King answered first. "Attacks against our northern islands have stopped. There have been a few mentions of fire fae with fangs settling above ground, but nothing to be concerned about."

Zaeth lifted a dark brow in his direction but didn't press the matter. "Likewise, the Dark Kingdom is now home to new creatures. It's been made clear killing won't be tolerated on our land."

"All those remaining have adapted well," El added, her hand coming to rest on Zaeth's thigh.

"Wonderful," Greer said as the door to the war room opened. A hesitant looking waiter peeked his head in, but Greer was waving him forward as if a grand dinner being served among the leaders of the seven kingdoms were as normal as the sun rising. "Now that work is done, we can enjoy the delicious dinner I had our talented cooks prepare."

Waitstaff eased in, rounding the room in waves as they delivered platters of food and drink, all of which was coordinated by Greer.

I accepted the glass of red wine offered to me as I watched the room transform into a place of beauty. In no time, glowing candles and golden decor accented by simple white flowers filled the space. All talk of war and monsters faded as decadent spices filled the air, the aroma causing my mouth to water.

Dishes were unveiled and everyone helped themselves as happy chatter rose around us.

We'd never forget all that we'd lost, but as I watched Greer laugh with El, the two of them smiling over something King Dante said, I knew that Pax was in good hands.

As if sensing my happiness, my sisters turned to me. El

smiled, her hazel-blue eyes softening while Greer raised her very full glass of wine.

"To defeating arrogant gods," Greer grinned. Low chuckles sounded around the table as glasses clinked.

"To fae and humans creating a better world together," El added, the table murmuring their approval.

I lifted my glass, letting the realness of this moment pulse down our sister bonds. Letting hope shine through.

"To the future."

EPILOGUE

ELARA

Many Years Later…

My entire body hurt. Bone-deep, muscles splitting apart, life-changing type of hurt.

"One more push, El." Lannie voice was calm and steady. She was the unyielding coast the waves broke against in a storm. A steady endurance.

But I wanted to give up. To just have this pain stop.

"Here it comes," Lannie said, her voice cutting through my spiraling thoughts. "Push!"

With a deep, shuddering breath, I did. An agonized scream sounded through the room. I knew it came from me, but there was a certain level of detachment—a surrealism—to this moment that nobody could've prepared me for.

"Oh my gods," Greer gasped from my side, sounding like she might pass out. She shared a loaded look with Zaeth as her grip on my hand tightened. "You're pushing out a whole baby. Like, an entire living creature is coming out of your—"

EPILOGUE

"One more push," Lannie interrupted, throwing Greer a glare.

"You said that last time," I panted, looking up at Zaeth. He hadn't left my side since the moment my water broke. I was exhausted and spent, but I could already feel my body contracting again, the urge to push overwhelming.

"That's it, El," Lannie encouraged as I screamed, feeling the pressure build, the pain searing through me—and then releasing.

A cry rocked through the air moments later. My chest heaved and my entire body hurt, but Lannie plopped a wrinkly, squirming baby wrapped in a soft blanket on my chest in the next heartbeat, and I somehow knew I'd do it all again just to hold her.

"She's beautiful, El."

Words escaped me as I held her tight, tears streaming down my cheeks. I cradled her to my chest while the placenta worked free, marveling at her small hands and tiny toes, at how she already had a full head of dark hair like her father.

Soon the worst of the bleeding had stopped and Zaeth was able to sit beside me on the bed as we stared at our daughter.

"Would you like to hold her?" I asked, relishing the post-labor haze as I secured her swaddle.

Zaeth adjusted his arms as I handed her over, his eyes shining as he tucked her in close to his chest.

I'd never seen him smile like that—disbelief, pride, shock... and maybe a little bit of fear, too. But he was beaming, his cinnamon eyes brimming with happy tears. And I thought in that moment I fell in love with him all over again.

My heart swelled as Zaeth leaned down, pressing a soft kiss to her head as she cooed.

"Hello, little love."

ACKNOWLEDGMENTS

Thank you.

Thank you to every person who joined El, Greer, and Lannie on their journey. I hope meeting these characters has lightened your world, just a little.

A special thank you to the readers who have been with me from the start. It has been a wild ride, but I'm not jumping off anytime soon.

Thank you to my mom for supporting me on my dream of becoming an author. Your support has been more valuable than you know and has also been a great way to flush out the trigger warnings.

To my husband, my own Dark King: I love you with every fiber of my being. We've some how managed to create three little humans, raise two puppies, survived the chaos of an average day, and are still obsessed with each other.

You are my forever.

My partner in this life an all others.

I love you.

ABOUT THE AUTHOR

C.L. Briar is a believer that books are always better than reality and one of the biggest offenses a person can commit is interrupting reading time. When she is not busy dreaming up dark fantasy worlds and plotting destruction, she can be found drinking coffee in her backyard with her husband, three young daughters, and hound dog.

Made in the USA
Middletown, DE
09 March 2024

50599453R00276